ANTHONY
BRUNO

BAD
MOON

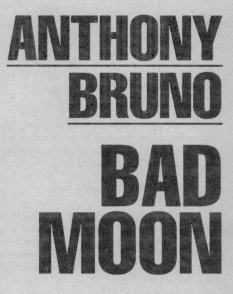

A DELL BOOK

Published by
Dell Publishing
a division of
Bantam Doubleday Dell Publishing Group, Inc.
1540 Broadway
New York, New York 10036

ISBN 0-440-21559-5

Reprinted by arrangement with Delacorte Press

Printed in the United States of America

Published simultaneously in Canada

July 1993

10 9 8 7 6 5 4 3 2 1

RAD

For Al Zuckerman

ONE

Sabatini Mistretta felt bad. Here he was sitting with Sal Immordino's own sister Cil, eating her cookies and drinking her awful coffee, and just the other day he'd given the okay for a hit on her brother. And what was worse, Cil was a nun, for chrissake. The old mob boss pressed his lips together. It just didn't seem right.

Mistretta took another pignoli cookie off the plate that was balanced on the arm of the sofa. The cookies were good, but he shouldn't eat so many. But with Cil's coffee you needed something to kill the taste.

"Would you like some more coffee, Mr. Mistretta?" Cil tilted her head and smiled like a saint, those big eyeglasses of hers flashing in the light.

Mistretta laid a hand on his belly and made a face. "No thanks, Cil. I'll be up all night as it is."

"How about you, Jerry?"

Jerry Rella, Mistretta's bodyguard and driver, shrugged and nodded. "Sure, Cil. Just half a cup." Jerry had a nice smile. He had the kind of rubbery face people trusted. Very kind watery blue eyes. And he actually was a nice guy if you didn't cross him.

Cil stood up from the other sofa and reached over for Jerry's cup and saucer. "I'll be right back." She turned and sailed back toward the kitchen, which was in the rear of this run-down brownstone—the Mary Magdalene Home for Unwed Mothers.

Mistretta glanced up at the water stains on the ceiling. The roof leaked. The whole place was a disaster. Even Goodwill wouldn't take furniture like she had in this parlor. He was surprised Cil hadn't hit him up for some money. She usually did, even though he always said no. The Church has plenty of money, he'd told her before. Look at the Vatican, for chrissake. Take a little gold outta that place and put the money into the Mary Magdalene Home, he'd told her. But she had a head as hard as her brother Sal. She didn't want to take money from the diocese. She wanted to remain independent, she said. And that's why she and all these poor girls with their babies had to live in this dump stuck in the ass-end of Jersey City. But Mistretta felt bad now, considering her brother was gonna die and all. Maybe he oughta give her a couple of thou. Just to fix the roof, at least.

Jerry reached over from the third couch and snatched a cookie from the plate. Mistretta watched him as he bit into it and got powdered sugar on the lapel of his suit jacket. He wondered whether Jerry was the guy who got the contract. Jerry used to do a lot of those jobs before he became Mistretta's bodyguard. He was good with a gun.

Who knows? They could've picked Jerry for the job. It'd be good if they did, but Mistretta wasn't gonna get involved. He was getting tired of all this shit. He was ready to take it easy, let the others take care of the day-to-day bullshit. But if Jerry does whack Sal Immordino, that'll put him in good with Juicy Vacarini, and then

Juicy'll take care of him when he starts taking over some of Mistretta's duties. That'll be nice. If it's Jerry.

But Mistretta told Juicy at the meet the other day—he didn't wanna know nothing about the details of this thing. He agreed with them that Sal was dangerous where he was now, locked up in the nuthouse down in Trenton. Sal had a big beef with Frank Bartolo because Mistretta gave him Sal's crew after they took Sal to the loony bin. Sal felt Frank owed him money for deals he put together for that crew, profits that came in after Sal was put away. But Frank had a big beef with Sal too. He said Sal was making bad blood between him and the guys in the crew. Loopy Lou, Gyp, Angie, Phil, Jimmy T.— they were all very loyal to Sal, and they stayed in touch with Sal, visited him at the bin. The way Frank Bartolo figured it, these guys would never earn for him the way they did for Sal as long as Sal was still around making them think he'd be back someday.

But it was Juicy who came up with the best reason for whacking Sal. The guy's miserable down there in Trenton, and there's no way he can get out. If he admits he's not nuts so he can get outta there, they'll try him on all his old murder and racketeering charges and throw him in jail, maybe even put him on death row. After all, they're always looking for white guys they can execute. So what's the only thing left for Sal to do? Sing, that's what. He talks to the state in exchange for a change in life-style. They'll put him in one of those nice country-club facilities if he starts ratting on the family. He names enough fucking names, they'll get him into witness protection, get him a place out in Kansas and make him a real fucking American. Juicy was right. Nothing against Sal, but he was too vulnerable where he was. The guy was ripe for the picking. He was too much of a risk. He had to go.

Mistretta looked sideways at Jerry brushing the powdered sugar off his lapel. Jerry was a nice guy, got along pretty good with everybody. Still, he was never bosom buddies with Sal, so Sal would know something was up if he showed up down at the bin. Maybe he wasn't the hit man.

Mistretta thought about it. Bartolo's kid, Frank Junior, he was a possibility. Violent son of a bitch, and almost as big as Sal. Would be a nice way to get the kid some respect in the family if he did Sal. Frank Junior wasn't too bright, though. Maybe he could sneak in dressed like another nut. The kid was a big jooch, he'd look the part.

Then there was always Joey D'Amico with that big ugly wart on the side of his nose. Mistretta never understood why the guy never went to a doctor and got rid of that thing. D'Amico was a pretty good earner, but he was a little ass-licker. Soon as Sal got put away, he started sucking up to his new boss, badmouthing Sal, talking about all the other guys in the crew. He'd do Sal just to earn a few brownie points with Bartolo, the sneaky little bastard.

Cil came back into the parlor, carrying the cup and saucer in front her. She floated like a ghost, it seemed, because you couldn't see her legs under the long habit. She set down Jerry's cup on the end table, then went back to her couch, folding her hands in her lap, smiling nicely for no particular reason. Mistretta figured she was getting ready to ask him for money again. She was gonna drop dead when he said yes this time.

"I have a little surprise for you, Mr. Mistretta."

He raised a bushy eyebrow. "Oh, yeah?"

She had this funny little smile. "It's in the basement."

"The basement?" Mistretta furrowed his brow and tugged on the flesh under his chin.

She smiled wider. "Yes. In the basement."

He looked at Jerry, who shrugged as he sipped his coffee. "What's down there, Cil?"

"I can't tell you. It's a secret." The glare was in her glasses. Mistretta wished he could see her eyes.

She stood up and pointed to the door under the staircase, the door to the basement. Mistretta looked over his shoulder, out the bay windows at the dark street. This was a bad neighborhood. You never knew who could be down there, for crying out loud.

"Why don't you just tell me what you got down there, Cil? You must have cock-a-roaches down there. I don't like cock-a-roaches."

"There are no cockroaches down there. Promise." She still had that giddy little smile on, like the Blessed Mother just came down and told her a joke.

Jerry was looking at him with his elbows on his knees, waiting for him to decide what they were gonna do.

Mistretta shrugged. "Awright, let's go down and see what you got." He got up off the couch, wincing as he put weight on his knees. Arthritis. It was a bitch getting old. Jerry followed him over to the basement door. He figured the girls who lived here must've made something. Last time he was here one of the pregnant girls gave him a bird feeder she made. Cil was trying to raise money having these kids make bird feeders. How many bird feeders you gonna sell in this neighborhood? People don't wanna live here, why should the birds want to? Cil was a nice girl, but she's the one who's the real loony tune in the Immordino family.

Jerry opened the door and started to go down. Mis-

tretta waited for Cil to go next, but she started heading
back for the kitchen. "Where ya going, Cil? I thought
you had a surprise for me."

She looked back over her shoulder. "It's down there.
You'll find it." She shrugged, and her eyebrows rose over
the tops of her big designer glasses. She bit her bottom
lip, still with that smile. "I have to go turn off the kettle.
I'm making more tea for myself."

She disappeared through the doorway again in a flut-
ter of black fabric.

He sighed, looked at Jerry, and tapped his temple.
"The lights aren't always on upstairs, Jer. Go 'head
down. Let's see what she's got these kids doing now."

Jerry nodded and flipped the light switch on the wall.
A dim, naked bulb at the top of the stairs went on. It
must've been a twenty-five-watter. Mistretta felt bad
again. Cil was always trying to save money any way she
could.

The staircase was narrow, and Jerry slid his hand
against the wall as he went down. There was a light on
down there, and Mistretta could hear a TV set going. It
sounded like that game show that's on Channel 7, the
one where the blonde turns over the letters—what's it
called?—*Wheels of Fortune.*

Mistretta leaned heavily on the railing as he started
down. He grit his teeth. Stairs were a bitch on his knees.

"So what's she got down there, Jer? Just tell me so I
don't have to go all the way down."

Jerry was just getting to the bottom of the staircase. "I
don't see nothing, Mr. Mis—"

Pfittt, pfittt!

Jerry spun around on his toe as he came off the last
step, and started to fall over like a tree. One hand was
inside his jacket where he kept his gun, the other was

holding the lapel. He landed hard on his side, like a side of beef hitting the slab.

"Jer!" Mistretta's chest was pounding. He stooped down on the steps and saw his bodyguard sprawled out on the black-and-white linoleum squares. His watery blue eyes were glassy. The only thing moving was the bloodstain spreading out on his shirtfront like a disease.

"How ya doin', Mr. Mistretta?"

The old boss jumped. "Who's that?" He squinted in the dim light. He could only hear the voice. He clenched his jaw because his knees were screaming with pain.

"You forgot me already? It hasn't even been two years. Why don't you come on down? We'll have a little talk, get reacquainted."

Mistretta spotted the long barrel peeking through the gloom at the edge of the stairs. It was a gun fitted with a friggin' silencer. The damn thing was looking him right in the eye. Mistretta winced. He couldn't even stand up straight, his knees hurt so bad. Even if he had the chance, he couldn't run upstairs to save himself.

"C'mon down, Mistretta. Let's catch up on old times. C'mon."

Mistretta struggled down to the next step. He could see the face behind the goddamn gun now. He couldn't believe it. It was Sal Immordino, Cil's brother.

"What the fuck you doing here? You're s'posed to be in the nuthouse!"

The big mameluke just smiled and shrugged, smiled like his goddamn sister. Mistretta glanced back up the stairs. "She set me up, goddamn it. A nun, for chrissake. That ain't right."

Sal shook his big fleshy face. "Cil didn't set you up. I told her I wanted to surprise you. And she believes everything I tell her. Christ, she still believes we're independent businessmen. I told her to get you here because I knew you'd be real happy to see me, Mistretta. Aren't you happy to see me?"

Mistretta was too angry to answer. Sal must've been hiding under the stairs, waiting for him and Jerry to come down. The big jerk looked like he'd gained even more weight since Mistretta last saw him. He must've been at least 270 now. Six foot five and 270. A big fucking bag of shit.

The old boss glared at the muzzle of the gun. "How the hell'd you get out of the bin, Sal? You flipped, didn't you? You made a deal with the state. You're gonna rat on me, ain'tcha?"

Sal stuck out his bottom lip and shook his head. "C'mon down. We'll talk about it."

"Talk my ass."

Mistretta heard footsteps behind him at the top of the stairs. *"Everything all right down there?"* It was Cil.

"N—" The silencer flew into Mistretta's mouth, banging into his front teeth and pressing against the back of his throat. The oily metal tasted worse than Cil's coffee, and it made him gag.

"Everything's fine, Cil," Sal said. "Go to bed."

"Okay, Sal. Good night, Mr. Mistretta. Good night, Jerry."

"Good night." Sal had a big grin on his puss.

The door at the top of the stairs closed.

Sal's grin turned mean. "I asked you to come down off those fucking steps, didn't I? Whattaya waiting for?"

Mistretta jerked his head back to get the gun out of his mouth. Who the hell did this guy think he was talking to? He fished around in his mouth with his finger. "You broke my fucking tooth, you big fucking jooch."

"You left me high and dry in the nuthouse for a year and a half. We s'posed to be even now?"

"You don't understand, Sal."

"Oh, I understand plenty. I understand that you okayed the contract Juicy and Bartolo put out on me."

Mistretta's heart started to pound. "Who told you that? That's bullshit."

"Never mind who told me. And don't say it's bullshit, because I know it ain't."

"You're all mixed up, Sal. You don't understand."

"I understand that you gave away my crew to Bartolo and let him keep a lotta goddamn money that's mine by rights, money that I coulda used for a good lawyer."

"You know how these things go, Sal. It was up to Bartolo to give you the money. It was his decision."

"You coulda made him. Aren't you boss anymore?"

"Don't make me mad now. You know I'm the boss."

"Well, you ain't a very good one. You don't take care of your people. I did so much for you, but when I was down, you forgot about me."

"I never forgot about you, Sal."

"Well, you never did anything *for* me," Sal shouted. He glared at Mistretta, fuming, then he looked over his shoulder. "Turn up the TV, Charles. I don't want my sister to hear."

Mistretta suddenly noticed two guys on the other side of the room in the glow of the television. The black guy was big, not as big as Sal, but big like a running back.

The other guy was slouched on a ratty couch, watching the little black-and-white TV perched on a plastic milk crate. He was scrawny and pale with a real goofball haircut, long on top but shaved close around the ears. He was mumbling something to himself, rocking back and forth, rocking and twitching, his eyes glued to the set. Every time he twitched, his eyes rolled back in his head and stayed there for a second.

"Hey! I thought I told you to get your ass down here, Mistretta."

Mistretta looked Sal in the eye. "This is your sister's place, for chrissake. It's holy. How could you pull this kind of shit in here?"

"Forget about my sister. She don't know what I do. And since when are you so worried about her? She's been asking you for a little donation for this place for years and you always told her to go screw. Go get it from the pope, you told her."

"You used to tell her the same thing, Sal. You never gave her a—" Mistretta winced. His front tooth was chipped, and the nerve must've been exposed because it hurt like a bastard when the cold air hit it. "So what's your beef, Sal? Just tell me. Maybe I can fix it."

Sal's eyes turned to slits as that mean grin pierced his cheeks. "You know, you make me laugh, Mistretta. You gonna tell me you can fix things? Bullshit. You ain't got the power anymore."

"You don't know what you're talking about."

"Oh, yeah? Bartolo doesn't listen to you. He listens to Juicy Vacarini now."

"Juicy?"

"Yeah, Juicy. Most of the captains listen to him. He's been running things lately because you don't care no more. Juicy might as well be the boss. He's just waiting for you to croak so he can take the title."

"You don't know what you're talking about."

"I know what I'm talking about. I know that Bartolo owes me four hundred grand and nothing you say is gonna make him give it up. I also know that he and Juicy got a contract out on me, and even if you cancel it, they ain't gonna listen."

"They'll listen. We'll have a sit-down and you'll tell them to their faces that you ain't talking to the prosecutors down in Trenton. We'll call off the hit."

"You ain't got the power." Sal extended his arm so that the muzzle was leveled on the knot in Mistretta's tie.

The old boss couldn't help swallowing. Getting shot in the throat was supposed to be very painful. He'd seen people suffer that way. He grit his teeth and cold air hit that tooth again. He glanced down at Jerry's body. His shirt was completely red now.

"Whad'ja kill Jerry for, Sal? He was a nice guy."

"He *was* a nice guy. I used to like him. But he woulda killed me if he saw me down here. Look at him. His hand is on his gun."

"He wouldn't have killed you. Not if I told him not to."

Sal's eyes flared. "Don't bullshit me, Mistretta." He lowered the gun and jabbed it into Mistretta's knee.

Pfittt!

It felt like a blasting cap went off on his knee. Mistretta instinctively went to clutch it, but he lost his balance and fell forward. He tumbled down the stairs, banging up his shoulder and back, and landed on top of Jerry. Spooked by all the blood, he rolled off fast, despite the pain, and pushed himself up against the wall. He was sitting up halfway, propped on one hand, his eyes blinking out of control. His knee looked like a fresh road kill.

"I was gonna retire," he mumbled. "I'm tired of all this shit. I just wanna retire and take it easy."

"This is bad. Very bad. Very bad." The scrawny guy on the couch was staring at him, wild-eyed, rocking back and forth, making the sign of the cross over and over again. In the name of the Father and the Son and the Holy Ghost, amen. In the name of the Father and the Son and the Holy Ghost, amen. In the name of the Father . . . Mistretta thought about doing that himself, but he was afraid he'd fall over if he moved his arm.

"Give him another pill," Sal said to the black guy.

"He's okay. Can't give him no more now anyway. Too soon."

"You sure he's all right?"

"He fine."

"Then keep him quiet." Sal glared down at Mistretta.

Mistretta held his chest. He was having a hard time breathing. "Whattaya want, Sal? Just tell me. You want the money from Bartolo? I'll help you get it."

"Fuck the money, Mistretta. I'll get that for myself. You wanna know what I really want?"

"What? Tell me."

"I want your job. I wanna be boss."

"You're crazy."

"I got guys still loyal to me. As many as Juicy's got. They thought I shoulda had your job a long time ago. Now I'm gonna get it."

"C'mon, Sal. Be for real here. Whattaya want? Let me help you."

Sal's nostrils flared. "I told you. I wanna be boss. And what I really want, I get. You wanna see how I'm gonna do it?"

Mistretta kept blinking. He couldn't focus on Sal's face. "C'mon, Sal. You're acting fucking crazy now."

"You think I'm crazy? Just watch."

Sal stepped over Jerry's body, straddling him. He squinted down the long barrel, holding the gun with both hands and taking aim. "Watch. I'm gonna give

Jerry his last rites. Extrem' unction." Sal put the silencer to Jerry's forehead. "In the name of the Father . . ."

Pfittt!

Jerry's head bounced.

Sal moved the gun to his belly.

"And the Son . . ."

Pfittt!

Jerry's whole body twitched.

Sal put the gun to the right shoulder.

"And the Holy . . ."

Pfittt!

The arm shot up and flopped back.

The left shoulder.

"Ghost . . ."

Pfittt!

The hand flipped open.

"Amen."

"A-men." The black guy was grinning like a chimpan-zee.

"Fucking bastard," Sal grumbled, staring down at Jerry's body. "I lent him twenty grand once for his daughter's wedding, and he was gonna kill me."

"No, Sal . . . no." Mistretta couldn't breathe right. "You're jumping to conclusions."

"This is bad. Very bad." The whites of the little scrawny guy's eyes flashed in the dim light as he stared at Jerry, rocking back and forth, crossing himself again and again.

When Mistretta looked up again Sal was smiling down at him. The big jooch hunkered down and whispered in his face. "Don't ever tell anyone I never gave you nothin', you old fart you."

Mistretta narrowed his eyes and glared up at him. "You do this, Immordino, you're gonna be sorry for the rest of your life. I'm gonna fucking haunt you. I swear to Christ I will."

The last thing Mistretta felt was the hot muzzle burning the skin on his forehead.

"In the name of the Father . . ."

"NO!"

Pfittt!

TWO

"**B**elieve me, it's no big deal, Tozzi." FBI Special Agent Cuthbert Gibbons took a sip from his beer bottle. He was sitting sideways on his stool, one elbow on the bar. Gilhooley's was hopping with the Friday happy-hour crowd. Gibbons was trying to cheer up his glum-faced partner. "It's not the end of the world, Toz. So you're gonna be forty. So what?"

Special Agent Mike Tozzi stared at Gibbons, then stared at the untouched bottle of Rolling Rock on the bar in front of him. He finally took a sip. He didn't need this shit.

"Trust me on this one, Tozzi. Turning forty is no big deal."

Tozzi stared at the green bottle in his hand. "How do *you* know? You probably don't even remember."

"Whattaya mean? It wasn't that long ago." Gibbons's voice suddenly got tight. He always got touchy whenever someone brought up the issue of *his* age.

Tozzi smirked at his partner and shook his head. Looking at the mirror behind the bar, he scanned the crowd. Gilhooley's was a favorite watering hole for people who worked for the city of New York since it was only a couple of blocks from City Hall. But tonight there was a roving pack of trial lawyers of the ambulance-chaser variety working the crowd, and there were even a few Wall Street types scattered here and there ogling the female secretaries and administrators. You could tell the Wall Street guys from the lawyers because they wore better suits and looked a little healthier, but not much.

A table of secretaries over by the wall caught Tozzi's eye. They were laughing and clucking over a frothy pitcher of whiskey sours, having a grand old time getting loaded. A couple of them were very cute—cheerleader cute—and they were definitely on the make, checking out all the guys they hoped were single. Tozzi was single, but they weren't looking for him. They were looking for guys in their late twenties, the guys with good suits. They sure weren't looking for soon-to-be-forty FBI street agents from the Manhattan field office's Organized Crime Unit.

He refocused and took a good look at himself sitting next to Gibbons in the mirror. He wasn't ugly, but he didn't think he looked like anybody's idea of a catch anymore. His dark, deep-set eyes always seemed to look tired now, even when he'd gotten enough sleep. He didn't have sagging jowls like Gibbons—not yet—but his face seemed longer and fleshier than he liked to think of it. His hair had thinned some on top, but he still had more than most guys his age. What did bother him, though, were the silver hairs. You could spot them from ten feet away now.

'Course, he had a long way to go before he looked like Gibbons. Gibbons *looked* like an old guy. Not an old man, but an older guy, an older middle-aged guy. His hair had gone south long before Tozzi had met him. All he had now were those thin gray strands that he combed back over his freckled head. Gibbons had jowls, too, real jowls. And that face. Nose hanging over his mouth like a big hot pepper, small mean eyes, and no lips. All that and the personality of a moray eel.

Tozzi studied both their faces side by side and shuddered. In fifteen, sixteen years, that could be him. Jesus.

But it wasn't his aging face that was bothering him or his graying hair. It was the fact that here he was in the middle of his life, and he hadn't done a single positive thing he could look back on and be proud of. Sure, putting bad guys away and keeping the mob at bay was something, but it didn't seem like it was enough. It wasn't like he had created something, something that would last, like a building or a great song. He didn't even have kids.

He glanced at Gibbons in the mirror. Gibbons didn't have any kids either. But at least he had a wife. Tozzi didn't even have that.

It was cool being single and free when he was in his twenties and thirties, going out with different women all the time, but the thought of being forty and still on the prowl seemed kinda sad and pathetic, very past tense. Too old for young babes, too immature for women his own age.

He took another swig from the bottle and looked up at the TV set over the bar. The local news was on, the black guy with the glasses on Channel 9. He was doing an update on a transit cop who'd been shot in the line of duty last month. The poor bastard was in a wheelchair, his arm in a sling, his wife trying to push him around their crowded little apartment, banging him into walls and furniture.

Tozzi shook his head and sighed. He glanced down at

the beer in his hand, then glanced at the cute secretaries getting shit-faced in the mirror.

Shit. He had to get outta here.

Gibbons turned in his seat and laid his forearms on the bar, lacing his fingers around his beer. "So what's the face for, Toz? I'm telling you. Turning forty is not a problem. It happens, and you feel like you want to kill yourself, but the next week you forget about it."

"It's not that."

"Yeah, right."

"I'm telling you. It's not."

"Then what is it? Your black-belt test? You're good. You'll do all right. Don't worry about it."

Tozzi stared at him. He resented the pep talk. "It's not that either." His black-belt test was only part of it.

"Then what's buggin' you, Toz? You can't tell me? I spend more friggin' time with you than I do with my own wife, and you can't talk to me? You know, Lorraine predicted a long time ago that you'd be terrible when you turned forty. She was right."

"How the hell would she know?"

"She's *your* cousin."

"Is that what you two do in bed at night before you turn out the lights? Talk about me?"

Gibbons looked at him blankly. "Who talks?" The crocodile smile broke open under his big hot-pepper nose. Wiseass bastard.

Tozzi slid off his stool. "I gotta go. I'll see you tomorrow."

Gibbons grabbed his sleeve. "Hey! Where you goin'?"

"I got paperwork to do on the Mistretta thing."

"It's eight o'clock. We put in a twelve-hour day. I

think the taxpayers got their money's worth today. Sit down and relax."

"No, really. Ivers said he wanted this report right away. I'll see you on Monday."

Gibbons layed a hand on Tozzi's shoulder. "Let me tell you something, Toz. One person cannot solve every crime in the city of New York by himself. Not even you. We did our part today. We covered the crime scene and collected the evidence. We spent the whole goddamn day with those two bodies. Now it's up to the lab techs to come up with something. See, each person has to take his own little square of turf and just deal with that. As you get older, you find out that that's what life is really all about. And now that you're about to be middle-aged, I think you ought to realize that." The bastard was laughing. He thought this was real funny.

"Fuck you, Gibbons."

"Hey, I'm just telling you the way it is, Toz."

"Look, Ivers told me he wanted the report ASAP. When a mob boss gets shot, the Bureau has to make some kind of statement to the press, and he wants to know what he's talking about for a change."

Roy, the regular bartender here, came toward them, wiping his way down the bar. Tozzi guessed Roy to be in his late twenties, maybe thirty. He had longish blond hair, big biceps, and a small waist, and he always looked happy. Tozzi watched his big arm running the rag along the bar. Why the hell shouldn't the guy be happy? He's not gonna be forty.

"Another round, gentlemen?" Roy asked.

Gibbons picked up Tozzi's beer. It had hardly been touched. "Another one for me, Roy. Maybe a cup of herb tea for my friend here since he's not drinking tonight. He must be watching his health."

Roy snorted out a laugh and revealed an army of perfect white teeth. He laughed like a donkey, but a good-looking donkey. Tozzi made up his mind then and there that he really did hate this guy's guts.

The muscle-bound donkey was still laughing as he brought up another bottle of Rolling Rock from under the bar. Gibbons drained his old one, then looked at his watch. Roy caught his eye and suddenly went poker-faced, nodding once.

Tozzi frowned. Were these two supposed to be subtle or what? He swore to Christ that if someone came out with a friggin' birthday cake, he was walking outta here. Poor sport or not, he wasn't in the mood. Anyway, his birthday was still two weeks away.

Roy went down to the end of the bar and reached up to turn up the sound on the TV. He looked like a goddamn orangutan with those arms of his. On the screen, the anchorman was kibitzing with the sportscaster and the weatherman. They cut away for a commercial then, and the sound was suddenly blaring as a red convertible raced through fall leaves on a country road.

"What's the story, Gib? Why's he got that thing turned up like that?"

"What? I can't hear you."

"You're not funny, Gibbons. Not funny at all."

"Whad'ja say?"

The car commercial played out, and the next one began. As soon as Tozzi heard the music—the sinewy beat against a thumping, gyrating bass—he knew what it was. The camera panned that huge weight room with all the sparkling chrome-plated exercise equipment. Tozzi didn't even have to look. Everyone knew this commercial.

"Is this supposed to be for my benefit, Gibbons?"

"Shut up, Tozzi, I'm trying to listen to this."

Tozzi looked back up at the TV. The camera stopped panning, and there she was in her metallic purple Lycra tights, the tits hanging out of her matching purple tank top with the fuchsia thunderbolts zapping down her lateral obliques, the pouty red lips, the come-hither eyes, the curly mess of long, two-tone blond hair spilling over her shoulders and down her back as she worked that crooked barbell up and down, doing her curls up and down, up and down, making her tits bobble with each jerk.

Gibbons was wearing a big shit-eating grin, and Roy had his thumb and forefinger over his eyes, trying not to laugh.

". . . *Knickerbocker Spas,*" the voice-over shouted, "*with fourteen convenient locations in Manhattan, Brooklyn, Queens, Staten Island, and New Jersey. At Knickerbocker Spas, we invite you to come on in and—*"

"PUMP IT UP!" Everyone at the bar yelled out the tag line, the line that the blonde always said with that look in her eye, that come-on-big-boy-I-dare-you-to-pump-it-up-for-*me* look. They even called her the Pump-It-Up Girl. Knickerbocker Spas had been blitzing the airwaves with this commercial all spring, and every straight guy in New York was in lust with this girl. Even Tozzi had to admit that she gave him a hard-on the first time he saw her. But what the hell was this all about, turning up the TV and making everyone deaf? What the hell was this, a pervert bar, for chrissake?

Tozzi shrugged and looked at Gibbons. "I don't get it. Is this supposed to be funny?"

"This is your favorite commercial, isn't it, Toz? Didn't you tell me that?"

Tozzi closed his eyes and shook his head. He couldn't

believe this. This was fucking juvenile. No, it was worse
than juvenile coming from an old guy like Gibbons. It
was senile. Anything to bust balls. Ha, ha, ha.

"Now, tell me the truth, Tozzi, and be honest. Have
you or have you not been telling me for the past month
that if you could have one wish before you died, it was to
have fifteen minutes alone with the Pump-It-Up Girl?
Tell the truth now. Did you say that or am I crazy?"

Roy was howling. The music on the commercial was
still thumping as the two-tone blonde worked that barbell, showing off that incredible bod as the voice-over
described the spa's facilities.

"All right, all right. I admit it. I did say she was nice.
So what of it?"

"But did you say that you wanted fifteen minutes
alone with her?"

Tozzi just looked at him. Roy was splitting a gut as he
reached up to turn down the volume on the TV. Everyone at the bar was watching them, flashing these big
dopey smiles, like they expected something else to happen.

Tozzi lowered his voice. "Yeah, okay, if it'll make you
happy, Gib. That's what I said. I said I wouldn't mind
having fifteen minutes alone with the Pump-It-Up Girl.
Okay? You happy now?" He glanced up quickly at the
two-tone blonde before the commercial ended and
sighed. His young-babe days were over. He wouldn't
know what to do with a girl like that.

Gibbons was smiling with his teeth. "Well, Toz, your
wish is my command."

Someone tapped Tozzi on the shoulder then. He
closed his eyes and started to turn around, expecting to
see a goddamn cake shaped like the Pump-It-Up Girl

with a million candles sticking out of the boobs like two flaming porcupines. But he was wrong.

"What the—?"

She rested her forearms on his shoulders and played with the hair at the back of his neck. The tawny come-hither eyes were calling to him. The pouty ruby lips were right there in front of him. That two-tone, bronze-gold hair was all over the place. And those incredible boobs—they just floated there, suspended in space right under his chin. He tried not to stare down her cleavage, but it was a real struggle.

"Hi, Tozzi," she said.

"Uh . . . hi."

Gibbons and Roy were in tears. The crowd closed in, the lawyers and the Wall Street types going bug-eyed to get a good look at her chest. The horny bastards were drooling all over the floor.

"Jesus Christ, that really is her," Tozzi heard one of them say. "It's the Pump-It-Up Girl."

"*That's* her boyfriend?"

"Lucky bastard."

Tozzi turned toward the envious voices, but she turned his face back around with one finger on his chin and leaned her forehead into his. "I've heard a lot about you, Tozzi." She had the kind of pouty voice you'd expect to come out of those lips.

Tozzi could feel his face heating up like a toaster.

"My name is Stacy. Stacy Viera."

"Nice to meet you . . . Stacy."

"Hey, c'mon, Toz, is that the best you can do?" Gibbons was having a fucking ball.

It was at that moment that Tozzi realized he had his hands on the Pump-It-Up Girl's waist. He suddenly became very self-conscious of them, so he quickly put them on her bare arms and gently undid the embrace. The touch of her skin felt very nice, firm but soft at the same time. He could feel himself getting hard. The goddamn thing had a mind of its own. He stared into her face and decided she couldn't be more than twenty. Exactly half the age he was going to be in two weeks. Old enough to be her goddamn father. All of a sudden he wasn't hard anymore.

Stacy's pout got a little juicier. Her eyes darted over his face. She looked upset.

Gibbons nudged him with an elbow. "Hey, Toz, whatsa matter? We're trying to cheer you up here. You look like you're going to a funeral."

Stacy looked to Roy and frowned. "I don't think he got the joke."

Tozzi glared at Gibbons. His face was burning. "This is not funny."

"Lighten up, Toz. You been down in the mouth all winter. We figured you needed a boost." Gibbons eyed Stacy's tits whenever he saw she wasn't looking.

Roy flipped the towel over his shoulder and leaned over the bar to mediate. "I'm sorry if this embarrassed you, Toz, really. It was mostly my idea. I apologize. See, one night Gibbons was in here and the commercial came on and he mentioned that you thought Stacy was real hot. I told him that I knew her—see, I work out at the place in the Village where she teaches aerobics—and so we figured it would be a real hoot if we could set it up so you could meet her in the flesh. So I asked Stacy and she said it was cool with her, and she even found out when the commercial would be running tonight so we could set it up the way we did. But, jeez, we didn't mean to make you uncomfortable or anything like that. We were just kidding around."

"Yeah," Stacy said, "it was just supposed to be fun."

Tozzi zoomed in on those baby-doll lips and got very depressed. He was supposed to be getting a kick out of this, and now it was upsetting him that he wasn't. A scolding voice not unlike his cousin Lorraine's was echoing through his head. *Act your age, act your age.*

He looked at Roy, then at Gibbons, trying not to stare at Stacy. He took one last swig of his beer, then got off the stool. "Look, I'll see you later, Gib. I gotta go." He headed for the door.

"Hey, Toz, where ya goin'?"

"I'm sorry, man," Roy called out. "Lemme fix you a drink. On the house."

"You told me he was a good sport, Roy."

Stacy's words followed him out the door, like a rain cloud.

Outside, Tozzi shrugged into his trench coat as he walked down the sidewalk. A good sport, huh? His life was half over, for chrissake. He wasn't supposed to be chasing babes like Stacy Viera anymore. He was beyond being a good sport.

The night was cold and wet and miserable. You could see the drizzle coming down in the streetlights. Tozzi flipped up his collar and shoved his hands into his pockets, fingering his car keys, mulling over that stunt they'd pulled in the bar, upset with himself that it was upsetting him so much. Gibbons and Roy meant well, and Stacy was probably a good kid. It was just bad timing, that's all. He wasn't in the mood for kidding around. Sure, Stacy Viera was a walking wet dream, but that wasn't what he needed anymore. Gibbons and Roy didn't understand that. They didn't know that it was time for him to grow up.

He turned down the side street where his car was

parked. The street was empty and quiet except for the sound of his own footsteps muffled by the drizzle. It was the perfect setting for how he felt right now. He went toward his car and pulled out his keys, thinking that maybe he wouldn't go home right away. He'd just end up watching something stupid on TV if he went home. Maybe he'd drive around for a while in the rain. He stuck the key in the lock and considered crossing the George Washington Bridge and heading up the Palisades Parkway. Kill some time riding along the river, listening to the radio in the dark.

But as he turned the key in the lock, he suddenly felt something in his back, something small and hard. Something like a gun barrel.

"Don't move and don't turn around."

The guy sounded nervous. He kept prodding Tozzi with the gun even though Tozzi was doing what he was told. He waited for the guy to say something else. If he was a mugger, why wasn't he demanding money? If he was a killer, then he was an amateur. Professional shooters don't wait.

Tozzi didn't say a word. He didn't want to provoke him. He turned his head slightly to the left.

The guy pushed his face back around with his free hand. *"I said don't turn around!"*

Tozzi's heart was thumping with relief. Thank God he didn't shoot. Now he knew that the guy was holding the gun with his right hand.

He considered the possibility of an aikido move. Turn quick to the right toward the hand with the gun, and roll to the guy's shoulder, take his wrist at the same time and control the gun, pull his arm forward to take his balance, then swing it back up and fold it behind his head, pointing the hand and the gun to the ground, forcing him to fall over onto his back. Keep control of the gun and point it in his face. *Kote gaeshi* from a stick-'em-up attack. Not the easiest throw, but one he'd done before, one that could be on his black-belt test.

Tozzi took a breath and let it out slowly to calm himself. As the gunman pressed the barrel into his back again, he started his move, turning nice and smooth, quick but not rushing it, putting himself shoulder to shoulder with the guy, pulling him forward to take his balance, then swinging the arm up and over, twisting his hand behind his head until he fell backward and hit the pavement. The guy still had the gun, but Tozzi had a good grip over the hand so that the weapon was pointed back in the guy's shadowy face.

"Hey! What the f—"

"Let go of the gun," Tozzi said.

"Fuck you, man."

"Let go of the—"

"Tozzi? I'm sorry about what happened in there."

Tozzi looked up. He recognized the pouty voice calling to him. Stacy Viera was standing on the corner five car-lengths away, a stacked silhouette in heels under the streetlamp.

"Stacy, go get Gib—"

A loud wet crack cut him short. The gun had gone off. A hot poker seared through Tozzi's thigh. The powder burn singed his pants, and the stink filled his nostrils. Tozzi clutched his thigh and clenched his face. Shit! Stacy had distracted him. He'd let up on his grip and lost control of the gun. The bastard had pulled the friggin' trigger. Shit!

The gunman rolled over and scrambled to his feet. Tozzi couldn't be sure in the dark, but he just assumed the guy still had the gun. Stooped over, holding his leg,

Tozzi dropped to one knee, the blood draining out of his face. He groped for the gun in his ankle holster.

"*Tozzi! What happened? Are you all right?*"

Stacy was running toward them. He could hear her heels clicking on the pavement. Jesus Christ!

"Get down! Get behind a car!"

Tozzi expected the bastard to plug her, then empty his gun into him. But when he glanced up, he saw that the guy had his hands to his sides. Tozzi couldn't make out his face in the dark, but it seemed like the guy was just staring at her.

"Holy shit . . ." the bastard whispered.

"This is bad. Very bad."

Tozzi whipped his head toward this second voice. He squinted into the shadows between the parked cars. He struggled to get his gun, tearing at the holster and ripping the Velcro straps. He was getting light-headed and he felt like throwing up, but he was determined to keep it together.

He got his gun out and pointed it up at his attacker. "Freeze," he croaked.

The bastard suddenly fired down at him, the muzzle flash lighting the street for a microsecond. Tozzi heard the *ping* of the bullet piercing the car door just above his head.

"*Freeze!*" Tozzi shouted.

The gunman turned to bolt. Tozzi fired over the man's head, but he didn't stop. Tozzi leaned on the car and hauled himself up to pursue, but his leg couldn't take the weight and it gave way under him. He collapsed to the ground, flat on his belly, his cheek pressed against the wet asphalt. He heard running footsteps splashing through puddles down the block. Under the streetlights in the distance, he saw two running figures, one big, the other small. The big guy seemed to be pushing the small guy ahead of him. Then he heard Stacy's clicking heels coming up behind him.

She knelt down beside him, her knees in his face. "Oh, my God! Are you all right? Are you all right?"

Tozzi tried to push himself up, but the leg hurt like a bitch. He tried to move it, but it wasn't responding, so he eased himself down onto his side. "Get Gibbons," he grunted.

"Oh, God!" she kept saying. "Oh, God!" She was chewing on her pouty lips, on the verge of hysteria. "Oh, God!"

"Go get Gibbons," he grunted again. "Don't worry. I'm all right. Just go get Gibbons. Go *now!*"

Reluctantly she got to her feet and staggered toward the bar, stopping to look back at him with every step she took, afraid to leave him alone.

"Go ahead, Stacy. Get Gibbons. Go ahead now. And call for an ambulance." He tried to sound as reassuring as he could even though he felt like he was gonna pass out.

He lowered his head back down to the asphalt and squeezed his eyes shut as he reached for the wound.

Shit! he thought. Now I'm gonna miss my black-belt test. *Shit!*

THREE

Sal Immordino sat hunched over on a folding chair, looking intently at his fists, making like he was talking to them. He always talked to his hands when he was putting on the nut. It was what he did.

Loopy Lou Nardone was sitting next to him with his fingers joined on top of the table. They were in the visitors' room, a small cubicle built into one corner of Sal's ward at the Vroom Building, the dungeon where the criminally insane were kept at the state psychiatric hospital in Trenton, New Jersey. Visits weren't monitored here the way they were at a regular prison because no one here at the nuthouse had been officially convicted of anything. But the walls were made of that thick security glass, the kind that has the thin wire mesh inside it, and the guards were always watching.

Sal furrowed his brow and frowned at his left hand. "So did you find out who the hitter was?"

Loopy Lou threw his hands up and shook his head. His jet-black hair looked like a used Brillo pad, his mouth was lopsided, and he was walleyed, but he was the top soldier in Sal's old crew, loyal like a brother. He was the one who should've taken over the crew after Sal got sent here, not that ass-licking Frank Bartolo. "It's a big fucking secret, Sal. I got my ear to the ground, but nobody knows nothing. It must be somebody nobody ever used before."

Sal raised an eyebrow and examined the knuckles of his right hand. "Not Bartolo's kid?"

Loopy Lou's wandering eye shot open. "Whatta you, kidding? You think that dumb fuck could sneak his way in here and pull off a hit? You'd spot him a mile away."

"Hmmm. Maybe. What about Joey D'Amico? He'd volunteer."

"D'Amico couldn't shoot himself. You know what they say. He didn't even make his bones by himself. He hired some kid to do his hit for him so he could get made. I don't think it's D'Amico."

"Maybe." Sal glanced out at the ward on the other side of the glass. The nut cases, the real ones, were shuffling around in their bathrobes and baggy jeans. A big TV set was mounted high up on the wall where no one could reach it. It was on, but no one was watching it. There was a guard leaning back on a folding chair, reading a paper by the door, and another one just outside the door to this room who kept his eye on Sal and Loopy Lou.

Loopy Lou threw up his hands again. "I just can't figure it, Sal. Either they hired somebody nobody knows, or they called off the hit."

Sal spread his fingers and studied them. "They didn't call off the hit." He was sure about that.

He stared out at the Thorazine Boys, the other nine patients on this ward, and wondered if any of them might be faking it to beat a rap the same way he was. But if one of them was, he'd never say so. That was the whole deal. You had to act like a nut to be declared mentally incompetent in the eyes of the court. Problem was, you had to act like a nut all the time because if a doctor or a guard or anyone ever saw you not acting like a nut, they'd boot your ass the hell outta here and haul you back into court to face your charges. That's why Sal had to act like one of them. But what if one of the Thorazine Boys was faking it too? What if one of them wasn't nuts and Juicy and Bartolo had gotten to him, given him the contract to kill their old buddy Sal? Wouldn't have to worry about sneaking the hitter into the hospital that way. It would be perfect. Sal tried to remember if any of these guys had visitors recently, a messenger who might've brought the deal in from Juicy and Bartolo. Sal scanned their blank, pale faces. You can't be too paranoid when you know there's a contract out on you.

Up on the TV, Phil Donahue was talking to a bunch of old bags about something or other. If Donahue was on, that meant it was after four. Charles should be here by now. Sal suppressed a grin. He couldn't wait for Charles to give him the details.

Sal glanced back at his soldier. "So whatta they saying about Mistretta's hit?"

Loopy Lou's eyebrows shot up and his bad eye rolled. "They're going nuts. The cops still got the old man's body, you know, and they're saying they won't be finished doing the autopsy for at least two weeks. Mrs. Mistretta's having conniption fits. Can you imagine? Poor woman's gonna hafta wait all that time to bury her husband. That's a shame."

"My name been mentioned?"

"Not that I heard, but I wouldn't be surprised. I

mean, like it wasn't no secret how you felt about Mistretta."

Sal squinted at his thumb. "Well, at least one of my problems is gone." He raised his index finger and squinted at that one. "One down, three to go."

Loopy Lou mumbled out of the side of his mouth. "Juicy, Frank Bartolo—who's the third one?"

Sal raised his middle finger. "That FBI guy, Tozzi. Dudley fucking Do-right."

Sal caught his own angry expression in the glass wall's reflection, and immediately he let his face go slack before the guard saw him. He saw red whenever he thought about Tozzi. Fucking Tozzi. Life was sweet before Tozzi came along. Back when he was out on the street, Sal used to play dumb all the time whenever people were looking, act like a punch-drunk retard and get away with murder. It had kept him out of jail for twenty years. But then Tozzi came along and caught him with his guard down in Atlantic City, saw him act normal. And that's how he ended up here in the bin. He had no choice but to take the insanity plea or face charges. But the charges were murder this time, so that friggin' old bastard of a judge said he had to put Sal in the nuthouse with the real nuts.

Loopy Lou looked all around before he spoke. "You really gonna do Tozzi, too, Sal?"

Sal let half a grin sneak out. "He may already be done."

Loopy Lou smiled on one side of his face. "And so that means you can check yourself outta here?"

"Yup."

"Tremendous."

Sal looked Loopy Lou in his good eye and bit the insides of his cheeks to suppress his joy. The only thing

the state had on Sal was Tozzi's testimony that he wit-
nessed Sal acting normal. With Tozzi gone, there was no
testimony and the state had no case. He could check
himself out into his sister's custody and he'd be as free as
a bird. He could be outta here as soon as the day after
tomorrow, the way he figured. All he needed was for
Charles to get here and give him the word that the deed
was done. He scanned the ward again. Where the hell
was he?

There were commercials on the TV now. Sal let his
jaw go slack and looked blank just in case someone was
watching him through that one-way mirror on the other
side of the ward. Sal couldn't hear the sound, but he
could see that they were playing that commercial for
that health club in New York, the one with the blonde
with the long corkscrew curls and the jiggly tits. What
the hell did they call her? The Pump-It-Up Girl, yeah.
Sal squinted and zeroed in on her jiggly tits. Yeah, baby.
Day after tomorrow, you can pump me up anytime.

Sal stared at the thunderbolt stripes on the Pump-It-
Up Girl's leotards and remembered that night at Cil's
place last week, how they dragged Mistretta and Jerry
out of the basement, how Mistretta left this long, bloody
brushstroke on the floor when Charles dragged him out
by the ankles like he was a rickshaw. Fucking pain in the
ass bled all over the place. Took them an hour to clean
the place up, that loony bird Emerick saying "This is
bad, this is bad, this is bad" over and over and over again
the whole time. Even dead, Mistretta was a pain. But
now he was gone, and Tozzi was too. Just two more to
go and the way would be clear for Sal to take over.

Sal caught himself smiling then, and he wiped it right
off.

"Tell me something, Sal," Loopy Lou mumbled.

"When you become boss, is it gonna be like it was when you took over for Mistretta that time when he was at Lewisburg? Gyp and Jimmy T. asked me to ask you."

Sal looked him in the good eye and shook his head slightly.

Loopy Lou's face dropped.

"Nope. This time it's gonna be better."

A lopsided grin reached out for Loopy Lou's earlobe. "You're gonna make some guys very happy, Sal. *Very* happy."

Sal thought back to the time when Mistretta made him acting boss. That was when things started to fall apart between them because the old man didn't like the way he was doing things. The old fart thought Sal's ideas were too big. Mistretta liked the old ways, the safe bets, things he understood: girls, dope, hijacking, gambling, unions, loan-sharking. Sal had taken the family into new ventures when the old man was away: gas tax scams, insurance scams, school bus contracts, asbestos dumping, payola. Mistretta didn't understand those kinds of things so he didn't trust them. He said they weren't reliable. The old bastard was a throwback to the past; he ran the family like a fucking dictator. If Sal had stayed on as boss, they would've made money, *real* money, not this nickel-and-dime whores and bookie crap they made now. Well, that was gonna be old news. Sal was ready to bring the family back up to speed. All he had to do was get outta here and take care of those other two assholes.

Loopy Lou scratched his Brillo head. "You know, I just thought of something, Sal. Aren't you safer in here as long as the contract is still out on you? Won't it be easier for them to get you on the outside?"

Sal made fists and boxed with the air. "Theoretically,

yeah. But as soon as I take care of Juicy and Bartolo, that won't be a problem anymore."

"Why not?"

"Would you go through with a hit if the guys who hired you weren't around to pay you? Think about it."

A light bulb went on over Loopy Lou's head. "Yeah . . . you're right."

Sal kept sparring with the air. "So how's Bartolo been treating you guys?"

Loopy Lou made a disgusted face. "You know what he did now? You remember that Dominican guy Gyp used to work with all the time, Raoul, the fence up in the Bronx?"

"Yeah, I remember him."

"Bartolo tells Gyp he can't do no more deals with him, none of us can."

"Why not?"

"Bartolo hates spics, that's why."

"He's crazy."

"I know he's crazy. And the sad part is Raoul's got a kid with leukemia. He really needs the dough, and Gyp told Bartolo that. But Bartolo didn't wanna hear nothing about it. He stuck to his guns and said no more deals with no spics, no matter how much money's involved. Can you beat that shit?"

Sal shook his head. The way he figured, somebody oughta give him a public service award when he finally gets rid of that fat-ass, baldheaded fuck. Frank Bartolo had been a nothing, a hanger-on, never earned a penny for the family in his whole goddamn life. But he was a good ass-kisser, and he sure knew how to suck up to Mistretta. *Right away, Mr. Mistretta. No problem, Mr. Mistretta. Don't worry 'bout a thing, Mr. Mistretta. Whatever you want, Mr. Mistretta.* And in the end it paid off for him. Not only did he get himself a crew, he got a good crew, *Sal's crew*. All good earners, each one of them. None of them really wanted to go with Bartolo, but what could they do? Complain to the old man? Lotta good that woulda done. It was no wonder those guys were saying rosaries every night, praying for Sal to come back. And there were guys in other crews who wanted him back as boss too. The way he and Loopy Lou figured, at the very worst they could count on half the family backing Sal. And in Sal's mind, that was the half worth having.

Sal tightened his fists, gritted his teeth, and kept punching air. The useless half belonged to that fucking pervert Juicy Vacarini, Mistretta's favorite capo, his hand-picked successor. But all that guy knows about is girls. Girls, girls, girls. Vacarini wouldn't know how to diversify the family if somebody told him. Sure, the guy makes good money with all those pros of his, but that's all he's got. He makes steady money, but he don't go nowhere with it. He doesn't know how to build with it. But old Mistretta, he thought Juicy was Mr. Wonderful. Juicy was his boy. And to his credit, Juicy may look like a sleepy momo with those Elvis Presley eyes and those stupid silk shirts of his, but he is a shrewd son of a bitch. Only thing is, he thinks he's got a lock on being the new boss. But he don't know how strong the competition is yet.

Sal threw a hard roundhouse.

"Hey, Sal, what's this guy looking at over here?" Loopy Lou nodded at the glass door. Charles Tate was standing there in his gray guard uniform, poker-faced, waiting to be noticed. The other guard who'd been watching the door was gone. "This *moolinyam* got a problem or what?"

Sal covered his mouth and grinned. He'd never thought of Charles as a *moolinyam*, an eggplant. His skin wasn't that dark. 'Course, now that he thought about it, if you looked at his head from a certain angle, it was sort of shaped like an eggplant. Charles thought he was a tough guy, but that was all in his head. Half the time he tried to come off like Run DMC, but underneath he was Bill Cosby. Sal had to laugh. Mr. Black Mafia, this guy. Wants to be a wiseguy. Stupid *moolinyam*. Now that he's made his bones shooting Tozzi, he must think he can be an honorary member. Yeah, sure. Just wait.

Sal hunched over his hands and didn't look at Loopy Lou as he spoke to him. "Why don'cha take off now? I gotta talk to this guy. If you wanna find out when I'm getting out, call my sister. Otherwise, stay away for a while. The feds'll be watching me."

"Whatever you want, Sal." Loopy Lou stood up and went to the door.

Sal compared his thumbs. "And keep your ear to the ground about the hitter. It'd be nice to take care of him, whoever he is, in case it takes me a while to get Juicy. You know what I mean?"

"I know what you mean." Loopy Lou's face got serious all of a sudden. He stood there like a big iguana with a Brillo pad on its head. Sal didn't know which eye was looking at him. "You be careful, Sal, you hear? A lotta us guys are depending on you."

"Don't worry. I'll be okay."

The big iguana nodded and went out the glass door into the hallway. Charles followed him with his eyes until he was out of sight, then he opened the door and came in.

Sal glanced over at the one-way mirror across the ward.

"Ain't nobody in there looking," Charles said. "I just checked." He pulled up a chair and propped his foot on it.

Sal rocked in his seat and looked straight ahead, just in case someone was watching. "So what happened? Tell me." He bent over his lap and squeezed his eyes shut, gritting his teeth and grinning. He couldn't wait to hear the details.

But the *moolinyam* wasn't saying anything. Sal turned his head and looked up at him. The guy looked guilty as sin.

"No good, man. I had a problem. I don't think I got him."

Sal's stomach bottomed out. His eyes went out of focus. This was what he didn't want to hear. "Whattaya mean you don't think you got him?"

"I mighta got him once, Sal. I dunno. But I don't think he dead."

Sal's fists were clenched. He wanted to smack this son of a bitch right in the mouth. He should never have agreed to let him go out and try it on his own. Sal glanced at the mirror again and leaned forward over his fists, mumbling to them frantically, just in case.

"It wasn't my fault, Sal. You ain't gonna believe this, but I got distracted. And you ain't gonna believe by who."

Sal glared up at him from under his eyebrows. "Don't start telling me stories, Charles. It's fucking bad enough already."

"I swear to God, Sal. This ain't no story. That girl from that commercial on TV, the Pump-It-Up Girl. She must be Tozzi's girlfriend or something. She showed up outta nowhere with that body of hers and I got distracted, man."

Sal's knuckles were white. He stole another glance at the mirror. Sweat was dripping from his forehead onto his pants. He was tempted to haul off and punch the shit outta this lying bastard.

"It's true, Sal. I was all set to do him, but then she showed up yelling to Tozzi and I looked up at her and then Tozzi grabbed the gun."

Panic zinged through Sal's chest. "You mean he has the gun?"

"No, no, don't worry 'bout that. I got it at home. He never took it away from me."

Sal stared down at the sweat spots on his pants. He couldn't believe this. Tozzi was fucking charmed. And what the hell was the Pump-It-Up Girl supposed to be? His fairy godmother?

Sal wiped his forehead with his sleeve. "This is bull-shit, Charles. You're lying. You didn't even try. Pump-It-Up Girl, my ass. She wasn't there."

"I swear to God, Sal. She was there. And if it wasn't for her, Tozzi'd be dead now."

Sal grit his teeth and frowned, his chest heaving. "What about Emerick? Where's he?"

"Donnie? He's home too. Don't worry. He's okay."

"Don't tell me not to worry. You fucked up. I got plenty to worry about now."

"No, Sal, no. I'll fix it. I'll find Tozzi and I'll get him this time. I promise."

"Emerick leave any prints?"

Charles shook his head. "No time. Happened too fast."

Sal grumbled at his fists. "Shit."

"Look, Sal, I know you mad already, but I got another problem. You know, it ain't easy keeping Donnie at my place, man. Even with his pills, he's all over the place. Them pills only keep him doped up so long."

"So double the dosage."

"Can't do that. What if he die?"

"So whattaya telling me here? Just say it."

"I'm afraid he gonna get loose one of these days while I'm here at work. If I had some money, maybe I could get somebody to come in and give Donnie his pill, put him to bed. But I need cash, Sal."

"I told you from the very beginning, Charles. There wasn't gonna be no cash till this was all over. When I can walk outta here, then you'll get paid."

Charles's face froze. He was looking at Sal through slit eyes, like he knew Sal was lying.

"Look, Charles, I can't leave here till Tozzi's dead. It's as simple as that. With him around, there's nothing I can do for you."

"I told you, Sal. I'll find him and I'll do him. But I need some money now."

Sal's stomach was in agony. It was one big knot. He couldn't lose Emerick. Jesus, everything depended on that little fruitcake. Everything. Sal stared at his thighs and shook his head.

"Whattaya shaking your head for, Sal? Sal? You listening to me, Sal?"

Sal mumbled in a trance. "You fucked up once. That's once too many. You ain't gonna do nothing no more. *I'll* do it."

"That's crazy, man. I can't get you out again." Charles creased up his face like he was in pain.

"You did it once. You'll do it again."

"Can't do that no more. Everybody jumpy enough around here with Donnie gone. They find you missing, all kindsa shit'll come down."

"Hey! You wanna get paid or not? You want them nice clothes and the Lincoln and all that shit you told me you wanted? You wanna keep working for me? Then you get me outta here to do the hits. You ain't no hitter, Charles. Face it. And I can't afford any more fuckups. Tozzi has to go, fast." Sal thought about the contract they had on him. If Loopy Lou was right and they got a hitter nobody knows, he's a sitting duck cooped up in here. He had to whack Tozzi so he could get out as soon as possible.

"Yeah, but Sal, you really think—"

"Yeah but nothing, Charles. That guard downstairs who watches the video monitors? And the other guy who works the all-night shift on this ward? Your friends?"

"Yeah, Buster and Ramon."

"Right, Buster and Ramon. You told me they both got little habits, the two of them. So they need money for coke, right?"

"Yeah, but—"

"Shut up and listen for a change. I want you to go buy them some shit. Give 'em a taste for free. Let 'em know, when they do something for us, you'll give 'em another toot. They'll get me out and they'll get me back in, just like the last time. You watch."

"But, Sal—"

"I don't wanna hear it, Charles."

Sal curled into himself as he pulled his St. Anthony medal out of his undershirt. He glanced at the mirror and turned his back on it completely before he slipped his thumbnail into the back of the gold medal and pried it open. Tucking in his chin to see what he was doing, he opened the locket and picked at the folded bill inside until it came out. He unfolded it and smoothed it out on his thigh.

The whites of Charles's eyes were showing. He was grinning like a wiseass monkey. Sal was pretty sure the *moolinyam* had never seen this president before. Grover Cleveland.

Sal folded the thousand-dollar bill in half and kept it close to his chest. "Take this and get your friends some good shit. Then you give it to them a little at a time so they do what you tell them to. You listening to me, Charles?"

The *moolinyam* was nodding, smiling and nodding. His hand crept over his knee, reaching out for the money. His fingers were like tarantula legs. "Don't you worry, Sal. I fix everything this time. This time I do it like a pro. Money-back guarantee. Tozzi be so dead he won't even know it."

The tarantula snagged a corner of the bill, but Sal wasn't letting go. "You're not listening to me, Charles. I said I don't want you to do it. *I'm* gonna do it. Tozzi's too tricky."

"Don't sweat it, man. You leave it to me. Better for you to just chill out here. You know, just in case they do a surprise night check or something like that. If they find you gone the same night Tozzi die, then maybe they blame you. You stay cool and let me take care of it." The tarantula tugged on the grand.

Sal looked up at his smiling monkey face and released his grip. But as the tarantula snatched up the cash, Sal went for the *moolinyam*'s crotch with his other hand and grabbed him by the balls. He got a good grip through the gray uniform twills, squeezed hard, and put a clamp on. He wanted to make sure he had the man's attention.

"Now, tell me, Charles. Whattaya gonna do with that grand?"

Charles's voice was high and hoarse. "Don't worry, Sal. I'm gonna fix—"

Sal squeezed.

Charles shut his eyes and groaned.

"You and your two friends got me and Emerick out before, so I know you can do it again. You'll get me out, I'll do what I have to do, and then you'll get me back in before anybody misses me. Same way we did it with Mistretta. Okay? Do we understand each other?"

Sal kept the pressure on. He could feel the throb of Charles's pulse through his fingers. His own heart was throbbing just as hard.

Charles's face was creased and tight, his eyes squeezed shut. "Okay, Sal, okay. If that's the way you wanna do it."

"That's the way I wanna do it." Sal let him go. He could see that Charles wanted to double over, but he was fighting it. Didn't want to show that he was in pain.

Sal glanced down and saw that Grover Cleveland was on the floor, right next to his foot. Charles must've dropped it. "Why don't you pick up the money, Charles. It'll make you feel better."

Charles hunkered down and let out a groan.

Sal let his face go slack and glanced at the one-way mirror again. He wiped his sweaty face and took a few deep breaths. Friggin' Tozzi. It wasn't like the guy was magic, he told himself. If he could kill a boss, then killing a stupid little fed like Tozzi shouldn't be that hard. All you needed was an experienced hitter.

He sat up and looked at his fists, nodding to himself. It shouldn't be that hard, he thought. He had plenty of experience. Plenty.

He kept staring at his fists, and his thumping heart started to calm down a little.

FOUR

Gibbons sat back in the blue vinyl armchair and cracked his knuckles one by one as his wife, Lorraine, fussed over her dear cousin Tozzi, scolding him for hopping around the hospital room on one foot the way he was. They were making such a scene, Tozzi's sick-looking roommate put on his robe and slippers and wheeled his IV bottle down the hall to the dayroom to get out of their way. Tozzi was just trying to collect his things and get dressed, but Lorraine wanted to *help* him get dressed and he didn't want to be helped. Gibbons understood how he felt. Women don't have the same sense of dignity men do. What do women always talk about when they get together? Their plumbing, their feelings, and their underwear. Men talk about sports.

He looked out the open window at the noisy intersection of Greenwich and Seventh Avenue South. It was a good thing St. Vincent's Hospital was right here. This was supposed to be one of the most dangerous intersections in the city, people getting killed here all the time. He thought about the guy who tried to kill Tozzi and wondered if the guy was really a mugger. Maybe the guy really was out to get Tozzi. Maybe the guy had been sent to kill him. Maybe whoever it was who sent the guy wanted Gibbons done too. They were partners, after all. Gibbons tugged on his nose and frowned.

Lorraine was still chasing Tozzi around the room, scolding him like a mother hen. Her long, dark hair was wild today, and the bright sunlight streaming through the windows picked up the silver threads every time she passed through it. She hadn't bothered to tie it back this morning, she was so worried about her cousin. Just threw on a blouse and a skirt, brushed her hair a little, and rushed Gibbons out the door. She looked nice. Sort of wanton but stern.

The hospital had kept Tozzi here overnight for observation, even though according to Tozzi it wasn't much more than a flesh wound. They were letting him out this morning, and Lorraine insisted they both go pick him up and take him home, meaning *their* home. Gibbons didn't put up an argument, even though he hated having houseguests, even when he liked the person. If someone was gunning for Tozzi, he shouldn't go back to his place right away, not alone. Still, the thought of having Tozzi around the house didn't thrill Gibbons. The moody son of a bitch was just gonna make everybody crazy. Gibbons couldn't wait for Lorraine to break the news to her cousin that she was bringing him home to take care of him. Tozzi was gonna have a fit.

Lorraine was standing in the middle of the room with her hand on her hip, exasperated. "Michael, will you please stop bouncing around like that and use the crutches?"

"I'm fine, Lorraine. I'm fine." Tozzi was holding the crutches in one hand, hopping around on his good foot, trying to collect his things. He was already making Lorraine crazy. Wait'll he's around the house for a while.

Gibbons closed his eyes and rolled his neck on his shoulders, listening for the old familiar crick on the left side. There was gonna be one good thing about having Tozzi stay over. Lorraine could bust someone else's balls for a change.

"Michael! Will you please sit down and let me help you?"

Gibbons winced. She could etch glass with that voice.

Tozzi kept hopping around like an idiot. "I'm okay, Lorraine. I'm fine. I can do it for myself." Tozzi bounced over to the other blue vinyl armchair in the room, plopped himself down, and started to put his socks on. He managed the left one okay, but you could tell from his face that the right was a struggle.

"Here. Let me do that." Lorraine reached for the sock, but Tozzi pulled it away.

"I said I'm okay. I can do it." He was gritting his teeth.

"No you can't. Give it to me."

He waved the sock over his head, out of her reach. "It's dirty, Lorraine. It's the same one I wore last night."

"Will you give it to me and stop acting like an ass? I can see it hurts you to bend that leg. Let me help you."

"I'm not helpless, Lorraine. I can do it."

She was steaming. "You're not helpless, you're hopeless. Gibbons, will you tell him to be sensible? Maybe he'll listen to you."

Gibbons shook his head. He didn't want any part of this catfight. No use talking to either of them. They both had those hard guinea heads.

Tozzi managed to get the sock over his toes, but now he was having a hell of a time pulling it over his heel.

His face was red and he was biting his bottom lip. Lorraine was biting her bottom lip too. Gibbons didn't understand what she was getting so cooked up about. If the guy wanted to be a jackass, let him. He's only hurting himself. 'Course, Gibbons wouldn't want anybody putting his socks on for him. To hell with the socks. He'd just step into the shoes and stick the socks in his pocket.

"Michael, can I ask you something?" Lorraine's voice dropped to a slightly more conciliatory pitch.

"Sure. What?"

Gibbons inspected his fingernails. He had a feeling he knew what was coming.

"I talked to your mother this morning. She wants to know if you intend to give up aikido now."

Tozzi's forehead bulged and his eyes slipped farther under his brow, like rattlesnakes ready to strike. "No, Lorraine, I am not going to give up aikido now. And my mother can go—"

"But she's worried about you, Michael. She doesn't want you to do something stupid and end up a cripple."

Tozzi pointed to his thigh. "I did not do this on the mat doing aikido, Lorraine. I was shot on the street by a mugger."

"But your aikido didn't help you fight him off, did it?"

Gibbons pinched his nose to keep from laughing out loud. She had no mercy. But she did have a point.

Tozzi's face was an angry red ball, but he chose not to argue with her, which was unusual for him. He was, no doubt, following the supposed first rule of the martial arts: Avoid the fight. Either that, or he didn't have a good answer.

Tozzi tried a clever tactic then. He ignored Lorraine's original question and answered the one he wished she'd asked in the first place. "I keep telling you, Lorraine, it's just a flesh wound," he said. "The bullet went in and came out, didn't hit bone or anything. I'll be back on my feet in a week and a half, maybe sooner."

Lorraine put on the mournful face. This was one of those Italian specialties reserved for people in the hospital. Illness was an Italian delicacy, like baccalà. In fact, the death-and-dying report was a daily bulletin with the older members of the Tozzi clan, and Tozzi's old lady was the editor in chief.

"Michael, we all know how bullheaded you are. Your mother and I are afraid you're not going to let this heal properly. Look at yourself. You're not treating it properly now. And remember, the body doesn't heal as quickly at your age."

Gibbons rolled his eyes to the ceiling. Oh, boy.

"What do you mean, at my age? I'm thirty-nine. What's that? Is that supposed to be old?"

"You're going to be forty in two weeks, Michael. Face it, you're not a kid anymore. This martial-arts stuff is for young people."

"You don't know what you're talking about, Lorraine. You don't know the first thing about aikido."

"I may not know anything about aikido, but I do know you. You're dying to test for your black belt, and you'll risk anything to do it. Including the use of that leg. For God's sake, Michael, you have nothing to prove."

"I'm getting mad now, Lorraine. You know why? Because you and my mother both belong in a nuthouse. You must think I'm stupid. You think I don't know I've got nothing to prove? I'm a goddamn street agent, for chrissake. I've been shot at, stabbed, kicked, clubbed, beaten up, pistol-whipped, stomped. I've had guys try to run me over. A crackhead tried to chop me up with an ax in East Harlem one time. Another time some union goon came at me with a circular saw. I've even had to put up with attack dogs. Not just once, *three* times. So I know I don't have anything to prove. I've already proved it, a hundred times over. What I get out of aikido is something else entirely. Something I don't think I can make you or my mother understand."

Lorraine folded her arms. "Try."

Tozzi's nostrils flared. "Well, for one thing, it brings me peace. Which is something I'm not getting from you right now."

"Well, I'm sorry about that, Michael. Why don't you arrest me for disturbing your peace?" Lorraine's voice was back up in the chicken-screech range.

Gibbons screwed a pinkie into his ear. This was getting boring.

"Am I disturbing something?"

Gibbons glanced at the doorway. Brant Ivers, Assistant Director in Charge of the Manhattan FBI field office, was standing on the threshold. The boss was here to visit the fallen soldier. Gibbons sat up. This ought to be moving.

Ivers's square frame filled the doorway just about right. His head was square, his jaw was square, and his shoulders were square. He was artfully gray at the temples, and Gibbons always wondered if he had that done at some fancy men's salon somewhere uptown. He probably thought it looked commanding on camera, gave him a glint of wisdom and authority. A powerful enhancement for the figurehead. Now that Gibbons thought about it, Ivers *was* sort of like the hood ornament on a fancy old car—silver and stiff.

Ivers nodded to Lorraine and Gibbons, then fixed his authoritative gaze on Tozzi, who was sitting there with his sock hanging off his bare foot like a wool cap on one of Santa's elves. "How are you feeling, Tozzi?" It sounded more like an accusation than a question.

Tozzi snapped the sock off his foot and lowered it tenderly to the floor. "Fine. It's still sore and a little stiff, but I can get around. A couple of days home on the couch and I'll be functional."

Lorraine shot him the death-ray stare, but she knew enough to hold her tongue in front of Ivers.

"I've spoken with your doctor," Ivers said. "They think it's a bit more serious than that."

Lorraine beamed. She had her argument ready for when Tozzi told her he didn't want to recuperate over at their place.

Ivers spoke with stern authority. "The doctor wants you off that leg for more than just a few days. I told him there'd be no problem. I'm putting you in for four weeks' sick leave. If you need more time, you can have it. But I want you to use the time to rest. Do you understand?"

Gibbons could see the muscles working in Tozzi's jaw. The same muscles were working in Ivers's. To say these two didn't see eye-to-eye on certain things would be like saying Jews and Arabs tend to have differences of opinion.

Tozzi thought Ivers was an ass-kissing paper pusher whose top priorities were his own image and his next promotion. He was right about that, but Ivers was also the boss and they had to live with him. It was one of those realities Tozzi had a hard time swallowing.

Ivers thought Tozzi was a hot dog, a disciplinary problem, an embarrassment to the Bureau. He was right, too. Only problem was, Tozzi had a nasty habit of getting results, which prevented Ivers from doing the one thing he wanted to do most in his tenure at the Manhattan field office: Shit-can Tozzi.

It was a cozy relationship, sort of like grit in a clam's mouth. The irritation often produced pearls.

These two could butt heads like this for hours if you let them, but Gibbons decided to break it up before it got ugly. "Have the police gotten anything on the mugger?"

Ivers pursed his lips and shook his head. "They've promised to send me a report today, but they don't seem to have much. Ballistics will analyze the slugs, for whatever it's worth."

"Which probably isn't much."

Ivers ignored Gibbons's observation. He didn't think much of opinions that didn't come out of his own mouth. "The detectives assigned to the case will want to talk to you, Tozzi. They're working on the theory that it wasn't a simple mugging. They want to know if you have any enemies."

Both Gibbons and Tozzi snorted out a bitter laugh at the same time.

Lorraine frowned.

Ivers stared at them from under his bushy eyebrows. "Am I missing something?"

Tozzi looked at Gibbons. "Do we have any enemies, Gib?"

Gibbons shrugged. "Only if you count all the wiseguys and mob associates in the five families. What's that? Fifteen hundred, two thousand guys. That's all."

"Yeah, that's all."

Lorraine looked ill.

Ivers stood there like a high school principal, coughing to get the unruly class's attention. "How about specific suspects? They want names."

Tozzi rolled his eyes up. "Phew! Where do I begin? Well . . . Richie Varga, Juicy Vacarini, Sal Immordino, Ugo Salamandra, Emilio Zucchetti, Jules Collesano, Phillie Giovinazzo . . ." Tozzi ticked them off on his fingers. "Christ, everybody hates me."

"Don't sound so proud of it." Ivers crossed his arms. The stone on his Yale class ring glinted in the sunlight.

Gibbons cupped his chin and considered Tozzi's short list. Every one of those guys had a reason to want Tozzi six feet under. Him, too.

"Mr. Ivers?" A woman's voice came in from the hallway.

Ivers stepped out of the doorway, and a smartly dressed black woman came in—glasses, navy suit, pearl-gray silk blouse, black leather shoulder bag. Gibbons guessed she was somewhere between thirty-three and forty-five, attractive in an executive sort of way. She wore her hair straight back and chopped at the neckline, a tortoiseshell hair band holding it in place. The glasses were stylish but sedate, purple-gray plastic frames, half-moons hanging from a heavy crossbar that covered her eyebrows. Gibbons wondered why she was dressed for business on a Saturday morning.

"Madeleine Cummings," she said, and offered her hand to Ivers. "I was told I could find you here."

Ivers shook her hand. "I didn't expect you until Monday. Welcome to New York, Agent Cummings."

Gibbons raised an eyebrow. *Agent* Cummings?

"I prefer *Dr.* Cummings, sir."

Ivers nodded. "Of course." He was smiling, which was unusual. He usually disdained correction from underlings.

"I arrived last night," she said. "No sense in my wasting the weekend when I could be getting acquainted with my new assignment."

Ivers smiled and nodded, proud of the new kid in class. Gibbons was waiting for her to pull a polished apple out of her purse to put on his desk.

"You must be Agent Tozzi," Cummings said. Her gaze sank from Tozzi's face to his bare foot. "I'm sorry to hear about your injury."

She didn't sound very sorry.

Tozzi reached up and shook her hand. "Nice to meet you."

Ivers extended his arm to bring Gibbons and Lorraine into the circle. "Dr. Cummings, this is Agent Cuthbert Gibbons and Lorraine Bernstein."

Gibbons instinctively clenched his jaw at the sound of his first name. He hated it, and he hated having to explain to people that he hated it. He preferred to be called Gibbons, just Gibbons, but he decided not to bother setting Dr. Cummings straight. He wouldn't be seeing much of her since he never had much contact with people outside of the Organized Crime Unit, thank God.

Cummings shook his hand, then took Lorraine's. "And may I ask what your interest is here, Ms. Bernstein?"

Lorraine was thrown off by the bluntness of her question. "Well . . . I'm Gibbons's wife and Michael's cousin."

"I see." Dr. Cummings turned back to Ivers, dismissing the husband-and-wife team.

"And by the way," Lorraine added, "that's *Professor* Bernstein." Lorraine flashed her cordial de' Medici smile.

Dr. Cummings's head snapped back around. She offered a small smile of her own, nodding in approval.

"Dr. Cummings is with the Bureau's Behavioral Science Unit at Quantico," Ivers explained. "She's going to be with us for a while."

"To analyze Tozzi?" Gibbons smiled like a crocodile. "I always said he needed his head examined."

Tozzi gave him the drop-dead stare. "I never heard you say that."

"You never listen."

"Actually, gentlemen," Cummings said, "my specialty is aberrant psychology that expresses itself in compulsively violent manifestations."

Gibbons exhaled a laugh. "Sounds like my partner's last job evaluation."

Lorraine shot him the hairy eyeball. That meant she wanted him to behave. She couldn't pick on Tozzi in front of company so she probably figured she had to make do with picking on her husband because she could do that without talking, just dirty looks and signals. It's a skill wives seem to develop naturally. Give her a few more years and she'd be using mental telepathy to chew him out, screaming into his head from out of the blue. It was too bad he loved her so much. Love can be a goddamn liability sometimes.

"Dr. Cummings is here as part of an internal exchange program the Bureau has instituted," Ivers said. "Agents who normally work in the labs or at desk jobs will be getting some field experience in order to get a better understanding of how the system functions as a whole. Dr. Cummings will be working as a street agent for the next six weeks, getting a feel for the front line, as it were."

Ivers and Cummings smiled and nodded, apparently

pleased with each other. Gibbons nodded, but he wasn't smiling. Another bullshit program from the brass in Washington. Let the executive agents tour the trenches for a month and a half so they'll have something to talk about at their Georgetown dinner parties. Grade-A bullshit.

"I had planned to put Dr. Cummings with Robertson and Kelso," Ivers said, "but since Tozzi will be on sick leave for at least a month, I think I'll let her partner with you, Bert."

Gibbons's face went slack. "What?"

"Yes." Ivers nodded, confirming his own decision. "It makes sense in terms of manpower allotment. By the time Tozzi is ready to return to duty, Dr. Cummings's stint here will almost be up." Ivers smoothed the lapels of his camel sport jacket, proud of himself, the prick.

Gibbons's stomach growled. "I don't think that's such a great idea. You can't just slot anybody into an LCN investigation. I'm working full-time on the Mistretta rubout, for chrissake. This is no time for on-the-job training. I've got informants who trust me. They see a new face, they'll clam right up. How'm I gonna get anything done with her hanging around?"

Cummings raised her chin and clasped her hands behind her back. "Agent Gibbons, do you think I'll be an impediment to your La Cosa Nostra investigation because I'm a woman or because I'm black?"

Gibbons bared his teeth. "You'll be an impediment because you don't know a goddamn thing about working the street."

She stared him in the eye, absolutely expressionless. "My race and sex have nothing to do with it?"

He stared back. "Your race and sex have everything to do with it. A wiseguy won't think twice about whacking a black chick. To those people, you're worth about as much as used coffee grounds."

"Gibbons!" Lorraine's eyebrows shot up into her hairline. The usual outrage of the politically correct.

"I'm just telling you the way it is out there. They know who I am, and they know not to dick around with a fed. They don't know who the hell you are, Cummings. And *these* sunny Italians don't welcome visitors with open arms."

"Well, you can introduce me." She was very confident. "Once they know I'm a fed, they won't *dick* with me either." She cussed like a college girl smoking in front of her parents for the first time. Look at me, I'm a grown-up.

"Bert, I can't think of a better man to put with Dr. Cummings than you," Ivers said. "You're the most senior agent in the field office."

Gibbons bristled.

Tozzi was snickering, his bare foot crossed over his knee. Gibbons glared at him. Another asshole. This was his fault. If he hadn't let himself get shot, Ivers would never have thought of this.

Gibbons was itching to yell at someone, but considering the company, he decided he might do better if he took a rational tack. "Look, Doc, no offense to you, but I just can't afford to have you standing around collecting data while I'm trying to figure out who ordered the hit on Sabatini Mistretta. It'll be dangerous for you, and counterproductive for me. I'm sorry, but what I do is not a game for intellectuals."

"Obviously."

Gibbons scowled at her placid face. Bad enough he was married to a female egghead, he didn't need another one around his neck on the job.

A skinny Hispanic kid came into the room pushing an empty wheelchair. "I'll be back for you in five minutes," he said to Tozzi. "I just have to get the nurse with your release papers." After the orderly left, Tozzi hauled himself out of the chair, using one of his crutches like a pole. Gibbons noticed that he'd slipped his shoe on without the sock.

Ivers moved over next to Gibbons and spoke into his ear. "I'm sorry, Bert, but this is from Washington. It's out of my hands, really. Just bear with it for a few weeks and I'll see what I can do."

Gibbons chewed on his upper lip. He knew exactly what Ivers would do—the usual, nothing.

Cummings watched Tozzi wincing and twisting to get comfortable in the wheelchair. "May I ask you something, Agent Tozzi?"

"Sure. What?"

"Where will you be convalescing?"

"You mean, where am I going now?"

"Yes."

Tozzi shrugged. "Home. Where else would I be going?"

She looked to Ivers. "Do you think that's wise? The attacker exhibited deadly force with Agent Tozzi. Suppose his intention was murder. A determined personality will pursue his or her target until the goal has been achieved."

Ivers raised his eyebrows. "You've got a good point."

Lorraine covered her mouth with her hand. "Oh, my God . . ."

Tozzi shook his head. "The guy was just a mugger. No one's out to get me."

"But you don't know that for sure."

"Well, no, you can't be absolutely sure about anything, but logically—"

"Dr. Cummings is right," Ivers interrupted. "I'll put a man at your apartment for a while."

Cummings adjusted her glasses. "If you're suffering a genuine manpower shortage, you probably don't want to lose another body to mere guard duty. I have an alternative suggestion."

"Yes?"

"I'm borrowing an apartment just a few blocks from here from an old Barnard classmate of mine."

Gibbons glanced at Lorraine. Her face lit up when she heard Barnard. Old school tie and all that crap. Cummings would be all right in her book now.

"Tozzi can stay at my friend's apartment while he's recuperating and I'll stay at his place."

Tozzi shook his head. "I really don't think that'll be necessary. No."

Ivers rubbed his chin. "You just ticked off a whole laundry list of mobsters who might want to see you dead. Maybe your attacker *was* sent to kill you. As you said, you can't be absolutely sure about anything."

"Believe me," Tozzi said. "This guy was not a shooter. If he was a pro, he wouldn't have wasted any time. It would've happened so fast I wouldn't have known he was there."

Cummings folded her arms. "Maybe they'll send someone better the next time."

Tozzi dug the crutch into the floor like a paddle and turned the wheelchair to face her. "It's very nice of you to offer, Dr. Cummings, but what about you? What if some guy does show up at my place looking for me and he finds you instead? You think he's just gonna go away?"

"Well—" Cummings had an answer, but Lorraine cut her off.

"You could stay at our house, Dr. Cummings. We have room."

Gibbons just looked at her. If Ivers hadn't been standing between them, he would've strangled her on the spot. He hated having houseguests, and Lorraine knew that.

"I couldn't impose, Professor Bernstein."

Gibbons's chest was heaving. You're damn right you can't impose. Not in my fucking house.

Lorraine smiled sweetly and shook her head. "It won't be an imposition. We were already planning to have Michael stay with us, but this way I think it'll work out better for everyone. Michael will be able to recuperate safely with his precious independence intact, and Gibbons will be able to prep you in the evenings for the next day's work. It'll be total immersion for you."

Gibbons bared his teeth. I'll give you total immersion, the both of you. Total fucking immersion till I don't see any more bubbles coming out of your mouths.

"Why don't we think this over," Gibbons said.

Ivers shrugged. "Sounds good to me. Does this sound viable to you, Tozzi?"

Tozzi looked disgusted. "All I want to do is go home and take it easy by myself for a while. I know my place in Hoboken is gonna be a lot quieter than anyplace in Greenwich Village. More conducive to rest. And I have a hard time sleeping in unfamiliar places. You know what I mean?"

"You can rest fine in the Village," Ivers said. "Try it for a few days and see how it goes." Ivers's tone made it clear that Tozzi didn't have any options.

"But I—"

"Tozzi! Thank God you're still here."

Stacy Viera tripped into the room, tits first. She was wearing a black motorcycle jacket over shiny aerobics tights with wide red-and-white diagonal stripes—a life-size candy cane with boobs and gams. She whipped that curly mass of bronze hair over her shoulder as she squatted down on her heels to get on Tozzi's level in the wheelchair. The ass end wasn't bad either.

"I'm glad I caught you before you checked out. Roy told me they took you here to St. Vincent's. I wanted to come see how you were doing, but they just told me at the nurses' station that you were checking out. Don't you think you should stay here for a few more days? Roy said he thought you lived alone. You shouldn't be going home to an empty house. Loneliness creates bad energy, and that slows healing."

"Oh, really?" Lorraine was looking down at her with the schoolmarm face.

Cummings looked sideways at Lorraine. "Bad energy?"

Ivers coughed and covered his mouth. He was trying not to stare down Stacy's cleavage.

"Gee . . . it was nice of you to worry about me, Stacy. I, ah, appreciate it."

She was gazing into his eyes. "I'm *very* concerned about you. You were shot, for God's sake."

"Well . . . yeah." Tozzi was flummoxed. He didn't know how to respond to all this concern. When he noticed all the eyes staring down at Stacy, he quickly started to make introductions. "Stacy, this is my boss, Brant Ivers. You know Gibbons. This is my cousin Lorraine. And this is Dr. Madeleine Cummings."

"Hi!" Stacy stood up and flipped the hair over her

shoulder. She did it that way models do, real loose and sexy.

Gibbons was having a hard time not staring at her himself, but the girl really was something to see.

Ivers smiled pleasantly as he shook Stacy's hand, but Lorraine and Cummings eyeballed her like a couple of border guards.

All of a sudden Lorraine turned and glared at Gibbons as if she knew what he was thinking. Cummings was glaring at him, too. Gibbons glared right back at her. Whatever he'd done wrong, it was between him and his wife. What the hell business was it of hers?

Stacy must've felt all the bad energy they were generating because she looked a little dismayed all of a sudden.

"Don't mind these two, Stacy," Gibbons said. "They went to Barnard."

"Really?" Stacy wheeled around to face the border guards, but she moved too fast and the aftershock bobbled her boobs. She did that hair flip thing again. Her eyes were wide and sparkling, like dark amber jewels. "God, I went to Barnard, too. I graduated last year." She ran a hand through her hair and looked at Lorraine and Cummings in disbelief. "Wow, alumnae."

A mean grin stretched across Gibbons's face. The border guards were not amused. But neither was he, really. His face sank as he remembered that he was gonna have to live with the two of them for the next month and a half. He balled one hand inside the other and looked for another knuckle to crack, but he was all cracked out.

Crap.

FIVE

The hallway smelled like rotten fruit, and the walls were spray-painted with graffiti so stylized Sal couldn't make out what the words said. Probably kids' names, he figured. They always do their names, these kids. Somewhere in this dump someone was playing a stereo loud enough for Sal to hear that it was that shit rap music. He could never make out those words either. Two o'clock in the morning and some jerk's playing that shit like that. He shook his head as he followed Charles down the scuzzy hall to the *moolinyam*'s apartment. Things crunched under his feet as he walked. Sal frowned. They live like animals, these people. Animals.

Charles was jingling a big key ring that was on the end of a chain attached to his belt. "Man, I hope he being good. He shoulda had his pill two hours ago."

"He better be good," Sal muttered. He needed Emerick. Christ, this whole thing hinged on him.

"This gonna be all your fault if he gone cuckoo in there. There ain't no reason for you to be coming out tonight. Just a waste of time. We ain't gonna do nobody tonight."

"No, Charles, this is your buddies' fault. Ramon and Buster. What the hell took so long? You guys were supposed to get me out by midnight."

"I already told you, Sal. Cops brought some guy down from Newark who shot his wife, then wanted to kill hisself. We didn't know they was coming. Couldn't get you out with all them cops around." Charles turned down another long corridor.

"Jesus. Where the hell is your place?" Sal was anxious to see Emerick. He had to see for himself if the nut was all right.

Charles started picking through his key ring as he walked. "It's true, you know. You ain't got no business being out tonight, Sal."

"I got plenty of business. You keep telling me Emerick's a problem for you. I'm gonna have a little talk with him. Nut or no nut, Donnie boy's gotta start listening." Sal chewed on his bottom lip. Emerick had to straighten up and fly right, at least for a little while. If he acted too nuts, no one would ever believe he pulled off all the hits Sal had planned. You had to be at least partly rational to shoot four people and give them the sign of the cross.

"You gonna talk to him, huh? You think it's easy handling Donnie. You wait. You'll see." Charles stopped in front of a dented metal door. The apartment numbers were gone, but the outline from the last paint job was still visible. 5L.

Charles unlocked the door and opened it a few inches. He put his mouth to the crack. "Donnie. Donnie. It's me, Charles. I'm home." He looked back at Sal. "Gotta let him know I'm here. He starts screaming if you sneaks up on him."

Sal could see that the lights were on inside.

"I'm home, Donnie. It's me. . . ."

Charles opened the door all the way, and they both saw it together.

"What the—"

"Shit!"

Sal had to squint against the glare. It looked like every light in the apartment was on, and the shades were missing from all the lamps. The living room walls were covered, baseboard to ceiling, with pictures cut out of magazines and newspapers, all pictures of women. Crotch-shot pinups from raunchy nudie magazines. Housewives from Betty Crocker cake-mix ads. The Breck girl. A cute telephone operator with headphones on. Madonna. Mrs. Gorbachev. Leona Helmsley. Dr. Ruth. They were pinned up with all kinds of things—straight pins, safety pins, nails, forks, knives, the handle end of spoons, a corkscrew, wooden matches, pencils, pens, screwdrivers, anything that would go through the plaster walls—and each picture was pinned four times, through the forehead, the belly, and each shoulder. A *Playboy* Pet of the Month had an open pair of scissors piercing both her shoulders. An unwound coat hanger was sproinging out of the Pump-It-Up Girl's belly button in a newspaper ad for Knickerbocker Spas. An aluminum turkey baster was embedded in the forehead of the vice president's wife.

Donald Emerick was squatting in a corner of the room, his shirt off, staring at them like a kitten, total innocence. His skin was so white it was less than white, and he was so skinny his chest looked like it was caving in. His light brown hair was all mussed on top. A gooney smile crept around his face, but his eyes stayed dull and ignorant. He started nodding his head and his hair flopped around like a rooster's comb. "God is happy," he whispered.

"Goddammit, Donnie. I'm gonna break your muthafuckin' head for this."

Charles rushed the little guy, but Sal reached out and grabbed a fistful of jacket. "Leave him alone. Lemme talk to him."

Charles shrugged his shoulder away and huffed. "Muthafuckin' little geek." He wanted a piece of the kid, but he wasn't gonna get it. Sal didn't want him messed up.

"Go get his pill," Sal said. "Go 'head."

"I'll get him a fucking cyanide pill." Charles grumbled as he went into the kitchen.

After Charles left the room, Sal looked the little fruit-cake in the eye. "You remember me, Donnie?"

The kitten eyes just stared back at him.

"You don't remember me? Sal? From the hospital? We took a ride together last week. You remember? We were in that basement and you were on the couch watching TV?"

Sal took a step forward, and out of the blue the nut case freaked. He jumped up on the couch and started screaming like a broad. "Get away, get away! You're bad! You want to kill me!"

"No, Donnie. No." Sal held his palms up to show he wasn't up to anything, but he kept inching toward the guy. "I don't wanna kill you. I'm your friend, Donnie. I'm not gonna hurt you."

"Get away! Get away!" he screamed. Emerick started to press up against the back wall, but there was too much junk sticking out of it.

"Stop yelling, Donnie. C'mon, it's too late for this. People are trying to sleep." Sal moved closer. He figured he'd get the little nut around the neck and pin him to the couch. Hold him down so he could talk to him. "C'mere, Donnie. I wanna talk to you."

Sal reached out to grab Emerick by the hair, but the nut suddenly bounced on the cushion and kicked Sal's arm.

"Why, you son of a—"

Sal snatched Emerick's arm, but the nut leapt on him and sent him toppling back. He crashed over the coffee table and broke it, banging his head hard on the floor. Sal saw red. He was ready to break this little shitass's nose. Then he stopped himself. He needed this guy.

Charles ran into the room. "What happened?"

"He's crazy," Sal said, getting to his feet.

"Shit, I know that."

The skinny nut was running around the room, jumping on the furniture, screaming like a monkey in a cage.

"Shut him the fuck up before someone calls the cops."

Charles knew how to handle nuts. He went after him, got him into a corner, and grabbed his wrist, but Emerick was wiry and he wormed his way out, screaming as he jumped up on a wooden chair.

Sal moved in fast and tried to kick the chair out from under Emerick, but the guy dove into the air like he thought he could fly, and would've sailed right over Sal's head if Sal hadn't caught him by the ankles and tackled him to the smelly rug.

"Gimme a hand here, Charles. I can't hold him by myself."

"Wha'd I tell you? I told you he strong when he off the pills." Charles threw his body over Emerick's.

Emerick screamed and struggled, got one leg free and started kicking.

Sal took a heel in the face before he was able to grab the ankle again and hold down both legs. "Christ Almighty, together we must outweigh this guy by about four hundred pounds."

"I told you."

Emerick let out a scream like he was Ella Fitzgerald trying to break a glass. It startled Sal, and the nut broke free from his grip. Kicking his legs, Emerick was able to squirm out from under Charles's weight and retreat to the couch. On his way he picked up a hammer from the pile of splintered wood that had been the coffee table. He must've used it on his decorating job.

"You're bad! Get away! You're very bad!" Emerick swung wild with the hammer.

Sal scowled. "What the hell's he talking about?"

"I think he remember you. He remember you killing Mistretta and that other guy. He scared."

"He should be." Sal snatched up a leg from the broken coffee table on the floor. "You got the pills?"

"Yeah. Right here." Charles had a capsule in his palm. Sal recognized the colors—orange on one end, pink and white granules on the clear end. It was Thorazine, but this one looked a lot bigger than the ones they used to try to give him at the hospital.

"Get away! Get away from me! You're bad!" The guy's eyes were frantic, like something out of a monster movie.

Sal kept his eye on that swinging hammer. "Okay, listen to me, Charles. I'll grab the hammer, and you pull his feet out from under him. Then we sit on him and get the pill down his throat. Okay?"

"Okay. We can try it." Charles moved away from Sal and positioned himself for the attack, but he didn't sound hopeful.

Sal watched the hammer swinging right and left, right and left. He waited for Emerick to swing left again, then he made his move. As Emerick started his backswing, Sal lunged forward and batted the nut's hand with the coffee table leg. Emerick screamed and Sal clubbed his hand again, then grabbed the shaft of the hammer.

Emerick's eyes were white and his mouth was wide open. Suddenly thinking of Dracula, Sal panicked and raised the table leg over his head. The fucking freak was gonna bite him. He was just about to bash Emerick's brains out when the vampire vanished. Charles had pulled the rug out from under him, and Emerick was on his back on the couch, flashing the whites of his eyes.

"You're bad!" Emerick shrieked. "You want to kill me! You're bad!"

Sal dropped his knee to Emerick's chest and slapped the nut's clawing hands away as he worked the wooden hammer shaft into his mouth. Emerick bit it like a mad dog.

Sal was breathing hard, sweat pouring down his face. He'd almost bashed Emerick's head in. Christ Almighty, he could've killed the guy and fucked himself royally. He needed Emerick. Emerick had to take the rap for killing Mistretta, Bartolo, Juicy, and Tozzi. That's why they were bringing Emerick along on the hits, to make him leave his fingerprints. Emerick was Sal's made-to-order psycho. If they asked, Sal was gonna say Emerick got the idea when they were on the ward together. Emerick heard him mumbling about things and took over his personality, flew the coop, and killed all Sal's enemies. That's exactly what Sal was gonna have his old shrink say when the cops came around asking why this nut Emerick did Sal's dirty work for him. But Christ Almighty, Sal couldn't believe he could be so stupid. He almost killed his baby here, his ticket to freedom, to power. He swallowed on a dry throat as he struggled to keep Emerick

down, trying not to hurt him. He needed Emerick, but
he needed him under control, and not next year. Sal had
to finish off his hit list this week, especially Juicy and
Bartolo, before their hit man found him first.

"Give him the goddamn pill, Charles. Hurry up."

Emerick was struggling, screaming like he was being
raped. Charles was sitting on his thighs. He reached over
and tried to figure out how to get the pill down Emerick's throat, but his teeth were clenched on the hammer
handle.

"Whattaya waiting for? Just stick it down the side."

"That won't do no good. He won't swallow it."

"We'll hold him here till it melts in his mouth."

"Can't wait that long. People be calling the cops
pretty soon. Think we killing some girl in here."

"Shit." Sal gritted his teeth. Then something caught
his eye on the wall. With one hand holding the hammer
steady in Emerick's mouth, he reached over and pulled
the aluminum turkey baster out of the vice president's
wife's head. He shook out the plaster dust, then worked
the small end into Emerick's mouth between the hammer and his lower teeth, prying his jaw open.

"C'mon, Donnie. Open up. Be a good boy now."

Emerick fought him, his eyes squeezed tight, but Sal
put his knee to the skinny nut's face and managed to pin
his head against the back of the couch. Sal worked the
metal tube in little by little, getting it down farther and
farther until Emerick started to gag.

"Okay, drop the pill in. Hurry up."

Charles dropped the capsule into the wide end of the
turkey baster, then he reached around and clamped
Emerick's nose closed. "Swallow, you goddamn little
freak. Swallow it."

Emerick stopped struggling and started gurgling and

grunting. They couldn't tell if he had swallowed the pill or not.

"Blow on it," Sal said.

"Wha'?"

"I said blow on it. Like a blowgun."

Charles made a face. "Man, what if he got AIDS? What if he blow back and spit in my mouth?"

Sal growled in his face. "Hurry up and blow that god-damn pill down his throat or you're gonna fucking wish you had AIDS."

"Aw, man . . ." Charles complained, but he did what he was told, bending forward and blowing on the wide end of the tube.

"Did he get it?"

"I dunno. What you want me to do? Stick my finger down there?"

Emerick was bucking and choking, his face turning blue. Sal pulled out the baster, afraid that he was gonna choke to death and ruin everything. He dropped the baster but kept the hammer in place, still afraid that Emerick might bite.

After a few minutes, Emerick stopped bucking. His body relaxed and his eyes gradually glazed over. When his lips were wet and loose on the wooden handle, Sal removed the hammer.

Sal's heart started to pound. Jesus Christ! He's dead!

He leapt off Emerick's chest and reached into the guy's shirt to feel for a heartbeat, but when the little nut blinked and looked up at him, Sal nearly had a heart attack.

"Jesus! I thought he was dead."

Charles got off Emerick's legs. "Three hundred milli-grams of Thorazine? Man, you might as well be dead."

Tears were streaming down the sides of Emerick's

face, running into his hairline. "This is bad," he mumbled. He was pathetic now.

"C'mon, sit up, Donnie. Sit up." Charles pulled Emerick up by the arms and sat him up on the couch. "Turn on the TV."

Sal was puzzled. "What for?"

"TV mellows him out."

"He looks pretty mellow to me."

"Yeah, but he gets into a crying jag, he'll cry all night long. Can't let him do that. Ain't fair."

Sal felt bad for the little guy. The television was sitting on one of those cheap TV carts with the imitation brass-finish legs. Pieces of aluminum foil were wrapped around the ends of the rabbit ears. Sal turned it on.

As the picture came on, Sal stood back to see what it was. A lot of shining chrome. Nautilus machines and crap. Then the camera found that friggin' blonde with the long, curly hair and the jiggly tits, the Pump-It-Up Girl again.

"Hey, Charles, here's your friend."

Emerick's face twitched as he let out a long, pitiful moan. "Bad . . . Very bad . . ."

"Turn that off." Charles was sitting on the edge of the couch next to Emerick. He pulled the nut's face into his chest to keep him from seeing the TV. "Can't let him see that. Sexy girls like that get him all upset."

Sal switched the channel. The first thing he found was an old World War II movie, guys shooting rifles and throwing hand grenades and shit. That was no good. He switched it again. Black kids with big heads bawling their eyes out, flies getting in their eyes and noses. Kids starving in Africa. Sal changed the channel. That stuff made *him* upset.

"Put on Channel Nine." Charles was still cradling Emerick's head against his chest.

Sal turned the dial to nine. A close-up of a can of paint came on the screen. *"Yes, friends, this portion of our show is brought to you by Martin Paint."*

"What's this?"

"It should be *Joe Franklin*." Charles was letting Emerick watch now. "He like *Joe Franklin*. Old white people talking shit make him mellow, keep him calm."

Sal looked at the screen. Joe Franklin was sitting behind his desk, talking to some blowzy old redhead who looked like she just came back from a USO dance in the forties. Sal couldn't believe it. Joe Franklin must be about ninety years old now. Little short guy with that dyed hair of his and the gooney moon face. Jesus, Joe Franklin. Sal just assumed the guy had to be dead by now. But there he was. Joe Franklin. Son of a bitch.

On the couch, Emerick was zoned out, not moving a muscle, just staring at the TV. Those pills really did the trick. He was like putty now.

Then Sal noticed the turkey baster on the rug. There were teeth marks on the metal tube. *Deep* teeth marks. Sal stared at the pinwheels in Emerick's eyes, and his heart started to pound again.

Sal knew he shouldn't be surprised, though. Technically Emerick was a serial killer.

SIX

Tozzi was sitting on the floor with his back against the sofa, his bum leg up on two pillows. Magazines and newspapers were spread out all around him, but he'd read them all and now he was bored. That's why he was winding up these Zoid things, the little Japanese wind-up robot animals that Stacy had bought for him, letting them go on the coffee table. They came unassembled and putting them together helped pass the time, but now they really weren't so interesting. Tozzi kept winding them up and letting them go, though, because it was like eating peanuts from a candy dish. You only did it because they were there.

He finished winding up the bull Zoid and set it down so that it would charge the lumbering gorilla Zoid. The turtle Zoid was on the other side of the table, scaling a staggered stack of *Time* magazines. When it reached the Bart Simpson coffee mug that Stacy had bought, the turtle butted its head against the ceramic wall and walked in place, grinding its little motor until it wound down.

Tozzi looked at his watch. His buddy, John Palasky, from his aikido class said he'd be stopping by after work.

He reached for the turtle and started to wind the stem. He wished John would get here soon. Recuperation was driving him batty.

He let the turtle Zoid go and watched it walk the length of the coffee table. It climbed over that morning's *New York Times* and crossed the ad for Knickerbocker Spas, the one with Stacy in it. He wished he could stop thinking about Stacy. She was only twenty-two, for chrissake.

But she was unbelievable.

The doorbell rang then.

"Finally," Tozzi mumbled as he reached for his five-foot *jo* stick on the floor next to him. It was one of the practice weapons they used in aikido. He extended the wooden stick to the intercom buzzer on the wall and pressed the button to let John in.

Dr. Cummings's friend's apartment was on the first floor, so Tozzi knew John would be right outside the door by now. "Come on in, John. It's open."

Tozzi heard the door open in the short hallway.

"Who's John?" Stacy walked into the living room. She was wearing her black leather motorcycle jacket over a black leotard top and tight blue jeans with those pseudo cowboy boots that had gotten popular, the ones that are really low-tops under the pants cuff. She was smiling, pushing the hair out of her face, those bronze ringlets spilling down over one breast.

Tozzi sucked in his breath. "You're not John."

She shrugged. "I guess not. You'll have to make do with me until he gets here. So who's John? Another FBI guy?"

"No. John's one of my aikido buddies. He said he'd stop by this afternoon."

She took off her jacket and threw it on a chair. "You must be depressed about missing your black-belt test."

Tozzi shrugged. "Not much I can do about it. I'll just test next time. That's all. There's beer and soda in the refrigerator. Help yourself, if you want."

"Thanks." As she went into the tiny galley kitchen, Tozzi watched her backside. God, did he want her. She was incredible. Not only great-looking, but she was smart and hip and funny. But every time he thought about doing something with her, he thought about her age. She was just barely in her twenties, and he was gonna be forty. He was old enough to be her father. *That* was depressing. It wasn't like it was unheard-of for guys to date girls much younger than themselves—you saw it all the time. It was just that he kept hearing that voice in the back of his head, the one that sounded sort of like Lorraine: *Grow up. Act your age.*

She came back out with a bottle of Dock Street in her hand. Gibbons had bought him a case. She kicked off her boots and sat down on the floor on the other side of the coffee table. Her tawny eyes gave him the once-over as she tipped the bottle to her lips. "You look antsy. You must be getting bored."

"Yeah, you could say that."

"Why don't you go out? This is the Village, after all. Plenty to do around here."

"I'm supposed to stay off the leg for another day. Doctor's orders." He frowned down at the leg as if it were a lazy dog. "Had to be the right leg, too. Can't drive either."

"Did you ask your boss about taking home some paperwork?"

Tozzi shook his head. "I called Ivers this morning.

'Absolutely not,' he said. He told me sick leave means no work. At all."

"You planning on listening to him?" She took another sip.

"No."

She grinned. "That's what I like about you. You seem like a straight arrow, but you aren't. You're really a pretty cool guy."

"Get outta here. Forty-year-old guys are not cool. They only think they are."

"Not true. Not true at all. You're gonna be a black belt and you chase all these Mafia guys for a living and you carry a gun and all. I mean, you do all this macho stuff, but you're not macho. You're really a nice guy. That's cool."

"Well, I'm flattered that you think so."

"But you don't believe it."

Tozzi shook his head. "Nope."

"See, that's what I mean. You're cool because you don't think you're cool."

Tozzi nodded, trying to understand, but he could see the generation gap opening up in front of him like a sinkhole.

Stacy took another sip and flipped the hair over her shoulder. "So have the police made any headway in finding out who shot you?"

"Nope. I still think it was just a mugger. Had to be."

He reached over for the gorilla Zoid and started to wind it up. In all probability it was just a mugger. But maybe it wasn't. He'd been mulling this over ever since Ivers had asked him at the hospital if he had any enemies. Three possibilities kept nagging at him.

Richie Varga had been running a very lucrative insurance scam while he was supposed to be in the Witness

Protection Program. Tozzi and Gibbons had uncovered him, but Varga's conviction had recently been overturned. He was out now, and he was a crafty son of a bitch. He might be looking for some payback. He could've sent a shooter after Tozzi.

Emilio Zucchetti was the king of the Sicilian heroin importers. He'd lost a lot of money thanks to Tozzi, and he was an old Mustache Pete. The old-timers lived by the Mafia code of honor, so he would demand revenge the old-fashioned way. By rights, Tozzi should definitely be on his hit list.

Then there was Sal Immordino, who had more reason than anyone to want Tozzi dead. It was Tozzi's testimony that would put him away forever because Tozzi was the only law-enforcement agent ever to witness Immordino acting sane. Of course, Sal was stuck in the bin down in Trenton, forced to play numskull or face charges. But if Sal could somehow get rid of Tozzi, his path to freedom would be clear.

Tozzi exhaled slowly. Any one of these guys could've sent a killer after him. And they wouldn't stop with one try.

He'd talked to Gibbons that morning after he hung up with Ivers. Gibbons promised to look into these three and get updates on their recent activities, then get back to him.

Tozzi positioned the gorilla on top of the magazines so that it would attack the bull. Out of the corner of his eye, he could see that Stacy was staring at him. He kept his eyes on the toys.

"Do I make you nervous, Tozzi?"

"No. Of course not. What makes you say that?"

"I dunno. It's just the impression I get."

"No. You don't make me nervous." He flashed a quick smile at her, then glanced down at the Zoids.

She put the beer bottle to her lips and grinned. "Ah-huh."

Tozzi didn't say anything. He adjusted the bull's direction so that he'd charge the gorilla head-on.

"Do you think I'm attractive?"

Tozzi coughed up a nervous laugh. "What, you don't have a mirror at your house? Of course you're attractive. Don't you think you're attractive?"

She shrugged. "I dunno." Her eyes were sly slits.

"C'mon. You don't think you're beautiful?"

She was grinning like a cat. "I want to know what *you* think. What's your criteria for a beautiful woman?"

He caught himself staring at her lips. They were juicy and plum-red. He coughed into his fist, then returned the sly grin. "Well . . . if you really want to know my personal test for judging a beautiful woman, it's this. A truly beautiful woman is beautiful when she's sopping wet. The hair's not done. She's not wearing makeup. No flattering clothes to accentuate this or that. No heels. Nothing. If she can turn me on coming out of the shower, *that's* a beautiful woman."

Stacy raised an eyebrow. "Do you think I'd pass the test?"

Tozzi smiled and shrugged. "I dunno."

She nodded and slowly twirled the beer bottle on the tabletop. The bull Zoid and the gorilla Zoid were toe-to-toe, grinding away, neither one giving any ground. Stacy looked up at him. Her eyes were full of mischief. "So which way's the shower?"

Tozzi's heart fluttered. Then he heard that voice in his head. *Act your age.* He looked down at the Zoids.

He felt her hand on his shin under the coffee table

then. It was walking up his good leg. She started circling his kneecap with her finger as she gazed into his eyes, raised her eyebrows, and bit her bottom lip.

Tozzi felt light-headed. *Jesus, help me.*

Her fingers did the walking up the inside of his thigh. She paused and ran her fingernails along the inseam of his jeans, going up and down, reaching a little higher with each run.

He swallowed hard.

She lowered her shoulder so she could reach those last few inches. But as he watched her curls tumbling to one side as she went for it, Tozzi suddenly realized something. He wasn't hard. He wasn't even starting to get hard, nothing.

Then he heard the voice scolding him. *Grow up. Act your age.*

He blinked, spooked by the voice. He should've been hard by now, but he wasn't. Not even close. It was the first time this had ever happened to him in his life. Christ, he was always hard. He wanted to give it a little help with his hand, but he was afraid he'd run into hers down there. His heart started to beat faster and his breath got short. He couldn't get it up. Maybe it was because of his injury. The blood was all going to the bad leg. Or maybe this is what happens when you turn forty. Oh, shit. What if he started something with her, and when the time came, he couldn't get it up? Oh, no . . . No . . .

Stacy took her hand off his thigh then and reached across the table, dragging her palm over his cheek. "You never answered the question," she moaned. "Do you find me attractive or not?" Her face was serious. She meant business.

But what if he couldn't get it up? Oh, Jesus . . .

She touched his lips. "Do you?"

"Well, Stacy . . . ah . . . I . . ." There was no graceful way out of this. He was stuck there on the floor with his bum leg. If he put her off, she'd think he was gay. If he went for it, and then he couldn't do it, he'd kill himself. That's all there was to it. He could never deal with that. He'd just have to end it all.

"Tozzi?"

Act your age.

"Toz-zee?"

Grow up.

"Tozzi?!"

He swallowed hard. Please, God. Whatever you want. Anything. Please.

The doorbell rang.

Thank you, God.

Stacy pouted.

Tozzi shrugged apologetically. "Must be John."

"Don't answer. He'll go away."

"I told him I'd be here."

It rang again.

She sighed.

It rang again.

He pressed his lips together and shrugged as he picked up the *jo* stick and pressed the buzzer.

She sighed out loud as she stood up. "I'll let him in," she said, going toward the door, walking backward and giving him those pouty eyes. When she disappeared down the hallway, Tozzi felt his crotch. Still nothing. Shit. He was cursed.

"Hi." He heard John's voice coming in from the hall-way.

"Hi. You must be John." Stacy was vaguely sarcastic.

"Yeah. How'd you know?"

"I'm just a good guesser, I guess. Come on in."

John followed Stacy into the living room. He was wearing a conservative blue suit, his banker getup. Stacy rolled her eyes and smirked behind his back. It was obvious what she thought of guys who looked like bankers. Not cool enough.

"Hey, Toz, how you feeling?" John put out his hand.

Tozzi reached up and shook it. With his back to Stacy, John bugged his eyes out. They were miniature versions of Stacy's breasts, gazanga eyes. Tozzi looked past John to Stacy. She crossed her eyes and stuck her finger down her throat.

"John, this is Stacy Viera. Stacy, John Palasky. John and I take aikido together."

"You told me." She shook his hand and forced a smile.

John's tongue was on the floor. If he only knew what an asshole he looked like right now.

"Tozzi and I started aikido at the same time," John explained. "We came up through the ranks together."

Tozzi laughed, trying to lighten things up. "Yeah, they say we're like a tag team. Some people actually think we look alike."

Stacy looked skeptical. "Maybe in a police report."

Tozzi leaned his elbow on the sofa and started to push himself up off the floor. "You wanna beer, John?"

"No, I'm fine. Sit down, sit down."

Stacy looked at her wristwatch. "Listen, I've got a five-thirty high-impact class. I'd better start heading back to the gym."

"Oh." Tozzi didn't like that look on her face. He felt like he'd done something wrong.

"Maybe I'll stop by later on," she said.

"Oh . . . Okay . . . I'll be here." But will my dick be here?

She picked up her motorcycle jacket from the arm-chair and shrugged into it.

John was grinning at her like an idiot. "It was nice meeting you, Stacy."

"Yeah, you too, John." She looked down at Tozzi, like she expected something. He wished to God he could give her what she wanted. "Bye," she finally said, flipping her hair over her shoulder and heading for the door.

John waited for the door to close before he sat down in the armchair and loosened his tie. "I'll make you a deal, Toz. You give me Stacy's phone number and I won't test next week. I'll wait for you so we can be black belts together."

"Forget it, John."

"C'mon, Toz. I thought we were friends."

"Forget about it." He wasn't thinking about the test.

"Tozzi, I'm in love here. She wants me. I can tell."

Tozzi started winding the bull Zoid. "Go fuck yourself, will ya, John?"

"That's what I do all the time, Tozzi. C'mon, you're not interested in her. You're too old for her."

Tozzi glared at his friend. He set the bull down on the coffee table and it charged across the magazines. "Go fuck yourself, John."

"Please, Tozzi, I'm begging you. I'm only thirty-four. It wouldn't be cradle-robbing if I went out with her."

"Go fuck yourself, John."

Forty isn't old. It's a fucking curse, is what it is. I'm cursed.

The bull chugged its way over the pile of magazines, tripped, and did a header off the coffee table. John leaned over and picked it up. He had the body in one hand, the head in the other. "It's broke, Toz. The head fell off."

Tozzi glanced out the bay window. He could see Stacy walking up the street, her long blond curls bouncing down her black leather back.

"I said, the head came off, Toz."

"Go fuck yourself, John." Tozzi's teeth were clenched. His forehead was beaded with sweat.

"Oh . . . Maybe I will have that beer after all, Toz."

John went into the kitchen while Tozzi stared out the bay window and watched Stacy walking down the sidewalk, her corkscrew curls bouncing as she grew smaller and smaller in the distance.

He put his hand over his crotch. Still nothing. It was a fucking curse. It had to be. He was being punished for something.

Tozzi dropped his chin to his chest and spotted the headless bull on the coffee table.

Shit.

SEVEN

Gibbons shuffled into the kitchen, all dressed for work except for his tie, which was draped around his neck. He opened the dishwasher and grabbed a clean cup. He was worried about Tozzi. He was worried about himself, too.

Tozzi kept saying it was a mugger who shot him, but Gibbons didn't buy it. Tozzi had too many enemies in the mob—they both had—wiseguys they'd investigated together and brought to trial. So it was only logical that if some wiseguy had a vendetta against Tozzi, he had it against Gibbons, too. Trouble was figuring out which wiseguy. Tozzi had come up with three likely suspects off the top of his head, but Gibbons had been thinking about it and he'd come up with at least a couple of dozen. He wasn't gonna tell this to his boss, Ivers, though. Ivers might do the chickenshit thing and try to put them under protection until someone was apprehended. That could take forever, and the police might never find anybody. No, Gibbons planned to handle this the way he would any other investigation: Run down the most likely suspects, eliminate the unlikely ones, then squeeze whoever's left until he finds out who wants them dead. And hope that he doesn't get shot first.

The morning light was streaming through the window over the sink as he poured himself a cup of coffee. Lorraine was at the stove, stirring a pot. Gibbons looked over her shoulder to see what she was making, then backed off when he saw the swirling, gritty white glop. He didn't want to get too close.

"What's that?"

"Cream of wheat." Lorraine didn't look up, just kept stirring.

Gibbons made a face. "Whattaya making that for?"

"I like it."

"I don't remember you ever making it before."

"That's because you hate hot cereal, and it's too much bother to make it for one."

"So whattaya making it now for?"

"Madeleine told me she loves cream of wheat, but she never has time to make it. I thought I'd surprise her this morning."

Gibbons plopped some milk into his coffee from a cardboard quart. Madeleine, was it? They were getting real chummy, her and Cummings. They were also turning the place into a goddamn girls' dormitory. Last night Lorraine had rented an opera from the video store, some humongous black woman making the god-awfullest noise—Haystack Calhoun in drag with rhinestones all over her head. The two of them were riveted to the set, drinking herb tea and eating dried apricots. Cummings snuck those in. They looked like two zombies eating dried-up ears, staring at the Momma Witch Doctor on TV. And the worst part about it was that the Mets had played Cincinnati last night. He had to listen to it on the radio in the bedroom. Christ Almighty. Cummings had only been there a couple of nights and he was already fed up with this goddamn arrangement.

"Good morning." Cummings waltzed in, chipper as a bird.

"Morning." Gibbons sipped his coffee and gave her the once-over. She was wearing a tobacco-green suit with a big paisley shawl or scarf or kerchief—whatever the hell you called that rag women wear—pinned to one shoulder and looped under the other armpit. Gibbons pointed at it with his cup. "Don't wear that."

Her chipper face went dead. She adjusted her glasses, then laid her hand on the rag. "Why shouldn't I wear this?"

" 'Cause we're going to the bin today."

Her mouth got shorter. "I find your reference to a state mental hospital as the 'bin' offensive. And your implication that a patient might try to strangle me with my own scarf is even more offensive. I assume *you* will be wearing your tie."

Gibbons shrugged and took another sip. "That's different."

"And why is that?"

Gibbons pulled his gun out of the holster under his jacket. "Because I carry one of these and you don't."

The morning sun sparkled off Excalibur's metal finish. Excalibur was a vintage .38 Colt Cobra, the weapon Gibbons had carried his entire career as an FBI agent. Gibbons forced himself to keep the barrel pointed up. Cummings wasn't worthy of a slug from a weapon as fine as Excalibur, though he was sorely tempted to wing her so he wouldn't have to partner with her.

Cummings's face didn't move as he put his gun back in the holster. "Comparing penises again, are we?"

Gibbons stared at her over the rim of his cup. He

wasn't even gonna answer that one. It was just another lead-in to more of her bogus psychology crap. No matter what they talked about, she knew all the "underlying reasons" for why people did what they did, and in Cummings's world view, men had a lot more underlying reasons for their unacceptable behavior than women did. She'd been having a field day analyzing Tozzi. He was practically a mental leper with all his scabby unacceptable behavior and his nasty underlying reasons. He lived alone in an apartment that got cleaned only when one of his female relatives did it for him; he only kept beer, ketchup, and eggs in his refrigerator; he lived on takeout; he wasn't married; he dated a lot of different women; and he was basically paranoid. He was barely worth the air he breathed.

Gibbons assumed Cummings felt he was just as bad as Tozzi. He preferred baseball to opera, after all. Cummings just wasn't saying it in so many words because she was a guest in his house. Of course, Lorraine didn't help matters. She lapped this psychology shit right up, and that just encouraged Cummings to spout out more of it. According to the good doctor's latest assessment, which Lorraine related to him with more than a few giggles before they turned out the lights last night, he and Tozzi had the egos of Fred Flintstone and Barney Rubble with the ids of Frank and Jesse James. Very insightful.

Lorraine started pouring out that glop from the pot into two bowls. She was humming, probably some tune from that opera video. Gibbons dropped two slices of rye bread into the toaster. Lorraine was really being weird about this whole situation. He and Cummings had been sniping at each other since she got here, but Lorraine was determined not to get involved. The odd thing was that the bickering didn't seem to upset her very much. It was like she was quietly enjoying having her Barnard buddy on the premises throwing digs at him all the time and generally making his life miserable. Sort of like having a surrogate witch around the house to do the dirty wife business.

Lorraine put the empty pot in the sink and brought the steaming bowls of glop to the table. Gibbons grabbed the edge of the table and braced himself.

Cummings clasped her hands together. "Oh, my God! Cream of wheat. Lorraine, you are a sweetheart."

Lorraine shrugged and smiled. "A little treat. For both of us."

Cummings sniffed the rising steam and savored the experience, carefully stirring in a pat of butter and sprinkling cinnamon on top. Gibbons waited for her to spoon up her first taste.

He stared down into her bowl. "You really like that stuff?"

"Ummm." She nodded and spooned up some more. "I love it."

"Aren't you worried, though?"

"What about?"

"What your colleagues might think."

"What do you mean?"

He nodded at the spoon as she put it in her mouth. "Looks like a bad case of semen envy to me."

Cummings gagged on her glop.

Lorraine slammed down her spoon.

The toast popped.

Gibbons smiled like a crocodile.

Lorraine was bound and determined not to yell at him. Barnard girls are above that. You could see in her crimson face how hard she was trying to be unaffected. Gibbons started buttering his toast.

"Why are you going down to the state hospital today?" Lorraine asked, changing the subject. "I thought Ivers had you two on the Sabatini Mistretta case."

"Gonna go talk to Sal Immordino." Gibbons spread butter on the second piece of toast. "He might know something about who killed Mistretta. He might also know something about who plugged Tozzi."

Cummings looked up from her glop. "It would be more helpful if he knew something about Donald Emerick."

"You still pushing that theory, huh? It's a little too *Twilight Zone*, if you ask me. More than a little."

"Who's Donald Emerick?" Lorraine asked.

Cummings adjusted her glasses. "He was a patient on Sal Immordino's ward who was reported missing the day before Sabatini Mistretta was murdered. I believe Mr. Emerick could be our killer."

Gibbons rolled his eyes and bit into a piece of toast.

Lorraine leaned toward her buddy. "Why do you think this Emerick person is the killer?"

"He's killed before. Two women, both in the same week. One was a prostitute. The other was a housewife whom he happened to see parking in a handicapped space at the supermarket. He stalked them both and cornered them where they lived."

"So naturally he'd whack a mob boss next time he had a chance to kill. The pattern is obvious, right?"

Cummings ignored his sarcasm and continued her explanation to Lorraine. "He nailed the prostitute to a wall with five-and-a-half-inch nails, through the head, shoulders, and abdomen. He did exactly the same to the housewife, except that he used the woman's kitchen knives in that case. After he was apprehended, he told the police he was 'blessing' them because they were sinners and they needed absolution. He said he had to give them the sign of the cross."

Gibbons got up to get the marmalade from the refrigerator. "This is her only good point, Lorraine. Don't blink, you'll miss it."

Cummings continued to ignore him. "Sabatini Mistretta and his bodyguard, Jerry Rella, were slain with the same wound pattern. They were both given the sign of the cross."

"However," Gibbons said as the refrigerator door slammed shut, "Emerick used nails and knives to kill those women. Mistretta and Rella were shot, and the wounds may not have been the cause of death. In Rella's case, they appear to have been inflicted *after* death. So it's *not* the same."

"I beg to differ, but in essence it *is* the same. Assuming that career criminals like these two Mafiosi would put up significantly more resistance than two terrified women unused to violent confrontation, Emerick simply may have had to kill them first to accomplish his goal. And as for the weapon, whether it was bullets, knives, or nails, in each case the same goal was achieved, which apparently was to satisfy some distorted inner need."

Gibbons shook his head. "First of all, that hooker Emerick killed? She had been working the trade for quite some time, so she was probably no stranger to violent confrontation. I'll bet she put up more of a fight than a seventy-four-year-old mob boss with more aches and pains than Carter's got little liver pills. As for the wounds, my guess is that they're some kind of bullshit Mafia symbolism. I've seen stuff like this before. Dead canaries in the mouth, balls cut off and stuffed down the throat, tongues up the ass, eyes gouged out—there's nothing new about this."

Lorraine looked a little green. She pushed her bowl of mush away.

"I've checked the archives on symbolic maimings connected with La Cosa Nostra murders. There actually aren't that many, and none of them come close to resembling this."

"You think wiseguys consult the archives before they do what they do?"

"The bodies were found in a sandpile under the West Side Highway, but it's been established that those men weren't killed there. They were moved, which to me indicates some kind of compulsive behavior. Generally, mobsters leave them where they fall. No?"

Lorraine looked out the window.

"I just told you. Wiseguys don't follow rules. So what if they moved the bodies? All that says to me is that wherever they whacked Mistretta was too incriminating. They did it too close to home."

"Can we change the subject?" Lorraine was still looking out the window. Both her legs and arms were crossed.

"What about the thumbprint on Mistretta's watch and the partial palm print on the bodyguard's neck? Wouldn't mobsters take precautions against leaving prints? A psychotic killer doesn't worry about leaving fingerprints. Getting caught doesn't even enter his mind because he feels perfectly justified in what he's doing."

Gibbons shook his head. "We haven't gotten anything back on those prints yet. They could be the victims' own prints, or their wives' or their girlfriends' or their kids'. It's too soon to tell."

Cummings folded her arms and stared at him. "You cannot be so stupid as to think that there's no connection between those wounds and Donald Emerick."

Gibbons leveled a stare right back at her. "Did it ever occur to you that maybe Immordino got the idea from Emerick? You ever think of that?"

Cummings frowned. "Mental institutions are not like prisons. Psychotics like Mr. Emerick and Mr. Immordino don't compare notes. Now, I know you don't believe that there's anything wrong with Mr. Immordino and you feel that he's faking his condition, but he has been diagnosed paranoid schizophrenic by a court-ordered psychiatrist, and several doctors have supported that evaluation under oath. That's why he's been incarcerated at the state hospital for the past nineteen months. Those were all reputable doctors, and I accept their findings. From the reports I've read, Mr. Immordino could not possibly have murdered anyone. He isn't capable."

Gibbons looked at his wife. She raised her eyebrows and shrugged. Even Lorraine knew that Cummings was wet behind the ears on this one. Incarceration never keeps mob guys from pulling off hits. Putting out a contract on someone is no problem for them. It's like calling out for pizza.

He wondered if Immordino had ordered a large with Gibbons and Tozzi on it.

Gibbons reached back for the coffeepot on the counter and refilled his cup. "You know, speaking of reports, I took a look at Emerick's file. Those women he killed were both blondes. At the time that he killed them, he'd just been asked to leave the seminary where he was studying to be a priest. According to the file, he had been acting pretty nutty at the seminary, doing stuff like breaking into people's rooms to look for light switches in the wastepaper baskets because he thought someone was stealing his. They finally decided they had to do something with him when he tried to crucify himself to an apple tree, so they sent him home to his parents. No one could really figure out what was bothering him until he murdered those two women. Seems he was at a mall one night a few months earlier when he happened to see one of the priests from the seminary in his civies going into the movies with his girlfriend. Apparently Emerick really looked up to this particular priest, thought he was a real saintly guy. The girlfriend just happened to be a blonde. Emerick followed them in and watched the priest put his arm around the girl. After the movie, he followed them and saw them kissing in the priest's car. That's what set Emerick off. The woman was a sinner, he told his shrink afterward, and she had to be absolved with the sign of the cross. Problem was, he didn't get a real good look at the girlfriend, so he kept mistaking other blondes for her."

"Yes, I know all that. I read the file. Do you have a point?"

"Yeah, I do have a point. If Emerick's mission in life is to save the soul of some wayward blonde, why would he shoot a couple of wiseguys? Doesn't exactly fit his profile, does it?"

"The man's life is circumscribed by irrational behavior. His 'mission,' as you put it, may have evolved since the initial murders. He may be going after bigger sinners now. Mistretta certainly qualifies under that category."

"I don't buy it, Doc." Gibbons sipped his coffee.

Cummings narrowed her eyes and stared at him, turning on the arctic blast, total attitude. "Then you're being deliberately ignorant."

He put down his cup and pointed at her. "You know what your trouble is, Cummings? You bought the psychology franchise a long time ago, and now you expect people to buy your version of things no matter what. Give me a little credit for my specialty, why don'cha? I've been chasing down wiseguys for almost thirty years now. I've seen 'em come and go. When a boss is shot, it's no accident. It's a hit. Believe me."

"Why is your past experience worth more than mine? Because you're a tough guy and you carry a gun? I've participated in forty-one serial killer investigations with the FBI. I've seen how they mutilate flesh. I've reconstructed their patterns and preferences. Serial killers are fussy people. They want things just so. This killer fired eight bullets into two victims, repeating a specific pattern twice. He then moved those two bodies. That takes time and forethought, and it takes a good stomach. Mob hits are done fast, in and out. Am I correct? This one was *savored*. This was done to satisfy an inner need."

"Wait a minute. Are you telling me Emerick is a serial killer now?"

"He exhibits all the signs. If he did kill Mistretta and Rella, then we definitely have a serial killer on our hands."

"I don't think he did it. Only mob guys kill mob guys."

And FBI agents sometimes. Gibbons glanced out the sunny window.

"Gibbons, I don't care how many years you've been on the street chasing mobsters. This is *my* kind of killer. I know it. I can feel it."

"Hey, if you're so sure there's a serial killer on the loose, follow up on it on your own time. But as far as I'm concerned, you're Tozzi's replacement and I'm senior man on this team, so I call the shots."

Cummings knit her brows. "Which means what exactly?"

"It means we're treating this case the way it should be treated, as a mob rubout."

Lorraine turned back and faced the table. She wasn't so green now. "Madeleine did receive her doctorate from Johns Hopkins. She had years of clinical experience before she entered the Bureau. Don't you think you're being a little bit pigheaded in refusing even to consider her ideas in this case?"

Gibbons stared at his wife. "No. I don't." He knew he sounded like an asshole, but there was no time to dick around looking for this Emerick character, not if there was someone out there gunning for Tozzi. And maybe him, too. But he couldn't tell Lorraine that. She'd go nuts, and he didn't want her to worry.

Gibbons drained his cup, stood up, and looked at Cummings. "I wanna be on the road by quarter of eight." He sawed his tie under his shirt collar and decided not to tell either of them that he was bringing Tozzi along to interview Immordino. Cummings would object and Lorraine would have a shit-fit.

He left the kitchen and headed down the hall to the bathroom for his morning sit-down, wondering whether Lorraine picked up on the fact that he'd worn his gun to breakfast. He usually didn't do that. But with mob guys, you could never be too careful.

Sal Immordino sat hunched over in a folding chair next to his favorite table on the ward, the one with the checkerboard printed on the Formica top. He was staring at his hands, elbows on his knees, mumbling to them, deep in a three-way conversation. He was trying his damnedest to ignore Tozzi, who was sitting right in front of his face. Tozzi hadn't said a word to him since he came in five minutes ago, just sat there staring at him, tapping his cane on the floor, the son of a bitch.

Sal studied his pinkies. He wanted to know what the fuck this bastard wanted. Did he know it was him who tried to whack him or what? Or was it because of Mistretta that he was here? Either way, it didn't matter. Sal wasn't gonna tell him anything. He wasn't even gonna look at him. Mr. Magic, this guy. He dodges bullets and has a fairy godmother who protects him from harm. Mr. fucking Magic the fed.

Tozzi stopped tapping the cane. In his peripheral vision, Sal watched Tozzi reach into the inside pocket of his jacket and pull something out. Son of a bitch. It was one of those little tape recorders, like the one Tozzi had hidden on his body that time in Atlantic City two years ago when Sal dropped his guard and threatened to kill Tozzi. Thank God, Tozzi sweats a lot. It screwed up the works and they didn't get Sal down on tape. If Tozzi had gotten that down on tape, getting rid of the bastard wouldn't do Sal any good because there would've been physical evidence against him. But as it was, only Tozzi's testimony could put Sal away. That's why he was gonna die.

Tozzi reached over and snatched Sal's left wrist. Sal flinched, but he didn't resist. He was supposed to be mental. Tozzi forced the little tape recorder into his hand.

"Here, take it," Tozzi said.

Sal just stared at it in his hand, deliberately looking puzzled. He kept his eyes down and didn't look at the one-way mirror on the wall across the room. Tozzi's buddy Gibbons was in there. Sal was willing to bet money on that.

"This is so you know I'm not taping you this time. Okay, Sal?"

Sal almost laughed in his face. *How do I know you don't have another one taped to your back? You must think I really am stupid.*

"Now, let's cut the shit, okay, Sal? I know there's nothing wrong with you, and you know that I know, so let's stop playing games here. My deposition attesting to your mental competency is on file with the court, and there's nothing either of us can do about that. But if you cooperate with me now, I can talk to the guys at the U.S. Attorney's Office, see if they want to cut you some slack for helping us out."

Sal glanced from the tape recorder to Tozzi to the one-way mirror. *Fuck you, Tozzi. Mistretta said you guys would try to get me to flip. This is just what Juicy is afraid of. Get outta my face, Tozzi.*

Tozzi rested his chin on the cane. "You could also turn state's witness. Give the prosecutors enough good dirt that they can use and maybe, just maybe, you could end up in witness protection. If they think they can get some solid convictions out of it, they'll drop some of the prior charges against you, make you a deal on the heavy ones. Maybe you'll end up with a coupla years on the worst charges with credit for time served here. I dunno. I'm not a prosecutor. But it's worth a shot. No?"

Sal looked Tozzi in the eye. He let the tape recorder slip out of his hand and smash to the floor.

Tozzi glanced down at the pieces, then slowly grinned up at him. "I know what you're thinking, Sal. 'I'm not gonna rat on my buddies, no way, not me. And I'm sure as hell not gonna go live in some shitty little split-level in the middle of nowhere where the only mozzarell' you can get is the A&P brand and all the kids are blue-eyed blondes.' That's what you're thinking. But is that any worse than what you got here?" Tozzi looked around at the nuts shuffling around the ward. "Don't look like the Fontainebleau to me, Sal. And your buddies back in the family haven't done too much to help you get outta here, have they? The way I hear it, Mistretta really cut you off at the knees. You used up most of your own money on lawyers, then the old man wouldn't help you out. Some godfather, huh?"

Not exactly, Tozzi. I got a little stashed away that nobody knows about, not even my sister. Sal stirred the broken pieces of the tape recorder with his toe.

"Whattaya think, Sal? Was it Juicy Vacarini who did Mistretta? Juicy doing a Gotti so he can be boss?"

Sal didn't look up.

"Or was it *you* who ordered the hit, Sal? Scraped up your pennies and hired a shooter? Is that the way it went down? I mean, if anyone wanted Mistretta dead, it was you more than Juicy. Right? The old man definitely had his favorites, but somehow you got bumped from that list. So maybe *you* had him whacked. Whattaya think, Sal?"

Sal kept his head down. His heart was bashing against his chest.

"Maybe I oughta ask Juicy what he thinks. I'll tell him I asked you, but you didn't have an opinion on that subject. You think Juicy'll have any ideas?"

Sal's heart was going nuts. He kept his chin on his chest, opening and closing his hands, first one, then the other, real slow. He wanted to strangle this son of a bitch. Tozzi thought he was cute, but he knew damn well what Juicy would think—that Sal was cooperating with the feds because that's what Juicy and Bartolo and all those guys wanted to believe. That's why they had a friggin' contract out on him. Shit!

Sal heard footsteps coming this way, normal-people footsteps. He kept his head down in case it was that other fuck, Gibbons.

"You the one wanted to see me?"

Sal knew the voice. He squeezed his eyes shut and stopped breathing.

"You Charles Tate?"

"That's me."

Tozzi pulled out his I.D. "Special Agent Mike Tozzi, FBI." He reached up from his seat and shook Charles's hand. "Thanks for coming in. I understand this is your day off." Tozzi pointed to an empty chair.

"No problem, man. No problem at'all."

As Charles sat down, Sal noticed that he was wearing royal-blue sweats and high-top Reeboks, the ones with the air pump inside. Those shoes go for about a hundred fifty bucks or more. They looked pretty new, too. Sal hoped to hell those shoes fell off the truck. This bastard better not be using that grand on fucking sneakers or he's gonna be one very sorry dude.

Tozzi took a small notepad out of his pocket and flipped it open. "For the past two months you've been the guard on duty on the third shift. Is that correct?"

"No, O'Connor's got the graveyard. I'm second shift."

Tozzi pulled out a pen and crossed something out. "While you were on duty, did you notice anything unusual going on with Mr. Immordino here?"

Sal's eyes bulged. *The* moolinyam *better say the right thing*.

"How 'xactly do you mean 'unusual'?"

Tozzi drummed on the pad with his pen. "Anything

different from his usual routine. New visitors, phone calls. Did he act funny in any way? You know what I mean."

"Well, let's see . . ."

Sal gritted his teeth. *Think before you talk, Charles.*

"Well, Sal don't never use the phone, and the only visitor I ever seen him get is his sister, the nun." Charles laughed that growly hissing laugh of his. "And Sal, he *always* act funny. Everybody act funny on this ward."

Sal's gut clenched as something suddenly occurred to him. What if Tozzi recognizes Charles's voice from that night the *moolinyam* tried to kill him? What if he already knows Charles was the guy? Why the hell did he call Charles in here? Sal froze, waiting for Gibbons to run in with a gang of state cops to bust the two of them.

Tozzi flipped a page in his notepad. "The guy who escaped, Donald Emerick. Did he and Mr. Immordino here ever pal around together?"

"Well, I wouldn't call it palling around."

Shut the fuck up, Charles. Just say you don't know.

"What would you call it, then?"

"I dunno. Sal never pays attention to nobody. Just talks to his hands, all day long, just like he doing now. Emerick, he the kind of dude who goes up and down with his medication. Give him his pill, he mellows right out, easy as could be. But when the medication starts wearing off, he perks right up and gets real curious. Every once in a while I'd see him sitting over here next to Sal, listening to him mumble to his hands. But Sal never talked to him. I always figured Emerick thought Sal was saying his prayers. See, Emerick, he prayed a lot, prayed all the time. The one thing he wanted most was a string of them rosary beads. Every day he'd be asking me to get him some rosary beads. But the doctors said no way, too dangerous."

"Were they afraid he'd hurt himself or the other patients?"

"Both. Emerick's a little dude, but he one of the worst ones here. They shoulda had him in a room downstairs by hisself. He killed two ladies, you know. That's how he got in here. I bet he tries to kill somebody again. You watch."

Sal clenched his fists. He wished to hell Tozzi would disappear. Charles was talking too much.

Tozzi wrote something down on the pad, ripped out the page, and handed it to Charles. "This is a number where you can reach me. If you see Mr. Immordino doing anything out of the ordinary, anything that strikes you as different for him, anything at all, I'd appreciate it if you'd give me a call."

"Will do." Tate slipped the phone number into the front pouch of his sweatshirt.

"Thanks for coming. Sorry to disturb you on your day off."

"No problem." Tate got up and walked back across the ward, his new high-tops squeaking on the linoleum.

Tozzi leaned into Sal's face. "Last chance, Sal. You got anything you want to tell me?"

Sal clenched his fists again. He was so mad, they were shaking. He wanted to punch Tozzi's head off and piss down his throat, he was so mad. But he was afraid to move a muscle, afraid to do anything that might make him look sane. They must have a video camera going behind that one-way mirror, filming this whole thing. On top of that, Sal couldn't figure out if Tozzi actually knew something about him and Charles and Emerick, or he was just acting like he knew something, hoping he

could scare Sal into talking. He oughta know better by
now, the bastard.

Tozzi stood up and leaned on his cane. "Nothing to
say, huh? Well, it's been nice talking to you, Sal." He
turned to go, but then stopped and turned back. "By the
way, you want me to give Juicy your love when I see
him?"

Sal kept his head down, gritted his teeth, and squeezed
his fists so hard they hurt. *Fuck you, Tozzi.*

"That's what I thought." Tozzi walked through the
ward, dragging his bum leg behind him.

Sal followed Tozzi out with his eyes. His face was as
tight as his fists.

You're fucking dead, Tozzi!

EIGHT

Tozzi helped Stacy out of her leather motorcycle jacket
and handed it to the hatcheck girl. Stacy looked incredible tonight. Little black dress cut up to the middle of her
thigh, black suede heels, and all that incredible hair. She
was a walking dream, and he wasn't the only one who
thought so.

A couple of guys at the bar were giving her the eye
right now, showing their appreciation in their gaga faces.
They waved the bartender over and asked for his opinion. It was the same. Tozzi was willing to bet they were
wondering whether this was really the Pump-It-Up Girl.
All three of them probably had hard-ons for her. He
wished he could have one for her. His equipment still
wasn't responding, and it was driving him nuts. There
was no good reason for this, but he sure as hell wasn't
going to go to a doctor. It wasn't like that. It was all
mental, and he was pretty sure he could fix it himself. If
he stayed around Stacy, the blood was bound to start
circulating again. With the right stimulation, it would
happen. He was almost positive.

He got the ticket from the hatcheck girl, and leaning

on his cane, escorted Stacy over to the maître d's register. The skin on her bare shoulder was soft and firm.

The restaurant was a classy Italian place on East Seventy-first Street called Pompeii. Tozzi scanned the dining room and checked the back tables, where the preferred customers were usually seated. He spotted Frank Bartolo's shiny bald head right away. Juicy Vacarini was sitting next to him, just the two of them at a table for four in the corner near the piano. Hey, why not? Juicy owned the place.

Watching Juicy light a cigarette, Tozzi began to have second thoughts about bringing Stacy here. Juicy was definitely gonna have a hard-on for her. He had a special appreciation for beautiful women. He ought to. Juicy was the biggest whoremeister in the Northeast. He supposedly had a gift for recruitment.

Stacy smiled sweetly at Tozzi and spoke through her teeth. "This looks like one of those places where they do mob rubouts, Tozzi. I don't want to end up on the front page of tomorrow's *Post* facedown in a plate of linguine."

Tozzi smiled back pleasantly. "Then order something else."

"Very funny." Her smile turned sarcastic. "I don't like the energy in this place. Why don't we go home? I'll make something for us."

He could tell she was nervous. "Don't worry. Nothing's gonna happen. We're just here to check out the scene, that's all. Besides, the food is actually very good here." It always was in mob joints. He took her hand and patted it.

The maître d' weaved his way through the dining room, coming toward them. He had a face like a corpse.

"Do you have a reservation, sir?"

"Yes. For Thompson."

The maitre d' checked the register and nodded. "Right this way."

As they followed the maître d', Stacy furrowed her brows. "Thompson?" she whispered.

"You never use your real name for a reservation," he murmured. "It's an invitation for a setup. But don't worry," he added quickly. "Nothing's gonna happen here tonight." He sneaked a look at her face to see if she believed him.

Tozzi kept his eye on the maître d'. He knew who the guy was, but he couldn't remember his name. The guy did some time for hijacking a truckload of fur coats at Kennedy a while back, took the rap for a made guy in Juicy's crew. This restaurant job must've been his reward for being a stand-up guy. His utter joy and gratitude was written all over his petrified face.

They followed Happy the maître d' around a big table of fat couples eating pastries and drinking cappuccinos. Tozzi made sure he didn't stare at Juicy and Bartolo, but he kept them in his peripheral vision. No one was gonna believe this was a coincidence, but he still had to make it look like it was.

Happy showed them to a table across the room from the two capos. At a table on the other side of the piano from Juicy and Bartolo, three soldiers from Bartolo's crew were eating with three women too young and sexy to be their wives. Louis "Loopy Lou" Nardone, Domenico "Gyp" Giambella, and Jimmy Turano had been key men in that crew when it was Sal Immordino's.

Little Jimmy T. had made a mint setting up dummy gasoline brokerages that bought and sold hundreds of thousands of gallons of gas, then disappeared before it was time to pay the federal taxes. By beating Uncle Sam out of his cut, Jimmy was able to sell his gas to retailers at a big discount and walk away with a nice profit.

Cockeyed Loopy Lou had been running a couple of asbestos-removal companies under different names out on Long Island. He hired illegal Polish immigrants hungry for work who were willing to take their chances ripping out asbestos ceilings and pipe insulation without adequate safety equipment, then dumped the toxic material on a farm near Albany in the middle of the night.

Gyp ran a private school-bus company in Queens that specialized in transporting handicapped kids. Gyp had managed to finagle an exclusive contract for all the public schools in the boroughs of Brooklyn, Queens, and Manhattan. Without competition, he was able to charge whatever he wanted. And he did.

But according to the latest intelligence reports on these guys, they weren't too happy with their new captain. Gyp still had his fleet of school buses, but Frank Bartolo pulled the reins in on Loopy Lou and Jimmy T. On Bartolo's orders, they were concentrating on loansharking now, and they weren't making nearly as much money as they had been under Sal. Apparently Bartolo didn't want to owe Sal anything, so all enterprises started under his leadership were now terminated.

Tozzi watched the faces of the three wiseguys. They didn't look unhappy now, but he had a feeling the girls had a lot to do with that. What Tozzi found interesting was that Bartolo wasn't sitting with his soldiers. It looked like he was deliberately ignoring them and they were ignoring him. Supposedly Bartolo didn't like to rub elbows with his men. Supposedly he felt he was above that. Interesting.

Tozzi felt his bandaged thigh under his pants and he thought about Sal Immordino playing dumb with him

yesterday. Gibbons had checked on the other two mobsters he thought might have tried to have him killed. Old
man Zucchetti was on a farm deep in the rain forests of
Brazil, hiding out from a Sicilian drug rival who'd made
an unsuccessful attempt on his life, and the Los Angeles
field office had confirmed that Richie Varga was in Cali-
fornia, trying to produce movies. As far as they knew
Varga wasn't doing anything illegitimate, and he hadn't
been out of the state in eight months. That didn't guarantee anything, of course, but Tozzi and Gibbons agreed
that Varga and Zucchetti were too far removed from
things in New York to care about an FBI agent who had
given them some trouble once upon a time. That left Sal
Immordino, and considering that the boss of Immordino's family had just been whacked, Tozzi couldn't
help feeling that there was a connection between the
Mistretta killings and his own "mugging." If Sal was
behind all this, he was setting himself up to go head-to-
head against Juicy for control of the family, so Juicy
might have something to say about that. The mob vow
of silence was all well and good, but if Juicy thought the
FBI could take care of his main competition, he might
drop a few subtle hints. It was known to happen.

When Tozzi looked back at Bartolo and Juicy, he saw
that Juicy was looking this way, but he wasn't looking at
Tozzi. It was Stacy he was focused on. Tozzi pressed his
lips together and let out his breath. He hadn't planned
on using Stacy as bait, but . . .

He waved to Juicy and worked up a nice big smile.
"There's somebody I know over there," he said to Stacy.
"Let's go say hello."

Tozzi stood up, pulled out Stacy's chair, and led her
toward Juicy's table.

"They don't look very happy to see you," Stacy said through her teeth.

"Don't worry. That's just the way these people are. They're not very demonstrative."

"Who are they? Are they killers?"

He put his hand on her shoulder. "Just smile. Nothing will happen."

"Excuse me, sir." Happy the maître d' moved into their path just as they got to Juicy's table. "Your table is over there, sir."

Tozzi looked past him to the proprietor.

Juicy Vacarini was leisurely sucking on a cigarette, elbows on the table, hands clasped in front of his face. He squinted through the rising smoke, his gaze fixed on Stacy. He was a thin guy with a long horse face and styled steel-gray hair that swept laterally over his ears, defying gravity. His clothes were impeccable, and his skin had that peculiar waxy sheen Tozzi had seen on Hollywood types, guys who've had face-lifts. Juicy had young features, but Tozzi knew he wasn't that young— early to mid-fifties. Tozzi thought of him as a Lamborghini—fast and sharp to look at, but constant maintenance.

Frank Bartolo, on the other hand, was a gas-guzzling, bottom-of-the-line, stripped-down domestic sedan. Hunched over a mountain of golden fried calamari with a fork in his chubby fist, Bartolo glared up at Tozzi from under hairy caterpillar eyebrows. With that cue-ball head of his, he looked like a mad egg.

Juicy squinted up at Stacy and took another slow drag off his cigarette. "I've seen you on television, haven't I?"

Stacy sighed, rolled her eyes, and nodded. She didn't mind being the Pump-It-Up Girl. It was the loss of anonymity that bothered her.

"You know, every time I see your commercial, I say to myself, 'This is a very talented person.' And I wonder, Why is this person wasting her time with these low-rent commercials?" He shook the two fingers holding the cigarette at her. "You should be acting. You know that?" Swirls of smoke rose from his hand like a lasso. "Film."

Tozzi's jaw tightened. Juicy had a genuinely engaging smile, and Tozzi could see that it was working its charm on Stacy. He shouldn't have brought her here.

"How's it going, Juicy?"

The capo ignored Tozzi, giving Stacy his undivided attention. "Please, sit down." He indicated the chair opposite himself.

She looked at Tozzi to see if it was all right. It wasn't, but he nodded anyway as he pulled out the chair for her, then took the one opposite Bartolo.

The egg snarled. "Who invited you, Tozzi?"

Tozzi sat down and hooked his cane on the edge of the table. "We're a package deal."

"Oh, yeah? She a fed, too?"

Tozzi glanced at her. "She look like a fed to you?"

Stacy glared at them both. "Why don't you ask me yourself?"

The egg grumbled as he speared another forkful of calamari rings.

Juicy looked up at Happy the maître d'. "Bring us a bottle of Cristal."

Happy nodded and made tracks for the bar.

Juicy looked into Stacy's eyes. "I prefer Cristal. I think it's a little more sophisticated than Dom P."

Tozzi smirked. "Or is that the brand that happened to fall off the truck this week?"

Juicy acted as if Tozzi wasn't even there. He only had eyes for Stacy. So did every other guy in the place, except for Bartolo who kept cramming calamari into his mean little mouth as he gave Tozzi the evil eye.

They stared at each other for a minute, then Bartolo suddenly erupted. "So whattaya want?"

"Dinner."

"Then go sit at your own table."

"I like this table better."

"You know something? This is government harrassment, pal. You're giving me *acida* here. I'm gonna get my lawyer on you guys."

Tozzi held up his cane and twirled the hook. "I'm on sick leave, Frank. So I'm not on duty now. Which means I'm just being friendly."

The egg scowled. "Bullshit you are."

Juicy frowned at them, very displeased. He didn't like them using bad language in front of the lady. He shrugged and shook his head apologetically to Stacy, still ignoring Tozzi.

The piano player came back then, and Juicy made eye contact with him. He sat down at the keyboard, poker-faced, and started to play "Fascination." Juicy leaned over the table and spoke softly, just to Stacy. Tozzi couldn't hear what he was saying over the piano. This was the way it was gonna be: Stacy would get all of Juicy's attention while he had to make do with the mad egg. Okay, fine. He could deal with that.

"So how's it hanging, Frank?"

Bartolo stared down at his plate and kept eating.

"Tell me something, Frank. All this stuff I've been reading in the papers—should I believe any of it?"

The mad egg reached for his wineglass and took a glug, then went back to the calamari.

Tozzi leaned in closer and whispered, "Some of the

papers are saying that Juicy did Mistretta, that he's the new boss now. That true?"

"Get the fuck outta my face, will ya?"

Tozzi leaned back. "Hey, I'm just asking, Frank. See, I haven't been to the office lately. I don't know what's going on."

Bartolo pointed his fork at Tozzi. "Listen, wiseass, don't get cute with me. You think I don't know what's going on here? You guys are warming up to pin this thing on us 'cause you jerk-offs can't find the real killer. You're not fooling anybody, Tozzi. Some fucking crazy person did Jerry and the old man. Anybody can see that. Only a crazy person would pull that kind of sick shit, shooting up their bodies like that."

"You mean, *you* wouldn't do it like that. You'd do it clean. One to the back of the head, maybe two to be sure, then get out quick."

"Hey! Don't miscombobulate my words, okay? I would never kill nobody. And neither would Juicy."

"Okay, fine. I believe you, Frank. I do. . . . But how about Sal Immordino? You think he coulda done it?"

At the mention of Sal's name, Juicy quickly glanced at them, then looked away. He was listening. Good.

Bartolo stopped chewing and stared at Tozzi. "Sal Immordino's supposed to be in the nuthouse. What, he got out?"

Tozzi shrugged. "I don't think so. I mean, I just saw him there the other day."

The egg's mouth dropped. "He talk to you?"

Tozzi ignored the question. Let them think Sal did talk to him. "So do you think Sal could've done something like that? He is supposed to be a 'crazy person,' after all."

The egg threw down his fork, bunched his fingers,

and gestured with his hand. "How? How could he do it?"

"Whattaya mean, 'how could he do it'? He hired a shooter, put out a contract. How else do you kill somebody?"

Bartolo joined his palms and shook his hands as if he were praying to God. "The man's a fucking fruitcake. How's he gonna order a hit? He can't order coffee, for chrissake."

Tozzi looked at Juicy, but he was looking at Stacy. "How do you know, Frank? He's been in the hospital almost two years now. Maybe he got better."

Bartolo waved him away. "Get the fuck outta here. Where's he gonna get better?"

Tozzi was surprised that Bartolo was insisting that Sal really was mental. He figured Bartolo would've jumped at the chance to pin Mistretta's murder on Sal and bury him. He hated Sal. It would also take the heat off Juicy if it was him who sent the hit man. Maybe Sal, Juicy, and Bartolo were in this together. Tozzi doubted it, though. Somehow that kind of reconciliation didn't seem likely, not with their histories.

Happy came back with a bottle of champagne in a silver ice bucket and four tall glasses. He started to set down the glasses when Juicy stopped him. "Just two," he said loud enough for Tozzi to hear as he pointed to the space between Stacy and himself.

Stacy glanced at Tozzi. She looked a little nervous. Tozzi wondered what kind of bullshit Juicy was feeding her. He wasn't worried, though. She was smart enough to see through a sleazebag like him. A sleazebag with a big friggin' hard-on. Shit.

As Happy went to work uncorking the champagne,

Tozzi turned back to Bartolo. "So, Frank, if it wasn't Sal who had Mistretta whacked, who do you think did?"

"How the hell should I know?"

Tozzi lowered his voice. "C'mon, Frank. Don't play dumb. You know who did it."

"I don't know nothing." Bartolo went back to his calamari.

Tozzi leaned in close. "How about this, Frank? What if I told you we could protect you? We could relocate you and change your identity, give you a new life. Your son, too—your whole family. Your name ever comes up in a felony investigation—with the exception of murder, of course—you'll be immune. We'll make the deal, I'll arrange the whole thing. Just tell me who did Mistretta."

Bartolo stopped chewing and looked him in the eye. "If we make this 'deal,' you gonna get me a house next door to Sal?"

Tozzi shrugged. Let him think Sal's flipped, that he's talking to the feds. It'll make them crazy. And that's when they'll screw up.

The cork popped, and Tozzi looked over toward Happy. He noticed that the muscle had arrived. A big hunk of meat crammed into a pearl-gray double-breasted suit was loitering by the piano, staring at him. The guy stood there like a buffalo, mean but dumb. It was hard to tell what he was thinking, if he was thinking anything at all. He laid his big pale hands on the piano. They looked like a pair of uncooked chickens.

The piano player finished up "Fascination" and segued right into "Strangers in the Night." Juicy stood up then and moved around the table. He held Stacy's chair as she got up, then took her hand and led her to the cramped space between the table and the piano where they started to dance. The restaurant wasn't the kind of place where people danced, but Juicy was dancing with Stacy anyway and the whole place was watching, except for four fat couples at a big table in the middle of the room who were busy scarfing down cannolis and cheesecake. The muscles in Tozzi's jaw started to flex by themselves. He kept his eye on Juicy's hand on the small of Stacy's back, the son of a bitch.

Bartolo reached for his wineglass and let out a snide laugh. "What's-a-matta, Tozzi? You look jealous."

"Of what?"

"Juicy. You think he's gonna steal your girl?" Bartolo was sucking his teeth and grinning.

Tozzi ignored him. He wasn't jealous. He just didn't want that pig touching her.

Bartolo snickered. "Better watch out, Tozzi. Juicy's got a way with women. He don't even have to try. They chase him."

Tozzi looked Bartolo in the eye. "Yeah, we should be so lucky. Huh, Frank? Ugly guys like us."

Bartolo just sucked his teeth and grinned.

Tozzi glanced back at Stacy and Juicy. They were dancing awfully close, but she didn't seem to mind. Strangers in the night, huh? Tozzi waited for them to turn around again so he could see where Juicy's hand was. He was shocked to see that it was still up on her back. Juicy's restraint was amazing.

Bartolo picked up his fork and started eating again. "So what've you and Sal been talking about lately? The weather?"

"Total immunity from prosecution on anything that happened before today, Frank. Think about that, Frank. I don't think you appreciate what a good deal I'm making you here."

Bartolo smiled and chewed. "You're a real piss, you know that, Tozzi?"

"You're not thinking ahead, Frank. Juicy's no Mistretta. Yeah, he's a flashy guy and all, but he don't know half of what Mistretta knew and the whole family's gonna suffer. Including you. Think about it, Frank. What does Juicy know? Pussy. That's all he knows. You're backing the wrong horse, Frank. Any family with a pimp for a boss is in big trouble. Nobody's gonna respect him."

The egg swiped his mean little mouth with a napkin and nodded toward the dancers. "You know, for someone who don't know nothing but pussy, Juicy's getting to know yours pretty good, Tozzi."

Tozzi looked up and saw Juicy's hand down on Stacy's ass, pulling her pelvis into his. She was pushing off his lapels, beginning to resist. He bit his bottom lip. That fucking pig.

Tozzi grabbed his cane by the bottom end and reached over, hooking Juicy's wrist and yanking his hand off Stacy's ass.

"Hey!" Juicy grabbed the hook and pulled, but Tozzi pushed at the same time, and the sleazebag went crashing into the piano where he just barely caught himself on his elbow before he fell on his ass.

The buffalo came charging around the piano. Tozzi stood up, flipped the cane, and stuck the rubber tip into the buffalo's windpipe, letting the side of beef's own momentum pull the rug out from under him. He hit the floor so hard, glasses and plates in the whole room rattled. The buffalo lay there, flat on his back, eyes squeezed tight in pain. Happy the maître d' rushed over to help him up while some lone patron at the bar applauded from the front room.

Juicy was on his feet, straightening his tie and smoothing the hair over his ears, venom in his eyes for Tozzi. Stacy stood between them, looking from one to the other. Her eyes were huge. She must've thought they were gonna start shooting. The whole restaurant was still.

Tozzi took her arm. "Let's go, Stacy. I don't feel like Italian tonight."

Juicy stayed where he was by the piano. He lit a cigarette, still glaring at Tozzi. "Play something," he snapped at the piano player.

The piano started to tinkle. It took Tozzi a moment to recognize the tune. "Makin' Whoopie." Hushed conversations started up around the room. The four chubby couples had stopped eating their desserts. They all had big eyes and small mouths as Stacy and Tozzi passed by.

"Hey, Tozzi." Bartolo was wiping his mouth with a napkin as he walked over to them. "I thought you were supposed to be a bright guy, Tozzi. You don't act too bright. This ain't no joint." He nodded toward Juicy. "You embarrassed the owner."

"Tell the owner he had it coming. Tell him if he wants to cop a cheap feel on the dance floor, he should take one of his pros to Roseland."

Bartolo stuck his pinkie in his mouth and picked his teeth. "Not smart, Tozzi. You come into a man's place of business and rough him up—not smart."

"Is this a threat, Frank?"

Bartolo shrugged. "You can take it any way you want it."

"Don't worry. I will." Tozzi turned to leave. His leg was throbbing. He'd twisted it the wrong way when he stood up fast to deck the buffalo.

Stacy could see that he was in pain. "You all right?"

"Are *you* all right?"

She looked confused. "Of course I'm all right. I'm not the one who was fighting."

"What was that pig trying to do? I saw him with his hands all over you."

She flipped the hair over her shoulder and gave him a weary look. "He had the same line of bullshit I've been hearing about twice a day ever since they started running the commercial. 'You have so much talent, you should be in the movies. Why don't you let me help you? I know people on the Coast.' It's all crap. I hear it from horny old guys all the time."

"You didn't give him your phone number or anything?"

"Are you crazy?" She was about to get angry, but then a sly grin spread across her face. "Are you jealous of that slimebucket? I never thought I'd see *you* get jealous. I thought you were cooler than that." She was wearing a sly grin, trying to give him grief.

"I *am* cooler than that."

"Yeah, sure." She was still grinning, the tip of her tongue peeking out of her lips.

When they got to the hatcheck girl and Tozzi gave her their ticket, Stacy suddenly ran the palm of her hand over his cheek, turned his face around, and planted her lips over his, grinding in a kiss to end all kisses. Out of the corner of his eye he could see Juicy and Bartolo huddled at their table, grumbling and bitching about something. Him and Sal Immordino, no doubt.

The hatcheck girl returned. "Your coats, sir."

But Stacy wasn't coming up for air. Tozzi put his hands on her hips and tried to get into it, but it wasn't working for him. He couldn't figure out what the hell was wrong with him. He couldn't concentrate anymore. The throbbing was all in his thigh, not his pants.

He gently pulled away from her lips. "Not here," he murmured as he took their coats.

She looked down, grinning, full of mischief.

He helped her on with her motorcycle jacket, staring at all that incredible hair, those incredible legs.

But there was nothing going on downstairs. Nothing at all.

NINE

"**K**eep eating, Frank. Keep eating." Sal mumbled to himself as he peered through the binoculars. He was facing the starting gate down on the track where the trotters were taking their positions, but he wasn't looking at them. He was looking down the stands, two sections over, about fifteen, twenty rows down from where he was sitting, focusing on Frank Bartolo's shiny head. Frank was eating a sausage-and-pepper sandwich, eating it like there was no tomorrow. He'd already had a cup of clam chowder, a shrimp cocktail, a hot dog, and a pastrami sandwich. He was also working on his third cup of beer, the milk-shake size. The man was a human garbage disposal. He didn't even know what the hell he was eating, he ate so fast. Sal narrowed his eyes as he watched the last three inches of the sausage sandwich disappear down Bartolo's gullet. He wanted him to eat more. "Keep eating, Frank."

"Whad'ja say?"

The *moolinyam* was looking at the racing page in the sports section of the *Star-Ledger*. He wasn't checking the stats on the ponies, though. He was checking out the ad on the bottom of the page, the ad for Knickerbocker Health Spas, the ad with that broad with the tits in it.

"So who do you like, Charles?" Sal kept his eye on Bartolo.

"Huh?"

"In the next race. Who do you like?"

"Oh . . . lemme see. . . ." Charles ruffled the paper and went to the top of the page. "In the sixth, right? The sixth . . . How about . . . ? Here. Quick Sand. Number three."

Sal put down the binoculars and looked at the paper where Charles's finger was. "Quick Sand's not running here. Quick Sand's running at Aqueduct. You're looking at the wrong listing, genius. This is the Meadowlands."

Charles glared at the listing as if it were the paper's fault. He didn't like being wrong.

"Forget about that girl, will ya, Charles? She's pumping up your brain, that's what she's pumping up. She's making you stupid."

"You still don't believe me, do you? You think I'm making it up. Well, she *was* there that night. I'm telling you, it was her. If she didn't show up and distract me, Tozzi would be dead—"

"Shut up, for chrissake. We're in a crowd." Sal glared at him, then looked to one side, then the other. You could never tell who might be around, and he was nervous enough being out here. He was still worried about that shooter Juicy hired.

He took the paper out of Charles's hand and looked down at the picture of the Pump-It-Up Girl. Charles was dreaming. He didn't see her that night. Maybe he *thought* he saw her, but he didn't see *her*. He must've seen some blonde and thought it was her. That's the way these *moolinyams* are. As long as it's blond, they love it, even if the broad's a dog. But Charles didn't see anybody that night. This whole story about the girl was bullshit. He was just trying to cover his ass for blowing it with Tozzi.

Sal smacked the page with the back of his hand. "Tell me the truth, Charles. You really think a girl like this would ever go for a guy like you?"

"Shit, yeah." Charles looked insulted.

"Why? Whatta you got that's so special?"

Charles grabbed his crotch. "The only advantage God ever gave the black man. The object of white man's envy." He was smiling like a chimp again.

"You mean slam-dunking a basketball?"

"You know what I mean, Sal. The black man got the heavy artillery. We got them love cannons."

"Oh, yeah? Who told you that?"

"Every bitch I ever been with."

"Well, then those women never did it with an Italian guy."

"Get the fuck outta here."

"I'm serious. Next time you get a woman in the sack, you ask her first if she ever had any Italian *sauseege*. See what she says."

"Why? What she gonna say?"

"She'll tell you God loves the Italians better. She'll tell you God *is* Italian."

"Get the fuck . . . Why would she say that?"

"Because He may have given you guys the love cannons, but he gave us the cannons and the cannon *balls*." Sal grabbed his crotch and shook it.

"Get the fuck outta here." The chimp wasn't smiling.

Neither was Sal really. He was trying to stop worrying about that shooter so he could just do what he came here to do.

Sal turned around in his seat and looked at the time clock on the big board where the odds were posted. It was six minutes to post time. The last trickle of bettors were wandering up the aisles, heading for the windows. These were the serious bettors, the ones who waited to see the final odds before they placed their bets.

Sal blinked. All this smoke in here was making his eyes sting. The indoor stands at the track were like the dayroom at the fucking hospital, except there were about a million times the number of smokers here, and a lot of them were smoking cigars. Bartolo smoked cigars.

Sal picked up the binoculars. Bartolo's big joochy kid was standing up in his seat, holding his hand out. Frank was peeling off bills for him. The kid looked just like his old man, round and grouchy, except the kid was taller and he still had some hair. Sal was still trying to figure out if Junior was the one they gave the contract to. Frank might've pushed for his kid, but Sal couldn't see Juicy going along with it. Sal knew who the kid was, and he was convinced that Juicy would want a stranger, someone Sal would never see coming. Anyway, Junior was too stupid. Even his father treated him like a retard.

Through the binoculars, Sal watched Bartolo jerk his thumb up the stairs toward the betting windows. He was sending Junior upstairs to place their bets and bring back more food. They'd done it this way with every race so far. It was their routine. Sal fine-tuned the focus, trying to see how much money Bartolo was giving the kid. It was hard to tell, but it looked like a lot. Frank liked to play the ponies almost as much as he liked to eat. The poor kid wasn't getting to see any of the races, though, because he was always up getting food for his old man. But Bartolo didn't give a shit about the kid. He didn't give a shit about anybody but himself.

Why don'cha bring your father back a coupla prune Danishes while you're up there, kid? And another sausage and peppers. He needs it.

Charles leaned over and spoke low into Sal's ear. "How's he doing, Sal?"

Sal kept looking through the binoculars. "I dunno. I forgot how much this son of a bitch could eat."

"Gotta go sooner or later. Or did God give you guineas big-ass stomachs, too?"

Sal didn't answer. Bartolo was aggravating him now, sitting there yawning, working his jaw like it was feeding time at the zoo again. The smoke was burning the hell out of Sal's eyes, and the gun was digging into his side. There was no comfortable place to put it with that damn silencer screwed on. He could've taken the silencer off, but he didn't like the idea of having to take time out to put the damn thing on again when he needed it. But the way it was, it wouldn't stay put in his waistband, and it was irritating his skin.

"*Five minutes to post time.*" The familiar announcement echoed through the track. "*Place your bets, ladies and gentlemen. Windows will be closing in five minutes. Five minutes to post time.*"

"Whattaya think of Hilary's Blue Flame?" Charles was reading the paper again.

Sal shrugged, binoculars on his face. "I don't know nothing about the ponies."

"I like the name. Hilary's Blue Flame. Sound like a hot bitch."

"Sounds like the pilot light in some old Irish lady's kitchen."

Charles stood up. "I think I'll put down two bucks to show. And if I win, I ain't giving you nothing."

"Sit down." Sal grabbed Charles's sleeve and yanked

him back down into his seat. Through the binoculars he could see Bartolo getting up, frowning and rubbing his belly, ballooning his cheeks and blowing air out of his lips as he shuffled out of his row.

Finally. The son of a bitch finally had to go to the john. Unbelievable.

Sal handed the binoculars to Charles and tugged the brim of his golf cap down over his brow. "There he goes."

Bartolo hauled himself up the steps, working his way against the crowd rushing back to catch the race. He looked like he was in pain, wincing with his hand over his gut.

Sal waited for Bartolo to get to the main floor at the top of the stairs before he got up. "C'mon, Charles. Let's go." He glanced at the big board: four minutes and thirteen seconds left till post time.

Sal shuffled through the row and tried to squeeze past the two old bags who were bored stiff and annoyed as hell that their husbands had taken them here. They'd been squawking all night, and everyone in that section could hear them. They were up here from Florida visiting their families, but they did not want to be here at the track. *You boys got Hialeah at home*, they kept telling the old guys. *You got the track at Hallendale and the one at Hollywood, too. Whattaya need to come here for?* They were so pissed, they didn't even want to move and let Sal and Charles by. The blazing redhead glared up at Sal like a crab in a boiling pot as he asked nicely if she'd let him by. As he stepped over her, he thought about stepping on her old goddamn foot, but she looked like the type who'd make a scene.

Sal and Charles moved quickly up the concrete steps. The track hounds heading back to their seats made way for them. Together they were pretty imposing, like a couple of pro football players, which worried Sal. He tugged the brim of his hat down lower and hoped they didn't stick out too much. All he needed now was for someone to mistake them for two guys from the Giants and start asking for autographs. Christ, a crowd like that would be a perfect setup for pulling off a hit. He could feel the gun sinking into his gut—five, six shots at point-blank range. Lot of screaming, he don't see nothing but his life passing before his eyes, and the shooter disappears. Sal put his head down and walked a little faster.

Up on the main floor, the lines in front of the betting windows were still long. Except at the fifty- and hundred-dollar windows. They were never that busy.

Sal scanned the crowd. "You see him?"

Charles shook his head. "I don't see him."

Sal looked up at the board. Lines of yellow-white lights formed the numbers, and they were changing fast now as last-minute bets shuffled the odds. At the top of the board, the time left till post time ticked down. 3:41, 3:40, 3:39 . . .

Heading through the crowd, Sal felt the gun in his belt, the long silencer rubbing against his thigh. He had a full load in the clip, thirteen shots. That should be more than enough to do Frank. Unless someone gets in the way and he has to "bless" him, too. That could be a problem. He wanted to be in and out fast. He didn't want to have to reload.

They made their way around to the back of the betting windows, where the lounges and the food concessions were. And the bathrooms.

"There he is." Charles pulled on his arm.

Sal shrugged him off. "Quiet down. I see him."

Bartolo was shuffling toward the bathroom, skating

across the floor with his hands on his belly. The sourpuss was more sour than usual. He looked like he had to go bad.

Sal looked up at the board. Two fifty-eight till post time.

"You remember what you're supposed to do?"

Charles smirked at him. "This s'posed to be hard or something? 'Course I know what I'm s'posed to do."

"You better."

Charles was acting cool, but Sal had a feeling he wasn't so cool inside. He blew it with Tozzi, he could do the same here. Sal was beginning to think that maybe it wasn't even him who shot Tozzi in the leg. Maybe Charles hired someone else to do it, paid some stupid crackhead fifty bucks to do it. Sal definitely didn't buy this shit with the Pump-It-Up Girl. Well, we'll see what kind of killer the *moolinyam* is now. Ten to one, Charles pisses his pants. And if he does, he can fucking walk home 'cause Sal wasn't gonna ride all the way back to Trenton shut up in a car that smelled of piss. No way.

They headed toward the bathroom, walking slow, but not too slow, trying to blend in. Bartolo had just gone into the men's room, pushing his way past the guys rushing out so they wouldn't miss the race.

That low, soothing voice emanated from the ceiling speakers again. *"Two minutes to post time, ladies and gentlemen. Two minutes."*

Sal and Charles entered the crowded men's room. The room was tiled in a gray-and-white checkerboard pattern. A long line of urinals was against one wall, stalls on the opposite wall. The sinks were on the wall next to the door, and that's where the attendant was set up with his bottles of colognes and cans of hair spray, all this shit arranged just so on the counter. Sal had never seen anybody use any of that stuff in a public bathroom, but these old guys were always here peddling it. This attendant was about ninety years old, a black guy with Coke-bottle glasses, brown-and-white patent leather shoes, and no teeth. On the edge of the counter there was an open Te Amo cigar box filled with change and a few singles, his tip box.

Charles moved into the room and got in line for a urinal, which is exactly what Sal had told him to do. There were at least twenty guys waiting for their turn to pee. Sal coughed into his fist to cover his face and scanned the faces around the room, looking for possible hit men. It didn't seem likely, but someone could've followed him here from the hospital—it wasn't impossible —and a crowded bathroom was a good place for a hit. The guy could be waiting for him right now, making like he was fiddling with his zipper when he was really getting his gun out. Sal's head started to throb. He knew he wouldn't recognize the guy if he was here. He couldn't even get his own piece out fast enough to defend himself, not with that goddamn silencer attached. Only thing he could do now was go on with his own business and hope no one in here was out to get him.

Bartolo was just going into a stall, the second one from the end. Sal grabbed a Kleenex from the attendant's box and blew his nose. He kept it there until Bartolo closed the stall door.

"One minute to post time, ladies and gentlemen." The mellow voice oozed out of the ceiling in here, too. *"Place your bets. Windows will be closing in one minute. One minute to post time."*

Sal shuffled past the guys waiting for urinals and stood by the stall next to Bartolo's. A skinny geek with long, greasy hair and a black T-shirt came right out, and Sal

moved in. He closed the door and locked it, then sat
down on the toilet. Under the partition, he could see
Bartolo's doubleknits down around his ankles. Bartolo
was grunting and straining, but he didn't have to work at
it very long. All of a sudden it sounded like someone was
dumping a bucket of slop into the water. Sal made a face.
It didn't take long for the fumes to drift over to Sal's
stall, and he had to hold his breath. Jesus Christ. The
guy was rotten inside.

He pulled the gun out of his belt, breathing through
his mouth.

Mr. Mellow came back. *"The windows are now closed.
No further bets will be taken on this race. The betting windows are now closed."*

Sal stopped and listened. Bartolo was moaning
"aaahhh" in relief. Feet shuffled on the tiles outside.
Loose change clinked into the cigar box. "Thank ya, sir.
Thank ya, sir." That was the old guy.

Sal rested his hand over the gun, coughed loud and
racked the slide at the same time, then froze and listened. His face was drenched with sweat. More slop hit
the water. Bartolo moaned. Sal got another whiff of the
bastard and nearly threw up. The bastard deserved to
die. He was an environmental hazard.

"The horses are in the gates. And they'rrrrrre off!"

Sal leaned forward and peered through the crack in
the stall door. There was no one left at the urinals that
he could see except Charles, who was standing there
holding his dick.

*"Time Traveler takes the lead, followed by Snicker, Corne-
lius B., Nor'easter . . ."*

"Y'all missing the race, son."

"Yeah, I know, Pappy." Charles was pulling up his fly,
looking right at Sal.

Sal pinched his nose against the stink. *Go 'head, Charles. You said you knew what to do.*

Sal slid the bolt on the door, opened it a crack, and watched Charles moving toward the sinks. When he got to the old man's counter, he faked a slip and caught himself on the edge, knocking over the cigar box in the process. Change hit the tile floor and rolled all over the place. A quarter hit Sal's shoe.

"God*damn*!" the old guy cussed.

"Sorry, Pappy. Floor's wet."

The old guy muttered and struggled to his knees, grumbling and groaning.

"Don't worry, Pappy. I'll help you. Don't you worry. We'll get it all."

"*Coming 'round the bend it's Time Traveler by a length, Snicker, Nor'easter moving ahead, Cornelius B. . . .*"

Charles was down on his knees next to the old guy, looking up at Sal.

Sal pantomimed taking off a pair of glasses. It took Charles a second to understand that Sal wanted him to take the old guy's glasses. If he didn't, they were gonna have to kill him, too, and that might not fit in with Emerick's profile. He was supposed to kill for a reason, not just for the hell of it.

Charles hooked his long tarantula finger behind the hinge of the old guy's glasses and flipped them off his face.

"Hey!"

"You lost your glasses, Pappy. Lemme help you." Charles tossed the glasses onto the counter with the bottles of cologne and the cans of hair spray. "Now where'd those devils go?"

"*On the backstretch it's Time Traveler, Nor'easter, Cornelius B., Snicker, Footloose, Hilary's Blue Flame . . .*"

"My glasses! I need my glasses." The old man was frantic, pawing at the floor.

Sal came out of his stall and pointed the long barrel of his gun at Bartolo's door. He listened for someone hiding in another stall, but Charles came up behind him and shook his head. He'd already checked the stalls.

Charles waited for Sal to make his move. He'd said he was gonna watch just to show Sal that he wasn't chickenshit. The *moolinyam* could do whatever the hell he wanted, Sal didn't care. He was thinking about Bartolo now, Bartolo and the goddamn hitter. He couldn't wait to see the look on Bartolo's face when the fat fuck saw him standing there. Sal raised his leg slowly, held it there for a second, then kicked the door in. It banged against the inside wall and vibrated in place.

Bartolo was sitting on the can with his bare legs exposed and his pants down over his shoes. But he didn't looked surprised or scared or anything like that. Just real pissed off, the way he usually looked. Then Sal realized that what Bartolo was holding in his lap wasn't his dick. The son of a bitch had a fucking gun, a revolver pointed up at Sal's face. Jesus!

"You stupid fuck, Immordino. Go 'head, try it."

Sal's gun hand trembled. He couldn't stop blinking. He couldn't fucking believe this. "How the—"

Bartolo scowled at him. "You think I didn't see those big mameluke feet of yours under the stall? Only you and Frankenstein got feet like that."

"Shit, man." Charles started backstepping to the door.

Bartolo extended his arm and pointed the revolver at Charles. "Don't move, Jackson. Unless you wanna be a chocolate doughnut."

Sal could feel his heart thumping. He struggled to keep his eyes focused and his gun trained on Bartolo.

"Since when did you start carrying a piece to the track, Frank?"

"Since your old FBI pal, Tozzi, told me you might be coming around. Now drop it, Sal."

Sal saw double. That fucking little shit Tozzi.

"Coming 'round the bend, it's Nor'easter and Time Traveler out front, Footloose three lengths behind, and Hilary's Blue Flame coming up fast . . ."

Charles was looking up at the speaker in the ceiling. "Sheeeet."

Bartolo was sitting there with his piece and his hairy white legs, stinking up the whole place, like he was King Farouk. "I said drop the fucking gun, Sal."

"I need my glasses, boy. What you do with my glasses?" The old man was on the floor, spitting mad. He couldn't see what was going on.

Sal glanced at the old man out of the corner of his eye. He on his knees, feeling around under the sink, feeling around up under the counter.

"Hey, Sal, you fucking deaf or what? I said drop the gun."

Sal grit his teeth. *"You* drop the gun."

"I ain't dropping nothing."

"Then we both die. How's that sound, Frank? I'll shoot you and you can shoot me. You like that?" Sal was so mad thinking about that fuck Tozzi, he was willing to take his chances. He had the automatic, he could get off more shots.

"In the stretch it's Nor'easter, Time Traveler falling back, and Hilary's Blue Flame charging hard . . ."

"This is the last time I'm gonna fucking tell you, Sal."

"Hey, I'll make you a deal, Frank. I'll drop the gun if you tell me who the shooter is Juicy hired to get me."

"Yeah? And then what? I get to blow your head off?"

"So there is a contract out on me?"

"I didn't say that, Sal."

"You don't have to. I know all about it." Sal squeezed the butt of his gun, dying to pull the trigger.

"I don't know nothing about no contracts, Sal."

"You lying bastard—"

Boom!!!

Sal ducked. The gunshot reverberated off the tile walls and made his ears pop. Bartolo jumped off the toilet and hit the deck with his pants around his ankles.

"Ain't no one gonna steal my tips, goddammit."

Sal looked back at the old black guy kneeling by the sink. He had a gun, too, some old Wild West six-shooter thing, something Tom Mix woulda used. Pieces of duct tape were stuck to the long barrel. He must've kept it taped up under the sink, just in case.

Bam!!!

The old man yelped and collapsed to the tiles, banging his hip. He started wailing like a sick cat.

Bartolo was on his big fat belly, holding his gun two-handed like some kind of infantry commando. *Bam!!!* He plugged the old guy again, and the cat wails stopped.

Sal didn't hesitate. He leveled his gun and fired. *Pfittt, pfittt!!!*

Bartolo's body jumped like a couple thousand volts of electricity just went through it, and his fat ass jiggled. There were two bullet holes in his back, one high, one low. Charles scrambled to snatch the fat ass's gun away.

Charles was spooked. "He dead?"

Sal's heart was going nuts, but he tried to sound cool. "Turn him over and find out."

Charles grabbed a fistful of Bartolo's shirt and hauled him over on his back. Sal watched the glassy eyes staring up at the ceiling. He still might not be dead yet. He could be faking.

Sal clenched his teeth. No problem.

He put the silencer to Bartolo's forehead. *Pfittt!*

Belly button. *Pfittt!*

Shoulder. *Pfittt!*

Other shoulder. *Pfittt!*

Amen.

Blood oozed across the tiles. The smell of gun powder burns covered up Bartolo's stink. Sal's ears were throbbing. His shirt was drenched.

"And coming into the finish, it's Nor'easter out front by a head, Time Traveler and Hilary's Blue Flame neck and neck. Nor'easter, Time Traveler, Hilary's Blue Flame. Nor'easter out front by a head, Hilary's Blue Flame by a nose, and Time Traveler. Nor'easter, Hilary's Blue Flame, and Time Traveler. Nor'easter, Hilary's Blue Flame, and Time Traveler falling back now. At the finish, it's Nor'easter, Hilary's Blue Flame, and Time Traveler. Nor'easter, Hilary's Blue Flame, and Time Traveler . . . That's a final, ladies and gentlemen. Nor'easter, Hilary's Blue Flame, and Time Traveler."

"Shit, Sal! I told you I shoulda played that horse."

"Shut up!" Sal's head was pounding like a jackhammer in the morning. He was trying to figure out whether he should give the old man the sign of the cross, too. But he couldn't stop thinking about Tozzi, that fucking bastard, warning Bartolo and Juicy that he might be coming. How the hell did he know? What, could he read minds now? One way or another, the goddamn guy was always ending up in his face. How the hell could Tozzi know what he had planned? Charles? Couldn't be. If Charles was working with the FBI, he wouldn't have helped him whack Bartolo. They don't let their people do that kind of stuff. At least, they never used to.

"Sal, Sal, we gotta get outta here, man. Guys be coming in to go to the bathroom."

Sal rubbed his forehead for a moment, thinking hard, then he jammed his gun back into his pants. The barrel was hot against his skin. "You got Bartolo's gun?"

"It's in my pocket."

"Take the old man's piece, too."

"Why?"

"To fuck 'em up. The cops always wanna get the murder weapons." Sal went to the door.

Charles took the six-shooter out of the old man's dead hand and stuck it in his pants, covering the butt with his sweatshirt.

Sal glanced back at Bartolo's body and the cartridges on the floor all around him, then pulled the door handle with his knuckles so as not to leave fingerprints and walked out with Charles right behind him.

The main floor was starting to get crowded again, the winners collecting their money, other people getting stuff to eat, some heading for the bathrooms. Sal and Charles headed straight for the escalators. Sal worried that someone would notice that his shirt was soaked and it was coming through his jacket. They were halfway down on the escalator when they heard the commotion starting. A lot of yelling, then the hubbub of the curious. Sal imagined that it would be pretty crowded in there now, all the nosybodies pushing and shoving to get a peek at the bodies, the old black guy and the fat ugly bald man all shot to hell, caught with his pants down. It would take a few minutes for the cops to come, and it would take even longer to clear the room and figure out what had happened. By that time they'd be on the turnpike, heading south.

Sal stepped off the escalator and didn't look back. He

wasn't thinking about Bartolo anymore. That was done. He was thinking about Tozzi and how he was itching to give that son of a bitch his "blessing." He was thinking about the shooter, too, wondering whether he could've gotten Bartolo to tell him who it was. Bartolo had to know who it was, but he never would've told. Not in a million years.

Outside, as they walked through the parking lot, Sal told himself it didn't make any difference. Soon as they took care of Juicy, it would be a moot point. The contract is void as soon as the guy who takes it out dies, and Juicy was gonna go soon.

But Sal was still dying to know who the son of a bitch was. Who knows? Maybe it was Tozzi? Coming up to Charles's car, Sal got light-headed considering that possibility.

Charles unlocked the driver's door and got in. Sal waited for him to unlock his side, his hand on the handle.

Tozzi? Nah. Couldn't be.

Could it?

"C'mon, Sal! Get in! Hurry up!"

Sirens screamed across the parking lot in the distance. Revolving red-and-blue dome lights raced through the night, heading for the entrance to the track.

Sal got in and slammed the door shut. "Let's go."

TEN

tacy sat on the edge of her chair, hugging herself.
The room was cramped with too many folding chairs
and a long conference table. It was also dim and chilly,
too air-conditioned. She sat in the corner against the
back wall, trying to stay out of the draft coming from
the air duct on the ceiling. This whole place gave her the
creeps. She wished Tozzi hadn't brought her down here.
Yes, she wanted to be with him, but not at a state mental
hospital.

Looking through the one-way glass mirror that covered one wall, she scanned the ward on the other side.
This was the room where the doctors observed the patients. It was like watching fish at the aquarium. Men in
bathrobes and pajamas shuffled across the floor, wandering aimlessly. Other men in baggy blue jeans and white
T-shirts smoked and stared out into space. One guy
rubbed his crotch and rocked back and forth while he
smoked, puffing, rubbing, rocking, puffing, rubbing,
rocking. A fat guard in a gray uniform sat tipped back in
a folding chair by the door, reading the paper. Tozzi
leaned on the edge of a table, bouncing his cane on the

floor impatiently. He was waiting for that guy Sal Immordino he kept talking about.

Except for the drone of the TV mounted high on the wall, it was fairly quiet in there. She strained to see what was on TV, but it was too far away. Some old black-and-white movie maybe. She could hear what was going on in there through the speaker that hung over the one-way glass in here, and she'd just overheard the guard telling Tozzi that Sal Immordino had been taken to the infirmary, but that he was due back soon. Tozzi was itching to talk to him. Even though she didn't like being here, she had to admit she was more than a little curious to see this Mafia guy he kept talking about.

A video camera sitting on a tripod was pointed at the glass. Tozzi had set it up, hoping he could get Immordino to say something or do something to prove that he wasn't insane. A red light on the camera kept flashing to show that it was recording. He'd told her not to touch it, just let it go by itself. But the silent, pulsing light was making her nervous. It was creepy.

She studied Tozzi's face as he waited out there. His brow was furrowed, his mouth serious. He was like an eagle perched on a cliff, waiting to pounce. He'd asked her to drive him down here because his leg got stiff and weak when he tried to drive. Gibbons couldn't drive him because this place was now officially off limits to them. Tozzi had said something about Dr. Cummings complaining to their boss, Mr. Ivers, about how they had treated Immordino last time they were here and Ivers had read them the riot act. But Tozzi never listened. He said he wasn't on duty now, he was on sick leave, so this wouldn't be an official FBI interview. It was just a visit.

Stacy couldn't help but smile. That's what she liked about him. He didn't put up with any bullshit. He knew what had to be done and he just went ahead and did it. At least, with most things.

She rubbed her bare arms and sighed. She wished he was a little more take-charge when it came to her. It was so weird. He knew exactly what he wanted with everything else, but with her . . . Well, she just couldn't figure him out. On the one hand, he always wanted to be with her. He'd been calling her and they'd been going out, but whenever they were together, it always started out just fine, then it would get . . . well, weird. He always said all the right things and he seemed to like her, but they were stuck in the heavy-petting stage, which seemed pretty odd for a guy his age. They'd make out like teenagers, but it never got any further than that, and he was the one who was always cutting it short. She couldn't figure it out. What was holding him back? He said he wasn't religious or anything like that. Maybe he had AIDS and he was afraid he'd pass it on to her. But he wouldn't hide something like that. At least, she didn't think he would. She didn't know what to think.

Except that she really liked him and that she wished he'd stop acting so weird.

He was the first guy she'd known since seventh grade who didn't try to put the moves on her the first time he met her. In fact, he didn't even seem to be interested in her at all that night at Gilhooley's. Too bad. Maybe if he had stuck around and drooled all over her the way most guys did, he wouldn't have been shot.

She thought back to the scene on the street that night when she'd gone after him wanting to apologize, worried that she might've hurt his feelings. She remembered the drizzle in her hair and how you could see it in the streetlights. Then the flash of the gun in the dark and Tozzi yelling to her. That's about all she remembered.

That and the sight of Tozzi lying on the ground. They kept asking her afterward if she remembered seeing anybody else there, but she didn't see anything but the gun flash. It was too dark, and it happened so fast.

She looked through the glass and focused on Tozzi's bad leg. He said the bullet got him in the thigh, but she'd never actually seen the wound, let alone the bandage. What if the bullet hit a little higher? She stared at his crotch and crinkled her face. Oh, my God. Maybe that's his problem.

The door opened then. Stacy was sitting behind it, so she didn't see who it was right away.

"Will ya look at this? Must be *America's Funniest Home Videos.*"

"Shut that fucking thing off."

"Want me to break it?"

"Just shut it off."

A black man in a gray guard's uniform came into the room, reaching out for the video camera. An enormous sallow-faced white man in a plaid flannel shirt and baggy khakis followed him in.

Stacy coughed to announce her presence.

Both men froze like deer caught in the headlights. The big white guy immediately stooped over and looked at the floor. It was only then that Stacy noticed the restraining belt around his waist, a wide leather belt with two additional straps that kept his wrists bound to his hips. His clenched hands were huge. They reminded her of pit-bull heads in studded collars.

The guard smiled at her. "Sorry about barging in on you like this. Didn't know anybody was in here." His eyes were all over her.

She flashed a phony smile and rubbed her arms. Her skin was hard with goose bumps.

The white man looked up at the guard from under his brows and mumbled something. The guard went over and closed the door.

Her heartbeat went into double time. She glanced at the nameplate pinned to the guard's shirt pocket. It was Charles something, she couldn't make out the last name. The lettering was small, and the lighting was bad. She wanted to know his last name so she could memorize it, just in case something happened.

The guard looked through the one-way mirror for a few seconds, then turned his attention back to her. He tilted his head to one side, narrowed his eyes, and started shaking his finger at her. "Ain't you that girl on TV? The one with the dumbbell?"

Stacy flipped her hair over her shoulder and avoided his gaze. Men came on to her this way all the time, and she usually didn't have any problem telling them to go to hell. But in here she was afraid to say anything to him, afraid of what might happen if she said yes, she was the Pump-It-Up Girl, afraid of what might happen if she said no and disappointed him. She glanced at Tozzi out on the ward and wondered whether he'd be able to hear her if she yelled.

"You that Pump-It-Up Girl, ain'tcha?" The guard was shaking his head like he couldn't believe his eyes. "Damn. It sure as hell is you."

Stacy started to shake her head no. "I don't think . . ." Her words trailed off.

"Hell, I gotta get your autograph. You famous."

"No . . . I'm not really . . ." Her throat was dry.

He turned to the huge white guy. "This here is the Pump-It-Up Girl, man. Can you beat that?"

The big man didn't seem to care one way or the other.

He was busy working his fists, flexing them in their restraints.

"Hey, look!" The guard was all excited, pointing at the glass. "I think that's you right now."

Stacy didn't know what he was talking about until her eye found the television set out on the ward. Shit. Of all times to play that goddamn commercial. There she was curling the barbell. She didn't need a good look to tell it was her commercial. Christ.

"I tol' you that's her," he said to the white guy. "C'mere and get a better look."

The guard pulled the big man over to the camera. He seemed reluctant to look, but he bent forward and peered into the viewfinder. "Look at the TV, man. Here, I'll work the zoom for you. It's like a telescope. Go 'head. You'll see. It's her."

The big man bent his knees and squinted one eye as he looked into the camera. He turned around and looked over his shoulder, stared at her face, then turned back to the camera and looked through the viewfinder until the commercial was over. When he stood up again, he stared at her face. Her stomach was solid ice.

It was then that she noticed that his hands weren't in the restraints anymore. They were hanging loose by his sides. When he saw that she'd noticed, he calmly slipped them back into the belt restraints as if he were putting them in his pockets. His grim face didn't move the whole time. Only his eyes did.

Stacy thought about running out of there, but the room was jammed with chairs and the two men were between her and the door. She crossed her legs and hugged herself tighter.

The guard jerked his thumb at the glass. "Ain't that Mr. Tozzi, the FBI man? Sure it is. I 'member him walking with that cane last time he was here." He pointed his thumb at her. "Then you *must* be the Pump-It-Up Girl. I read about you in the paper. It said some FBI agent got his leg shot up saving you from a mugger in New York City. Yeah . . . That must've been him. Am I right?"

Stacy nodded and mumbled. "Right." One of the gossip columns in the *Daily News* ran something about her a few days ago. Someone spotted her at the hospital visiting Tozzi and whoever it was called it in to the paper. The paper called her at the spa to confirm the story, but she didn't realize that when she took the call. She got flustered when the columnist started firing questions at her and instead of just saying "no comment," she altered the story a little and said she was being mugged when an FBI agent happened to come by and he saved her.

"That musta been some scary scene. Tozzi shooting it out with that mugger."

She pressed her lips together and nodded. "Yeah . . . it was."

"And you really was there, saw the whole thing, huh?"

She was puzzled by the question. "Well, yeah. Of course I was there."

A goofy smile crept around the guard's face as he made eye contact with the white guy. "You sure it wasn't one of those publicity stories you famous people make up just to get yourselves in the news?"

She shook her head. "No, it really happened." All of a sudden the guard seemed more loony than threatening with all these dumb questions. He kept looking at the white guy, nodding his head with this strangely confident "I-told-you-so" look on his face. The guard seemed like the one who should've been wearing the restraining belt.

But it was the big guy who was really making her

nervous. His face hadn't changed at all since he realized she was in here, and he kept staring at her—and not at her body, at *her*. She kept her eyes down, trying not to look at him, but he was hard to ignore for long. When she glanced over at him again, she was surprised but relieved to see that he wasn't staring at her anymore. He was staring at the video camera.

She glanced up at the camera. The red light wasn't blinking.

"Hey," she said to the guard. "Did you turn that off?"

The guard didn't answer. He was too busy rummaging around the room, examining the case the video equipment came in.

"What're you looking for?"

The big white guy slipped his hands out of the leather restraints again and scratched his cheek. He walked around the table and took a seat across from her, staring at her the whole time.

"What do you want with me?" She didn't want him to think she was frightened, but it was in her voice. She coughed and repeated herself. "What do you want?"

He raised an eyebrow and shrugged. The guard was poking around behind her. Her heart started to pound. Out of the corner of her eye, she could see Tozzi on the other side of the glass, still waiting out on the ward. She thought about yelling, then wondered if she might be overreacting. But why was this guy wearing a restraining belt with his hands free like that?

The white guy looked up at the guard, then looked down at something on the floor. Stacy followed his eyes to the black camera case open on the floor. It was as big as a small trunk. Big enough to put a small body in, she thought. Her throat suddenly got so tight it ached.

The guard looked very serious all of a sudden, serious

and disapproving. He was shaking his head at the white guy.

The white guy nodded his head yes. His face still didn't move.

Stacy stood up. She felt a little queasy. "Where's the women's room?"

The guard didn't answer. Instead he moved toward the door and stood in front of it.

Jesus. What the hell did they want? Stacy tried to remember all the things you're supposed to do when you're confronted with a rapist, but her mind drew a blank. All she could think was that there were two of them, they were both big, and the room was closing in on her.

She stood up and stepped through the crowd of chairs toward the door. "I have to go to the—"

"Did you hear us when we came in?"

"What?"

The guard had his head tilted back, looking at her down the angle of his cheeks. He was smiling, but it wasn't a very nice smile.

"Excuse me. I need a bathroom."

She stepped closer to the door, but the guard didn't budge.

"I axed you a question. Did you hear us when we came in?"

"Please let me by. I have to go."

The white guy was looking up at her from under his brows. His big hands were on the table, waiting.

"Excuse me, please. I want to get out." She tried to be assertive, but the strain in her voice gave her away.

The guard folded his arms over his chest and flared his nostrils. "Answer me first."

The big white guy got to his feet. He was moving around the table.

Her chest was heaving. It was freezing cold. She wanted to scream, but she stopped herself. What if Tozzi didn't hear her? It would just provoke them. The big guy would go berserk, strangle her, stuff her body in that case. The guard would sneak it out of the hospital, dump her in the woods somewhere. Animals would chew through the case to eat her. Whatever was left of her would be rotten before it was ever discovered.

She looked from one to the other. They weren't moving. She felt faint and she felt nauseated, but not enough to throw up. She wished she could as she suddenly remembered that that was a recommended strategy for dealing with a rapist. Puke on him. But these guys were as big as professional wrestlers and they were on opposite sides of the room. She couldn't possibly have enough in her.

The guard growled at her. "Lady, I axed you a simple question. Did you hear—"

Suddenly the door swung open and banged into the guard's back.

The man jumped. "What the—"

The door opened all the way. Tozzi was standing on the threshold, holding his cane in one hand like a sword. His eyes swept the room, then settled on the big white guy.

"What the hell you doing in here, Sal?"

Stacy's jaw dropped. Sal? This is Sal Immordino?

Tozzi glared at the guard. "What're you doing in here?"

"Well, uh . . . I thought you wanted to talk to Sal."

"I've been waiting for you out on the ward for the past twenty minutes. Whattaya doing with him in here?"

"I thought they said you wanted to talk to him in here, that you wanted privacy. Guess I didn't understand."

Tozzi raised an eyebrow and exhaled out loud. He was making it obvious that he thought the guard was full of shit. He glanced at Immordino, who was swaying on his feet, mumbling to his hands, then looked to her. "You all right?"

She pressed her lips together and nodded. "I'm okay." She hadn't meant to whisper.

Tozzi barked at the guard. "Get him outta here. Take him to the ward and wait for me."

The guard shrugged, unfazed. "Whatever you say, man. C'mon, Sal. Let's go." He took Immordino by the arm and started to lead him out.

Stacy found her voice. "He's not strapped," she said to Tozzi. "The straps are loose. His hands are free." She sounded panicky again.

The guard heard her. He checked the belt and tugged on the straps. "Must've forgot to tighten them after Sal went to the bathroom." He shrugged. "He don't need that thing. He gentle. Just another dumb hospital rule. Patients in transit gotta wear the belt." He fixed the straps and led Sal out of the room.

Stacy felt much better after they were gone.

Tozzi put his hand on her shoulder. "You sure you're all right? Did they do anything to you?"

She shook her head and shivered. "I think the guard messed around with the camera. I'm not sure. I didn't actually see him do anything to it, but the light's not blinking."

Tozzi examined the camera, then did something to it. The red light started flashing again.

"They say anything to you?"

"The guard kept asking me if I heard them come in. I

didn't know what he was talking about. I guess he wanted to know if I heard Immordino say anything."

"Did you?"

"I heard two voices, but I didn't actually see him talking."

"What did he say?"

"Something about turning 'that fucking thing' off. He was talking about the camera."

"But you didn't see him say anything."

"No."

"Shit." Tozzi sighed.

"Why? What's wrong?"

"If you'd seen him say that, we could've used you to testify against him. You heard him, but unfortunately you didn't *see* him talking. Wouldn't do us any good. Besides, I'd have to explain what you were doing here and that could be a problem in terms of procedure. Shit."

"Over here, Sal. C'mon. There's your table over there."

In the one-way mirror Charles was leading Sal across the ward.

"I'll be as quick as I can. You wait here." Tozzi started to go, but Stacy held on to his hand.

She looked into his eyes. "I have to pee."

He looked into hers. "Oh. Then go."

"Come with me."

"You can't go alone?"

"Keep walkin', Sal. Keep walkin'."

Tozzi couldn't keep his eyes off the glass.

"Just come with me and wait outside. I'll be fast."

He shrugged, a little puzzled. "Okay." His avenging-eagle face switched to a fatherly expression of extreme concern for her well-being. She liked him better the other way.

She rubbed her arms again, thinking about Sal Immordino's expressionless face. He put his arm around her shoulder as they left the room and went out into the hallway. It was a little warmer in the hallway, but she still had goose bumps. She walked a little faster and picked up their pace as they went down the hallway. She really did have to pee.

ELEVEN

Gibbons cupped his hands over the windowpane in the front door of the Mary Magdalene Home for Unwed Mothers and looked in. A skinny guy was right there in the hallway, painting the wall with a roller. Gibbons frowned. What the hell was his problem? Couldn't he hear the doorbell? Gibbons rang it again.

Madeleine Cummings tilted her head to one side and gave him that sarcastic little grin of hers. "Shall we break it down?"

He ignored the remark. He was trying not to fight with her. Actually, he was trying not to even talk to her. He was here for a reason, even though she didn't think so. Sal Immordino wouldn't talk to Tozzi yesterday, which was no surprise, but Tozzi had a bad feeling about him now. He'd scared the hell out of Stacy, and she believed that either Sal or that guard Charles Tate had tampered with the video camera Tozzi had set up. Gibbons figured that it might be worthwhile to squeeze Immordino's sister Cil, the nun. She always seemed to be in a fog when it came to her brother's criminal enterprises, but she might let something drop without even knowing it. It was worth a try. After all, if that was a hit man who shot Tozzi, the contract was still open, and the way Gibbons figured, if Immordino was the one who put out the contract on Tozzi, there was probably one out on him, too. Gibbons sucked in his breath and pressed the doorbell again.

"Why don't you give them a chance?" Her exasperated voice now.

He kept peering through the window. "There's a guy standing right there, for chrissake. What is he, deaf?"

Cummings shrugged. "Maybe he is."

Gibbons just looked at her. He knew what she was thinking, that he was insensitive to the plight of the disabled. She'd been going on and on about how he and Tozzi had "brutalized" Immordino at the nuthouse, even squealed on them to Ivers, and Lorraine had been lapping this crap up, looking at him across the kitchen table every morning like he was Hermann Göring or something. Gibbons wished to hell Charles Manson would escape, so Cummings would be called back to her old job down at Quantico.

He was about to start pounding on the door when he spotted a girl inside coming down the hall. She slid the chain on before she unlocked the door.

"Yeah?" She peered under the taut chain. Her eyes were light brown and very wary. Her face was pasty.

Gibbons held up his I.D. so she could see it. "Special Agent Gibbons, Federal Bureau of Investigation. This is Agent Cummings. We'd like to talk to Sister Cil."

The girl stared blankly at his I.D. Her bottom lip hung slack, and she looked like she had too many teeth for her mouth.

Cummings lowered Gibbons's hand and looked into the gap in the door. "Please tell Sister Cil that we're sorry to show up unannounced and that we won't take up too much of her time."

Gibbons glared at her. What the hell does she think they do, call ahead? Sure, why not give suspects enough time to get their stories down pat before you get there? The way Cummings figured things, that would be the polite thing to do, and with her, civilized behavior counted for a lot. Jesus, she was an ass.

The girl closed the door and slid the chain off. When she opened it again, Gibbons noticed that she was pregnant—not real pregnant, just starting to show. Her mousy brown hair stood up straight over her forehead, glued that way with that mousse crap these kids all wear. The rest of her hair was an awful-looking rat's nest. He figured her to be fourteen, maybe fifteen.

"I'll go get her," the kid said. She went back through the hall and disappeared into the back of the building.

The smell of wet paint drifted out through the open door. The painter looked like a real halfwit, staring straight ahead at the wall in front of him, rolling over the same strip, up and down, up and down, not going back to the pan for more paint, not moving on to a new spot, just moving that roller up and down, up and down.

Gibbons knew Cummings was waiting for him to say something about the guy. He wasn't going to give her the satisfaction.

"So where's Tozzi today?" she said.

Gibbons shrugged. "I dunno."

"I'm surprised you didn't bring him along. Having seen how he deals with the mentally disturbed, I can't imagine what he'd do to a nun."

Gibbons raised his eyebrows and shrugged. He wasn't gonna say a word.

"Or is he too preoccupied with that girl now?"

"What girl?"

"That young girl, the one on TV."

Gibbons knit his brows and deliberately looked puzzled.

"Stacy Viera."

Gibbons grinned. He knew who Cummings was talking about; he just wanted to hear her say Stacy's name. She and Lorraine had been referring to Stacy as "that young girl" ever since they met her at the hospital.

"So? Is he still seeing Stacy?"

Gibbons shrugged. "I dunno what Tozzi does on his own time."

But it wouldn't take too much imagination.

Cummings frowned. "You may not realize it, but Lorraine is pretty upset about this. She thinks her cousin is just leading Stacy on."

Gibbons shrugged again. "The girl's over twenty-one . . . I think."

"Age has nothing to do with it. It's Tozzi's attitude. You can see it in his face. He thinks of Stacy as his personal pinup girl."

"Did he tell you that?"

"No."

"Then how do you know that's the way he feels about her? Maybe he respects her for her mind."

Cummings folded her arms and looked over her glasses. "Not likely."

"You're just assuming he's up to no good. But you don't know for sure. And neither does Lorraine."

"I'm not *assuming* anything. What I *see* is a special agent of the Federal Bureau of Investigation carrying on with a television personality of some local repute whose popularity is based on her sex appeal and implied lasciviousness. This association does not fit in with the circumspect image the Bureau expects from its personnel. And I'm not entirely sure Tozzi has the moral fiber to keep his relationship with Stacy from becoming a serious embarrassment to the Bureau."

Gibbons bit the insides of his cheeks before he cursed. "How would you know what kind of 'moral fiber' Tozzi has?"

"I've seen the great qualms he had in belittling Sal Immordino. Dating Stacy doesn't seem to pose much of dilemma for him. I realize Tozzi's your friend, but face it, he's an oral personality. He takes what he wants when he wants it with little regard for others."

"You don't know what the hell you're talking about."

Cummings pointed at the backward words painted on the glass in the front door: The Mary Magdalene Home for Unwed Mothers. "Places like this exist because of people who can't control their wants and desires."

"You saying Tozzi would knock Stacy up and then abandon her? Is that what you're saying?"

If Tozzi did, he'd kill him.

Cummings closed her eyes and shrugged. "I'm not saying he would. I don't really know him well enough to state a professional opinion. But the potential for unacceptable behavior exists in every personality."

"You don't know what you're talking about."

She held her chin and studied him for a moment. "Your adamant defense of your partner couldn't stem from a vicarious thrill you're getting out of Tozzi's relationship with Stacy, could it? Armchair quarterbacking in a psychosexual sense?"

Gibbons ground his molars. "Save the psychology for the real nuts, okay?" Bitch.

"Very bad. This is very bad."

They both stared at the painter as he kept rolling over

that same spot. He was shaking his head and mumbling to himself, eyes glued to the wall.

"This is bad." The guy didn't seem to know they were there.

Suddenly Sister Cil appeared, swooping down the hallway like Batman. She was wearing the heavy-duty habit, the black one that went down to her ankles. A bad sign. She usually wore the more modern version, the knee-length skirt and the little headpiece that showed her hairline. Gibbons knew that when she wore this getup, she was going to be filled with the spirit of the Lord her God, which meant she'd evade all his questions and stonewall it.

The nun stopped by the painter and admired his work, then took his arm and moved the roller a foot to the right. "Very good, Donald. Now try using some more paint."

Sister Cil swooshed toward the door to greet them in a flurry of black cloth, head-tilted smiles, and glinting glasses. The Catholic caped crusader. Gibbons could understand why people who went to parochial school never get over the experience.

"Agent Gibbons, how *are* you?"

"You remember me."

"Of course I remember you." She turned her high beams on Cummings. "And you are . . . ?"

"Madeleine Cummings. I'm also with the FBI."

The nun nodded and smiled. At what, no one knew.

"I apologize for just showing up like this, Sister"— Cummings glanced sideways at Gibbons—"but my partner insisted. We'd just like to ask you a couple of questions, if you can spare a few moments."

"Of course, of course. Come into the parlor. And watch out for the wet paint."

The caped crusader led the way to the front room off the hallway. It was a dark, dingy room with big bay windows covered with heavy drapes drawn halfway. Rather than taking advantage of the daylight, the room had ice cube–tray fluorescent fixtures buzzing on the ceiling. These walls needed a paint job even more than the hallway, but the way their painter was going, it was gonna be a while.

Three worn, mismatched sofas were arranged around the old brownstone's white marble mantelpiece. A television set was inside the fireplace. The kid who'd answered the door was sitting on the sofa closest to the TV, engrossed in a soap opera. Another kid, an out-of-the-bottle blonde with a rat's nest of her own, was sitting next to her, holding an infant. Gibbons could only see the baby's legs because his head was under his mother's oversized T-shirt, sucking away. Neither of the girls paid any attention to the visitors. The soap was more important.

"Please sit down." Sister Cil indicated the green brocade sofa directly opposite the two kids.

Gibbons caught Cummings staring at him again. She thought she could read his mind. She was probably thinking he was getting all bent out of shape because the kid was breast-feeding over there. He didn't give a shit. You couldn't see anything anyway—just a little bit of her bare belly and the baby kicking his legs, having a ball under there. It was no big deal. What the hell did she think he was gonna do? Throw a blanket over them? Make the kid leave the room? Christ, the poor girl's life was miserable enough. Let her have her soaps in peace.

Sister Cil sat with her hands clasped in her lap. "So how have you been, Mr. Gibbons?"

"Fine, Sister. Fine." Gibbons watched for signs of sarcasm in her relentlessly pleasant demeanor. He and Tozzi were the ones who had arrested her brother in Atlantic City two years ago. She knew he was here to ask about Sal.

"And how is Mr. Tozzi doing these days?"

Gibbons nodded. "He's fine."

"I take it he's not your partner anymore. You're with Agent Cummings now?"

Gibbons and Cummings answered together. "Temporarily."

"Oh." Sister Cil smiled and nodded. "Before we get to your business, may I ask you something, Ms. Cummings?"

"Yes?"

"Now, you don't have to give me an answer right this moment, but I would be terribly grateful if you could come back some evening and speak to the girls. They have so few good role models, and I think meeting a successful woman from the real world would make a big difference to some of them." Sister Cil nodded in the direction of the two kids zoned out on the other couch.

On TV, a rich-bitch blonde was huffing and puffing around an office, talking down to her little brunette secretary. The blonde seemed to be warning the brunette about seeing some guy, saying it wasn't "very smart" for her to be seen with him. The brunette cowered a lot and had a good "distressed" face. The blonde acted mainly with her shoulders. The kids were riveted.

The nun sighed. "I wish I could afford more stimulating diversions for the girls than this trash. But I suppose I should be grateful that we even have a television. Money has always been a problem for us, but donations are down and it's become particularly difficult."

Cummings turned from the soap opera back to Sister

Cil adjusting her glasses. "Media images are very problematic for adolescents. Young women seem to be especially vulnerable to misleading messages, particularly those concerning idealized concepts of romance. These messages have largely become the operating subtext of most commercial television programming. Young women become so eager for the kind of glamorous romance they see in the media, they become easy prey for manipulative men." She adjusted her glasses again and looked Gibbons in the eye.

Gibbons rubbed his jaw, looked at the ceiling, and sighed. Give me a break, will ya?

Sister Cil laid her hand on her chest and pursed her lips. "You are so right, Ms. Cummings. I hear virtually the same thing from every young woman I talk to. They want to be loved so badly that they will submit themselves to any boy who shows them the slightest bit of attention. Men seem to have an animal instinct when it comes to finding girls like this. They seem to be able to smell them. I'm sure they're not evil people, because they must be subject to equally distorting influences of their own. But when it comes to innocent young girls, men do become sinful. It may be nature's way, but it's not right." Cil was all choked up by the time she finished her little spiel.

"This is bad. Very bad! Very bad!"

The painter wasn't facing the wall. He was staring at Cil, his face crumpled and fretting, a lot more distressed than that brunette on TV. He reached into his pocket and took out a set of rosary beads, black wooden ones. He was getting paint on them. "This is bad! Very bad!"

Cil shot up off the sofa and went to him, putting her arms around his shoulders to comfort him, shushing him and telling him it was all right, it was all right. He grazed her skirt with the roller and left a pale yellow smudge. She plucked the roller out of his hand and set it down in the tray on the floor. "Come with me, dear. It's time for a break. Maybe Lucy will make you a cup of tea. How does that sound? A nice cup of tea." She led him through a doorway to the back of the house, his agitated mumbling trailing behind. "This is bad. Very bad! Very bad!"

The kids on the couch hadn't moved. They were still glued to the set. The baby under the blonde's shirt had stopped kicking.

When Gibbons turned back, he caught Cummings staring at him again. "You may as well say it," she said. "I know what you're thinking."

"How the hell do you know what I'm thinking?"

She smirked. "Come on. I know what you think of people like that man. You're prejudiced against people who have problems."

"I didn't say a word."

"You don't have to. It's all over your face."

Gibbons looked at the ceiling and bit his upper lip. Working with her was like having a goddamn wife on the job. Even Lorraine wouldn't be this bad. He raised his finger and was just about to tell Cummings off when Sister Cil swooped back into the room and resettled herself on the sofa, rearranging the folds of her habit to cover the paint smudge.

"I apologize for the outburst," she said, clasping her hands in her lap again. "He's a very sweet man, but certain things upset him without warning. I'm afraid with my dwindling budget, we can't afford to hire professional help." She broke out into a beatific smile. "But the paint is very good quality and it was a donation.

That's something to be thankful for." She bowed her head. Amen.

Gibbons smiled and nodded, wanting to stick his finger down his throat. "Speaking of money, Sister, that's something I want to ask you about." He sat forward and leaned toward her. "From what I understand, you run this place on your own, and the diocese doesn't provide you with any funding. Is that correct?"

Cil nodded, her glasses glinting. "Yes, this is a private charity."

"Why's that? Wouldn't you do better hitching your wagon to the diocese? In terms of funding, I mean."

The nun tilted her head and paused for a moment before she answered. "Yes and no. We would receive money from the diocese if we chose to be under their auspices, but we would also be subject to their scrutiny as well."

"Is there anything wrong with that?"

"Well, Mr. Gibbons, you must understand that I greatly admire Archbishop Leahy. He is truly a wonderful human being, and it's my opinion that the policies of his administration do not reflect his own personal feelings of Christian love and charity. But there are certain people in the diocese who are not hospitable to my goals here at Mary Magdalene. They feel that the work we carry on here is better done by secular social service agencies, and that we are—well, frankly, they don't feel that we're necessary. The thrust of the diocese's efforts today is education—which is a worthwhile goal, I don't argue with that. What I do find objectionable is their implied policy that some people are beyond the Church's concern, that when a young girl makes a grave mistake, she should be thrown on the scrap heap and left to the uncertainties of the secular agencies."

"In other words, the diocese would shut you down."

The nun tilted her head a bit more. She looked like a mynah bird, all black and just as vague, searching for one of her memorized phrases. "The diocese might do that, yes. If we took money from them."

"So where *does* your funding come from?" Cummings asked.

Gibbons almost dropped dead. For once, Cummings was being helpful.

"Mostly private donations."

"And have these donations been able to sustain you here, Sister?"

The beatific smile returned, more radiant than before. "We get by, Ms. Cummings. The past couple of years have been difficult for us, but God provides."

Gibbons pulled on his lower lip. "How about your brother Sal? Does he help you out?"

The saintly smile dimmed as the corners of Cil's mouth drooped. Her eyeglasses flashed. "How do you mean, Mr. Gibbons?"

"Up until two years ago, your brother was involved with several lucrative business enterprises. He must've socked away a nice little bundle. I would think Sal would be your guardian angel."

"My brother has never had any 'business enterprises,' Mr. Gibbons. He is a very ill man. He has very few assets of his own."

"Yeah, that's what they tell me, but I find that hard to believe. We do know that he has at least one numbered bank account in Switzerland and a holding company in Panama."

Cil's back stiffened. "Oh, really?"

Gibbons puckered his lips and nodded. "Really."

"I think you're mistaken, Mr. Gibbons. I am my

brother's legal guardian, so I know what he has. About fifteen thousand dollars that came from an inheritance. I put that money into long-term certificates of deposit for him in order to earn the highest interest rate available."

Gibbons just stared at her and let it get uncomfortable, the overwrought dialogue from the soap opera filling the room. "How about we level with each other now, okay, Sister?"

The nun looked puzzled. She was good at looking puzzled. Gibbons had seen that face plenty of times. It was especially good when she was in custody. Sister Cil had been there that night they arrested Sal in Atlantic City. She looked real puzzled in handcuffs.

Gibbons tried to see her eyes past the glare in her glasses. Fifteen grand, my ass. Sal had to have more cash than that to hire a shooter.

"Lying is a sin, Sister. Even when you're trying to protect your own brother."

"I don't lie, Mr. Gibbons. You should know that." Her mouth was a short, flat line.

"This place has really gone downhill since the last time I was here. About two years ago, just before Sal was arrested. Could it be, Sister, that this appearance of poverty is all for show? Like Sal's supposed mental illness?"

She was seething, but keeping a lid on it. "I can assure you, Mr. Gibbons, that I would not subject these young women to any degree of hardship if I had the means to afford better. As I said, Sal has the certificates of deposit, and we maintain a small joint savings account—not quite two thousand dollars—which we agreed to use only for dire emergencies. I can show you all the papers."

"Hmmm . . ." Gibbons nodded. "When you say that you and your brother agreed to use this savings account only for dire emergencies, does that mean you discussed it with him?"

"I *informed* him, Mr. Gibbons. You know he's not capable of understanding such matters. He's a very ill man." Her glasses were beaming death rays.

Gibbons nodded and looked at her through lizard lids. He knew she was full of shit, and he wanted to make sure she knew that he knew.

Cummings coughed. "Sister, I'd like to point out for the record that Gibbons and I do not agree on the state of your brother's mental health, and his opinion that your brother is faking his condition is just that, an opinion. The Bureau does not officially stand behind it."

Gibbons wanted to get his hands around her neck. What the fuck did she think she was doing? She was cutting his legs out from under him, that's what she was doing, goddamn her.

"And *I'd* like to state for the record, Sister, that Dr. Cummings is only an observer in this investigation, and *her* opinions in said investigation are worth about as much as a cup of pigeon—" He stopped short and glared at the nun. "Never mind."

Cil's chin sunk into her neck. "Excuse me? What investigation? You didn't say anything about an investigation."

Cummings spoke. "We're investigating the recent murders of a Mr. Sabatini Mistretta, Mr. Mistretta's bodyguard Jerry Rella, a Mr. Frank Bartolo, and a Mr. Lucas Witherspoon." She ticked off the list like recipe ingredients.

The nun looked puzzled again. "Who's the last one?"

Dr. Cummings clarified. "Mr. Witherspoon was an employee at the Meadowlands racetrack, where the Bartolo murder took place. He appears to have been an unfortunate innocent bystander."

Gibbons couldn't take any more of her shit. "You don't know that for sure, Cummings. No one does yet. And where the hell did you learn how to conduct a field interview? *We* ask the questions, not her. The Bureau doesn't provide customer service."

Cummings inhaled sharply and hardened her face. She turned to Sister Cil. "Agent Gibbons and I have a difference of opinion concerning the nature of these homicides. He contends that these were La Cosa Nostra–related killings. I believe that they are the work of a serial killer."

Sister Cil slapped her chest. "A serial killer?! Mother of God, pray for us."

Gibbons chewed on his upper lip. He wanted to strangle them both.

The nun stared at him. "Are you suggesting that my brother is a serial killer now?" Cil was up on her high horse.

Cummings suddenly had nothing to say. She sat there with her arms folded, looking at him with one eyebrow arched over the top of her glasses, waiting for him to clean up the mess she'd made bringing up that serial killer bullshit. She probably didn't even realize how badly she'd botched this up. Cil was spooked. She wasn't gonna tell them anything now. May as well just leave. It'll just be denials from here on in—denials and testimonials as to the saintliness of her dear brother the numskull. Shit.

Gibbons heard something familiar then—a pounding bass and drums. He looked at the television set and saw the camera panning that big, sparkling chrome weight room. It was Stacy's commercial. The camera found

Stacy working her barbell up and down, up and down, jiggling her jugs.

"Wow, she's pretty." The brown rat's nest on the other couch stared at Stacy in a buck-toothed, slack-mouthed trance.

The blond rat's nest with the kid on her tit moaned in agreement. "Yeah . . ."

"Looks aren't everything, girls," Sister Cil said, trying to get their attention.

Cummings put her two cents in. "Physical beauty seldom guarantees happiness in life."

The girls paid no attention to them. The Pump-It-Up Girl was their idol, and they didn't want to hear anything bad about her. Actually, Stacy was the one Sister Cil ought to get to come talk to these girls. Minor celebrity, very attractive, Barnard grad. She'd be a hell of a better role model than friggin' "Loose Lips" Cummings. At least she's good at her job.

"It's true," Cummings said to the girls, trying to talk over the television. "Television images are not reality. I've met that woman, and I know that she—"

"This is bad. Very bad."

The weirdo painter was standing in the doorway, staring at the television. A mug was dangling from his finger. His pant leg was wet, and there was a puddle on the floor at his feet. He was holding a screwdriver in his other hand.

Sister Cil bolted up from the couch. "It's all right, it's all right. Your pants will dry. Let's go find Lucy now." She led him back where he'd come from.

"*At Knickerbocker Spas, we invite you to come on in and . . .*"

"PUMP IT UP!" the two girls shouted in unison. It

was the first time either of them had shown any sign of brain activity. They were both beaming at the TV.

Cummings watched them, shaking her head.

Gibbons watched her face. It was like watching milk curdle. Amazing how someone with diarrhea of the mouth could always look so constipated.

He looked at his watch, then glanced at the doorway where Cil had taken the weirdo. No use hanging around here, he thought. She wasn't gonna say anything to them. May as well go back to the field office. He hauled himself out of the sunken couch.

Shit.

TWELVE

Sal clamped his fingers under his armpits. It was friggin' cold sitting out here in Charles's Chevy. The wind was kicking up, and the people outside on the street were all hunched over with their hands in their pockets. Too fucking cold for April. He blew into his fist. "So, Charles, what're we doing here?"

"Waiting."

They were parked in a no-parking zone on Bleecker Street in the Village, outside a place called Blue Monday's, one of those NYU hangouts. Charles was turned away, looking out his window, and blue neon light from the sign in the bar's window tinted the side of his face and neck. The neon letters reflected across the hood of the car, like slithery blue snakes.

Either the *moolinyam* was looking at something, Sal figured, or he was deliberately *not* looking at him. Sal had a feeling he was pissed off about something.

Sal rubbed his hands together as he watched the people passing by. His eyes darted from face to face. He was worried about the contract. Any one of these people could be a shooter. It made him nervous being out here.

He wouldn't feel safe until Juicy was dead. But that one was gonna take a little planning. First things first.

He glanced at Charles's blue face. "So what're we waiting for? I thought you knew where she was."

"I know where she's s'posed to be." Charles still wasn't looking at him. He'd been moody all night, hardly said a thing all the way up here from the hospital. What the hell was his problem now?

"So let's go find her."

Charles didn't answer.

"You're fulla shit. You didn't find her."

Charles finally turned and faced him. "I found her, I found her. Whattaya think I been doing all week driving up here after work? Checking her out and chasing her down, that's what I been doing. I found her, man. Over there." He pointed across the street. At the far end of the block, sandwiched between a Greek coffee shop and a hippie leather boutique, was a Knickerbocker Spa, one of the franchises.

Sal shrugged. "So what?"

"So that's the one where she works."

"And?"

"And she's teaching one of her aerobics classes right now. She's in there."

Sal grinned. "Nice going, Charles."

Charles turned away and grumbled something under his breath.

Sal wanted to smack him one. Charles was getting to be a real pain with this attitude of his. He got resentful whenever Sal told him to go do something. The other night on the ward he was like a broad on the rag, all because one of these Arnold Schwarzenegger guys with the muscles threw him out of some spa uptown when he started asking too many questions about the Pump-It-Up Girl. He was too sensitive, this guy.

The fucking guy's problem was that he thought Sal was gonna stiff him. These past couple of days he'd been moaning and groaning, dragging his ass, complaining that he wasn't getting nothing out of this. But for chrissake, he knew what the hell had to be done before he could get paid. Mistretta, Bartolo, Juicy, and Tozzi all had to become history, then Sal would be able to get to his money and give him his hundred grand. Then Charles could go get himself that Caddy he'd been dreaming about, fill it full of pussy, Colt .45, and Kools, and drive himself to *moolinyam* heaven. But not until the job was done, the whole job.

Sal bit his fingernail. Money—that's all this guy worried about. He didn't know what worries were. Charles didn't have a contract out on his head. He didn't have someone out there itching to put a bullet in the back of his head. He didn't—

Sal's heart leapt as he spotted a big joochy guy pass in front of the car. For a second, he thought it was Bartolo's kid, but it wasn't. He wiped his brow with his sleeve. Jesus.

Charles let out another one of his long, exasperated sighs.

Sal glared at him. He knew this was all for his benefit, but with Charles acting like a goddamn baby, they'd never get anything done tonight, and Sal didn't have time for any more dry runs. Charles propped his chin on his fist and sighed again, real loud and melancholy. Sal couldn't hold his tongue any longer. The *moolinyam* didn't understand that it was his life that was on the line here. It was time to get a few things straight with this guy. "What the hell's eating you tonight, Charles? You got a beef? Say it."

"Nothing wrong with me." The guy still wouldn't look at him.

Sal bit his bottom lip. "C'mon, Charles, spill it. I can see you're not happy."

Charles shrugged, still looking out that window. A moody, blue *moolinyam*. Wonderful. Just what I need right now.

Sal peered through the windshield and focused on the double front doors of the Knickerbocker Spa across the street. This bastard knew more than he was saying. If he knew the Pump-It-Up Girl was teaching a class right now, then he had to know more. What if she always left by some back door, but out of spite Charles was keeping that little piece of information to himself? Then what? Then they'd lose her, that's what. Sal stared at Charles's blue face. This guy probably already knew where Tozzi was. One day when he was up here this week, he probably followed the Pump-It-Up Girl to wherever Tozzi was staying. Charles was holding out on him, holding out for his money. But he didn't even know how to ask for what he wanted, the dumb fuck. That's why he was acting this way. Sal squinted at the front of the spa again. Son of a bitch! He was gonna lose Tozzi again.

"You know where Tozzi is, don'cha, Charles?"

"I dunno know where he is." Charles shrugged, unconcerned.

Sal glanced at his watch, then looked at the spa. "If you know where he is and you're holding out on me, Charles, you're gonna be fucking sorry."

Charles rolled his head on the seatback and stared at Sal. His eyes gleamed wet in the blue light. "Oh, yeah? Whattaya gonna do about it?"

Sal laid his hand on the gun in his belt. "I'll stick this up your ass and give you a lead enema, how about that?"

"Bullshit. You ain't gonna shoot me. Not out here on the street. Cops pick you up like a bug on a pizza, throw your big ass in jail. And you know what happens they find you out here shooting niggers. You s'posed to be nuts. You s'posed to be locked up at the hospital. They find you out here, man, you fucked."

Sal's fingers were freezing. The bastard was right. If he ever got caught out of the nuthouse, he was screwed. Especially if Tozzi was still around to testify against him. He definitely couldn't depend on those two cokehead guards at the hospital to keep quiet about helping him get out in exchange for dope. He really did need Charles. Shit.

"So whattaya want, Charles? What is it? How can I make you happy?"

Charles snorted up a humorless laugh. "Happy? You don't give a shit about me. I'm the slave here. You just tell me what to do. Shit, I oughta kick your butt outta this car right now. Then wha'chu do? Huh? Gonna take the train back to the hospital, check yourself back in? Hell no! You need *me* to get you back in."

"Hey, Charles, let's not talk crazy—"

"They oughta find you gone in the morning. Then we see what happens. Cops, FBI, they'll all go hunting for you. You'll have to run like a dog, man. Serve you right, too. 'Cause that's how you treat me. Like a dog."

Sal glanced over toward the spa. A bunch of women came out carrying gym bags. None of them looked like Stacy, he didn't think. They could be from her class, though, which meant it was over. If they were gonna find Tozzi tonight, they had to get moving soon, but this moody bastard was still pouting, goddammit.

Sal's stomach was in a knot. "What the hell do you want, Charles? Just say it. C'mon, talk!"

Charles banged on the steering wheel. "What'm *I* getting outta all this? Bullshit, that's what I'm getting. I tell you I need some money, you tell me I gotta wait. That's bullshit, man. When you kill Tozzi and that Juicy guy, how do I know you ain't gonna kill me, too? Huh? You tell me. How do I know?"

"C'mon, Charles. Don't talk stupid."

"You wanna know what I want?" Charles bounced on the squeaky seat and turned to face Sal all the way. "You really wanna know what I want? I wanna guarantee."

"A wha'?"

"A guarantee. You ain't giving me no money. You don't give me nothing but more things to do. That's why I wanna guarantee that you ain't gonna fuck me when this is all over."

Sal had to laugh. This guy was crazy, he had to be. "Okay, sure, Charles. You write it up and I'll sign it." Sal kept his eye on the spa, waiting for that big head of blond curls to come out the glass doors.

"I don't want no fucking papers, Sal. I want to get made."

"Wha'?" Sal wasn't listening.

"Stop looking over there and look at me. You axed me what I want. This is what I want. I want you to make me. I wanna be a card-carrying, made member of the Mafia."

Sal just looked at him. He couldn't believe what he was hearing. This guy wanted to get made? What was this supposed to be, funny? There ain't no nigger wiseguys. Never were and never will be. Can't happen.

"I said, stop looking over there for that girl, man. Don't worry about her. Worry about me. I wanna be a made man. Make me or find your own way home."

Sal's fists were tight, and his chest was heaving. He was ready to go for his gun. He didn't give a shit. Where the hell did this guy get off talking to him this way?

"You gonna do it or not? Tell me now."

Sal turned away to look for Stacy, but Charles grabbed his face and turned him back around. "You gonna do it? I gotta know."

Sal reared back. His hand was on the butt of the gun. He was ready to plug this bastard through the heart and leave him here. . . . Yeah, but how was he gonna get back to the nuthouse? Who'd get the cokeheads to let him in? Shit!

"There she is, Sal. Look." Charles was smug. He was a real wiseass now.

Sal spotted her right away. The hair and those legs. Denim jacket, miniskirt, dark stockings. "Start the car. C'mon now. No more fooling around. I don't wanna lose her."

"Not until I get made." Charles pulled the keys out of the ignition and rolled down his window halfway. "I'll throw 'em down the sewer. I swear."

Stacy started walking up the block.

"Start the fucking car, Charles. She's gonna jump in a cab and we're gonna lose her." A python bulged in Sal's stomach.

"She ain't gonna take no taxicab. Look."

Stacy walked into the open bay of an underground parking garage. Sal could see her going up to the attendant's booth.

"She gotta car, Sal. I know what kinda car. I know the plate number, too." Charles was smiling, like he was holding all the cards.

Sal tried to peer into the parking garage, but he couldn't see her now. A car pulled out of the garage, a big black sedan, but it couldn't be hers. Too soon, and anyway, it wasn't the kind of thing she'd drive. But how the hell would he know which one was her car? They were too far away to make out a driver's face through a glaring windshield. Shit.

"So whattaya say, Sal? You gonna make me or not?"

Sal wanted to go for his gun so bad . . .

"Well?"

Make *this*, asshole.

"*Well?*"

Sal squinted at the garage. "All right, all right, all right."

"All right, what?"

"You got it. Soon as we get back to the hospital, I'll make you. Now hurry up and start the car."

"No." Charles was shaking his head, dangling the keys out the open window. "Do it now."

"Right here?" A white VW Rabbit poked its nose out of the garage. "Whattaya, kidding?" Sal watched as the VW waited for a chance to pull out into traffic.

"Take it easy, man. That ain't her car. C'mon. We'll do it right now."

"Charles, there are rules. You gotta be Sicilian to be a made guy. At least Italian. You oughta know that."

"You gonna be the boss, Sal. That's what you keep telling me. A boss can make who he wanna make."

Sal chomped his teeth, staring at the garage. "I can't do it now. Not here. You need certain things. You gotta have 'em or else it's not official."

"We got everything we need right here. All you needs is a gun and a knife. I read all about it in a book."

A lipstick-red Trans Am shot out of the garage and screeched up the street. Sal wiped the sweat from his nose. "That her?"

Charles closed his eyes and shrugged. "Make me and I'll tell you."

The python was doing a rumba in Sal's stomach as he watched the Trans Am disappear around a corner. "Look, Charles, I would do the ceremony for you, but we don't have everything we need. The way I was made, you need a picture of a saint. You got a picture of a saint? Can't do it without a saint."

Charles reached into the back of the car and rummaged through the junk on the backseat. He came up with a ratty-looking back issue of *Ebony* magazine. James Brown was on the cover. "We can use this."

"Who? James Brown? He ain't no fucking saint."

"He's the godfather of soul. Close enough." Charles ripped the cover off the magazine.

A little yellow Honda two-seater eased out of the bay. Sal strained to make out the driver, but he couldn't see through the glare in the windshield. Shit. Charles was holding out the picture of James Brown.

Sal snapped it out of his hand. "All right, all right. You win."

"*Molto benny.*" Charles smiled and showed all his teeth.

"Gimme the knife. Hurry up." Sal looked all around to see who was near the car before he pulled out his gun and held it in the shadows under the dashboard. He took the knife from Charles and unfolded it. "Gimme your finger." Sal squeezed the tip of Charles's index finger, looked around again, then jabbed it with the knife.

"Ooooww!"

"Shut up. This is sacred." Sal pulled Charles's hand out of the shadows. "You see this blood?" It was blue in the neon light. "This means we're family now."

Sal swallowed. A nigger wiseguy. Mistretta must be spinning in his grave now.

He held the knife and the gun together in his other hand. He didn't dare take them out of the shadows. "You see these? From now on you live by the gun and the knife, and you die by the gun and the knife."

Sal laid the weapons down on the rubber mat and picked up the picture of Charles's saint. He held Charles's bloody finger over it. You were supposed to make a cross in blood, but that didn't seem right under the circumstances, so instead Sal traced an X with Charles's finger. James Brown had a wet blue X over his face. Sal hoped to Christ this bastard didn't have AIDS.

He pushed in the cigarette lighter then.

"It don't work," Charles said.

"You gotta match?"

"I dunno." Charles started looking on the floor. "I quit smoking for New Year's."

"You're supposed to burn the saint."

"Yeah, I know. . . ." Charles felt around under his seat.

A maroon Subaru wagon pulled out of the garage. "All right, never mind. Forget about it. That part's not important." Sal crumpled up the picture and threw it on the floor. He couldn't believe he'd actually done this. He just made a *moolinyam*.

"Now listen, Charles, we got just two rules, and you must never disobey them. First, you must never ever ever tell anybody family secrets."

"What secrets?"

"Any secrets that another made guy might tell you in the future."

"Oh . . . Don't I get no instruction book or nothing?"

Sal's stomach screamed. "No, there's no friggin' book. If someone in the family tells you a secret, he'll tell you it's a secret and then you'll know. Okay? You got it?"

"Got it. Now, what's the second thing?"

"The second thing is you're not allowed to screw around with another made guy's wife. You understand? That's a no-no."

Charles nodded. "Okay."

"All right, now you're a made guy. Congratulations. Now start the car."

"That's it? That ain't much of a ceremony, Sal. Ain't you s'posed to kiss me or something like that?"

A limo pulled into the parking garage. Sal's hands were trembling. "No, Charles. If I kiss you, that means I'm gonna kill you."

"Oh."

"Now start the goddamn car."

A red Toyota Celica zipped out of the garage.

"C'mon!"

"Chill out, Sal." Charles stuck the key in the ignition and turned the engine over.

Sal wanted to break his friggin' neck, he was moving so slow, but instead he jammed his freezing fingers under his armpits and held his tongue.

A black Jeep Cherokee with pink windshield wipers and ski racks on the roof emerged from the parking garage.

Charles put it in gear. "That's her." He looked in his side mirror and cut in front of the next car coming up Bleecker Street. There was only a cab between them and the black Cherokee as they cruised down Bleecker. The Cherokee turned left at LaGuardia Place, heading uptown.

Sal's gut was in agony. He'd just thought of something. "How do you know she's going to see Tozzi? How do you know she's not just going home?"

Charles grinned like a wiseass chimp. "Because she lives in that building over the garage."

Sal clenched his fists, but he didn't say a word.

"By the way, Sal, can I still call you Sal, or do I have to call you 'boss' now?"

Sal shut his eyes and pressed his forearm into his aching gut. "Just watch the friggin' road, will ya?"

THIRTEEN

Tozzi scanned the bleachers around him. They were filled with wives and kids, girlfriends, a few boyfriends, some parents. The room was huge, two basketball courts side by side with their nets folded up out of the way, the ceiling at least two stories high. The lights in the gym were bright but not harsh, illuminating the small army of people down on the gym floor in their white *gi* uniforms sitting *seiza* on their knees, arranged by rank—white belts, then orange belts, then blue, then brown. The black belts in their black *hakama* skirt pants outlined the near edge of the mat. High-ranking black belts, third and fourth *dan* level, sat *seiza* in three corners of the open space, watching like referees. In the near left-hand corner, *Sensei* sat on a folding chair with his hands on his thighs. He was here from Japan to instruct and oversee testing, which he did only twice a year. To progress beyond blue belt in aikido, you had to test before *Sensei*.

Tozzi pretended to be watching what was going on down on the mat, but he was actually looking sideways at Stacy sitting next to him. She was really getting into this,

which surprised him. Most of the people he'd taken to
aikido testing in the past got bored after a while, but she
was riveted, clenching her fists, pounding her thighs, biting her lip, rooting for the candidates as they tested. But
he was a little disappointed that she was getting into it so
much because, to be honest, he was a little jealous. She
was getting all excited for all these other guys who were
testing. He would've been down there testing for black
belt right now if he hadn't been shot. She could've been
getting all excited over him. He glanced down at his
crotch and frowned. He wished he could get all excited
over her.

He'd been trying not to think about it, but his problem wasn't getting any better. His dick was shot. It was
depressed, lethargic, lazy, something. Maybe he got bit
in the pecker by a tsetse fly. But it wasn't funny, and he
was really starting to worry. He'd sworn he'd never go to
a doctor about something like this, but now he was beginning to think he'd better. Christ, if being with Stacy
couldn't make him stiff, what could?

Out of the corner of his eye, he watched her watching
the action on the mat, and he caught himself frowning.
His buddy John was down there testing now. It was his
shodan test, the big one, the first degree in the black-belt
ranks. Until you reach *shodan*, you're considered only a
guest on the mat. Your real study begins with black belt.
It took Tozzi and John five years to get to this point, but
Tozzi was going to have to wait another six months until
Sensei came for his next visit. He was happy for John—he
really was—but he also felt that he was being left behind,
that he was missing the boat, and these feelings put a
cloud over what should have been happiness for his
friend. It bothered him that he was being so self-cen-
tered.

On the mat, John was doing *bokken kata*, formal move-ment with the wooden practice sword. He'd just finished going through the formal techniques with a partner. The last part of the test, the part everyone looked for-ward to, was coming up next. It was the part you worried about most when you were testing: *randori*, free-style, five attackers against one.

Stacy leaned toward Tozzi and whispered, "John really looks good, doesn't he?"

"Yeah . . . he does."

Tozzi glanced at her sideways. How would she know good aikido from bad? She'd never seen it before to-night.

John finished his *kata* and handed his *bokken* to one of the black belts on the sidelines. He was then instructed to sit *seiza* in the middle of the mat by himself while *Sensei* selected the *ukes* for his test, the five guys who would be attacking him. Four black belts volunteered immediately and were all accepted by *Sensei*. The fifth was hand-picked: a first *kyu* brown belt from one of the upstate New York dojos. He was about six-three, full beard, very lean and muscular, athletic-looking, a run-ning-back type. *Sensei* liked to use him for testing be-cause of his speed and size. This guy tended to add a little extra drama to the event.

The five attackers lined up and sat *seiza* shoulder to shoulder facing John about twenty feet away.

Stacy wrapped her arm around Tozzi's. "I don't know if I want to watch this."

"Why not?"

"What if he gets hurt?"

"He won't get hurt."

Bodies had been flying around all night long. All of a sudden she was worried someone was gonna get hurt.

Tozzi studied her slanted brows. He thought she didn't like John.

He looked down at the mat. The crowd was still, but you could feel the contained excitement. All eyes were on John, waiting for him to bow to his attackers and start the *randori*. The room was silent except for a couple of nudgy kids climbing over the bleachers. Finally John bowed. The five attackers jumped to their feet and charged.

"Yikes!" Stacy dug her nails into Tozzi's forearm.

John was on his feet, waiting for his attackers to come to him, playing it smart and waiting, waiting. Just as the group was about to converge on him, he moved to his left and singled out the guy on the far end of the line who was coming at him with a *yokomen* attack, using the blade of his hand like a hatchet aimed at John's head. John ducked under the guy's arm as he swung and popped up behind his back, pulling him down by the shoulders onto his back.

The crowd cheered.

The next guy came at John with a *tsuki*, a punch to the gut. John deflected the oncoming punch to the side and again moved behind the attacker to pull him down by the shoulders.

The crowd yelled.

The third attacker came up fast with a *shomen* attack, the blade of the hand coming straight down toward the crown of John's head. John moved out of the way and let the hand whiz past his face so he could catch it down at belt level, then he pumped it once to get the guy's balance and threw him forward over his head, a clean "sledgehammer" *kokyu nage* that sent the attacker flying across the mat.

People down on the mat clapped and shouted.

Throwing an attacker far away gave you a little more time to breathe because it took the guy that much longer to get up and come at you again. Tozzi was impressed. John was looking good down there.

The fourth guy moved in with a left-handed *shomen* attack, but John was quick. He moved into the guy's space and intercepted the attacking arm while it was still high in the air and turned the guy right around, keeping control of that arm and leading him down on his belly with a commanding *ikkyo* response.

Tozzi was very impressed. John wasn't falling into the trap most people fall into, letting the attackers gang up on his back, forcing him to fight his way out. John wasn't letting himself get caught, turning as soon as he threw to face the next attacker. And he was mixing up his techniques nicely. It was the kind of *randori* Tozzi liked to visualize when he thought about testing.

Down on the mat, the big brown belt rushed up and reached out to grab John by the lapels with both hands, but John moved with the attack, not letting the big guy get a grip on him, guiding his outstretched arms until his balance was committed, then pushed off one elbow and threw from the hip, sending the big guy tumbling headfirst onto the mat.

Stacy kept squeezing his arm. "Way to go, John!"

Tozzi looked at her, then glanced down at his crotch. Yeah . . . way to go.

One of the black belts came back at John with a punch, and John responded with a nice *kote gaeshi*, spinning away from the punch and controlling the arm, leading the attacker forward in order to take his balance, then trapping the hand back over the wrist and pointing the fingers to the mat behind the attacker's head, forcing him to fall backward.

The attacks started getting wild and unfocused with more two-hand lunges for the shoulders, but John kept his cool, tossing them off his hip one after the other, alternating right and left. Then the big brown belt came back. He paused for a second and gave John a funny little smile, warming up for something, like a bull staring down the matador before the charge.

Suddenly the brown belt stepped forward and launched his attack, a *geri*, a forward kick aimed at John's chest. The sight was frightening. Given their height difference, it looked like John was gonna take it right in the face. The brown belt was like a big evil tree breaking out of the ground and going berserk. But John didn't flinch. He calmly stepped in as he moved to the side, tapping the big guy's raised leg to unsettle his mind as he passed, then slipped behind him and pulled him down by the shoulders.

"Did you see that?" Stacy screamed. "I can't believe it!"

Tozzi was impressed, too, but not for the same reason Stacy was. He knew the kind of damaging throw John could've done with that attack—grabbing his foot and shoving him back onto his tailbone, leaving him virtually no opportunity to cushion the fall. John had been charitable enough not to opt for the killer throw even though it would've been more efficient for himself. Tozzi was ashamed to admit that the killer throw was the first thing that came to mind as soon as he saw the kick coming. If it were him down there, he wouldn't have been so nice. It said a lot about his frame of mind. The object of aikido is to neutralize the attacker, not decimate him. Maybe he wasn't ready to test yet after all.

The attackers kept coming, and for the most part John kept them all at bay. The test was only a couple of minutes long, but it felt interminable when you were in the middle of it. The attackers were getting tired because they were doing all the running, so inevitably the attacks started getting sloppy. But John was getting tired, too, and he wasn't throwing them away as much as he would've liked to. The crowd shouted to him, encouraged him to keep turning, but the attackers swarmed and he fell into the trap. All five panting attackers clustered on his back, each one holding a fistful or two of John's *gi* jacket.

With pain and strain in his face, John mustered his *ki* and walked forward with the load on his back, got them moving, then bowed down and dropped to one knee, putting his head almost to the mat. All five flew over John's head in unison and tumbled forward like runaway hubcaps.

Stacy was bouncing in her seat, cheering John on.

Tozzi looked down at her heaving cleavage and chewed the inside of his lip. That wasn't exactly a real throw. Two of those guys were just being nice. He shifted in his seat to create some friction against his sleeping wiener.

The attackers were exhausted now, and their attacks were getting wimpy, which made doing real throws very difficult. Aikido techniques depend on committed, energetic attacks so that you can use the attacker's momentum against him. John dispensed with a few weak *yokomen* attacks with in-close *kokyu nage* throws, and Tozzi could see that *Sensei* in the corner was about to call for the end of the test. But all of a sudden the big brown belt circled back, and it looked like he'd found his second wind.

The brown belt shuffled his feet like a linebacker as he waited for the other attackers to get out of the way.

When he saw an opening, he charged, arm raised high, going for John's head with a *shomen* attack. John was exhausted, and he didn't see the brown belt coming. That big meaty hand was gonna bop him right over the head. But then at the last second, John spotted the attack coming, and he quickly slid back a step to make some space for himself. The big guy's hand slashed down in front of John, and he caught it but kept it moving, sending it to the side and raising the guy's arm high enough so that he could duck under it. Suddenly John had the big brown belt's open hand locked in a *sankyo* grip, one hand controlling his fingers, the other around his palm, elbow pointed up and level with the shoulder. It was an effective hold. The slightest twist on John's part would send excruciating pain up the guy's arm. It was a great way to get someone bigger than you to move. Tozzi grinned on one side of his face as he imagined himself moving Sal Immordino with a *sankyo* hold.

The crowd on the mat knew what was coming next, and they started going crazy, "Throw him away! Throw him away!" John was already cranking the guy's arm, forcing him to backstep in order to alleviate the pain. When John had him extended as far back as he needed, he switched directions and led the brown belt forward, casting his arm as if it were a fly rod. The big guy flew forward, left the ground and sailed over the mat like a 747 coming in for a landing. He rolled over one shoulder, crashing to the mat, and slid a good six feet into the assembly on the edge of the mat, scattering the front row of orange belts.

Sensei signaled the end of the test, and the black belt assisting him yelled "Ai-okay!" to call off the attackers. He had to repeat it several times, though, because the roar of the crowd was rocking the gym in the wake of

John's last throw. When they finally realized it was over, the attackers went over to John to shake his hand and congratulate him.

"You've completed your test," *Sensei*'s assistant announced.

The crowd cheered and clapped. The big brown belt was patting John on the back as they got off the mat. John was dripping with sweat and his face was a little pale, but his expression was a beautiful mixture of relief, exhaustion, joy, and wisdom gained.

"That was incredible. He's great." Stacy flipped her hair over her shoulder, still applauding.

"Yeah, I know. He is good." Tozzi was trying to be enthused, but he was afraid he sounded flat and phony. He really wanted to be down there testing, getting pumped for it, doing it, taking the challenge. He had a feeling that if he could only test and take on a *randori* attack, it would get his juices flowing again and perk him right up. He'd be radiating with positive energy, *ki* shooting out of every part of him. Including the part between his legs.

"You look a little green, Tozzi." Stacy was looking into his eyes.

"Hmmm? Whattaya mean? I feel all right."

"I don't mean sick. I mean green as in envious."

"Me? Nah. Not me." Tozzi's face felt hot all of a sudden.

She took his hand, a pained look of sympathy on her face. "This is what's been bothering you, your test, right? That's why you and I haven't been . . . I don't know, meshing. Between work and your leg and missing this test, you've been pretty distracted. I understand. But maybe now that the test has passed, we can . . . I don't know. Maybe we can . . ." Her hand was on his thigh. Her tawny eyes were melting into his.

He cleared his throat and forced himself not to look down at her hand on his leg. It was still nap time in his shorts, dammit.

Her hand inched up his thigh as she leaned in closer to him. His heart rate instantly shot up to its target rate. He didn't want her to find out he had a limp dick, for chrissake, that he couldn't get it up. Oh, man . . .

They were nose to nose, her lips brushing his.

"Stac—"

"Shhh. Don't talk."

Her tongue touched his teeth.

"Stacy, this isn't—"

"Don't talk."

Her hand was rounding his thigh. His brow was beaded with sweat. Oh, God.

Her hand went to the back of his head as her lips ground into his.

He grabbed her wrist. "Stacy," he mumbled through the kiss, "Stacy, this isn't—"

"*YEEEE-EEEE!*"

He pulled away from her and stared down in the direction of that thundering guttural yell. He recognized it immediately.

Sensei was turned around on his chair, glaring up at Tozzi. The woman who was on the mat doing her *bokken kata* stopped in the middle, and the whole gym was still. *Sensei* stared at him, grim-faced, for a long moment, then he smoothed the hair over his ears and turned back to the woman on the mat.

"Please continue," *Sensei's* assistant called out to the woman. She started the *kata* from the beginning.

Tozzi's face was on fire.

Stacy pushed away from him and sat with her knees together, her hands in her lap. Her face was red, too. "Sorry."

When Tozzi looked down at the mat again, his eye caught John sitting *seiza* on the edge. He wasn't smiling, and his face was green, the envious green.

Tozzi shrugged and looked away. John hadn't been kidding that day at the apartment. He really did like Stacy.

Wonderful. Just what he needed, another enemy.

He looked down at his crotch and frowned. This is all your fault.

Sal Immordino was getting butterflies standing out there in the hallway away from the gym door with his back against the wall. He didn't like being here. The place was unfamiliar, and there were too many lights. He felt like an easy target. "So you see 'em?"

Charles had his hands cupped over the glass, peering into the gym, looking for Tozzi and the Pump-It-Up Girl. Sal didn't want to risk putting his face to the glass. Tozzi might spot him first. "Yeah, I see 'em now, Sal. They smoochin' up in the bleachers. That Japanese guy just got mad at 'em."

"What the hell's goin' on in there?"

"People beating each other up."

"Still?"

"Yeah, they must like getting beat up, these people. Pretty stupid if you ask me."

Sal looked at Charles in that stupid thermal sweatshirt jacket and those high-top basketball sneakers. I'm the one who must be stupid, Sal thought. Who the hell ever heard of a *moolinyam* wiseguy? If it ever got out that he made this guy, there wouldn't be anybody in the family on his side. Christ, every family in the country would want his head on a stick. They wouldn't have to hire a shooter. Guys would volunteer to do it for free. Jesus. What the hell was he thinking?

Charles was frowning into the glass. "Man, she all over him again. The bitch is in heat. Damn."

"Stop pulling your pud over her, will ya, Charles? You're fogging up the window." Sal got off the wall and tugged the brim of his golf cap down. "C'mon, let's go."

Charles looked surprised. "Go? Where you wanna go?"

Sal rolled his eyes. "Use your head, Charles. Can't do it here. Too many witnesses."

"Then where we gonna do it?"

Sal bent down to look through the window, careful not to get too close. "That's up to them. C'mon. Let's wait in the car. I don't like it in here."

Sal started down the hall, but Charles still had his face to that window. He had the hots something bad for that girl. He couldn't wait for Sal to do Tozzi. This guy actually thought he had a shot at getting her once Tozzi was gone. Sal just shook his head. They didn't make dumb like this anymore. This was special-order dumb. And now he was a made man. Jesus.

"Hey, Charles!" he hissed. "Let's go, I said."

The *moolinyam* peeled himself off the glass. "I'm comin', man, I'm comin'."

Sal sighed. Jesus . . .

FOURTEEN

Sal shaded his eyes from the glare of the floodlights and looked into the front seat of Stacy's Jeep. "You serious, Charles? You really don't know how to do this? I thought all you people knew how to break into cars."

"I told you, man. I don't know how to do this shit. You white people think all niggers're bad. Ain't true." Charles was nervous. He was looking all over the place. "Where the hell are we, man?"

"Montclair, I think. Maybe Bloomfield. I'm not sure. Don't worry about it." Sal wished to hell he didn't need this guy as much as he did. Charles was really aggravating him.

The parking lot back at that gym in Belleville had been dark compared to this place. This place was lit up like Yankee Stadium. Bright floodlights beamed across the gravel lot from the long, low brick building. A painted sign lit with spots hung over the front door: Larry's Woodside Bar and Grill. It was nothing but a glorified pizza joint, the kind of place that had neon beer signs in the small front windows. Thank God there were no windows facing the lot.

Charles was jumpy, but Sal could relate. It was a dark night, no moon and no stars. With those freaking lights shining down on them, it felt like one of those Nazi prisoner-of-war camps you see in the movies. Not the *Hogan's Heroes* kind of camp either; the one Steve McQueen busted out of in that movie where he jumped the fence on a motorcycle. That kind of concentration camp.

Sal could see his breath as he scanned the lot, which was full of cars. It was the perfect place for a hit. A shooter could be anywhere out here. That's why he was jumpy.

Sal squinted through the side window into the shadows under the dashboard on the driver's side. He was looking for the hood release. If there was an alarm on this thing, he wanted to get the hood open quick and yank the battery cables before anyone inside paid attention. They wouldn't notice it right away—the jukebox was so goddamn loud you could hear it all the way out here—but someone would hear it eventually if they didn't kill it right away.

"You don't have a Slim Jim, huh?"

"You asked me that already, Sal. I *told* you. I don't know what the fuck a Slim Jim is."

"Hmmm. . . ."

Sal glanced at his long shadow on the gravel and considered the alternatives. The bar was about twenty, thirty yards away. Not as far from these freakin' lights as he'd like to be, but it could be worse. The Jeep was facing the building, which was excellent. When they came out, they wouldn't have to go around the Jeep to get in. Also, the front seats cast a nice shadow over the backseat, and way in the back it was even darker.

"Okay, gimme the pry bar and the cutters."

Charles pulled the pry bar and the bolt cutters out of his pants. The stupid mook looked like Harpo Marx.

"Whattaya gonna do, Sal?" Charles followed him around to the back of the Jeep.

Sal took the pry bar and stared at the lock on the back door for a minute. "Listen to me now. If this thing has an alarm and it goes off, I want you to dive in there as soon as I get this door open and pop the hood from under the dash. I'll go around and clip the battery cables to kill it."

"I dunno, Sal. What if somebody inside hears it?"

"People never come running out as soon as they hear these things. They always figure it's someone else's car."

"I dunno, Sal . . ."

"Just shut up and do what I tell you, okay? Jesus Christ."

Sal looked over his shoulder. He thought he saw a shadow move between the cars. He waited, frozen, nerves tingling in his gut. It could be the shooter waiting for him. It could be. But probably not. He'd been telling himself all night that logically it was very unlikely. If someone had followed them all the way up here from the hospital, he would've spotted the guy by now. Unless the shooter was really good. Or there was more than one. Sal tried to remember whether Juicy was the kind of guy who'd pay for a quality job. He wasn't sure.

Sal got down on one knee and examined the lock cylinder a little closer. He positioned the straight end of the pry bar next to the keyhole, hoping to get a little toehold, but the damn thing kept slipping off. He turned the bar around to the hook end and banged at the lock a little to get under the lip. He banged easy at first, then a little harder, then a little harder still until he was eventually smacking the shit out of it, denting the body all around the keyhole, trying to get a piece of that god-damn lock.

C'mon, goddammit!

"Guess there ain't no alarm, huh, Sal?"

The *moolinyam* thought he was funny now. Sal didn't say a word, just kept whacking away at it until he got the hook under the lock and was able to yank the whole cylinder out. He stuck the hook under the edge of the door then and pried it open. It didn't put up much resistance, just made a little metallic croak as it popped.

Sal handed the tools back to Charles, then reached into his belt for the gun.

"Whattaya gonna do, Sal?"

"Whattaya think I'm gonna do, Charles? I'm gonna wait in the back here until they come out. After they get in, I'm gonna shoot Tozzi right in his friggin' head, and that'll be the end of that." Sal checked the gun, popping the clip, then popping it back in.

"You gonna shoot him from behind?"

"How else?"

"Shouldn't you shoot him from the front? That's how you did all the others. I mean, if you want Emerick to take the rap for this, you gotta do 'em all the same way, don'cha?"

"Front, back, what's the difference? Just as long as I give him the sign of the cross, right? Just as long as Tozzi's fucking dead."

"Don't get hot, Sal. I'm just asking. I guess it's okay to do one from the back, I dunno. Serial killers don't always kill the same way. Don't think so. Now that I think about it, I saw this thing on TV once about Jack the Ripper. Man, he did 'em all different ways. Cut 'em up, pulled out their guts—"

"Enough, Charles. You're aggravating me. Just shut up and get outta the way."

"I was trying to help. After all, I'm your made man now."

Sal frowned into the shadows. "Yeah . . . I know."

Sal opened the hatch all the way and climbed into the back. The Jeep sank with his weight and Charles looked very dubious. Sal didn't want to hear about it.

"Go wait in the car, Charles, and stay down out of sight. But don't fall asleep, you hear me? When you see Tozzi's head blow apart, start up the car and come and get me quick. You understand? Don't start the car until you see him get it, but don't drag your ass either. You understand?"

"I understand, I understand. No problem." Charles was nodding like he was an old pro at this.

Sal shut his eyes. He didn't even want to think about all the ways this guy could fuck up.

"Now, shut the door, Charles, and get the fuck outta here."

"Just one thing, Sal."

"What?"

"You ain't gonna shoot the girl, are you?"

Sal knew this was coming. "Not unless I have to."

"You don't have to kill her, Sal. She don't know nothing. She didn't hear you talkin' at the hospital the other day. I know she didn't. Promise me you won't do nothing to her. Okay, Sal? Will you do that? For me?"

"Look, Charles. I don't know what she knows or what she don't know. But if she turns around and sees me, she has to go. If she minds her own business and doesn't turn around, no problem. But if she looks at me, I got no choice."

Charles nodded, but he didn't look happy. He had it

bad for that broad. No use getting him all upset now, but Sal had already made up his mind. The Pump-It-Up Girl definitely had to go. She had to have heard him talking to Charles at the hospital, and Sal couldn't risk leaving any witnesses after he whacked Tozzi. And besides, Emerick was a known blonde-killer. He wouldn't let a sexy bitch like her live if he had the chance to plug her. It wouldn't fit his profile.

'Course, if he did shoot her, Charles'd be hell to live with. And for the time being he still needed the guy. Sal pressed his lips together and thought about it. Maybe he didn't have to kill her. It was hard to decide. When the time came, he'd know whether to shoot her or not. If she turned around and he saw her looking at him, he'd just do it. Period. That's all there was to it.

He looked up at Charles's anxious face. "Don't worry about it. Just shut the door and go wait in the car."

"Okay." Charles nodded as he lowered the back door, but he didn't sound convinced.

Sal could hear Charles's departing footsteps on the gravel as he lay down in the shadows and tried to get comfortable. The space was tight for him, but there wasn't much he could do about it. They might see him if he tried to hide in the backseat. He tucked his knees in and curled up in the fetal position, clutching the gun between his knees as he twisted his body to get the silencer out of his jacket pocket. The sound of metal sliding over metal filled the quiet as he screwed the silencer onto the barrel.

The inside of the Jeep smelled like her, the Pump-It-Up Girl, a sweet, fresh smell rather than a heavy perfume smell, kinda like green apples or watermelon or something like that. Sal shifted his position to make room for his shoulders and he found something on the floor back there under his knees. A teddy bear. A soft white teddy bear. He jammed it between his shoulder and his head and used it as a pillow. The teddy bear smelled even more like her, kinda nice. From what little he'd seen of her, she seemed like a pretty nice kid. But he was still gonna shoot her if he had to. Too bad, but that's what you get for hanging out with a bum like Tozzi.

Tozzi felt terrible. Stacy and John were making him feel like a real shit, and he hadn't done a thing, really. She was sitting over here pouting, wondering why he kept putting her off, and John was down at the other end of the long row of tables, sneaking hostile looks at Tozzi from behind his beer mug, like a sniper. They were supposed to be celebrating, for chrissake. Everybody else here was. Beer was sloshing, waitresses were dropping pizzas down onto the table from overhead, the jukebox was playing Bruce. Testing was over, for crying out loud. You were supposed to take it easy now, get a little drunk, relax, have a good time. But not these two. John thought he was trying to put the screws to him, and he didn't know what the hell Stacy thought. They just didn't understand.

Under the table he ran his finger along the inseam of his pants near his crotch. It was becoming a nervous habit, constantly checking to see if there was any improvement. But there wasn't any.

Stacy flipped her hair over her shoulder and kept her eyes on her glass of ginger ale. She didn't want to be here. On the way over, she'd kept asking if they could skip the celebration and go somewhere quiet where they could talk. He knew she wanted to talk about them, and he didn't want to talk about it. How the hell do you tell a

woman you gotta problem with your equipment? He
glanced down her cleavage. The last thing he wanted
was her sympathy.

John was just being totally weird, acting like Tozzi had
stolen his girl. Tozzi had no idea John felt that strongly
about Stacy. He thought John understood that he was
kidding when he talked to him on the phone the other
night and said he might try to fix them up because he
thought maybe he was too old for her. Christ, what guy
in his right mind would want to pawn off Stacy? John
must've been expecting Tozzi to play Cupid, then he sees
them making out in the bleachers at testing. No wonder
the guy was acting like he wanted to challenge him to a
duel.

Tozzi was about to get up to go talk to him when he
felt a hand on his shoulder. He looked up and saw *Sensei*
standing behind him. He was wearing a long-sleeved
pinstripe shirt now with his usual multiple layers of
T-shirts underneath. *Sensei* always liked to brag that he
was only 135 pounds, but Tozzi could never figure out if
he wore all the T-shirts for warmth or to bulk himself
up.

Sensei squinted one eye, and a sly grin stretched out
his mustache. "Drink, Tozzi, drink," he whispered into
Tozzi's ear. "You look so sad, like old man. Why? You
have beautiful sweetie. Better than black belt."

"*Hai, Sensei.*" Tozzi's face was hot again. This was
Sensei's way of reminding him that he didn't appreciate
people kissing in the stands during testing.

"Next time, Tozzi, you get black belt, *Sensei* get girl."
He nodded and flashed that sly grin of his, then moved
back to his seat where a fresh Heineken was waiting for
him.

Stacy leaned toward him and yelled over the music. "What did he say?"

Tozzi yelled back. "He told me to drink up."

"Oh." She shrugged and took a sip of her ginger ale, then went back to pouting. "Why don't we get out of here?" she yelled. "I can't hear a thing in here."

"Don't you want any pizza?"

She shook her head.

"I am sort of hungry."

"I'll wait for you in the car then." She started to get up, but he took her wrist. He didn't want her to go away mad. He was afraid she'd just take off and leave him here with his friends.

"Forget about the pizza. I'm not that hungry. Just wait a second while I congratulate a few of the guys, then we can go."

She nodded, but she didn't look happy. "I'll wait here."

Tozzi pushed his chair back. "Don't go away."

She sipped her soda and nodded, but she was looking at her glass, not him.

"I'll be right back. Five minutes." Tozzi got up and carried his beer through the crowd. He had to talk to John.

This was getting ridiculous with Stacy. She thought he was jerking her around, and he couldn't bring himself to explain his problem to her. Sure, she was a wet dream, but maybe she *was* too young for him. Scanning the faces of the aikido crowd at the table, he realized that he was one of the oldest guys here. He was also the only guy here who got shot at on a regular basis. It was a cliché but in this case it really was true: He *was* no good for her. That really struck home after he found her in that room at the nuthouse the other day with Sal Immordino and that loony-tune guard. Stacy was in danger just being around him, and that wasn't right. She needed someone closer to her own age, someone who could make her feel safe. She needed a nice guy who'd stay with her, take her places, treat her right. A guy who wasn't out of order. Basically she needed a guy like John.

Tozzi worked his way through the crowd toward John, forcing himself from looking back at Stacy. If he did, he might change his mind about this.

Tozzi extended his hand across the table as he came up to his friend. "Hey, John. Congratulations."

John shook his hand. "Thank you." It wasn't the cold shoulder Tozzi had expected, but it wasn't exactly a hearty handshake either.

"You looked pretty good out there."

John shrugged. "Yeah, I got through it."

Tozzi moved around the table and hunkered down next to him. "Stacy was very impressed."

"Oh, really?" Now he was cold.

"Oh, yeah. She was. Really."

"From down on the mat, it looked like she only had eyes for you, Toz."

Tozzi knit his brows and shook his head. "Don't believe everything you see. She was just fooling around. She was goofing on me."

"C'mon, will ya, Tozzi? I'm not stupid. I know what I saw. Everybody saw you two up there."

"I swear to God, John. It's not that way. There's nothing going on between us."

"Who you trying to bullshit, Toz? She's with you all the time. You told me yourself."

"No, not really. I haven't been seeing her all that much. I took her to testing tonight only because she asked to come. You know, 'cause she's interested in exercise and sports and that kind of thing." Tozzi could tell from John's face that he wasn't buying any of this.

John nodded toward Stacy. "She doesn't look very happy. What'd you have, a fight?"

Tozzi ignored the question. "Why don't you come over and say hi? C'mon."

"Nah, I don't think so."

"C'mon, will ya? She wants to ask you about your test."

John looked him in the eye. "You're fulla shit, Tozzi, you know that? What's she gonna ask me that you can't tell her?"

"All right, you're right. I am fulla shit. But will you come over and talk to her? What do I need, a blackboard with you? I'm trying to fix you up."

"I don't wanna be fixed up, okay? She wants you, not me."

"She doesn't *know* you, for chrissake. Come get to know her and maybe she'll like you better."

"Why would she like me better?"

Tozzi bit his knuckle and looked up at the ceiling. "Because you're a black belt now and I'm only a brown belt. How's that?"

"Forget it, Toz."

"Why?"

"Because she's leaving. Look."

Tozzi looked up. John was right. Stacy was leaving. He stood up and sidled around the table. "I'll be right back. Don't go anywhere."

When he caught up with Stacy, she was pushing through the front door, going outside. He reached out and touched her shoulder. "Stacy, where ya goin'?"

She pulled away from his touch, then spun around and turned on him. "You must think I'm a real bimbo."

The floodlights over the front door put a golden aura around her head. Her face was mostly in shadow, but he could still see that she was angry from the attitude of her posture. "I don't think you're a bimbo, Stacy. I've never thought that."

"Then why do you treat me like one?"

"When have I ever treated you like a bimbo?"

"Come off it, Tozzi. What were you doing just now with John? I didn't have to hear what you were saying. It was in your face. You're trying to fix him up with me. You were egging him on. What am I, a cow? You think you can trade me to your buddies, pass me around?"

Tozzi's mouth hung open. "Stacy, I—I don't know what to tell you. You're misreading the whole situation here."

"The only thing I'm misreading is you. I don't know what the hell's going on with you, and you aren't telling me. Are you gay? Is that it?"

The question hit him like a cannonball in the chest. "No, I'm not gay."

"Then why do you treat me like I have a disease? Whenever we get close, you push me away."

"You don't understand."

"Then explain it to me."

"Well . . . It's difficult to explain. . . . I can't—"

"Never mind. Go back to your friends. I'm going home." She turned and headed for the parking lot.

"Wait a minute, wait a minute. Don't run away on me. You want to talk? Let's talk."

She spun around and turned on him again, her hair flying in the floodlights. "No. I don't think I do want to talk now. I mean, what've we got to say? You've made it pretty plain what you think of me. I'm a nice piece of ass that you don't want, but I'm okay for your friend."

Tozzi felt terrible. "Stacy, you are so wrong, I don't know where to begin with you."

"You and John weren't talking about me? Go on, deny it."

Tozzi spewed out a long breath that appeared like a storm cloud on the cold night air. "Okay, I'll level with you, Stacy. I didn't know how to say this to you before, but let's face facts. It's never gonna work out with us. You are half my age. You'll still be a good-looking babe when I'm in the old-age home waiting for a nurse to change my Depends. You should be going out with guys closer to your age." It tore him up inside to say this because he didn't believe any of it.

"And you think John is the guy for me. Is that it?"

"I didn't say that."

"You don't have to."

"Stacy, look at me, for chrissake. I'm only old enough to be your father."

"Oh, please. Does that really matter to you?"

"Well . . ." He swallowed hard. "Yes. It does matter. There's a moral issue involved here. I am Catholic, you know."

Or used to be. He was gonna burn in hell for that one.

"Fine. Then good-bye. I'm going." She turned and stomped off to the parking lot.

"Stacy! Will you hold up?"

"No!" She kept walking.

Tozzi rubbed his arms. It was cold out there. "Stacy, wait in the car for me. I'm just gonna go in to get my jacket. I'll be right out."

She didn't answer. All he could hear were her angry footsteps on the gravel.

"Stacy, please. Just wait one minute for me. I just have

to get my jacket. I'll be right out. I don't wanna leave it like this."

No answer.

"I'll be right back. Don't leave." He hobbled back to the front door and rushed in.

Sal stopped breathing when he heard the key going into the lock. The driver's door opened. He couldn't see it, but he could feel it. His grip tightened on the butt of the gun.

The Jeep shook a little as someone got in.

"Bastard!"

It was her, muttering to herself. She was mad about something.

He took little breaths, not daring to move, wondering whether Tozzi was coming, wondering whether she'd take off without the son of a bitch and with him stuck there in the back. His heart started pounding as he waited for the other door to open, waiting for Tozzi. He listened, not moving a muscle. All he could hear was her sniffling. She was crying. What'd that bastard do, smack her around? Yeah, Dudley Do-right, the FBI man. See what you get for hanging out with guys like that, honey? And they talk about wiseguys.

He heard footsteps on the gravel outside then. He stopped breathing again.

"Oh, shit," she grumbled.

The footsteps stopped on the passenger side. Sal heard him trying the door handle, but it must've been locked.

"Go away," she said, real POed.

Sal pressed his lips together. No, honey. Let him in.

He heard the door handle again. "Stacy?" The muffled voice came from outside.

Sal's face was dripping. C'mon, kid. Let 'im in. Open the door before he spots me back here.

She mumbled something under her breath, and Sal felt the Jeep jiggle a little, then he heard her unlocking the door for him. It opened and Sal felt the weight of a bigger body getting in. Neither one of them said anything, but you could feel how pissed off she was.

Sal moved very slowly, very carefully, getting up on his elbow just far enough so that he could peer over the seatback. There were two silhouettes up front, their profiles obscured by the headrests. Sal grinned. Bingo.

"Why don't you get out?" the girl said. "I don't have anything to say to you."

"Stacy—"

Pfittt-pfittt!

Inside the closed Jeep, the first shots made Sal's eardrums pop despite the silencer, and it startled him. Couldn't stop now, though.

Pfittt!

The holes in the vinyl upholstery on the back of the passenger seat smoldered. Sal could see the body slumped to one side. Sal scrambled to his knees, extended his arm, and took aim at the head.

In the name of the Father . . .

Pfittt!

And the Son . . .

Pfittt!

And the Holy . . .

Pfittt!

Ghost . . .

Pfittt!

Amen.

Sal swung the barrel to the driver's side and took aim at all that blond hair on the other side of the headrest.

She was frozen, her hands cramped like claws on the steering wheel, looking at the dead guy in her car, not believing it had happened, frozen in the half second before the scream. She didn't look back. She just stared at her lover boy. Sal suddenly thought about Charles and how much he still needed him.

Shit.

Sal rolled over on his back, kicked the hatch open, and jumped out. He hit the ground running. Charles's Chevy raced up to the Jeep, and Sal got in.

"Go! Go! Drive!"

Charles gunned the accelerator and kicked up gravel. "You kill her?"

"Wha'?" Sal felt like he had cotton in his ears.

Charles raised his voice. "Did you kill her?"

Sal shook his head. "Didn't have to. She didn't see me. Got him, though. Got him good." Sal's heart was doing a slam dance against his rib cage. He was excited as hell.

As Charles pulled out of the lot onto the road, Sal thought he could just barely make out the girl's screams. They must've been pretty loud for him to hear through closed windows all the way out here in the street.

Charles sped off down the road, gripping the wheel tight with both hands. His face was drenched.

"Slow down, Charles, slow down. Just do the limit. You don't wanna look obvious." Sal turned around in his seat and watched Larry's Woodside Bar and Grill until it disappeared around a bend. When he turned back around, he frowned at the road ahead. "How about turning your headlights on, genius?"

Charles fumbled with the switch and turned on the windshield wipers before he finally found the lights. The mook was scared shitless. Sal half expected him to turn white.

Sal closed his eyes and shook his head. *I should have my fuckin' head examined.*

FIFTEEN

"**Y**ou wanna juice, Sal? Here, take it."

The attendant's voice crackled through the speakers on the wall. Through the one-way mirror, Tozzi could see the man carrying a cardboard box full of paper juice packs, handing them out to the patients on the ward. Sal Immordino was sitting at his favorite table, the one with the checkerboard printed right on the tabletop. As usual, he was mumbling to his hands, oblivious to the attendant standing over him trying to give him his juice.

Bastard!

Leaning back in his chair, head against the wall, Tozzi stared at Immordino's face, hearing the sound of that zipper over and over again. He felt washed out, empty inside, beyond anger. He couldn't stop thinking about John, his head on the dashboard of Stacy's Jeep, the blood puddle on the floor mat, and he couldn't stop thinking that Sal was the son of a bitch behind it. The mob hits could've been Juicy Vacarini's work, could've been anybody's work actually, anybody who had a beef with the Mistretta family. But not killing John. That had nothing to do with anything. It was obvious to Tozzi that those shots were meant for him, and only Sal Immordino needed him dead that badly. The sound of that zipper kept ripping through Tozzi's head, the zipper on the body bag they put John in. Immordino was definitely behind it, Tozzi was convinced. The only question was how they were gonna nail the big ugly bastard. Tozzi had already made up his mind that Sal was going down one way or another, and the law wasn't gonna get in his way.

"Are you all right, Tozzi?"

Madeleine Cummings sat down next to him. He was still trying to get used to her in her undercover disguise. It wasn't just the white nurse's uniform. It was the henna-brown bouffant wig Gibbons had insisted she wear because her own hairstyle didn't look right for a loony-bin nurse. It was too boring and sedate for someone in the real world, according to Gibbons. Then there were the glasses, the big pink plastic frames. Gibbons thought her own glasses looked too classy and expensive. These pink ones were as big as Sister Cil's, but not as impenetrable. Cummings looked perfect now. The only thing wrong was her Ph.D. manner of speaking.

"You've been through quite an ordeal. Are you sure there isn't anything I can do for you?"

"No, really. I'm okay." Tozzi glanced at Gibbons sitting at the long table, hunched over the reel-to-reel with a pair of headphones on his head. He was checking out the equipment, making sure it worked right before they sent Cummings out on the ward.

"You're thinking about your friend John, aren't you?"

Tozzi rolled his head against the wall and looked at her. "How can I not think about him? That was supposed to be me."

"Yes, obviously. But it wasn't your fault that it happened. You're not to blame."

Tozzi pressed his lips together and shook his head. "John was just trying to be decent. I'd just had this big fight with Stacy, and John was kind of in the middle of it, even though I don't think he even realized it. He felt bad that she was pissed off because I was trying to push him and Stacy together. All he wanted was to go out and apologize to her, let her know that he hadn't asked me to fix them up. When John got into the car to talk to her, the son of a bitch must've figured it was me. Seven shots. Three in the head." Tozzi looked up at the ceiling and blinked away the tears.

Cummings took off the glasses and held them in her lap. "How about Stacy? How's she taking this?"

"She was sitting right next to him, for chrissake. How do you think she's taking it?"

"I would imagine she's shaky, nervous, anxious, frightened."

"Try hysterical."

"Yes, I'm sure." Cummings nodded and grunted like a hundred-dollar-an-hour shrink, which was almost funny with her in this nurse getup. "Have you done anything for her?"

Tozzi crossed his brows. "Whattaya mean, have I done anything for her?"

"Did you at least stay with her last night?"

He hesitated before he answered, wondering if this was a trick question. Was she digging for dirt so she could run back and tell Lorraine? "Yeah," he finally admitted. "I did stay with her last night. At a hotel. With another agent. A woman agent."

"Good. She's going to need a lot of support now."

Tozzi just looked at her. He could see the analytical Dr. Cummings through the wig and the pink glasses, and although she seemed genuinely concerned, he was still suspicious of her. In a lot of ways, she was worse than Lorraine. He felt that she was always judging him.

Gibbons sniffed and snorted, swiping his nose with a handkerchief, still fooling with the tape recorder. Cummings was looking at Tozzi as if she expected him to say something.

"I didn't sleep with her, if that's what you want to know. I've never slept with her, okay?"

Not that I haven't wanted to.

Cummings's face remained placid. "It makes no difference to me whether you have or you haven't slept with her."

"Yeah, right." Tozzi looked back at the ward through the one-way mirror.

"It does bother your cousin Lorraine, yes, but I don't see anything that wrong with your relationship with Stacy."

He squinted at her.

"Actually I've been trying to convince Lorraine that she's been prejudging you on this."

"Really?" He was suspicious.

"Yes. Really."

Gibbons honked into his handkerchief. He pulled off the headphones. "She's all set. You ready to go check some heads, Doc?"

Cummings put her hands on her knees and stood up, but she didn't acknowledge his question. He was getting a big charge out of seeing her dressed like a nurse. Gibbons had been dying to knock her down a few pegs.

Gibbons stuffed the handkerchief back into his pocket. "Let's just hope Sal has something to say today. Maybe when his sister shows up to get him. Judge Newburry wasn't all that keen on issuing the warrant for this. Had to bring out the dog and pony show, explain to him that Sal was checking outta here today because he thinks you're dead, Toz, and this could be our last chance to get anything out of him. I finally convinced Newburry to give me the warrant, but he wasn't happy about it. He thought I was stretching probable cause a little too far."

"Frankly I agree with him," Cummings said.

Gibbons rolled his eyes up at her. "Don't complain. You're getting to go undercover. That's what you wanted, wasn't it? Now you'll be able to tell your grandchildren about it."

She ignored him.

He didn't give a shit. "You wanna go over it again? Just one more time? For me?"

"No. I know what I have to do. I go out on the ward and start checking the men for head lice." She tried not to make a face. "When I get to Mr. Immordino's table, I drop my comb, stoop down to pick it up, and place the electronic bug under the table."

"Have you got the move down?"

She smirked at Gibbons, but demonstrated anyway to show him that she'd practiced, stooping down and steadying herself on the edge of the table, her thumb on top, her fingers on the bottom. She'd hold the bug between her index and middle fingers. It had an adhesive backing so it would stick wherever she put it.

"You got the bug?"

"Yes."

"Where is it?"

"It's in my pocket." Testy.

"Check."

She jammed her hand in her skirt pocket. "It's there." She was determined not to lose her cool.

Gibbons nodded. "All right, but just remember to be

natural when you're out there. Don't rush, but don't drag your ass either. Remember, you're a nurse. You've got work to do. You're there to check heads and move on."

Cummings inhaled sharply. She was dying to tell him off.

Gibbons pointed at her head. "Fix your wig. It's crooked."

Cummings bit her tongue and adjusted the wig. Tozzi could see that she was burning up inside. She turned and marched toward the door then, chin up, shoulders back. But before she went out, she paused and let her drop-dead gaze settle on Gibbons. She looked like she was about to say something, but then changed her mind and left, banging the door closed behind her.

Gibbons shook his head. "That woman wants to tell me to go fuck myself in the worst way, but she just can't bring herself to do it. Never met such a tight-ass in my life. Ivers included."

"Aren't you being a little hard on her, Gib?"

"Nope."

"C'mon. You started busting her balls the minute you laid eyes on her."

"That's a two-way street, Tozzi. She's been busting mine, too. And she's got help."

"You mean Lorraine?"

Gibbons blew his nose again and nodded. "They're a real pair, those two. It's like a freakin' girls' school over at our place. It's like they're back at Barnard again. They stay up all night talking about all kinds of shit, stuff I don't even *want* to understand. If I turn on the TV, they give me shit about what I watch. I pick up the newspaper, they wanna know why I don't read the *Times*. When I won't eat the health-food crap they make for dinner,

I'm no good again. I'm telling you, Toz, I'm ready to move in with you."

"You just like to complain."

"Easy for you to say. You don't have to live with them."

"What's the big deal? They enjoy each other's company. Anyway, it's not forever. Cummings goes back to Quantico in four or five weeks."

"I could be dead by then."

"Of what?"

"Left-wing pseudo-intellectual bullshit."

"Get outta here."

"Yeah, sure, Stacy doesn't drink oolong tea with alfalfa honey and yammer on about Leonard and Virginia Woolf at seven o'clock in the morning—whoever the fuck they are. I'll bet Stacy doesn't drive you nuts, rattling the windows with opera records on the hi-fi either."

"She does eat tofu."

Gibbons wiped his nose. "Hey, if Cummings looked like Stacy, Christ, *I'd* eat tofu."

"No you wouldn't."

Gibbons scrunched his mouth to one side and thought about it. "You're probably right. I wouldn't." He blew his nose again.

"You taking anything for that?"

"What, the hay fever? Never. The pills make you dopey. It's all the trees they got down this end of Jersey. Soon as we get back on the turnpike and hit the New Brunswick exit, my sinuses will start drying right up. By the time we get up around Linden, Elizabeth, the oil refineries and the airport and all that, I'll be perfect."

"You're just a Jersey kind of guy, huh, Gib?"

Gibbons shook out his handkerchief, looking for a dry

space. "I always wondered why they called this the Garden State. Now I know. Hey, look, there she is."

Through the one-way mirror, Tozzi could see Cummings at the far end of the ward, talking to the guard on duty. She was explaining what she was doing there, telling the guard about the bogus lice problem and which doctor had sent her to check the patients. The guards hadn't been told about this. Guards get chummy with certain patients, the ones that aren't completely out of it, the ones who do favors for them. According to Cummings, it happens at all mental institutions. They didn't want it getting around the ward that the new nurse with the funny wig was actually planting bugs, not looking for them.

They watched as Cummings moved into the room. She looked around and hesitated before she went up to one of the nuts sitting on a bench, staring out into space. Tozzi wished she were a little more bossy and matter-of-fact about it, a little more like a real nurse, determined to get the job done any way she had to. Cummings stood over the pale, unshaven man and picked around through his scalp with the comb. It was obvious that she didn't like touching his greasy hair.

"Jesus, look at her." Gibbons croaked into his handkerchief. "She's gonna fuck this up. I know it."

"Give her a chance. She'll get into it."

They watched her move around the room, going from one patient to the next. She picked all the docile ones first, the ones who lived in their own worlds. They didn't give her any trouble, and it seemed to bolster her confidence. She was starting to act more like a nurse.

Gibbons sneezed again. "Shit!" He stood up. "I gotta go find some toilet paper or something. I'll be right back." He went out the door, wiping his nose with the limp handkerchief.

On the ward Cummings was moving on to the more active patients, following one of the nervous pacers, walking behind him to get a look at his scalp. He was a grizzly-looking, gray-haired guy in his late fifties. Tozzi winced as she went through his thick, matted hair. It looked like it hadn't seen shampoo in some time. The guy kept pulling away from her, but she stayed with him. Suddenly he swung an elbow at her. Tozzi sat forward, worried that she'd been hit, but she seemed unfazed by the blow. Apparently it didn't have much power behind it. The guy was just lashing out in annoyance. Cummings stayed with him and finished her check, then moved on. Tozzi nodded at the glass. She was doing all right.

She started checking a guy with no teeth who was leaning against the windowsill near Sal's table. Sal was in his usual position, hunched over, staring at his hands. She'd have to check him next.

"*Okay,*" she said as she finished going through the toothless man's hair.

The man wiggled his eyebrows up and down, and worked his gums. He scratched behind his ear like a dog with fleas as she turned away.

"*You're next,*" she announced as she approached Immordino.

Sal turned his big head and looked up at her, like a hippo noticing that a bird had landed on his back, neither annoyed nor particularly concerned. She took her comb and started picking through his scalp. He shook his head and jostled his shoulders. The hippo didn't like being pecked at.

Cummings stepped back and put her fists on her hips.

"Come on, now. This doesn't hurt." She went back into his scalp, and he shook his head violently to drive her away. She dropped the comb then.

Tozzi grinned. She was smart to wait for him to react like this. It looked like he had made her drop the comb. She was really doing all right.

Cummings stooped down to pick it up. It had landed under the table, which was perfect. If she had the bug ready between her fingers, she should have no problem sticking it up there. But just as she reached down for the comb, another hand reached for it, too, and got her hand instead.

"Hey, baby."

It was that pain-in-the-ass guard, Charles Tate. What the hell was he doing here? He doesn't work this shift.

The guard was hunkered down next to Cummings, and he wasn't letting go of her hand. Her other hand was down at her side, closed tight. Charles was trying to take that one, too, but she wouldn't unclench the fist or unbend her elbow. That was the hand with the bug. Shit.

"Excuse me," she said. *"I've got work to do here."* She stood up and he stood up with her. He had her by the wrist.

The free hand was balled into a fist against her hip. She was broadcasting that she was hiding something. Tozzi chewed on his upper lip, wondering if Sal had noticed. He couldn't see Sal's face because Cummings and the guard were in the way.

"Let go of my hand. Right now." Her teeth were clenched, her nostrils were flaring, and she was way out of character. She sounded like Barnard now. The attitude was all wrong. She should've been cursing him out

or belittling him, but not this. She was up on her high horse, and it was all wrong.

Charles was stroking her arm. *"Why you so mean, sugar? All I want is for you to check my head, too."*

"Do you have head lice?"

"Don' know. But my head sure itch." Charles gyrated his hips, moving into hers. *"Yeah, sugar, it sure itch for you."* He laughed, low and dirty. *"Wanna check my head? Please?"*

"Let go of me right now or—"

"Or what, sugar? What's a sweet thing like you gonna do to me?" He went for her tit, grinding his palm into it.

When he mauled her breast, she automatically slapped his face with her free hand.

Tozzi's heart jumped. She'd dropped the bug. He heard it hit the floor.

Jesus. Get outta there, Cummings. Just get outta there.

"Why you so mean to me, baby? Why you so mean?" He laughed and squeezed her tit hard. Tozzi could see from her face that he was hurting her.

Get the hell outta there.

But Charles wasn't letting her go, and the other guard, the one who was supposed to be on duty in there, was nowhere to be seen. Tozzi stood up, ready to go out and rescue her, but his eye caught Sal sitting there, passively watching all this. Sal thought he was dead. That's what they wanted him to think. Tozzi couldn't run out and save Cummings, not with Sal there.

He glanced at the door. Where the fuck was Gibbons? He said he'd be right back.

"Stop!"

He turned back to the mirror. Cummings was struggling. Charles had his hips up against hers, pressing her against the table. Christ! It looked like he was gonna nail her right there.

Tozzi paced toward the door. Where the hell was Gibbons?

"*I'm warning you, mister. Let go of me right this instant.*" Her voice was strident. She was making things worse. Her high-and-mighty attitude was aggravating him. Tozzi could see it from the way he was gritting his teeth and squinting at her. He wanted to hurt her.

"*I am warning you!*"

"*I'm real scared, sugar.*" He nudged her back so that she was sitting on the table, her feet off the ground. "*I'm all shriveled up to a little pea.*"

Shit. The bastard was on top of her. He was gonna rape her.

Tozzi went for the door. To hell with Sal.

But just as he opened it, he heard Charles yell.

"*Hey!*"

Through the glass, Tozzi saw Charles with his hand over his eye, taking a knee in the nuts from Cummings. The way she was holding that comb it appeared that she'd either poked him in the eye or raked his face with it. He rolled off her and curled up on his side on top of the table, one hand on his face, the other on his groin. She stood up, squared her shoulders, and straightened her wig.

"*Bitch!*" Charles reached over to grab her and got her hand again.

Tozzi was ready to bolt, but Cummings thought fast, countergrabbing his wrist and pulling him off the table. He hit the floor right on his hip, yelping like a hound dog. "*Shit!*" His eyes were squeezed shut in pain.

Cummings glanced into the one-way mirror. She wasn't sure what she should do now.

"Get outta there," Tozzi breathed. "Come back!"

She was looking at the floor, looking for the bug.

Forget it! Just get out of there.

Charles was getting to his feet. Cummings hesitated only a moment before she turned and headed for the exit.

Tozzi was standing by the door when she came back in. "You all right?"

Cummings pulled the wig off, let out a long breath, and nodded. "I lost the bug, though. I blew it."

"Don't worry about it. You handled yourself very well out there. Forget about the bug."

"But I didn't plant it." She plopped down into one of the folding chairs, looking around for Gibbons. "I blew it."

"I'm telling you, don't worry about it. Be thankful you didn't get raped. You handled that jerk very well."

She glared up at him. "You sound surprised. I got through Quantico, too, you know. I had the same basic training you had, so don't patronize me."

Tozzi held up his palm in apology. "I'm sorry. I didn't mean to imply anything."

The door opened and Gibbons came in, blowing his nose into a wad of toilet paper. "What happened?" He looked at Cummings. "You do it already?"

She shook her head and made a face. "I blew it. I dropped the bug."

"What!"

"It wasn't her fault, Gib. That guard, Charles Tate, showed up out of the blue and started coming on real strong to her. He had her on the table. It wasn't her fault."

Gibbons looked from Tozzi to Cummings and back again. "So where is it? Did you see where it went?"

Cummings motioned toward the one-way mirror. "It's out there on the floor somewhere."

Charles was hunched over in a chair near Sal, catching his breath. Sal hadn't moved from his original position.

Tozzi nodded toward the tape recorder. "Turn it on. Maybe it rolled somewhere where they won't see it. Maybe we can still pick up something."

Tozzi turned down the volume on the wall speakers as Gibbons pulled out the headphone jack on the tape recorder so they could all hear through the main speaker on the unit. The hubbub of the ward came through the small machine. They were getting something.

They all furrowed their brows, listening closely, trying to figure out where the bug was. Then something came through very loud, a grating, scraping sound. It wasn't static. They looked out at the ward through the glass, trying to figure out what the hell it was.

Loud crunching. The red light on the tape recorder sputtered, then went out. The sound went dead.

Cummings pointed at the glass. "Look at Immordino. His foot."

Sal was twisting his shoe into the floor as if he were putting out a cigarette. He kept it up, grinding very slowly and deliberately for what seemed like a full minute. He lifted his head then and looked into the mirror. He stared right into it, right at them, as if he knew they were there watching him.

Tozzi shook his head. "Damn."

Gibbons wiped his nose. "Crap."

Cummings threw down the wig.

Gibbons looked at her. "You still think he's crazy?"

She snatched up the wig from the floor and met his gaze. "I have no reason to believe otherwise. Crushing an electronic bug proves nothing."

"Jesus! Do you hear this, Tozzi?"

But Tozzi wasn't listening. He was standing in front of the glass, staring at Sal's big dumb face, thinking about John and the blood all over Stacy's seats, hearing the zipper.

His jaw was clenched tight.

SIXTEEN

Sister Cil stood in the front parlor, scowling as she looked out the bay windows, glowering through the sheer curtains. She didn't dare touch the curtains, much less part them. They'd take her picture if they saw her in the window, and she didn't need that. She was going to be hearing from Archbishop Leahy's office as it was— that, she could count on. She didn't need having her picture taken. If those awful people out on the street managed to take her picture and the archbishop's people saw it, it would only make matters worse.

She shook her head and followed her brother Sal with her eyes as he paced up and down the sidewalk out front, talking to his hands, shuffling his feet, throwing punches at the air, making those ridiculous boxing moves of his. If she had known it would be like this, she would never have checked her brother out of the hospital. There were at least a dozen men out there watching him. She assumed the two younger men wearing suits were from the FBI. The beefy fellow in the tight tweed sport jacket was probably from the state police. The others were dressed in jeans and light nylon jackets; they looked more common for a poor neighborhood like this, except that they were white, which meant they were probably police. Three of them had cameras, and one had a video camera. They were taking pictures of Sal as he paced and mumbled and acted like an idiot. It was disgraceful.

She'd asked her brother not to do this. She'd asked him not to come here at all. But he never listens to her. No matter what she says to him, Sal always does exactly what he wants. Now he was going to ruin the good name of the Mary Magdalene Home, connect it with all the unsavory things that were connected with him. Why in God's name was he doing this? She'd asked him specifically not to go outside, not to draw any attention to this place. But did he listen?

No. Sal always has to do what Sal wants to do. Never thinks of anyone but himself. Sometimes she wondered if what they said about him might be true, a little bit.

Sal was no saint, she was well aware of that. He'd gotten into some trouble when he was younger, associated with a disreputable crowd and was dragged down by their bad influence. In her heart, she suspected that he was probably guilty of some of the things he'd been accused of, but he was certainly not the killer or the notorious hoodlum they made him out to be. No, not Sal. She knew him too well. He wasn't capable of such sinning. Not really.

But whatever sins Sal might have committed in the past could be forgiven. It's in God's nature to be merciful, and that's why she'd agreed to keep his little secret, to maintain the common belief that Sal was mentally ill. He'd told her a long time ago that it was his way of repenting for his sins, that by living this restrictive life, never acting sane and never being treated as sane, he was doing penance. His time at the state hospital was the ultimate penance, and originally she felt that it would be good for him, that it would be the same as retreating from the world and entering a monastery. But the hospital changed him, changed him in the wrong way. It did not purify his soul. It made him bitter and vengeful. It was evident in the way he'd been treating her ever since he'd been discharged to her custody.

Sister Cil's eyes started to water as she watched her brother making a fool of himself out on the sidewalk. Maybe his penance did him no good. Maybe he was still a sinner. Maybe he was a compulsive, inveterate sinner. Maybe he'd been lying to her all this time. Maybe she didn't really know him at all.

She was suddenly reminded of Mr. Gibbons's allegation that Sal had a great deal of money in a Swiss bank account and something else in Panama. She took off her glasses to wipe her eyes. She didn't know what to think about him anymore.

"Sister! Sister!"

Lucy, her helper, came running down the staircase. The poor woman was clutching her heaving chest. She could hardly breathe. She really should lose some weight.

"Calm down, Lucy. What is it?"

Lucy couldn't get the words out. She pointed up the stairs. Her eyes were bulging out of her head.

"Is it one of the girls? Has Shavon's water broken?" Lucy always panicked whenever one of the girls went into labor.

Lucy shook her head and kept pointing up the staircase. She finally gasped it out. "In your room! Donald! Go! Go! Hurry!"

Cil frowned. Donald? Donald was supposed to be cleaning the bathroom upstairs. Now what? She'd told

Sal several times already that they were running low on Donald's pills, but Sal just ignored her. She'd been trying to make them stretch by extending the time between dosages.

Cil held her skirt and ran upstairs. "Donald? Donald? What are you doing now, dear?"

When she turned the landing on the second floor, she could hear him crying. "Donald?"

She marched to her room at the back of the building. "Donald, I'm talking to you. Answer me." When she reached the threshold and looked at her bed, she nearly died.

"Donald!"

He was lying on the bed, practically naked, his clothes in a heap on the floor. Her other wimple, the one that went with her long habit, was askew on his head, tears streaming down his cheeks. His naked skin was pale, almost bluish, and totally hairless. He had one hand inside his underpants; the other was brandishing a pair of scissors, the big pair they kept in the kitchen, holding them open like a straight razor. An image of Christ on the cross flashed before Cil's eyes—bloody, emaciated, draped in a dirty loincloth. She crossed herself quickly as she rushed into the room.

"Donald, put those scissors down." She spoke calmly but firmly, the way she'd dealt with suicidal girls in the past.

He shook his head, weeping bitterly, wetting the starched wimple with his tears.

She stepped closer. "Donald, what do you intend to do with that?"

"I'm so bad," he wailed. "I'm very bad. I think about them, and I can't help it. I'm bad."

"You think about who, Donald?"

He rolled his head against the pillow in anguish. "I think about the girls." He looked down at his underpants. "I can't stop it. It pops up by itself. I'm so bad."

"No, Donald, you're not bad." She put out her hand. "Now, give me the scissors."

"*Noooo!*"

His shriek startled her. Her pulse was racing.

"No. No. No. I have to get rid of it. I don't want it. It's bad!"

She started to move closer, but he yanked down his underpants and put the blade to his . . .

Cil looked away, her face flushed. She forced herself to concentrate on his face.

"Donald, please listen to me. You're being much too hard on yourself. Sexual thoughts are sometimes normal—"

"*Noooo!*" The shriek made the room thrum in its wake. "I'm bad. I have to cut it off before it makes me do something bad."

Cil swallowed on a dry throat. Donald needed his medication, full dosage. She'd warned Sal that they needed to have the prescription refilled. Why didn't he ever listen to her? She'd never seen Donald this upset.

"Why are you doing this, Donald? You can tell me."

He writhed and wept. "Too much sinning. *Too much sinning!*"

"You're not a sinner, Donald. I've been with you every day since you came here. You're not a bad person. You're a very good person. You work very hard, you do what you're asked to do, and you don't complain. I think you're a very good person, Donald."

Cil clenched her fists. Donald hadn't been out of the house since Sal and that Mr. Tate from the hospital first brought him here. Sal insisted that he stay inside and not leave the home. No wonder the man was going stir-crazy. He needed to get out and breathe some fresh air.

"Please, Donald, listen to me. Don't do this to yourself. *This* would be a sin. Your body is the temple of God. Do you realize that mutilating yourself would be a sin against the Lord? Please, don't." She imagined all the blood. And in her bed.

He looked up at her. His eyes were raw and wet. "I have to." His voice was barely a squeak.

"Why? Why do you have to?"

"Too much sinning. I told you."

Cil glanced down at his groin. It was standing up, fully erect. He was holding the blade of the scissors right up against it as if he were going to slice a carrot. She looked away and crossed herself twice.

"I don't understand, Donald. What do you mean 'too much sinning'? Who's sinning? Not you. Explain it to me."

"Everybody!" he wailed. "Everybody's sinning."

"Who?"

"Me. I have bad thoughts."

"Who else?"

"The boys."

"Which boys?"

His expression turned furious. "The boys who get the girls pregnant."

"Yes, you're right about that, Donald. But is there anyone else sinning?"

"The girls." He was still angry. He assumed she should know all this. "They make themselves look like whores. They let the boys do it to them. They're sinners, too."

Cil nodded to calm him. "Yes, Donald, I know. There are a lot of sinners in the world."

"You *don't* know. There are so many. You can't know them all." He stared into her eyes. "You can't. You don't know about the girl on television, the blond girl. Do you?"

"What girl on television?"

He squeezed his eyes shut and shook his head from side to side. "See? You *don't* know. I hear the girls here talking about her all the time. They want to be just like her. She's tempting them into sin. I hear them talking about her all the time. Dolores, Faith, Shavon, Roberta, Yvonne—all of them. They all want to be like her."

Cil knit her brows. She didn't know what he was talking about. "Who, Donald? Who do you mean?"

"*The girl on television!*" he shouted. "*The dirty girl! The blond whore!*"

"Are you talking about someone on the soap operas?"

"*Nooooo!*" His wail was plaintive, annoyed that she was so ignorant.

She didn't know what to do. "Donald, please. Shall I get Sal? Would you like to talk to Sal?"

Donald's eyes flared. "Sal's a sinner, too. Sal and Charles. They're both sinners."

Cil's stomach sank. Dear God. She didn't want to hear anymore. Not about Sal.

She looked at him sternly. "No one likes a tattletale, Donald."

"But they *are* sinners! They killed those men!"

Cil clutched her throat. "What men?"

He squeezed his eyes shut and thrashed his head back and forth. "I don't know, I don't know. They just killed them. They did. Downstairs."

"Downstairs where?"

"*Here!*" The shriek from hell.

Her heart was on the rack, being pulled apart. "You

mean Mr. Tate killed someone. That's what you mean, don't you? Your friend Charles—Mr. Tate—he's the killer. Maybe Sal was there, but Mr. Tate—"

"*No!* It was Sal who shot them. With a gun. Two men."

"Who?"

"I don't know, I don't know. A little man, a little grumpy man, he never smiled. And another one who came with him."

A little grumpy man? Mr. Mistretta? And Jerry? Cil felt ill. She shut her eyes and pressed her forearm into her stomach, then sank to her knees, supporting herself on the edge of the bed. When she opened her eyes again, that fleshy thing was looking right at her. She turned away and sat back on her heels, clutching her stomach, trying to keep from throwing up.

But Donald was right. Everyone was sinning. The whole world was sinning. Mr. Tate—well, he had heathen written all over him. But Sal? Sal, too? Had he been lying to her that much all these years? Was it all true what they said about him? Was he really as bad as the government prosecutors and the FBI made him out to be? Could he have actually killed Mr. Mistretta himself? He did hate Mr. Mistretta—she knew that—and he does have a very nasty temper. But . . .

God in heaven, help us all.

Her eyes shot open. She crossed herself quickly, then gripped the pair of pants on the floor next to her and whipped them over the naked body on her bed. "Put your pants on, Donald. We have to pray."

"No! I have to get rid—"

"*Put those pants on right this minute, mister, and get down on your knees and pray with me.*"

"But—"

"NOW!" Her screech made the windows rattle.

He dropped the scissors to his side. He looked terrified.

"I said, get dressed now. And don't make me repeat myself."

"Yes, Sister," he said in a little voice. He lifted one knee and started to put the pants on.

She waited for him to zip his zipper. "Now, get down here with me."

He crawled off the bed like a bad dog and got on his knees next to her, folding his hands on top of the bed. Her wimple was still on his head, crooked.

"Pray with me, Donald. We have to pray for the souls of all these sinners."

"Yes, Sister." He started to mumble the Our Father very quietly, his head bowed.

She tried to join him, but she couldn't concentrate. Her mind was on Sal. Sal and his lies. She closed her eyes and bowed her head, forcing herself to say the words of the Our Father. It was Sal's soul they needed to pray for. He was going to be needing their prayers. A lot of prayers.

Donald's head was bent over his trembling folded hands, eyes shut tight. " '. . . and forgive us our trespasses,' " he whispered, " 'now and in the hour of our death. Amen.' "

She took the wimple off Donald's head. "Amen," she repeated.

SEVENTEEN

Tozzi sat on the edge of the couch in Gibbons's living room, biting a hangnail, staring at the television, thinking about John. On the screen, Sal Immordino paced up and down the sidewalk, shuffling his feet, mumbling to his hands, throwing shadow punches. It was a copy of the video the state police had taken that morning outside Sister Cil's place in Jersey City. The camera zoomed in on Sal's face. He kept his eyes down, never looked into the camera, just paced and mumbled, sparring with his invisible partner.

Gibbons got out of the armchair and went over to the VCR. "They told me it's all the same. Two hours of this shit." He reached over to shut it off.

"No, wait," Tozzi said. "I wanna see a little more."

Tozzi watched Sal, watched his face, waiting for him to slip, waiting for him to glance at the camera, to show that he really was aware of what was going on. But he never did. He was so good at this, so well-practiced. He should be. The bastard's been doing it long enough.

Gibbons was standing there, with his arm on the TV. "You seen enough?"

Tozzi sat back and nodded. Gibbons turned off the VCR and Sal disappeared from the screen. The green outfield of Shea Stadium under the lights took his place.

"It's him," Tozzi said. "I know it. Sal's the one. Mistretta, Bartolo—it makes sense. John was a mistake. He thought it was me. But Sal's definitely the one. It has to be." He checked his fingers for another hangnail to bite.

Gibbons changed the channel to a basketball game. The Sixers were playing Boston for the Eastern Conference title. Philly had the ball. Their geeky-looking center, that seven-and-a-half-foot African guy, looped the ball back out to the perimeter to Charles Barkley, who wasted no time shaking Larry Bird on a pick and muscling his way straight to the hoop, scoring *over* the Celtic center with a finger roll.

Gibbons switched back to the Mets game. They were playing the Dodgers. Dwight Gooden was on the mound. Darryl Strawberry was at the plate.

"You're not saying anything, Gib. You don't think it's Sal?"

Gibbons backed up to the armchair, his eyes on the game. "Sure, I think it's him."

"And?"

Gibbons looked at him sideways. "And nothing. We can't prove it. He's got all his bases covered. According to the hospital records, the last time he was out on the street was nineteen months ago. Until yesterday."

"So he hired someone."

"Who?"

"I dunno. Somebody from his old crew, maybe a freelance contractor, I dunno."

"I dunno either." Gibbons glanced at him, then went back to the game. "But that's the whole point. We don't have a shooter we can connect to Immordino, so basically we got nothing. All we can do is what we're doing right now. Sit tight and let him think you're dead, so he can go his merry way. If he is making a power play for Mistretta's old job, maybe he'll get reckless and we can catch him doing something to implicate himself. If we're lucky."

"Yeah . . . if we're lucky."

On TV, Gooden threw heat. Strawberry swung and missed. Strike three. The side was retired. The crowd at Shea cheered the hometown big-money player for striking out the multimillionaire Mets defector.

Tozzi closed his eyes and rubbed his face. He couldn't stop thinking about John. His wake was tonight. Tozzi hoped it wouldn't be an open coffin.

Goddamn Immordino.

Immordino, Immordino. Tozzi wished he could get the bastard out of his head for a little while. The guy was gnawing at his gut, keeping him awake at night, distracting him from everything. There *had* to be something they could do to nail him. There had to be.

Tozzi stared at Gibbons's profile in the armchair. "Where's your partner today?"

"Huh?" Gibbons was wrapped up in the ball game.

"Cummings. Where is she?"

Gibbons looked over his shoulder to see if Lorraine was around. "I don't know and I don't care. Haven't been able to watch a game in peace since she got here. I hope she's lost."

"Nice to see that you're getting along so well."

Gibbons grunted, his eyes glued to the set. Dave Magadan was at the plate. Ojeda was pitching for LA.

"*Michael?*" Lorraine called from the kitchen.

"Yeah?"

*"Would you come here for a minute? I want to ask you
something."*

Tozzi hauled himself off the couch and flexed his knee
before he headed for the kitchen. He was walking without the cane now, but the leg was still a little stiff.

Lorraine was sitting at the table in front of a steaming
coffee mug. She was wearing one of those Mexican
weave pullover things—orange, blue, and brown-gray
stripes. The dinner dishes were stacked in the sink.
"Would you like a cup?" she asked.

"No, thanks." He had caffeine jitters as it was, he'd
been drinking so much coffee. Drinking coffee and staring into space, thinking about Sal Immordino, wanting
to put him away so bad, wanting to make him pay for
what he did to John. Tozzi pulled out the chair opposite
his cousin. "So what's up?"

She puckered her mouth to one side for a moment.
"Can I ask you something?"

"Sure."

She puckered her lips again. She seemed uncertain
about how she should begin.

"Just say it, Lorraine."

She sighed before she started. "Michael, what are you
doing with that girl?"

The blood flared in his face. He held his tongue until
his temper burned back down. "By 'that girl,' do you
mean Stacy?"

"Yes. I'm sorry. Stacy."

"What do you mean, what'm I 'doing' with her?"

"Well, from what I've heard, Stacy is head over heels
for you. Are you—how should I say this?—are you recip-
rocating those feelings?"

Tozzi looked up at the ceiling. He wished to God he
could reciprocate those feelings.

"Who told you this? Cummings?"

Lorraine's brows slanted back in sympathy. "Madeleine and I are concerned about you—both of you."

"My personal life is none of her business, and it's none of yours either, Lorraine. So just don't worry about it, okay?"

"But, Michael, you're not being fair to Stacy."

"What do you mean, I'm not being 'fair'?"

"You seem to be leading her on, treating her like a . . . like a pet."

"Like a pet? Did you come up with this one by yourself? It sounds more like one of Dr. Cummings's analyses."

"Michael, I'm not accusing you of anything, but let's be honest. Your history with women is nothing to brag about. I'm afraid you're going to end up hurting Stacy and you don't even realize it."

Tozzi reached across the table for her coffee mug and took a sip. He made a face. It had sugar in it. "Lorraine, you don't understand the situation here. It's not what you think."

"Then explain it to me."

Tozzi just looked at her for a second and sighed. How could he tell her that his dick was broken?

She raised her eyebrows and shrugged, encouraging him to tell her what was on his mind.

But there was no way he could bring himself to tell her. Christ, he couldn't even bring himself to tell Gibbons. He'd thought about unloading it on John, but he could forget about that. Yesterday he finally worked up the courage to call the doctor who had treated his leg and asked if his impotence could be a side effect of the gunshot wound.

The doctor said he seriously doubted that his problem

was a physical ailment. According to the doctor, impotence is almost always the result of stress. Tozzi admitted that he was under a lot of stress, particularly with Stacy. When Tozzi told him that he'd been avoiding sex with her because he was afraid he'd fail, the doctor told him he'd never know whether he was truly impotent unless he tried to have intercourse. Tozzi just grunted when he said that. He knew his own body and he knew that normally he would get erect just standing next to a woman like Stacy. He didn't say anything to the doctor, but he wasn't willing to risk an experiment, not with Stacy. What if they got started and he couldn't make it happen? He could never live with himself after that. The doctor finally suggested that Tozzi might want to see a shrink if his problem persisted.

Great. Maybe he could get an hour on the couch with Dr. Cummings. He could tell her all about his limp dick and how it was driving him so crazy he couldn't respond to Stacy. That wouldn't be too stressful. Yeah, right.

The phone rang. Tozzi looked up at it, a white wall phone next to the refrigerator. Lorraine didn't move to pick it up. It stopped ringing. Gibbons must've answered the extension in the living room.

"Be fair to her, Michael. For once in your life don't be such a typical male."

"Whattaya talking about, Lorraine?"

"Michael, I know you. You've only known Stacy for what?—a week and a half?—and already you've fast-forwarded into the future, decided the relationship could never work, and now you're looking for the escape hatch. You've done this with every woman I've ever seen you with. Except in this case, Stacy's just too good-looking to let go of, so you're sitting on the fence."

"That's not true."

"Michael, I know you. Be honest. You're poison with women. You don't know how to treat a woman like a person first. You're doing it now with Stacy. You're treating her like the Pump-It-Up Girl."

"Lorraine, you really don't understand the situation."

"I understand perfectly."

Tozzi couldn't believe what he was hearing. This was Cummings talking, not Lorraine. "Lorraine, I'm under a lot of stress right now. I'm very confused about a lot of things and—"

"Don't make excuses, Michael. Stacy's probably even more confused, thanks to you. She's probably trying to figure out what the hell you want from her, and you're not giving her any clues. Remember, she's only—what? Twenty-one, twenty-two? She's looking to you to take the lead. That's why I think you should make up your mind about her, Michael. As they say, shit or get off the pot."

"But—"

Gibbons came into the kitchen, tying his tie as he walked. "Get up, Tozzi. We gotta go."

"Where?"

"The field office. That was Ivers. He wants to see us, right now."

"Us? I'm still on sick leave."

Gibbons shrugged. "He said he wanted you, too."

Tozzi looked at the clock on the stove. "It's eight-thirty. He's still at work?"

"Yup. He said a coupla lab reports just came in. C'mon. I told him we'd be there by nine."

Tozzi stood up and rotated his knee to loosen up the leg. Lorraine had a condemning stare fixed on him. He just shrugged. It was beyond his control, but she didn't understand that. And he didn't know how to explain it to her.

"We'll finish this some other time. Okay, Lorraine?"

"Yeah, I bet we will." Weary and sarcastic.

"Finish what?" Gibbons was putting on his jacket.

"Nothing." Tozzi pointed his foot and stretched the leg.

Lorraine was staring at him, accusing him with her eyes.

"I'll see you later." Gibbons bent over and pecked her on the cheek. Her eyes stayed on Tozzi.

"Yeah, see you around, Lorraine. And thanks for dinner." He didn't need this aggravation, not from his own cousin.

Tozzi turned and headed for the door with Gibbons right behind him.

Out in the hallway, Tozzi could hear the sound of plates and silverware clinking in the sink. Lorraine was starting to do the dinner dishes.

Shit or get off the pot, huh? She didn't understand. She never would. She's a woman. He let out a long sigh and followed Gibbons out the door.

Madeleine Cummings was flipping through a stack of printouts spread out next to her on the green leather couch in Ivers's office. Ivers was in one of the guest chairs, leaning over a mess of papers on the coffee table. It looked like they'd been here for a while. Gibbons glanced at Tozzi as they walked into the assistant director's office, then narrowed his eyes and clenched his jaw. He wanted to know what the hell Cummings was doing here.

Ivers looked up at them over his half glasses. "Pull up

a chair. We've come up with something on the Mistretta-Bartolo killings."

Gibbons looked at Tozzi again, but Tozzi just gave him a shrug. He glanced down at all the papers on the coffee table as he dragged up a chair. He didn't like the look of this.

Ivers sat back, took off his glasses, and rubbed the bridge of his nose. "Why don't you lay it all out for them, Madeleine?"

Gibbons's upper lip rose on one side. Madeleine? When did this happen?

Cummings sat up and faced them. She let her gaze settle on Gibbons. "I've been doing a little work on my own." She reached into a manila envelope and pulled out a black-and-white glossy. "This is our man. Donald Emerick."

Gibbons grabbed the photo. It showed a chubby little guy being led away by a cop. He looked like a distraught honey bear in a cartoon—smallish, round-faced, full bushy beard. Gibbons guessed that the picture had been taken at the time of his arrest because the guy was in handcuffs rather than a straitjacket or belt restraints. The little honey bear was crying in the picture, crying inconsolably from the contorted expression on his face— mouth open, lips sort of puckered, eyes slanted back in fear. Either that or he was howling at the moon.

"This is the only picture I could get of him right now. I'm told he's lost quite a bit of weight since he's been at the hospital. I've asked them to send me a more current picture. It's on its way."

Gibbons tossed the photo onto the pile of papers. "What makes you so sure Emerick's the killer?"

Cummings's face was impassive. "Fingerprint analysis. The lab has a possible match. The partial thumbprint that was lifted off Mistretta's watch crystal could be Emerick's.''

Gibbons smirked and shook his head. "So what? A *possible* match won't hold up in court. Not in a mob killing.''

"Why won't it?" Cummings was indignant.

"Because it's inconsistent."

"What are you talking about?"

"Why would the killer be so sloppy with Mistretta, then be so careful with Bartolo? If he didn't care about leaving his fingerprints on Mistretta's watch, why didn't we find any prints on the bullet casings we found in the men's room at the track? Doesn't make any sense. There should be prints all over those casings from when the shooter loaded the gun. Psycho killers don't give a shit about leaving prints. They're on a mission from God, right? But there weren't any prints on those casings from the Bartolo murder. They were clean as could be. So whoever loaded that gun *was* worried about leaving his prints.''

"Psychotic behavior by its very nature is unpredictable—''

Gibbons waved her away. "Save it for the term paper, Doc.''

Ivers intervened before she could retaliate. "As to the matter of the weapon, we've finally gotten some solid information.'' He glanced at Cummings, who was suddenly smug as a Siamese. Ivers opened a bound gray folder and put his glasses back on. "One cartridge was recovered intact from the scene of the Bartolo-Witherspoon killings. It seems that this bullet ricocheted off the door of the bathroom stall where Bartolo was''—he cleared his throat—"sitting, and lodged in the toilet paper roll. As a result, it was a very good specimen for analysis, and ballistics was able to determine that it came from a Browning BDA 380. We checked with Alcohol, Tobacco, and Firearms, and they informed us that a case of these handguns was stolen from a warehouse in Shreveport, Louisiana, in 1990. These guns were traced to a Mr. Richard Skinner of Bordentown, New Jersey, who operated a porno parlor there called Captain's Paradise, and sold firearms under the counter. Mr. Skinner was convicted this past winter on weapons charges and is now serving time. ATF was kind enough to check their case file on Skinner for us, and they came up with something very interesting. Among the credit card records seized in their search of the store, there were four slips totaling five hundred and fifty dollars, all of them dated in the same week last October. The purchases were described as 'videotapes.' The cardholder is a Mrs. Thelma Tate of Trenton, New Jersey. Mrs. Tate is seventy-two years old and legally blind. Her son, Charles Tate, is a guard on the ward at the state mental hospital where Donald Emerick was residing until he escaped. He's also the same guard who assaulted Madeleine earlier this week."

The smug little Siamese looked like she'd swallowed the canary and enjoyed it.

A mean grin crossed Gibbons's face. "You think Tate bought the gun for Emerick? You gotta be kidding."

"How much stronger do you want the evidence to be?" she said. "I don't think Emerick will be mailing us a signed confession, if that's what you want."

Tozzi's forehead was bulging. He was ready to explode. "How do you know Tate gave the gun to Emerick? How do you know Tate isn't Sal Immordino's hit man? Jesus, what do *you* need? A signed confession from Immordino?"

Cummings sat there with her hands in her lap, Miss Prim and Proper. "According to the files I've read, Emerick has an unusually weak personality. He's very easily influenced, even passively. For this reason, he was not allowed to have a radio, and all television programs had to be taped and screened before he could see them. In fact, he had a serious setback at the hospital due to unmonitored television viewing. After seeing a thirty-second commercial advertising the program *Twin Peaks*, he became convinced that he had murdered Laura Palmer, and he demanded to be punished accordingly."

Gibbons gestured with his hands. "Wait a minute, wait a minute. You're saying that Sal Immordino could be running this guy? That Immordino played with this Emerick's head so that he could get the kid to do his dirty work for him?"

"It's possible."

"You're nuts."

Cummings ignored the comment. "However, given Mr. Immordino's condition, I don't believe that he could be controlling Donald Emerick. My hunch is that Emerick overheard Immordino complaining about his perceived enemies when they were on the ward together, and that's how he became fixated on Mistretta and Bartolo. Emerick, being so impressionable, adopted Immordino's burden. Thus, Immordino's vendetta became Emerick's vendetta. Now, for reasons that are not entirely clear to me yet, Charles Tate procured the weapon and facilitated Emerick's escape. My gut feeling is that Tate has a sadistic personality and *he* likes to control people. Giving Emerick a gun may have temporarily satisfied some deviant psychosexual need that this man has. In other words, Charles Tate got a thrill out of turning Emerick into Sal Immordino's guided missile."

Gibbons shook his head. "You don't expect anybody to believe this, do you? If you do, then you've really got your head up your—"

"Gibbons!" Ivers's nostrils flared.

Gibbons flared his back. "Look, maybe you can swallow this horseshit, but I can't."

Tozzi piped up then. "We know Sal Immordino is a fake, and we know what he's capable of. He's the one behind all this, not some hospital guard."

Cummings raised one eyebrow. "How can you know?"

Tozzi pounded his fist on the coffee table. "Christ Almighty, I know how the guy thinks. I've seen how he operates. He wants me dead, but he ends up killing an innocent guy. It's him. I know it."

Tozzi's face was red, and his neck was tight and strained. He looked like he was ready for the nuthouse himself.

Gibbons decided to intervene before Tozzi said anymore. "Look, we know that Immordino is staying with his sister in Jersey City. Why don't we go pick him up and squeeze him for a while. Maybe he knows where we can find Emerick."

"You mean, 'squeeze' him the same way you've successfully 'squeezed' him in the past?" The doctor's sarcasm had surgical precision.

Ivers folded his glasses and put them in his pocket. "She's right, Gibbons. Immordino hasn't opened up for anyone in over twenty-five years. He's not about to start now." He stood up and buttoned his suit coat. "For the time being I'm shifting the focus of this investigation away from Immordino and onto Donald Emerick. Our first priority is to find Emerick before he strikes again. The New Jersey State Police are looking for Charles

Tate as we speak. As soon as they have him in custody, they'll let us know."

Tozzi bounced out of his seat. "But Immordino is out on the street, too, for chrissake. He's the one we should be concentrating on."

"There are local agencies keeping their eye on him, and we just don't have the manpower to spare. They'll keep us apprised of his activities. Emerick is the more immediate threat as far as I'm concerned, and so far we're the only ones who know about him."

Gibbons's upper lip exposed an eyetooth as he watched the assistant director's small, benevolent smile beam down on Cummings. This was all political. Ivers liked exclusives. There were mobsters in the papers every other day. The general public couldn't tell one from another. But if Ivers could bring in a serial killer before the guy hit the papers and got a nifty nickname, Ivers would pick up a few nice brownie points down in Washington for sparing the Bureau the inevitable embarrassment of having to tell reporters day after day that no, they haven't caught Donald the Ripper yet. It would be a great coup for Ivers, and when you came right down to it, boosting the man's career was what they were all there for. At least, that was how Ivers saw it. Asshole.

Ivers buttoned his shirt collar and pulled up his tie. "Given Madeleine's expertise in these matters, I'm making her coordinating agent in this case. Until Emerick is apprehended, Gibbons, you answer to her."

"What!"

"You heard me. And as for you, Tozzi, I want you to go home and rest. You're on sick leave, so get busy being sick. If I find out you've been sticking your nose in this investigation again, I'll arrange for a more permanent leave of absence. Do you read me?"

Tozzi glowered at him. "Yes, sir." The two syllables sounded like something else.

Ivers went to his desk, and Tozzi got up and stomped to the door. "I'll meet you downstairs, Gib." He was gonna be climbing the walls tonight.

Cummings started gathering up her precious printouts and files. "Gibbons, I'm going to be busy here putting together a complete profile of Emerick. I think it would be helpful if you went down to the hospital tomorrow morning. See if you can find anyone on staff who remembers hearing Sal Immordino talking to Emerick. Find out what Sal said to him if you can. Maybe the other guards on that ward can be of some help."

Gibbons glared at her. His gut was roasting. The "coordinating agent" was up on her high horse again.

When he didn't say anything, she looked up from her papers. "Do you have any questions?"

"Nope." He headed for the door.

"When can I expect your report?"

"When it's ready."

"When do you think that will be?"

He turned around and just stared at her. *When I fucking feel like it.*

Ivers was standing behind his desk, waiting to hear Gibbons's answer. "We'd like it as soon as you get back from the hospital," he said.

Gibbons grumbled. "Right."

The Siamese smiled. "Good."

Right. As soon as I get back. Whenever the hell that is.

Gibbons left Ivers's office and passed into the waiting room, a crooked grin on his face. He had to catch up with Tozzi so they could figure out how they were going to handle Immordino.

"And, Gibbons," the assistant director called through the doorway, "if you or Tozzi go anywhere near Sal Immordino, you can consider yourselves dismissed."

Don't do me any favors, asshole.

Gibbons kept walking. His gut was on fire. He was afraid to open his mouth for what he might say.

"Did you hear me, Gibbons? Gibbons?"

"I heard you."

The outer door slammed.

EIGHTEEN

Sal pulled the car over to the curb next to a dark loading dock, took it out of gear, and turned off the engine. He'd already switched the headlights off before he turned onto the street. It was one of those deserted blocks in the West Thirties, no apartments, just factories and warehouses from one end to the other. Sal ran his fingers along the bottom half of the steering wheel as he peered out the windshield at the red taillights moving slowly down the block. "A real freakin' stud, this guy," he muttered to himself.

He shook his head at Charles's shitty little Chevy as it crawled in and out of the streetlights. Mr. Badass Stud was checking out the meat. Hookers came out of the shadows as the Chevy approached, then disappeared just as fast when it passed them by. Charles was a fussy bastard. He didn't want any black chicks, and brunettes didn't seem to interest him very much either. It was the blondes he braked for. But he was being very picky with them, too.

Sal shook his head. A real freakin' stud. And a made

man, too. A made man with a mouth to match his big
moolinyam pecker. Jesus, what the hell was I thinking?

Sal rolled down the window all the way and stuck his
head out to get some air. He hated this fucking car. A
goddamn Datsun, for chrissake. They didn't even call
them Datsuns anymore. The thing belonged to Lucy,
the old lady who helped Cil out at the home, and it was a
real piece of shit. For one thing, it was too small for him,
and for another, it stunk of her perfume. He only hoped
Lucy didn't notice that it wasn't parked where she'd left
it in the alley out back of the home. Cil probably
wouldn't let her call the cops, though, because she'd figure he was the one who took it. But then who the hell
wanted to hear Cil when he got back? She'd be all over
him, screaming about how he should stay in and not risk
being seen. She was getting to be a real pain in the ass
with that. You'd think she'd just be happy that he was
out of the nuthouse. She didn't act happy, though, and
she was getting a little too bossy with him. He was
gonna have to set her straight. Not right now, later.
There were a few other people he had to set straight
first.

The brake lights flashed on Charles's Chevy as it
passed under another streetlight. Two pros came out
from the shadows. A couple of blondes.

One girl could hardly walk, her heels were so high.
She was wearing a long fur coat that went down to her
ankles, and her hair was done up high on her head, sort
of a moussed-up Bride of Frankenstein do, except that it
also hung down long over one shoulder. When Charles
came to a full stop, she opened her coat and showed her
booty. She wasn't wearing a thing underneath. Sal wasn't
impressed. She was long, tall, and bony. Nice tits, but
too bony.

The other pro had a perkier look to her. A punky haircut on a round face, a little more meat on the bone than the other one. She was wearing red spike heels, but she could navigate a lot better than her girlfriend could. She opened her white rabbit jacket for the customer and showed him some very nice cleavage under a skintight red halter top. Sal had to squint to see what she was wearing on the bottom. It looked like a red Ace bandage coming up under her crotch, barely covering the essentials. Sal wondered what the hell that thing was. He'd never seen anything like that before.

The two blondes moseyed on over to the Chevy. The perky one leaned into the passenger-side window. The bony one hung back and stayed up on the curb. She looked like she wouldn't be able to get back up on her stilts if she leaned over too far. The negotiations didn't take long, but Sal was surprised when the perky one stepped aside and the bony one got into the Chevy. Sal would've bet money that Charles was gonna take the other one. Sal would've. Hands down.

As he watched the Chevy's taillights, Sal rotated his head and hunched his shoulders. He was tense. These broads out here were all Juicy Vacarini's. If Charles opened his big yap and bragged to his pro that Sal Immordino had just made him, it could get back to Juicy, and the bastard could have a field day with that. Juicy would make a big stink about it, take it to the friggin' commission. Sal could hear him now: *Sal Immordino made a freakin' nigger!* Christ, there'd be an open contract on his head. Every family member around the world would be obligated to whack him if they got the chance. And there were always those ass-kissing go-getters who'd want to make their mark by hunting him down and bringing in his head. He wouldn't be safe anywhere.

Sal stared at the Chevy's taillights as he rubbed the muscles between his neck and shoulder. They were like rock. The brake lights went out then, and the Chevy pulled away from the curb.

Sal turned the key in the ignition and hit the gas pedal. The Datsun's starter spun, but the goddamn engine wouldn't turn over. He pumped the accelerator, but it didn't do any good. Sal let go of the key and cursed under his breath. The friggin' engine was flooded again. He'd have to give it a minute before it'd start now. Son of a fuckin' bitch. The Chevy was already at the end of the block. He was gonna lose the bastard.

Sal turned the key again. The starter whirred, but the engine wouldn't fire. The Chevy was waiting at the light, the left signal blinking. Charles was gonna turn down Ninth Avenue. Shit! Sal would never find him once he got into the flow of traffic on Ninth. Charles could hit it up on the avenue, then disappear down another side street, which was exactly what he was gonna do, find some nice dark side street where he could get his money's worth from the pro. Shit!

Sal put his hand on the key again. He wanted to try it again, see if he'd get lucky, but he knew it wouldn't start. You had to wait longer with this thing. At least a minute. But he didn't have a fucking minute. The red light turned green. Charles was gonna be gone in a second. Sal's neck muscles cramped. Shit!

But as the traffic light turned and Sal was about to turn the key and try it again, the white backup lights on the Chevy's tail flashed on.

The Chevy went into reverse and rolled back down the block. Sal could hear the transmission whining. The car jerked to a stop under the streetlight where Charles had picked up the bony blonde.

They were yelling, the two of them. Sal could hear them, but he couldn't make out what they were saying. The passenger door whipped open then, and the bony blonde got out in a huff.

"Kiss my ass, you cheap son of a bitch!"

She slammed the door and hammered the roof with her purse a few times before she clicked back into the shadows on her stilts.

The perky blonde with the Ace bandage on her crotch peeked out of the shadows like an alley cat. She slipped over to the car and hopped in next to Charles. Sal could see their silhouettes in the front seat. A little talk, then two heads nodding. They were in agreement. As the Chevy took off again, the pro's cigarette butt sailed out of the passenger window and hit the pavement in a spray of orange sparks.

Sal tried the ignition again. The starter whirred. Sal kept his foot off the gas. It kept whirring, wouldn't turn over. Fuck!

He stopped, counted to five, and tried it again, foot off the gas. It spun and spun. Nothing.

C'mon, dammit all!

Suddenly the engine coughed and sputtered to life. Sal gave her gas and gunned it, afraid that if she died out on him again, that would be it. The Chevy was waiting at the corner. The light was red again. Sal pulled out into the street and drove slow.

"Hey! Over here, honey!"

The bony blonde was waving to him, her coat open, shaking her bush. He got a good look at her face. It was brutal. Too damn skinny. She looked like a goddamn skeleton with tits.

"Hey, baby! C'mere! Wanna party?"

Sal waved her off and kept going.

She had one of those voices, too. Like steel wool and Ajax. Cil's voice was sort of like that sometimes.

The light changed and the Chevy turned left onto Ninth. Sal sped up to make the light. Charles was already cruising downtown in the right lane when Sal got to the corner, not too fast, not too slow. The girl was probably telling him where they could go park to do the deed.

Sal veered around a double-parked cab and wondered why Charles had changed his mind about the bony blonde. It couldn't have been the price. Juicy's street girls all charge the same—or at least they're supposed to. Maybe Charles got a good look at her face in the car and realized that all blondes are not beautiful. A lot of black guys must think that because you see an awful lot of doggy blondes walking down the street, holding hands with black guys. Maybe Charles was smartening up and developing some taste. It comes with being a made man —you get taste all of a sudden. Yeah, right. Sal stared at the Chevy's taillights and tried to grin. It really wasn't funny. The *moolinyam* could be bragging to the girl right now.

The Chevy hung a right onto Twenty-fifth Street without signaling. Sal stepped on the accelerator and raced down to Twenty-fourth, then Twenty-third, hung a right, went to the end of the block, hung another right on Tenth Avenue, then raced back up to Twenty-fifth. Cruising past the intersection, he looked up the block and saw a set of headlights going out. Charles was parked between the streetlights in the middle of the block in front of a loading dock. It was another dark factory street. Sal pulled into a parking space out of sight on Tenth and cut the engine. Charles and the pro needed their privacy.

He sat there for a minute, keeping his eye on the rearview mirror, trying to figure out what he should do. Charles didn't have much money so he probably wasn't going for the deluxe job, not in the front seat of the car. He'd want to do it in a room if he were going for the deluxe job. He was a made man, after all. Sal looked at his watch. He wondered how long it took to get a little head. He wasn't sure, but knowing that horny son of a bitch, it probably wouldn't take that long.

Sal got out of the car and started walking toward the corner, the oncoming headlights on the avenue shining in his face. There was a big mother of a pro hanging out on the next block, one of those Amazon girls. Sal spit into the gutter. Probably a guy in girl's clothes looking to roll the horny assholes who come in from Jersey.

As Sal turned the corner, he was suddenly startled by something moving in the shadows on the sidewalk next to a brick wall. He hit the pavement and scrambled to the next loading dock, thinking it was the shooter Juicy had hired to get him. But when he didn't hear any shots, he peeked around the edge of the loading dock and saw what looked like a giant cocoon wrapped in plastic garbage bags. It was some homeless guy trying to get some sleep. Sal stared at the plastic cocoon for a second, waiting to see if the big moth inside was waking up or settling down or what. It shifted around, rustling the plastic, but it didn't look like it had the energy to do anything more than that. Sal stood up slowly and moved on. His chest was pounding.

He crossed the street and headed toward the Chevy, looking all around just to make sure. He didn't think he'd been followed, but you could never tell. It was darker down this end of the block, and Sal's eye kept darting into the shadows up on the loading docks, expecting to see a muzzle flash, ready to hit the pavement again.

As he came up to the car, Sal could just barely make out Charles's face. His eyes must've been closed because he didn't react as Sal approached. His head was lolled back against the headrest. Sal looked in through the driver's side window. The perky blonde's head was in his lap. Charles was in ecstasy.

Sal knocked on the window, and Charles jumped. "What the—"

"Hey, calm down, Charles. It's just me."

The blonde lifted her head and wiped her mouth with the back of her hand as Charles rolled down the window. "You scared me, man. Whattaya doin' here, Sal?"

Sal smiled at the pro. She was cute. In a hard sort of way.

"I be wit' you in five minutes, Sal. Just go wait over there—"

"Open up, Charles. It's cold out here." Sal pointed to the lock on the back door.

Charles tried to cover his dong with the flap of his jacket, but he was too big. "But, Sal, can't you see I'm busy here? I'm sorta in the middle—"

Sal hunkered down and stuck his face in the window. "Hey, you're the one who wanted to be made, right?"

"Yeah, but—"

"So now you're a made guy. You forget who your boss is already?"

"No, Sal, I didn't forget. You're the boss—"

"Oh, so you do remember. Good. So what's that mean, me being the boss?"

"It means whatever you say goes."

"That's right. What I say goes. So I'm telling you to open the friggin' door." Sal pointed at the lock.

"No, no, bay-bee." The blonde had a thick accent. She started jabbering then. It sounded like Polish or Russian or something. She sat up and shook out her hair, and Sal could see that she really was very nice. He wondered why Juicy had her working the street. She should be in a house, not out here. Too bad. She was nice.

"Open the friggin' door, will ya, Charles? I told you, I'm cold."

Charles twisted around and unlocked it.

The pro started to complain. Sal could tell from the way she was jabbering.

Sal got in back and shut the door. "Don't worry about me, honey bun. Finish up what you were doing. I can wait."

"She don't speak no English, Sal."

"Whattaya mean she don't speak English?" He'd seen her and Charles negotiating in the Chevy.

"All she knows is money."

The blonde smiled and nodded. "*Da*, moh-nee. Sohk, feefty. Fohk, one honndred."

"That's very nice, honey. Now get back down there and finish. We gotta talk business here."

The blonde looked puzzled.

Sal pointed over the seat, down at Charles's crotch. "Don't look at me. Look at him. Go on. Get back down there and finish up what you were doing."

She looked dubious, but she knew what he meant. Her head disappeared in his lap. Charles coughed and squirmed. He glanced nervously in the rearview mirror. Sal could hear her sucking up a storm down there, but the sounds coming out of Charles weren't exactly the sounds of pleasure.

The blonde started jabbering again. She sounded disappointed.

Sal leaned forward and looked over the seatback. "What happened, superstud? I thought you brothers never had those kind of problems."

Charles muttered something under his breath.

"Did you pay her, Charles?"

"Yeah."

"Then take a hike, honey bun." Sal jerked his thumb. "He'll come find you later when he feels up to it. Go 'head, go."

The blonde was puzzled, but she got the idea when Sal tossed a twenty at her and pointed to her door. Lucky for her she didn't speak English. Pros usually keep their mouths shut anyway, and this one was probably here without papers. He didn't have to worry about her. As she closed the door outside, Sal got a close-up of that red Ace bandage thing over her crotch. Weird-looking thing.

The door slammed shut. In the quiet, Sal could feel Charles simmering. "Don't get moody on me now, will ya, Charles?"

"I was into something with her, Sal. Couldn't you wait outside just five minutes?"

Sal leaned over the seatback. "A boss does not wait, Charles. Not for nothin'. You're a man of honor now. You got responsibilities. You got obligations, obligations to *me*."

Charles turned around and glared at him. "Yeah, I got all these obligations, but I ain't got no pay, Sal. When do I get to see some cash?"

"You got a fresh mouth, Charles. You don't talk to a boss that way. You got a lot to learn, pal."

"Yeah, but what about—"

"Shhh." Sal put his finger to his lips. "Never mention money to me. It's disrespectful. It's out of line. You work for me and I take care of you. From now on I'm like your father, okay? Certain things you just don't ask. When I have it, I'll provide for you. That's all you need to know."

Charles zipped up his pants and tucked in his shirt-tails. He was pissed.

"Here." Sal reached into his jacket and pulled out the 380. He tossed the gun over the seat, then took the silencer out of his pocket and threw that over, too.

Charles frowned down at the hardware. "What's this for? What do I need this for?"

"I got something for you to do."

"What?"

"Don't say 'what?' like that. You don't say nothing when I tell you to do something. You just do it. That's all. You're lucky I'm such a fucking patient guy. You know that, Charles? Mistretta was your boss, you'd be facedown in the mud in Secaucus saying hello to the rats. You know what I'm saying, Charles?"

"Yeah, yeah, yeah. I know."

"Now, listen to me. We got one more guy to whack. Vacarini. You know who I mean?"

"Yeah, Juicy. I know."

"He's not gonna be a big problem. I'm not worried about him. What I am worried about is what happens *after* we do him."

"Whattaya mean, Sal?"

"I'm worried about Emerick. Oh, by the way, did you get me any more Thorazine for him?"

"No, sorry, I forgot again. I'll get you some this week. Don't worry. I won't forget."

"Jesus, Charles. My sister's having a hell of a time

keeping the guy under control. And he's talking too much now. He needs his pills."

"I'll get 'em. This week. I promise."

"Please. I don't wanna wake up one morning and find my sister nailed to the wall, for chrissake. You know what I mean? Now, what was I saying? Oh, yeah. Emerick. We gotta do Emerick after we do Juicy. Can't risk keeping him around. You know what'll happen if the cops catch him? They'll take him back down to the bin. What if he starts talking to the doctors down there? He knows them, he trusts some of them. What if he starts telling them things? What if he remembers too much about us and Mistretta? He could fuck us up. I was thinking maybe instead of just letting him go, we should do him, too, and make it look like he killed himself. Whattaya think? That fit in with his psychological profile? Would he do something like that?"

Charles shrugged. "I dunno. He's a nut. Nuts do all kinds of weird shit. Sure, I guess he's the kind who could do himself. Why not?"

"All right then. That's what we'll do. Right after we do Juicy."

"So how we gonna do Juicy?"

"He's not hard to find. Don't worry about it. I called a guy from my old crew today, guy named Loopy Lou. He's gonna find out where Juicy'll be this week. I'll let you know."

"You want me to whack him?"

"What else?"

"By myself?"

"Why not? Is that a problem?"

Charles shrugged. "No. No problem." He picked up the silencer. "I never used one of these things. How's it work?"

"Here. Gimme." Sal took the silencer from Sal. "Gimme the gun. I'll show you."

Charles passed the gun back and peered over the seat as Sal held the silencer to the barrel of the gun. "See? It goes on like this. Just screw it together, that's all. Only, don't strip the threads when you put it on. You put it on crooked, it could explode in your hand when you pull the trigger. Here. Put it away now." Sal handed the gun and the silencer back to Charles.

Charles sat behind the wheel, holding the gun and the silencer, nodding at them. Sal could hear him trying to screw in the silencer. "There a trick to this, Sal? I can't get it to go in."

Sal grinned. *Of course you can't, Charles. That one's not threaded.*

He reached into the pocket of his jacket and got his hand around the butt of the other 380, the gun he'd used on Mistretta and Bartolo, the one Charles shot Tozzi with. He flipped the safety with his thumb while it was still in his pocket.

"I really hate to see Emerick go, but you know how it is, Charles. Emerick's like a lotta people. He talks too much. Whether a guy's nuts or not, a lotta guys have this thing inside them that makes them want to spill their guts. I don't know what it is, but a lotta guys have it. That's why you should never trust too many people. There are very few people in this world who can really keep their mouths shut."

Charles nodded. He was still trying to get that silencer on.

"Sometimes you can't even trust a made guy. I seen it happen. Guys I never woulda believed would ever do such a thing."

"Ummm . . ." Charles wasn't listening. He was still trying to figure out how that silencer went on.

"Take my advice, Charles. Don't trust anybody you can't trust. You know what I'm saying? Now that you're a made guy, I want you to understand that you're part of my family. I treat you like a son, you treat me like a father. Understand?"

"Yeah, I understand."

"That's why I want to give you my blessing."

Sal looked around to see if there was anyone outside, any of those cocoon people. Then he put the barrel of the gun to the back of Charles's headrest.

"Hey, Charles." Sal looked at Charles's face in the rearview mirror.

"What?" They made eye contact in the mirror.

"Didn't you hear me? I said I wanna give you my blessing."

"Huh?"

In the name of the Father . . .

The explosion rocked the car. Sal's ears popped. Blood glistened on the dashboard. Charles started to slump forward, but Sal reached over the seat and caught him by the jacket before he leaned on the horn.

And the Son . . .

Sal fired through the seat. The body jolted.

And the Holy . . .

Sal pulled the trigger again. The head jerked back and slammed into the headrest. Sal couldn't hear a thing now.

Ghost . . .

Another jolt. Sal's ears ached.

Amen.

The vinyl on the seatback was smoking. He pushed the body over onto its side on the front seat. Charles would've looked like he was just sleeping it off if it weren't for the shine of all that wet blood in the darkness.

Sal got out of the car and opened the driver's door with his sleeve over his fingers. He leaned in and found the gun and the silencer on the floor under the steering wheel. Loopy Lou had gotten the gun for him and had it delivered to Cil's place baked in a loaf of bread from the bakery. As Sal bent down to get the hardware, his face was right next to Charles's lap.

Too bad you didn't come when you had the chance, Charles. The girl was doing her best. We coulda said you went happy. Too bad.

Sal stood up, shut the door with his hip, and started walking back to Lucy's little Datsun. He peered into the shadows, his hand on the warm gun in his pocket, ready to start shooting if he had to. But even though he was still tense, he was glad this was all done. He didn't need Charles anymore. The guy was just a goddamn liability. If he ever got caught, he was gonna talk himself silly. Sure as shit.

But as he walked back toward Tenth Avenue, Sal couldn't help wondering if maybe he should've done the pro, too. He wasn't that worried about her, though. He didn't think she saw him that well. What he was worried about was getting the hell out of there. He hoped to hell that goddamn Datsun didn't act up on him again. He didn't like being out here like this. Too many hiding places for a shooter. And with those fucking guys you could never be too careful.

NINETEEN

Sitting on the edge of the couch in his borrowed apartment, Tozzi stared at the headline on the *New York Post:* HOLY GHOST HIT MAN STRIKES AGAIN! The front-page photo was a classic rubout shot, the car door open, body slumped over the seat, one leg hanging out, blood trickling off the shoe. Tozzi had already read the article. It was real creative writing. The reporter had done some snooping around the local mental hospitals, and somehow he found out about Donald Emerick's escape. Since Sal Immordino had been incarcerated on the same ward as Emerick, and Charles Tate, this latest victim, had worked on that ward, all the reporter had to do was connect the dots. According to the article, Sal was doing a Svengali on Emerick, controlling his mind, sending the guy out to kill for him. It wasn't that different from the scenario Madeleine Cummings had come up with the other night in Ivers's office, and this guy from the *Post* didn't even have a Ph.D.

Tozzi shook his head and frowned. Reading Cummings's theory in the tabloid put it in its proper perspective. It was pure bullshit. It would've worked better as a plot for a grade-B mad-scientist movie with swirling pin-wheels and that weirdo singing-saw music they always used in the fifties.

To his credit, though, this genius from the *Post* had figured out that Sal was on a revenge trip, getting back at people who'd wronged him in the past. Mistretta and Bartolo were obvious targets. "Undoubtedly" Tate must have mistreated Sal in some way at the hospital, the reporter speculated. Undoubtedly. Another scene from a grade-B movie. Igor whips Frankenstein, Frankenstein gets loose and breaks every fucking bone in Igor's body. What this brilliant journalist didn't mention at all was the other victim, John Palasky. What the hell did he do to Immordino? "Undoubtedly" John must've done something to deserve seven slugs at near point-blank range.

Tozzi put down the paper and breathed deeply until his stomach unclenched. Actually, he was thankful that the press hadn't gotten wind of the fact that the "Holy Ghost" had struck a fourth time out in Jersey. He'd managed to keep the police from releasing the details of John's murder. Tozzi was even more thankful that they hadn't found out that it was the Pump-It-Up Girl who was sitting in the driver's seat next to John when it happened.

He glanced down at the pile of windup toys Stacy had brought him on the coffee table. He hadn't seen her since the night John was killed. They'd talked on the phone, but she was still freaked and she said she wasn't ready to see him yet. He had a feeling she was afraid of him now, afraid that being around him was dangerous. He wasn't worth the risk. He looked down at his crotch. He was still in his T-shirt and shorts. She was right. He wasn't worth the risk.

He stared out into space. Lorraine was probably right, too. He was poison with women. Stacy was a kid, she didn't need all his head trips. It was all for the best that she was scared off.

He caught himself staring at that picture on the front page again, Charles Tate's foot hanging out of the car. What Tozzi wanted to know was how this reporter found out about Emerick. Why would the hospital tell him anything? Admitting that they'd had an escape would just be embarrassing for them. Could Cummings have talked to the press? He didn't think she would, not on her own at least. He just wondered if this was some kind of ploy she had cooked up to flush Emerick out, something Ivers had approved that they weren't telling Gibbons about because he'd been sulking and dragging his ass, resenting the fact that Cummings was in charge of this investigation now.

Tozzi shifted his gaze and stared out the grimy window at the morning light coming through the iron security bars. It was the most light he'd seen in this place since he'd moved in here. He didn't think a first-floor apartment got this much sunlight, not in New York. Unconsciously he fingered the bullet scar on his bare thigh as he stared at the filthy sun-filled window and seriously considered doing what he'd been thinking about.

Ivers had ordered him to sit tight and stay out of this, to use his sick leave to recover. But when the hell did he ever listen to Ivers? Immordino was behind all this, he was sure of that, and the bastard wasn't mental and he wasn't Rasputin the mad monk either. He was a dethroned *capo* making a power play for control of the Mistretta family, a bold, desperate gambit. This was about power, not psychopaths.

The phone rang. Tozzi blinked, realizing that he'd

been staring at the sunlight. He reached for the receiver on the end table. At this hour he knew who it was.

"G'morning, Gib."

"Fuck good morning. You seen the paper yet?" Gibbons had a full head of steam going and it wasn't even seven o'clock.

"Yeah, I saw it. The Holy Ghost Hit Man. It was just a matter of time before they came up with a name. It's catchy. Lot better than Son of Sam, I think."

"Holy Ghost, my ass. It's Immordino."

"You don't have to convince me." Tozzi rubbed his eye. "You think it was Cummings who talked to the press about Emerick?"

"Shit, she doesn't talk to anyone about anything. Doesn't have to because she knows it all. She spends all her time on the phone now with Behavioral Science in Quantico and then huddles with Ivers in his office. They don't tell me bullshit."

"She still staying over your place?"

"Unfortunately."

"You home now?"

"Yeah."

"Isn't she gonna hear you?"

Gibbons raised his voice. "I don't give a good goddamn what she hears."

"You think you can shake her this morning?"

"Oh, I don't know about that, Toz. She may need me to go out for rubber bands or something crucial like that." He was more sarcastic than usual.

"Listen, why don't you ditch her and meet me this morning? I've got an idea."

"Meet you where?"

"Queens. Mistretta's funeral is this morning."

"I already told Ivers and the good doctor we should be

over there, but they said no, it's not that important. We can get an intelligence report from the NYPD people. Christ, Ivers'd eat shit if she told him it was a brownie."

"I bet Immordino will be there."

"You think so?"

"Of course. He'll be acting like an idiot, but he's gotta be there. If he's ready to make his move, he wants everybody to know that he's back on the scene, and Mistretta's funeral is the perfect place for his coming-out party. The whole family will be there."

"Yeah, but Juicy's running the show now. He's not gonna put up with Sal's shit. I bet he won't even let Sal into the church."

"Nah, Juicy's not gonna make a scene, not at Mistretta's funeral. They gotta pay their respects to the old man. Anyway, Sal can't afford not to go."

"How do you figure?"

"Sal's gotta get the hearts and minds of the rank and file. He hasn't been out of the bin long enough to go around and press the flesh, reestablish the old ties. If he knew he had enough guys he could really count on, he could say fuck it and just stay home. Let 'em think he had Mistretta killed, he wouldn't care. Staying away would be his challenge to Juicy. But I don't think he has that kind of manpower yet, so he has to go. Until he can make some promises and win some of these guys over, he's gotta watch himself. The soldiers are gonna stay loyal to Juicy until they hear what Sal's offering."

"Hmmm . . . you could be right, Toz."

"But I don't wanna go to the funeral to *see* anything. I wanna *be* seen."

"Whattaya talking about? Sal thinks you're dead. You gotta stay out of sight."

"No, that's the point. I wanna be the monkey wrench

in Sal's works. He sees me alive, he's gonna have to rethink his plans. Besides, a lot of those wiseguys know who I am. What'll they think if they see me sitting in church with Sal? I wanna get right up next to the big son of a bitch and act like we're old pals from way back. How many supporters do you think Sal will get once they see him cozying up with the FBI agent who supposedly can put him away? You know what they'll think? They'll think he's made a deal with the government, that he's talking to us. That's what they'll think. And that'll make him poison."

"Immordino's not gonna stay put for that."

"What's he gonna do? He's gotta keep up the numskull act because he's in public. He can't do anything to me. He's not gonna punch me out in church, not in front of all those people. He knows there's gonna be cops there watching. And just in case he happens to whisper sweet nothings in my ear, I'll be wearing a wire. We get him on tape telling me to get the fuck away from him, and he's screwed. We take it back to the judge, and Sal will have to stand trial on all the old charges."

"You got it all figured out, huh, Toz?"

Tozzi sighed into the phone. He could hear it coming. "Go 'head, say it. You don't like any of this. This is 'freelancing,' according to you. You think we should go ask Ivers for permission first. But you know what the hell he's gonna say. Cummings has him buffaloed with this serial-killer bullshit. Christ, if we call and ask him right now, Mistretta will be rotting in the ground by the time he gets around to giving us an answer."

Gibbons didn't say anything. Tozzi could hear him breathing. At least he was thinking about it.

"Look, we've got an opportunity here, Gib. We can possibly put Sal Immordino away for good. At the very least, we'll keep him from taking over the family. Face it, Juicy's no angel, but at least he's predictable. Sal, on the other hand, has big ideas. He always has. He takes over, and we've got problems. They'll be into shit we never even heard of."

Gibbons was still thinking.

"But we gotta act now, Gib. The funeral starts at ten. We got three hours. If you don't wanna come, don't come. I'll go alone. Stick with Cummings. I'll be all right."

"You got a wire?"

"Yeah, I got a Nagra here. I got surgical tape, fresh batteries—I'm ready to go."

"Where's the funeral?"

"Howard Beach. The church is St. Anthony's. It's on 159th Avenue."

"I know where it is." Gibbons sighed into the phone. "Okay. I'll be parked across the street at twenty after nine. You find me."

"I'll be there."

Tozzi hung up and stared at the phone. That was too easy.

He got off the couch and walked through the living room to the bedroom. The first thing that caught his eye when he entered the room was the folded black cloth belt on the dresser. It was John's black belt, brand-new, never worn. *Sensei* had given it to Tozzi, and he planned to put it in John's casket before they sealed it. His funeral was on Friday.

Tozzi picked up the belt and weighed it in his hand. *Sensei* had suggested that Tozzi hold on to it for himself, for when he finally made *shodan*. He could wear it in memory of John. But Tozzi didn't feel right about keeping it. He'd called John's father and asked him what he thought about burying John with his belt. Mr. Palasky said John probably would've wanted that. Aikido had meant a lot to him.

Tozzi looked at himself in the mirror over the dresser, standing there in his underwear, hair mussed, the belt in his hand. John was a good guy. It shouldn't have happened to him. Tozzi put the belt back on the dresser.

"Immordino's not gonna get away with this," he murmured to the belt. "I promise you, John."

Tozzi pulled the T-shirt over his head and picked up the Nagra mini-tape recorder from the dresser. He stood sideways in front of the mirror and held the Nagra to the small of his back. That's where he'd put it. Run the wire around his ribs and up his chest, then attach it to the tie-pin mike. He'd never liked wearing these things. They were an invitation for trouble. If a wiseguy ever caught you wearing one, you could just forget about it. But this time it was different. He wasn't going undercover, and he didn't think anyone would be frisking him in church, least of all Sal the dummy.

He took the roll of surgical tape, pulled out about six inches, ripped it off, stuck it to the dresser, then pulled off six more inches. He stuck the strips of tape to the slender tape recorder, then carefully brought it to his back, watching in the mirror. Positioning it in the crevice of the small of his back, Tozzi held the Nagra in place with one hand as he smoothed the tape against his skin. As he attached the last piece, the doorbell rang.

Tozzi frowned at the front door. "Who the hell . . . ?"

He snatched the T-shirt off the bed and put it on as he went to the intercom in the living room. "Yes?"

"Hi. It's me. Stacy."

"Oh . . . hi."

"Can I come in?"

Tozzi buzzed her in and glanced at the clock on the mantel. Five after seven. Why so early? he wondered. He grabbed the knob and started to open the door when he suddenly realized that he was still in his shorts. He rushed back into the bedroom and grabbed his suit pants.

When he came back out, Stacy was standing in the living room, wearing a black minidress made out of sweatshirt material under a tan trench coat. She flipped her long corkscrew curls over her shoulder and looked at him with sad eyes. She looked washed out, like she'd been crying a lot. "Hi," she said. It was little more than a whisper.

"Hi." He was buckling his belt as he stepped closer. "You want some coffee?"

She shook her head and pushed the hair out of her face. She kept looking at him as if she expected him to do something.

He felt strange standing there in his bare feet and T-shirt, her with her coat on. "So . . . how've you been?"

"Angry."

He nodded. "At me, I assume."

She nodded. "Yeah. At you."

"Look, Stacy, no one feels worse about this than I do. John was my friend—"

"I'm not angry about the . . . about John dying. I'm sad about that. It's *you* I'm angry at."

"Why?" He knew why. He just didn't know what else to say.

"Because you hurt me. I thought we had something together. I thought you were different."

"Stacy, you don't understand."

"Why did you try to pawn me off on John that night?"

Tozzi looked at his feet and sighed. He had incredibly ugly feet. "I know that's the way it seems, but believe me, I wasn't trying to pawn you off. I was only thinking of you. I just thought you needed someone more appropriate—"

"How the hell do you know what I need?" She whipped her hair back. "*I* know what I need. You don't know. I need . . ." She stared at him for a moment, then looked away.

"Stacy, I—I don't know what to say to you."

"Yeah, I know. You never know what to say to me. You have a lot to say to everybody else *about* me, but you never have anything to say *to* me."

Tozzi felt awful. He wanted her to understand that he wasn't deliberately trying to be a shit, but how could he tell her about his problem? It was humiliating. Besides, as incredible as she was, he'd already made up his mind that they were wrong for each other. Lorraine was right: He was incapable of sustaining a relationship with a woman. And face facts, he was old enough to be Stacy's father. It was all wrong. It wouldn't work.

"I came here to find out where I stand, Tozzi. If you want me to go away, then I'll go away. But if you want me to stick around, you've got to show me you're worth it. I've been showing you all my cards right along. Now it's your turn."

Tozzi looked down at his crotch and sighed. He wasn't holding any aces.

"Talk to me, Tozzi. I have to know how you really feel about me right now, or else I'm gone. For good."

Tozzi sighed. "Stacy . . . Look, I've gotta go to—"

She snapped her head back. "No more excuses, Tozzi. I want to know now, and I want to know for sure."

"Look, Stacy." He stepped closer, but she did, too, and suddenly he had his hands on her hips. The toe of her black suede miniboot was rubbing against his bare foot. She smelled like spearmint and honey.

"Well?" Her face was inches from his.

All of a sudden he felt a little faint. The spearmint-and-honey fragrance was making him high, it seemed. Then he felt it, in his underpants. He was getting hard. He was growing like Jack's beanstalk. The blood must've been rushing to his crotch, that's why he felt the way he did. It was the kind of hard-on you could do push-ups with. It was so big, it ached.

Oh, my God.

Without thinking he pulled her closer and touched her lips with his. His head was spinning. Their lips touched again, lightly, then not so lightly until they were pressed together. His brain was speeding down a mountain, out of control. He didn't want to let her go for fear that he'd lose it. He wanted that kiss to go on forever and ever.

Her hands were flat on his chest at first, but now they started to roam. He wasn't aware that they were on his butt until they started to drift up his back. Then suddenly she pulled away from his lips.

"What's that?" Her brow was furrowed.

"What?"

"That thing on your back."

"Oh, that. It's a tape recorder."

She looked puzzled, then pissed.

"No, Stacy, I'm not taping you. I was getting ready to go to work."

"You're back at work now? I thought you—"

"No, not officially. But I've got a little job to do this morning." He glanced at the mantel clock. Shit. He had to get moving if he was gonna make that funeral.

She pushed him away, frowning. "Now you're gonna tell me you don't have any time for me? You're too busy?"

"No. No. I wasn't thinking that."

Not exactly.

He pulled her close, trying to figure out how long it would take to get to Howard Beach by cab. He linked his fingers around the small of her back. He was so horny and confused, his hands were shaking. He wanted her badly, but he just got through telling himself he was no good for her. Shit.

Her eyes were liquid. "So? Are we going to?"

Tozzi's pulse was gushing.

"Well?" she whispered. "Are we?"

Tozzi couldn't speak. He most definitely wanted to, but he knew he shouldn't. But his pecker was in working order again, and you know what they say: Use it or lose it. But he had to get to that damn funeral, he had to stop Sal Immordino. But this was Stacy Viera he was holding, the Pump-It-Up Girl. But he just swore to himself that he wasn't gonna do to her what he'd done to all the other women who came before her. But on the other hand . . .

Their lips collided again, and his tongue went searching for hers. His head was flying around the room, bouncing off the walls, and it wasn't until they started to fall onto the bed that he realized they weren't in the living room anymore.

They grappled and kissed, out of their minds, rolling on the unmade bed. Tozzi was on his back, the Nagra digging into his flesh. He reached around and yanked it off, his skin smarting from the tape. He came up for air long enough to put the tape recorder on the night table, and in that instant he caught a glimpse of his suit jacket hanging on the closet door. The black pinstripe suit. His funeral suit.

Shit.

Stacy was on her knees, straddling him, her hair tumbling down over his face. She flipped it back and nuzzled his ear, licking the lobe.

"Tozzi?"

"Hmmm?" He was looking at the clock radio on the night table.

"Are you paying attention?"

"Of course I'm paying attention. Whattaya think?" He was so big he thought he was going to explode. He rolled her off him and onto her side, and one of those incredible breasts landed on his forearm. The erect nipple nestled in his chest hair.

"You should see your face." She was laughing, her bronze eyes sparkling.

Tozzi caught another whiff of spearmint. He looked into her eyes and she stopped laughing. Their lips had another collision. Tongues clashed. He was dizzy again.

The kiss went on and on and on. He was skiing straight down a mountain, a hundred miles an hour right in his face. Stacy murmured through their kiss then, and suddenly he was back in the bedroom. He opened his eyes a crack. His suit jacket was staring down at them, waiting.

TWENTY

The windshield wipers sounded like they were going to a funeral. One . . . two. One . . . two. One . . . two. Real bummed out. Sal leaned forward in the backseat and pointed. "Why don'cha park over there, Cil? Near the side door."

"Why don't you be quiet, Salvatore, and let me drive?" Cil was crawling down the block, looking for a space that was big enough for Lucy's little Datsun.

"I just wanna go in the side way, Cil, that's all. I think I saw a guy with a camera out in front of the church. I'm sick and tired of those guys."

"Oh, really? You weren't sick and tired of them yesterday or the day before that. You were parading up and down the sidewalk, *posing* for the cameras then."

Emerick started shivering again. "Where's Charles? I want Charles."

Sal put his arm around him to calm him down. "Don't worry, Donnie. We're gonna see Charles later. In a little while." He wished to hell Cil would stop with that testy tone of voice of hers. It was making Emerick all jittery and shaky, like one of those little toy poodles.

"C'mon, now, Donnie. Take it easy, take it easy. She doesn't mean it."

"This is so bad. So very very *very* bad." His face crumpled, and he spoke without breathing, as if he were bearing down to take a crap. Sal hoped he didn't start crying again.

"Why don'cha turn around, Cil? Park on the other side of the street near the church, by the side door over there. I see a space."

"I know how to drive, Salvatore. I'll park where I want to."

Cil was in a real mood today. She was wearing the heavy-duty habit, which she probably would've worn anyway on account of Mistretta's funeral, but it seemed that whenever she wore that thing, it made her crazy. The rest of the time she was pretty much okay, a little *bazingy* in the head, but basically okay. But when she put on that long black thing with the headpiece and all, that's when she really turned into a nun, a *real* nun, like the ones Sal remembered from Catholic school. Brutal.

She was mad because Emerick was here. She wanted him to stay home with Lucy, but Sal told her they had to bring him. After all, they were all out of pills and Donnie boy had been cold turkey for two days now. Couldn't leave him alone with an old lady and all those girls. Sure, he was a real sweetie pie when he had his pills, but you couldn't be too sure about him now. Look at how nervous he is. That's what he'd told Cil. She didn't want to believe that her nice little Donnie boy might do something naughty with her girls, but in her heart of hearts Cil believed that all men were filthy animals, and she wasn't about to risk it even though she kept saying that bringing Donnie to Mistretta's funeral was totally inappropriate, *totally* inappropriate.

Sal grinned on one side of his face and looked at his own eyes in the rearview mirror. "Inappropriate" wasn't exactly the word he'd use. Maybe "memorable." If everything went the way he planned it, they'd definitely remember Donnie Emerick after today. Sal wiped his forehead with his sleeve and looked at his watch. Another hour or so and it would be all done. Just one more hour.

Unless the shooter finds him first. He tried not to think about that, but it was hard not to. It would be considered very disrespectful to try to pull off a hit at a funeral, but you couldn't trust anybody these days. Nobody played by the friggin' rules anymore. Sal sighed, wishing the goddamn butterflies in his stomach would go away.

Cil made a U-turn at the end of the block and headed back toward the church. There was a nice big space not too far from the side door. Sal didn't say a word. She pulled up alongside the car in front of the space and started fighting with the wheel to parallel park this piece of crap. Sal kept his mouth shut. Cil liked to complain, but she always ended up doing what he told her to.

St. Anthony's loomed outside the windshield, the toast-colored bricks of the steeple reaching into a drizzly gray sky. It always seemed to rain for funerals. God must like to see people getting their feet all muddy at the cemetery when they put the stiff in the ground. Sal had always thought God had a weird sense of humor.

Emerick started shivering again. He was sobbing, his eyes squeezed shut. His mouth was open and down-turned, kidney-shaped. Sal hugged him closer and rubbed his arm. "It's okay, Donnie. Believe me. It's okay."

"Where's Charles? I haven't see him in so long. I want

him to take me back to the hospital. I don't like it here. I want Charles."

"Don't worry, Donnie. He's coming. Soon. He told me to take care of you until he gets back. Okay?"

Emerick crumpled his face, nodded, then put his head on Sal's shoulder.

Sal caught Cil staring at them in the rearview mirror. It was a mean nun stare. She knew Charles wasn't gonna be coming around to see anybody. It had been in all the papers and on TV.

Sal waited for Cil to nose the car up to the curb and cut the engine. "Look, Cil, why don't you go 'head in? I'll meet you inside."

She turned around and glared at him. "And what about . . . ?" Her lips were tight. She gestured with her eyes at Emerick.

"Don't worry about it. I'll take care of everything. It'll be okay. Trust me."

"Don't tell me to trust you."

"Why not?"

"Just don't."

She opened her door and got out, slamming it shut.

Sal wrinkled his brow. What the hell was her problem now?

"This is so bad."

"Easy, Donnie. Take it easy."

Sal hugged Emerick and rocked him a little as he looked out the window at the cars assembled in front of the church. The hearse and the limos for the family were parked there. Mistretta's wife and kids and their families were just starting to go up the steps now. The back door of the hearse was open, but they hadn't taken the casket out yet. The old man would be the last one in and the first one out.

The little parking lot behind the church was filling up with Caddies, Lincolns, and Mercedeses. Everybody was here, it looked like. Sal bent his head to get a better look out the rear window. He spotted some of the guys from his old crew, the guys he could count on. They were all standing together in one group, their wives all together in another group. Loopy Lou, Jimmy T., Angie, Phil, Gyp.

Jesus, was that Phil's wife? *Madonn'*, has she gained weight. Actually, except for Gyp's wife, they all looked pretty bad. They looked like . . . like wives. No wonder these guys all had girlfriends.

About a half-dozen cars away from this group, another group of guys were standing together, smoking, fixing their ties and their collars, all big eyes and pouty mouths. They looked like a bunch of Rodney Dangerfield impersonators. Zito, Nicky, Tom-Tom, Richie Provolone, Bobby Cigars—all Juicy's guys. Joey D'Amico was over there, too. He used to be in Sal's crew, the fucking little traitor.

Sal wondered how many of them were packing. Tom-Tom was. He never went anywhere without a gun, even though you weren't supposed to take one into church. It was disrespectful. Bobby Cigars might be carrying. He was another friggin' gun nut. Maybe even D'Amico—he was such a nervous bastard. Assholes like him need guns 'cause they make a lot of enemies. Sal nodded to himself, thinking. Two, maybe three guns. That was all right, but he wished he knew for sure there were gonna be more.

Unless one of those guns belonged to the shooter who was after him. He sighed again. The butterflies were back.

A long black Lincoln pulled into the parking lot then. Sal squinted to see who it was. As soon as he saw the driver—Tony Nig with that kinky Afro haircut of his—Sal knew who was inside. Juicy Vacarini, the man of the hour. But when Tony Nig went around to open the back door, Sal was very surprised to see who stepped out with the slimy son of a bitch: Frank Bartolo, Jr., with his mother Rose balling her eyes, hanging on the kid's arm.

A grin wrapped around Sal's face. Beautiful. He never expected to see the Bartolos here. Frank's funeral was gonna be on Wednesday, so he just figured they wouldn't show up to Mistretta's. But here they were, mourning with the rest of the family. Poor Rose was pathetic. She looked like she didn't know where the hell she was. Junior looked like a friggin' mountain gorilla stuffed into that suit. He was almost Sal's size, but beefier. The roll of fat on the back of his neck bulged out of his shirt, and his arms were putting a strain on the jacket. He could barely button the thing in front. But Sal was happy to see Junior. Junior had a real bad temper, lots of assault-and-battery charges on his yellow sheet. And Junior always carried something. Always.

Sal bit his bottom lip. But what if Junior decided Sal Immordino was the guy who had his old man whacked? It made sense, and Juicy was probably telling people Sal was the one behind these hits just to turn them against him. Then there was the fuckin' FBI. That's what these goddamn feds do. They go around telling stories about guys, trying to make bad blood. Bartolo's kid wasn't that smart, he was easily led. What if he started shooting at *him* in church? Sal hadn't thought of that. All of a sudden he had stomach cramps.

As the big gorilla led his poor inconsolable mother into church, Juicy hung back and lit a cigarette, scanning the parking lot with one eyebrow cocked, like a fox checking out the chickens. The Rodney Dangerfields shuffled right over to shake hands with their captain. D'Amico went with them.

The other group—Loopy Lou and those guys—waved and nodded to Juicy, but they followed Junior and Rose Bartolo, which was only proper. They were still Bartolo's crew, even if it was in name only, so they were supposed to stick with their captain's widow. Sal was actually happy that they were following the Bartolos. It showed they weren't ready to accept Juicy as *capo di capi* yet. Sal had called Loopy Lou earlier that morning and asked him to fill the guys in, tell them to stay cool for a while until after the funeral. Loopy Lou must've convinced them because usually in a situation like this, everybody'd go suck up to Juicy, treat him like the big boss before the old boss was even in the ground. But these guys weren't doing that. They were treating Juicy like he was just another captain, which is what he still was officially. Juicy stood there with his boys, smoke sifting out of his nose as he watched Loopy, Angie, Phil, Gyp, and Jimmy T. walking away with their wives trailing behind. Joey D'Amico was whispering in Juicy's ear. Juicy knew he was gonna have trouble with these guys.

Sal smiled with his teeth. "Don't worry about it, Juice. It'll all work out fine."

"It's not good. Not good at all." Emerick was staring out the rear window, sobbing, twisting his head around like a retard. He started breathing hard all of a sudden, squirming in his seat. "Look! She's crying! Sister Cil is crying! Why is she crying? What's wrong?"

Emerick bounced on the seat. He was all bent out of shape again. Without Charles around, he'd become very dependent on Cil. He didn't like to be out of her sight.

Cil had gone over to say hello to Juicy. The waterworks were going now, and she was dabbing her eyes

with a handkerchief. They were both looking down at
the ground, shaking their heads, the usual funeral routine. But they were fucking phonies, the two of them.
Neither one of them was sad to see the old man go. And
they were probably telling each other how much they
loved Mistretta, how much like a father he'd been to
them. Fucking phonies. Juicy couldn't be happier. He
was the big cheese now. And Cil, she'd never say anything bad about anyone, but deep down she hated Mistretta's guts. She had to. The old bastard never gave her
a penny for the Mary Magdalene Home, and she used to
beg with him. Shit. Behind the tears, these two were
fucking ecstatic the old man was dead.

Emerick threw his head back into the seat. His face
was drenched in tears. "Why's she crying?"

Sal hugged the nut tighter, but he kept his eye on Cil
and Juicy. They seemed to have a lot to talk about, those
two. Juicy reached out and took both her hands in his.

Watch out, Cil. You don't know where he's been.
You'll pick up a nice case of gonorrhea off those hands.

"She's crying. *Why?*"

"Well. I'll tell you, Donnie." Sal pointed out the window. "You see that guy she's talking to? The skinny guy?
He is a very bad man."

Emerick sat forward and stared. "He is?"

"Yes. His name is Juicy. You know what he does for a
living? He's a pimp. But he's like a big boss pimp. He's
got all these girls, hundreds of girls, that he's turned into
whores. Whores as in 'prostitutes,' Donnie. You know
what I'm talking about?"

Emerick didn't answer. Sal hoped he was getting
through to this nut.

"Yeah, Juicy is a very bad man, a terrible man. He
takes these poor young girls and forces them to have sex

with men, disgusting old men, then he keeps the money and doesn't give them anything. Only thing he gives them is sexy clothes, high-heel shoes, and drugs."

"Drugs?"

Sal closed his eyes and nodded. "That's right. How do you think he keeps these poor girls working for him? He turns 'em into dope addicts so they won't run away. They need to get high so bad, they can't leave him. They'd die without their dope. And if they don't treat him like a little tin god, he won't give 'em any dope. Isn't that awful? He thinks he's God, this guy."

Donnie scowled. "There's only *one* God."

"Exactly. Only, Juicy don't feel that way about it. He's a real pagan, that guy. I don't like him."

"Why's he making Sister Cil cry?"

"Well, lemme tell you. You know all the girls back at the home? You know, where we live? Linda and Luisa and Crystal and Shavon and Carmen and Francine and all the other girls. Juicy wants to turn them into prostitutes, too. That's why Cil's crying. She doesn't want him to do that, but he's telling her he's gonna do it anyway. He's gonna make them take drugs and turn 'em into drug addicts so that they'll do anything for him. He's gonna turn 'em into whores so they'll make money for him. So they'll treat him like God."

Emerick started to shiver. His eyes were bugged out, staring at Juicy. "No," he whispered. "No." There was a fury in that whisper.

"Tell you the truth, Donnie, I don't know what to do about him. Juicy's got a lotta guys working for him. They do what he says. He could send some guys over to the home, tell 'em to break down the door, grab the girls, and stick needles in their arms. Ten minutes later, they'll all be like zombies, screaming 'Juicy is God, Juicy is God.' "

"*No!*"

"Well, I'll tell ya, Donnie. There's only one solution I can see." Sal reached into his jacket and pulled out the gun. "Juicy has to go. I know killing is bad, it's against the Ten Commandments and all, but in this case I think it's the only thing to do. You know what I mean? I think it's what God would want you to do, Donnie. It's like taking one life to save a couple hundred other lives. Coupla thousand, if you count all the kids these girls abandon plus the poor guys they seduce and lead into sin. I mean, just think of all the sins that will never happen if Juicy weren't around anymore." He put the gun in Emerick's hands.

Emerick tossed the 380 back to Sal like a hot potato. "Nooooo!"

A sharp pain zinged through Sal's gut. He took Emerick's hand and placed the gun in it, held it closed. "It's okay, Donnie. It won't hurt you."

"Bad! Very bad!"

"You're right, Donnie. You're right. That man Juicy is bad, very bad. And it's all up to you, Donnie. It's not a nice thing to have to do, but it definitely has to be done. Juicy's too evil to just let him go on the way he is. You've gotta kill him." Sal pointed out the window at Cil dabbing her eyes. "Sister Cil would want you to do it. She'd be proud of you if you did."

Emerick kept staring at the gun in his hand.

Sal's stomach was in agony. The nut wasn't getting it. Shit!

"She'd be so happy if you saved the girls from that man. She'd stop crying, Donnie. She would."

Emerick started nodding to himself, staring and nodding, staring and nodding. He mumbled something under his breath.

"What's that you said, Donnie?"

"I have to do it," he mumbled. "She wants me to. I don't want her to cry anymore."

"Good, good, Donnie. I'm glad you feel that way." Sal hugged him close and rubbed his shoulder. "I'm proud of you, Donnie. You're doing the right thing."

Thank God.

Emerick suddenly frowned and stared up at him. "No one is God except God. No one. Just Him."

"No. I agree. You're absolutely right, Donnie. One hundred percent right. Now, I want you to take a good look at that man, Donnie. You gotta make sure you know who he is so you get the right guy. Go 'head, look at him."

Emerick nodded and stared out the window. The gun was tight in his fist.

"Okay, now lemme tell you how you should do this. Pay attention now."

Emerick nodded, staring intently at Juicy. "I've got to do it. For the girls. For Sister Cil."

Sal nodded. "That's right, Donnie. That's absolutely right." He took a deep breath. His stomach felt much better.

TWENTY-ONE

Gibbons checked his watch. It was five minutes to ten, and he was parked across the street from St. Anthony's, right where he'd said he'd be. So where the hell was Tozzi?

He scanned the front steps of the church. A bunch of wiseguys holding black umbrellas were milling around the open back of the hearse. These had to be the pall-bearers. Everyone else had gone inside, including Immordino and his sister the nun. Friggin' Tozzi. This was his goddamn idea. Where the hell was he?

A knock on the window next to Gibbons's face made him turn away from the church. It was about time. But when he saw who it was, he dug his fingers into the car seat. Shit.

He rolled down the window a few inches. "What the hell're you doing here?"

Madeleine Cummings gave him her dead face. "What the hell are *you* doing here?" She was standing on the curb holding a goddamn two-tone purple umbrella over her head.

"Get in the car," he said.

"I asked you—"

"*Get in the friggin' car!*"

For a change, she did what she was told, thank God. A black woman hanging around outside a mob funeral in Howard Beach with a purple umbrella. May as well carry a big sign—HERE I AM.

She got in on the passenger side and slammed the door shut. "I don't like your tone of voice, mister."

Gibbons looked up at the ceiling and bit his upper lip. Here comes the Seven Sisters Scolding. As if he hadn't heard it before. "Save your breath, Cummings. I don't need the aggravation."

"Have you forgotten who the coordinating agent is on this investigation?"

"How could I?" He groaned and rubbed the back of his neck. "By the way, I thought you were busy chasing down your psycho killer. Whattaya doing out here?"

She raised her chin and flared her nostrils. It was how Ivy League types let you know that they're pissed off. "I'm here looking for you, Gibbons. When I couldn't find you, I figured you were out doing your own thing again, so I checked the duty register to see where you were. This location isn't part of our investigation. I need you to go over to—"

"This location *is* part of the investigation as far as I'm concerned. Now, if you'd just do me one gigantic favor and get lost, I'll do my job and you can get back to the field office and continue doing whatever the hell it is you do."

"You know, I have just about had it with your deprecating remarks about my work. I'll have you know that—"

"Stop!" Gibbons was looking out the side window. Directly across the street, a cab pulled up to the curb.

Tozzi stepped out of it, flipping up the collar of his rain-coat and pulling a hat down over his brow. As he shut the door and the cab took off, he looked at Gibbons's car, but didn't come over. Instead he headed for the church steps. He must've spotted Cummings and figured she'd just cause more trouble if he had to deal with her. He was right.

"What's Tozzi doing here? He's supposed to be on sick leave." Cummings opened her door, ready to go after him.

Gibbons reached past her and pulled it closed. "Sit still."

Tozzi was climbing the church steps. The pallbearers were looking at him.

"Let him go," Gibbons said. "He knows what he's doing."

"I will *not* let him go. I'm the coordinating agent here, and Tozzi is not supposed to be working. It's my respon-sibility to—"

"You wanna get hit with a harassment suit?"

"Excuse me?"

"You go in there and start an argument with Tozzi in the middle of Mistretta's funeral, they'll hit the Bureau with a harassment suit like you've never seen. Guineas are real sensitive about weddings and funerals. You dis-turb the services in there and we'll be hearing from their lawyers by the end of the day. And as coordinating agent, it'll be *your* ass on the line, Cummings."

"Don't try to bully me."

"All right. Go 'head." Gibbons reached over and opened the door. "Do what you want. Why listen to me? What do I know? I've only been doing this friggin' job for twenty-five years. What the hell do I know?"

She pulled the door shut and glared at him. Her Seven

Sisters nostrils were flaring like mad. Gibbons waited for her to say something, but something across the street caught his eye. Another yellow cab whizzed up to the front of the church. A woman in a tan trench coat got out, rushed through the gang of pallbearers, and ran up the steps. Gibbons squinted and got a good look at the long blond corkscrew curls bouncing up and down on her back as she climbed the stairs. It was Stacy.

Cummings pointed out the window. "Isn't that—"

"Yeah, that's her. C'mon. I don't like this." Gibbons shouldered his door open and went out into the drizzle. Over the roof of the car, he saw Cummings opening her purple umbrella. "Leave that thing here," he said.

She frowned at him. "Why? It's raining."

"It's purple. Leave it."

She flared her nostrils again, then closed the umbrella and threw it back into the car, slamming the door.

Gibbons bared his teeth. Take it easy with the goddamn door.

He met her at the front of the car and took her by the elbow, trotting across the boulevard, holding up his hand to slow the oncoming traffic.

"I can walk by myself," she huffed as they stood on the median strip, wet wheels hissing past them in both directions.

He didn't let go. "Now, listen to me. If anybody tries to stop us from getting in, let me take care of it. You go on in by yourself. Find Stacy and get her the hell out of there. But don't let her make a scene. All we need is for her to start a lovers' quarrel with Tozzi in the middle of a boss's funeral. Christ, I can hear Ivers now."

"What if she won't cooperate?"

"Make her cooperate." There was a break in the traffic, and they ran across. "Just be discreet."

"Okay."

They walked fast along the sidewalk. He kept his eye on the church. "You carrying your weapon?"

"Of course."

"Don't take it out. No matter who hassles you, no guns in church."

"I'm not stupid, Gibbons."

He glanced at her sideways. "Yeah. You told me." He could see the headlines now.

As they approached the church steps, Gibbons touched Cummings's shoulder and sent her on ahead. Out of the corner of his eye, he could see one of the pallbearers rushing over to head them off. Gibbons picked up his pace so that he could get between the pallbearers and Cummings.

"Hey, where you think you're going?"

Gibbons recognized the wiseguy. It was Joey D'Amico. Gibbons had busted him one time over in Jersey. He had been fencing fur coats. Had a showroom set up in the back of a warehouse about a mile from Giants Stadium.

D'Amico pointed at Cummings as she mounted the steps. "Hey, I'm talking to you, nig—"

Gibbons grabbed him by the throat and made his eyes pop. "What's all the yelling for, Joey? Don't you have any respect for the dead? Huh?"

Joey couldn't answer. Gibbons had his thumb right on Joey's windpipe.

Over at the hearse, the undertakers were pulling out the casket. Raindrops were beading up on the polished metal top. Two of the wiseguy pallbearers started to come over to help Joey.

"Stay put," Gibbons said as he pushed D'Amico back toward the others.

D'Amico was coughing like crazy. "Fuckin' fed," he rasped.

At the top of the steps, the church doors were open. Gibbons could hear the organ music from inside filling in the gaps between Joey D'Amico's coughing and the wet hiss of the passing traffic.

"I think they're waiting for you guys," Gibbons said to the group. He nodded at the casket. "Never keep a boss waiting. Even a dead one." Gibbons backed toward the steps, then turned and climbed them two at a time. Instead of going in the open double doors, he pushed through the single heavy oak door on the far right.

The vestibule was cold and dark. These old Catholic churches always reminded Gibbons of medieval torture chambers with the iron bands and the exposed rivets on the doors, the high vaulted ceilings, the gloomy lighting. A guy in a black suit was looking outside through the open double doors. Gibbons guessed he was from the funeral parlor from the look of him. It was the way he stood there with his hands clasped in front of him. There was an empty gurney by the door, waiting for Mistretta's casket. Gibbons looked around for Cummings. She wasn't in the vestibule.

He walked toward the open doors in the middle of the vestibule. Outside, the eight pallbearers were just starting to come up the steps with the casket hoisted on their shoulders. Gibbons looked the other way, into the church. The altar was straight ahead, Jesus hanging high on a big wooden cross. Gibbons slipped in and stood behind the last pew.

The church was crowded. He scanned the assembly, but all he could see were the backs of heads. He moved over to the side aisle to get a better look, and he spotted one big head towering over the crowd on the other side of the church. He moved up the aisle a little to get a look at the profile and saw that it was who he thought it was, Sal Immordino. His sister the nun was next to him, on the center aisle. Tozzi was on Sal's other side. Gibbons craned his neck and made out an aureole of curly bronze locks next to Tozzi. Shit. Stacy was over there, too.

As the people in the pews nearby started to notice him, Gibbons retreated to the back of the church, wondering whether it was worth doing anything at all at this point. Tozzi was shoulder to shoulder with Immordino, whispering into his ear. Stacy was jammed up next to Tozzi on the other side, leaning into his ear. Gibbons wished he could see her face better, see if she was frantic or what. If she didn't look like she was gonna make a scene, better to just leave her be. Of course, if Stacy was blabbing at Tozzi, she might drown out anything Immordino might say on the tape, which would defeat the whole purpose of their being here.

Gibbons looked around for Cummings. Where the hell did she—

The organ music swelled then, and everybody immediately stood up. On the altar, a priest emerged from a side door, wearing a purple satin tunic thing over a white robe. This purple was way gaudier than Cummings's umbrella. When the priest turned his back to the assembly and genuflected in front of the altar, Gibbons saw that there was a big black satin cross sewn to the back of the tunic.

Gibbons noticed the smoke then. The priest was carrying one of those silver gravy boats on a chain that they burn incense in. He turned to the congregation and started swinging the gravy boat, making it clang against the chain with each swing. He did three swings to the middle, three to one side, three to the other side, then back to the middle. The smoke drifted up and up past the dim chandeliers to the high ceiling where God the Father was painted on the ceiling, a huge old guy with fiery eyes, no shirt, a snowy white beard down to his belly button, and a white pigeon doing a kamikaze dive into his head.

"Pssst!"

Gibbons looked around. Cummings was coming across the back aisle toward him. She was walking fast, waving at him.

He frowned at her as he moved in her direction. Cool it with the waving, will ya?

Gibbons stepped across the center aisle as if he were crossing a mine field. He glanced to his left and saw that the casket was resting on the gurney, waiting to be brought in.

"Whattaya waving at? You're gonna make a scene, goddammit."

Cummings looked gray. She started to point her finger, then used her head to gesture instead. The priest was walking slowly down the middle aisle, swinging his gravy boat, coming down to greet the dead man.

She dug her nails into Gibbons's forearm. "The priest!" she whispered. "It's him!"

"Who? What're you talking about?"

"The priest! It's Emerick!"

Gibbons looked at the guy in the purple tunic, smoke swirling in his wake and rising to the ceiling. He stared at the skinny guy's pale face, the translucent eyelids, and he remembered the picture he saw of Emerick in handcuffs. Mentally he erased the beard and put the guy on a diet. Gibbons's fingers went numb.

Holy shit.

TWENTY-TWO

Tozzi cleared his throat. The smell of incense always made him choke, even as a kid when he'd been an altar boy. Sal Immordino was on his right, playing dumb but looking at him out of the corner of his eye. His sister Cil was on Sal's other side, leaning over the pew in front and scowling at Tozzi, her big designer glasses glinting with disapproval. Stacy was on Tozzi's left, brows slanted back, moaning into his ear.

"Let's get out of here, Tozzi. We have to talk."

"Please, Stacy. Not now."

"This is disgraceful," Sister Cil hissed. "Why don't you take your friend and get out of here, Mr. Tozzi? I've never seen such disrespect in the house of God in my whole life."

Tozzi tried to ignore both women. It was Sal he was interested in. He sidled up to the big jooch and smiled into his ear for the benefit of the crowd. "So tell me, Sal, how'd you do it? Mistretta, I mean. How'd you pull it off?"

"Leave my brother alone."

Sal gave him a drop-dead stare.

Tozzi grinned at him. "C'mon, Sal. You can tell me. You already did it. It's done. The old man's gone. So whattaya gonna do now? Make peace with Juicy? Or shoot him, too? Huh?"

"Leave my brother alone. You're scaring him."

"Yeah, right."

"Toz-*zee*, let's get out of here."

"Stacy, please." He gave her a stern look. He hated when people whined.

He could feel the tape recorder against his skin under his clothes, the reels turning slowly, waiting for Sal to say something. So far, though, all he had on tape were the two women. He had to get Sal to say something, something coherent. "So what's the deal, Sal?"

Cil leaned past Sal and shook her finger. "How many times do you have to be told, Mr. Tozzi? I don't care what your position is. You have no right to be here."

When she called him "Mr. Tozzi" in that tone of voice, he suddenly remembered the day Sister Superior smelled the Mass wine on his breath when he was in fourth grade. The altar boys used to sneak swigs from the jug in the sacristy when they had to fill the cruets before morning Mass.

"*Toz-zeeeee.*"

He tried to ignore Stacy as he put his face up next to Sal's. "C'mon, Sal. How'd you do it? Obviously you hired someone. But your credit must be good, 'cause as far as we can tell, you haven't touched any of your overseas accounts since you been in the bin. 'Course, a guy like you must have money squirreled away all over the place. How many little savings accounts you got, Sal? You know, the under-ten-grand accounts that nobody pays much attention to. Is that how you paid your shooter?"

Sal's upper lip rose in a sneer of contempt. He growled something under his breath, but Tozzi couldn't make it out. He was sure it wouldn't sound like anything on the tape.

"You know what I can't figure out, Sal? Why you drag your sister into your dirty work, that's what I can't figure. I guess you don't care very much about her, 'cause she can face charges, too, you know. For one thing, she's harboring you, which automatically makes her an accomplice. And wait'll I get a search warrant for the Mary Magdalene Home. I'll find something there. You can bet on that. And you know what? Even if I can't pin anything on you, I'll make something stick to her. That's a promise. And there ain't no law in this country says a nun can't do time. You watch what I can do."

Sal kept giving him the hairy eyeball, but he kept his mouth shut.

Tozzi kept smiling. "You think I'm bluffing? Just watch what kind of shit I can pull. I'll fuck up your life so bad you *will* be mental when I get through with you. I'll make sure Juicy finds out what good pals you and I are, how you sang like Tweetie Bird for me, told me all kinds of things about the family. See, we're buddies now." Tozzi put his hand on Sal's shoulder. "I want everyone to see how close we are."

Sal shrugged Tozzi's hand off. "Get away from me." Sal spoke up this time. People in the pew in front turned around and stared at him. The tape had to have picked up that one. But so what? It didn't prove anything.

"*Toz-zeeee.*"

"Stop talking to my brother."

Tozzi put his arm around Sal again, hugged him close, and smiled in his face.

Sal went to wrap his big paw around Tozzi's throat,

but Tozzi grabbed his wrist. "What's this? You trying to kill me again? You already tried that twice, Sal, and you blew it both times. You can't touch me."

Sal countergrabbed Tozzi's wrist. He grumbled deep in his throat. "Y'were just lucky."

Tozzi's pulse started to race. He prayed the tape had gotten that one. Sal had just admitted it, at least by implication. Sal's response implied that he was the one who sent the guy who shot him in the leg as well as the guy who killed John. It was on tape. At least he hoped to hell it was. Sal's voice was pretty muddy. But if it *was* on tape, maybe it would be enough to convict him of John's death. Maybe . . . but maybe not. It was only four garbled words, not enough to prove the guy was sane. Even if they brought him to trial for John's murder, Sal could probably beat it with the insanity defense the way he always had. Tozzi's joy evaporated. Sal was too goddamn smart. He wasn't gonna talk, not *really* talk. Shit.

"Leave him alone!" Cil sputtered.

"*Toz-zeeee!*"

There was just the hint of a smug grin on Sal's blubbery lips.

Tozzi stared him in the eye as he coughed into his fist. The incense smoke was getting thicker. The priest was coming down the center aisle. When he reached their pew, the priest stopped and swung the burning incense at them, banging the silver censer against the chain. Cil reared back from the hot, swinging pot, and Sal pulled his chin in. Tozzi couldn't figure out what the hell the priest was doing this for. Then something occurred to him. Where were the altar boys? Why was the priest all alone? There should've been four altar boys for this service. At least, that was the way they did it when he used to serve at funerals.

The chain stopped banging. Tozzi rubbed his smarting eyes. Suddenly there were yelps and squeals all around him. A woman in the row behind gasped. "Oh, my God!" Stacy clutched his arm for dear life.

When Tozzi's eyes cleared, he finally saw what everyone was reacting to. The skinny priest was holding a gun in his hand. It was leveled at their pew. "Step out, please," the priest said. His face was sweaty. He couldn't stop blinking.

Sister Cil was outraged. "Donald, what do you think you're doing?"

"Please let them pass, Sister."

"Donald, this is a church. Take off those vestments right now and go outside with that gun."

He shoved the gun in Cil's face. "I said let them pass, Sister. Please." His voice was shaky. So was his hand.

Cil crossed herself quickly and moved out of the pew. Her tone changed. She pleaded with him. "Donald, please listen to me."

But he wasn't listening. The barrel of the gun roamed from Sal to Tozzi to Stacy and back.

"You, you, and you," he said, pointing to each of them. "Step out and go to the altar. You must do penance. You are all sinners."

Sal had his hands up in the air, but he wasn't moving.

Tozzi put his hands up, too. "Can we talk about this . . . Father?"

Stacy was shaking. "What's he gonna do, Tozzi?"

The priest was stern. "You have all sinned. *Now, get out here,*" he yelled.

Sal muttered under his breath. "Take it easy, Donnie. Just take it easy."

Tozzi stared at the priest's face. Donnie? Donald Emerick? Oh, shit.

"Go to the altar, I said. Move!"

"Easy, Donnie. Easy." Sal shuffled to the end of the pew and moved into the aisle.

Emerick swung the gun around and pointed it at Tozzi and Stacy. *"You, too. Move!"*

"Okay, okay, we're coming." Tozzi started to move toward the end of the pew.

Stacy froze, and Emerick screamed like a banshee. *"You too, harlot!"*

Her face crumpled. "Please, no. Please."

"You sinned with him." Emerick pointed the gun at Tozzi's head. "You two sinned together. I can tell from the way you act."

She was breathing fast, sobbing and hyperventilating. "No. No. That's not true. You don't understand—"

"Go to the altar. How many times do I have to repeat myself?"

Tozzi was in the aisle with Sal. He spoke softly and evenly. "Do what he says, Stacy."

Reluctantly she started to move, her face as pale as Emerick's, unsure whether to put her hands up or leave them on the pew in front.

Cil was on her knees in the aisle. She was in a real state, beating her chest with both fists. "Mother of God, do something. *Somebody,* do something. This is the house of the Lord."

Wiseguys all around stuck out their bottom lips and shrugged. A guy wearing tinted aviator glasses and a bad hairpiece on the other side of the aisle patted his jacket to show that he wasn't carrying a weapon. "Sorry, Cil," he said. "It's a funeral."

Stacy stepped out of the pew and stood next to Tozzi, trembling with her hands up.

Emerick jabbed the air with the automatic. *"Go . . .*

to . . . the . . . altar. The three of you. Go. Kneel before your Redeemer."

Tozzi looked at Sal. Sal's eyes were dead as he started shuffling toward the altar. Stacy was sobbing. "Just do what he says," he murmured to her. "It'll be all right." Tozzi glanced down at Emerick's gun hand as he followed her up the aisle.

They walked slowly up the center aisle and mounted the two marble steps that led to the altar. The three of them stood together on the red carpet facing the big crucifix.

"Kneel down! Why do you make me repeat myself?"

Stacy dropped to her knees. Sal lumbered down to his. Tozzi just stood there. He didn't move.

"Kneel!"

Tozzi swallowed on a dry throat. He stood there, motionless.

Emerick screamed, *"Kneel down, sinner! Kneel!"* He moved up behind Tozzi and jabbed the gun into his back.

Tozzi let out a slow breath, remembering the last time he tried this, on a dark, drizzly street in Manhattan, the night he first met Stacy. She'd distracted him that time and he fucked it up. Wound up with a slug in his leg and six weeks' sick leave. He'd better not fuck up now.

Emerick poked him with the gun barrel again and hit the tape recorder. Tozzi stopped breathing, waiting for Emerick to say something about the hard object under his clothes.

"Kneel!" Emerick screamed. *"Kneel down!"*

He didn't seem to notice. He poked Tozzi again and dug the muzzle into his back, trying to force him to his knees.

Tozzi made his move then, rolling to the right and

getting shoulder to shoulder with Emerick, taking his gun hand. He gripped Emerick's hand with his thumb over the knuckles, pointing the weapon away. Pulling the arm forward and swinging it down, Tozzi made a line in the carpet pile with the barrel, taking Emerick's balance, then he lifted the arm up and over Emerick's head. Emerick toppled backward, and Tozzi maneuvered his body before he hit the floor, flipping him over on his belly and pinning the arm up straight in the air over his head. Tozzi pressed down and put enough pressure on the wrist to make it hurt. Emerick released his grip. Tozzi took the gun and shoved it in his belt as he dropped to one knee on Emerick's lower back, pulling out his handcuffs and securing one wrist, then the other.

"You're sinners," Emerick wailed with his face pressed to the carpet. "You must confess. You're sinners. I know you have sinned."

Tozzi glanced down the long center aisle. Mistretta's casket was all by itself at the back of the church.

Emerick was rubbing his face into the carpet. "I know you have sinned together. I've seen this woman on television. I know she's bad. Sister said so."

"You're under arrest," Tozzi said. He knew he was supposed to read Emerick his rights, but he didn't think it would do much good. "You have the right to remain silent—"

Emerick wasn't listening. He was too distraught, weeping and wailing, floundering on his stomach. "I know you have sinned, too, Sal. I saw you. I saw you kill that old man. And his friend Jerry, too. That man was Sister Cil's friend. She told me so. She said she liked Mr. Mistretta. I saw you shoot him. I saw all the blood on the floor."

A woman in the front pew screamed. The wiseguys

started mumbling and grumbling. The discord spread through the pews like a brushfire. Tozzi scanned the crowd. Where the hell was Gibbons? He reached for Emerick's gun in his belt.

"Forget about it, Tozzi. Throw it down."

Tozzi looked up. The church was suddenly silent. Sal was standing behind Stacy. He had her arm pinned behind her back and a small automatic jammed under her chin.

Tozzi stood up slowly. "Take it easy, Sal."

"Drop the friggin' gun, Tozzi, or I'll do her right here."

Stacy moaned as he cranked her arm.

Tozzi showed Sal his open palms, then slowly he pulled out Emerick's gun from his waistband with two fingers. He tossed it away behind him. The clatter of metal on the marble floor echoed through the church.

Juicy Vacarini's voice rose from the pews. "Get outta here, Tozzi. Leave. Let us take care of this."

He looked at Stacy. "I'm not leaving without her."

Stacy's face was as white as the marble altar. She was terrified, too scared to move. Tozzi prayed that she'd faint. She'd make a lousy hostage if she were unconscious. But her eyes were wide open and she was breathing fast, panting. She wasn't gonna faint. Maybe she'd hyperventilate and pass out. He wished she would.

Juicy called out again. "I said, let us take care of this, Tozzi. It's a family matter."

Tozzi looked out at the pews. Juicy was on his feet, four or five rows back. A few other guys were standing with him, guys from his crew. Across the aisle, Frank Bartolo's son, Junior, was standing, too. His hand was inside his jacket.

Tozzi looked past them. Shit. Where the hell was Gibbons?

He looked back at Sal. "Let her go, Sal. It's the only way I can get you outta here alive."

Emerick was still on his belly, sobbing into the carpet. "There's too much sinning . . . too much sinning."

"Let her go, Sal."

"No fucking way, Tozzi. You're gonna get us outta here all right. You and me and her." His eyes were darting all around the church. He knew he was a dead man if he stayed here. He yelled out to the crowd. "Anybody comes near me, I shoot her first, then I start shooting at you. I got thirteen fucking bullets in this mother, and I swear to Christ I'll use every goddamn one before I go down. Every one."

Tozzi's breathing was shallow. All they needed was a firefight in church. They could have a great big funeral for all the victims, right here, right away. Tozzi scanned the side aisles. Where the hell was Gibbons?

"Wake up, Tozzi." Sal nodded at the center aisle. "Start walking. Nice and slow. We're getting outta here."

"Sal, listen to me—"

"Move! I'm gone. I'm gonna disappear."

"Listen. You surrender to me now, you can go back to Trenton. We—"

"Fuck that. I ain't going back there. Not me. Send Donnie boy back to Trenton. He likes it there. I ain't no fuckin' nut case. Now, get moving. Go."

Stacy squealed as Sal cranked her arm again. "Tozzi, please! Do what he wants." The gun was irritating the skin under her chin. Her neck was red and blotchy.

Tozzi's heart was thumping. They couldn't stay here. Sal was desperate, and he couldn't trust these wiseguys.

Who knew how many guns they had out there? They could start a shoot-out any second. People would get killed, and Stacy would be the first. No. He had to take this outside. At least if it was just him and Sal, it would be a little saner, the odds a little more even. Sort of.

Sal kneed Stacy in the backside to make her walk. "Get going, Tozzi."

"Okay, okay, I'm going." Tozzi kept his hands up as he turned to go down the aisle. Mistretta's casket was in the aisle at the other end of the church. No one else was back there. As he stepped down from the altar, he glanced back at Sal and Stacy, then looked up at the plaster Jesus bleeding on the cross. He let out a long sigh.

You got any good ideas?

TWENTY-THREE

"**J**ust stay put, all of you. You keep walking, Tozzi."
Sal moved down the aisle, holding Stacy close, the barrel
of that gun right up under her chin. Her eyes were
squeezed shut and her jaw was clenched, either in pain
or fear, probably both. She was up on her toes, Sal had
her jacked up so high. He was practically carrying her.

Tozzi walked backward down the aisle, facing them,
ten feet away. He glanced right and left, hoping to God
none of these idiot wiseguys decided to pull a gun. Sal
was desperate—you could see it in his face—and he
wasn't kidding about emptying his clip and taking people
down with him. Tozzi didn't give a shit if Sal took down
any of his goombahs. It was Stacy he was worried about.
She was gonna be the first casualty if they started shooting. Tozzi scanned the pews, but it was impossible to tell
if anybody out there was holding a gun.

Sal's eyes shot around the church, but they kept coming back to Tozzi. "Don't get any ideas, Tozzi. Just be
cool. Everybody be cool. We won't have no problems
that way. I'll be gone and you can have your funeral.
Okay?"

"What about her, Sal?" Tozzi stopped walking.

"Keep moving!"

Stacy groaned as Sal twisted her arm.

"Just keep going, Tozzi. You hear me? I'm not fooling around."

Hands in the air, Tozzi stepped back a little quicker to placate Sal. "Take it easy, Sal. I'm going, I'm—"

Tozzi's heart jumped as he bumped into something. He looked over his shoulder. It was Mistretta's casket in the middle of the aisle. He shoved it to the side with his hip to make room, banging it against a wooden pew. The collision boomed through the church like a bomb going off.

Tozzi's heart was pounding as he backed around the casket. There were too many goddamn variables here. Sal was fucked—there was no way he was gonna get out of here alive. These people were not about to let him live, not after what Emerick said about him. If Tozzi had some backups here, at least Gibbons, maybe—just maybe—they could apprehend Sal and cool things down. But Tozzi was all alone here, and Sal was focused on him, which meant he wasn't focused on that one wiseguy in the crowd who was gonna start the shooting. Sal was a dead man, he was history, that was definite. But what about Stacy? How was he gonna save her? Sal wasn't the issue anymore. Stacy was. Just Stacy. Tozzi could forget about taking Sal in and having him prosecuted. He could forget about testifying against Sal, assuring the court that the guy was really sane and that he always had been. He could forget about . . .

Something suddenly occurred to Tozzi. Everyone in this place knows Sal's fucked, except Sal. He still thinks he's got a chance. He thinks he can make it out of here.

He's got hope. And if he's got hope, Tozzi's got something he's gonna want.

"Hey, Sal. Hold it a minute."

"Screw you, Tozzi. Just keep walking."

"No, wait. I got something for you. No tricks. I swear to God. It's under my shirt. Okay? I wanna get it for you."

"Don't fuck around, Tozzi. I'll kill her. I swear I will."

"I'm just gonna take off my jacket and put it down right here. Okay?" Tozzi started taking it off as he asked for permission.

"Don't get wise, Tozzi. I'll make you sorry for the rest of your fucking life."

"I'm gonna unbutton my shirt now." Tozzi loosened his tie and started unbuttoning his shirt. He tossed the tie aside and opened his shirtfront. "Can you see what I got?"

He ripped the tape off the wire on his chest, wincing against the sting. He pulled off the strips of tape on his side. "See what it is, Sal?" He took off his shirt and let it drop to the floor, turning to the side so that Sal could see the Nagra tape recorder on his back. "You see what it is, Sal? A tape recorder. It's all on tape, Sal. You talking just now. Loud and clear, you talking natural. It proves you're not nuts."

"You little fuck. I'm gonna—"

"I'll make you a trade, Sal." Tozzi ripped the strips of tape off his back and held the tape recorder over his head. "Stacy for the tape recorder. An even trade. The girl for the tape recorder." He shivered, bare-chested in the cold, damp church.

Out of the corner of his eye, Tozzi spotted a statue of St. Sebastian on the side altar. The saint was wearing nothing but a dirty loincloth with about a million arrows sticking out of him. St. Sebastian, the martyr. Tozzi's throat ached.

"So whattaya say, Sal? I give you the tape recorder, you let her go."

Sal didn't answer. He was thinking about it.

"C'mon, Sal, whattaya say? It's the only hard evidence we've got that proves you're not insane. It's the only recording in existence of you talking normal, carrying on a real conversation. Without it, we can't put you away. We wouldn't be able to touch you."

"That's bullshit, Tozzi. *You* can testify against me. Whattaya think I am, stupid?"

"Yeah, but I *won't* testify. I promise you. If you don't hurt her, I won't testify."

"You're fulla shit."

"No, for real. Let her go and I will not testify against you." Tozzi swallowed hard. "I swear to Christ I won't."

"You're bad, Tozzi. Shouldn't swear like that in church when you don't mean it."

"I do mean it. I'm telling you. Let her go and I won't testify."

"Why?"

"Because I love her. I want to marry her." Tozzi's heart was thumping like crazy.

"You're lying."

"I'm not. Now, c'mon. Take the damn tape recorder. Here." He set the Nagra down on top of Mistretta's casket and stepped back, showing Sal his empty palms. "Take it, Sal. It's your ticket to freedom. Take the tape recorder, let her go, and just get outta here."

Sal inched forward, pushing Stacy with him. His face was a tight fist, eyes burning. "If this is a trick, Tozzi, you're gonna be fucking sorry."

"Please." Stacy's voice was small and pathetic. She

was at the other end of the casket, less than ten feet away. But he couldn't see her face very well. Her head was tipped back against Sal's shoulder, pinned there by the gun.

"C'mon, Sal. Please. I'm begging you. Please. Take it and let her go."

"Yeah. Break my fucking heart, Tozzi. You lie like a rug. You don't love this girl."

"I'm telling you, Sal, I do."

"Yeah, sure. You don't give a shit about her. You're just trying to—"

"*Salvatore!*"

The shriek echoed through the church. Sal turned around fast, whipping Stacy around with him. Tozzi's eyes shot open. His gut bottomed out, certain that Sal was gonna blow her head off. Then he saw who it was— Sister Cil standing in the aisle, a tight frown on her face, mad as a hornet.

"Salvatore, let go of that girl and get down on your knees this instant."

"Get away, Cil."

She stomped toward her brother, eyeglasses flashing thunderbolts. "Salvatore, get down on your knees and pray to God for forgiveness for all the lies you've told me."

"Get away, Cil. I'm telling you now."

Sal looked frantic. Tozzi started to move around the casket.

"Get back, Tozzi!" He dug the gun into Stacy's neck. His face was dripping, his hand shaking.

Tozzi froze, pulse racing, fingers numb. Shit!

"Look at me, Salvatore. Look at me. You lied to me. For years you lied to me. You swore to me that you were innocent, that you never killed or stole or cheated, that other people tried to blame you for their sins and make you suffer their punishments. But that isn't true, is it? You are what the papers say you are. You're worse because you lied about it. Lied to your own family. Lied about not having any money when you knew how badly my girls and their babies needed things. Lied to me time and time again, and after all that I did for you." Tears emerged from the bottom rims of the nun's glasses. "You killed Mr. Mistretta, didn't you? You killed Frank Bartolo. And Jerry. And Mr. Tate. Didn't you? And you took advantage of Donald. And—"

"*Shut up, Cil!*" Sal pointed the gun in his sister's face. "*Shut up! Shut up!*"

This was Tozzi's chance. The gun wasn't on Stacy. They were just eight feet away, the other side of the casket. He had to make his move right now!

But as he lunged for Sal's outstretched arm, the lid of the casket suddenly flew open and scared the living shit out of him. The tape recorder flew into the air, sailing past the chandeliers and dropping into the crowd of mourners.

"*Freeze, Immordino. FBI.*"

Gibbons was inside the casket, sitting up in a bed of ivory satin, both hands on Excalibur, his trusty .38. It was leveled at Sal's head.

Sister Cil screamed and staggered back in horror, her hand over her mouth. Screams and shouts rattled the organ pipes in the choir loft. Sal was shaking all over. He looked like he'd just seen a ghost. Tozzi held his chest. He knew how Sal felt. Fucking Gibbons.

Gibbons didn't take his eyes off Sal. "Take his gun, Tozzi. And don't get funny, Immordino. You twitch the wrong way, and I'll drop you where you stand." Even the silence was scared of Gibbons.

Tozzi approached Sal with caution and put his hand on the gun, but Sal wasn't letting go. Sal was staring at Gibbons, mesmerized, dumbfounded, but furious, breathing hard, his chest heaving.

Tozzi spoke softly. "Leggo, Sal. C'mon, leggo." He twisted the gun back and Sal finally let him take it.

He did a quick check of the weapon, then stuck the muzzle in Sal's neck. "Now, let her go."

Sal didn't respond. He still had Stacy's arm pinned behind her back.

Tozzi stuck the gun right in his ear and racked the slide. Sal winced. "I said let her go."

Sal dropped his arms to his side, and Stacy stumbled away from him, retreating into a pew.

Tozzi glanced at her. She sat down and curled up with her head in her lap. Tozzi sighed. Shit. She was gonna be a mess.

Gibbons hauled himself out of the casket and pulled out his handcuffs. Sal didn't put up any resistance as Gibbons cuffed him. He was doing his dummy act again. The son of a bitch.

"C'mon, let's go, Immordino." Gibbons started to march Sal down the aisle toward the vestibule.

Tozzi noticed Madeleine Cummings on the other side of the casket then. She was holding his shirt and jacket. In the pew, Stacy was sobbing into her hands. He wondered what the hell he was gonna say to her now.

"Here," Cummings said, handing him his clothes. "Go take care of Emerick. I'll stay with Stacy."

Tozzi looked at her and nodded. "Thanks," he whispered. She understood what was going on.

But as Tozzi started putting on his shirt, a loud thud and a terrified yell echoed through the church. He wheeled around, braced the gun with both hands, and aimed down the aisle toward the vestibule.

A body was sprawled on the floor, covering the threshold between the church and the vestibule, blocking the way for Gibbons and Sal. Tozzi recognized the lifeless frog face on the chunky corpse in the black suit. It was Mistretta. A string of rosary beads was clamped into his waxy hands.

Sal was staring down at the corpse. He was white, in a cold sweat.

Sister Cil, who'd been holding herself up on the edge of a pew, wobbled, then fell backward and made her own thud as she fainted and crashed onto the wooden bench.

Gibbons turned around and glared at Tozzi. He was pissed. "I told this son of a bitch to stay put where I left him. You friggin' guineas can never listen, can you?"

Tozzi just stared at him. He couldn't believe this guy. "Jesus, Gib. This is a church, for chrissake. It's the man's funeral."

Gibbons shrugged. "I had to put him somewhere."

Wiseguys started moving toward the back of the church to see what was going on. Sal mumbled something to Gibbons, then stepped over Mistretta's body.

Gibbons glanced back at Tozzi. He was smiling like a crocodile. "Later, Toz. Sal's anxious to go."

TWENTY-FOUR

"**C**'mon. Drink up, Toz. It's your birthday." Gibbons flashed a mean grin as he pressed the beer bottle to his lips.

Tozzi nodded and sipped from his bottle to make his partner happy, sneaking another look at the clock on Gilhooley's back wall. It was almost nine-thirty. They'd been here an hour and a half, and they'd just done the cake-and-candles bit, but Stacy never showed. It was the only reason he'd agreed to this stupid birthday party idea. Lorraine and Madeleine Cummings were sitting together on the other side of the booth, satisfied with themselves. This was their deal.

Tozzi looked down at the slice of birthday cake on a paper plate in front on him. He hadn't had a chance to talk to Stacy after they arrested Sal Immordino at St. Anthony's two days before, and she hadn't returned any of his calls. He had to talk to her about what happened that morning, why he ran out the way he had, why he hadn't gone to bed with her. God, he'd wanted her that morning, and he still did want her, but he didn't think she really understood how urgent the situation with Immordino was.

Lorraine raised her eyebrows and examined his plate. "Michael, you've barely touched your cake. I thought chocolate was your favorite," she said.

"Actually, it's not chocolate." Cummings was cutting herself a second sliver. "It's carob sweetened with pear and white grape juice."

Gibbons made a face and pushed his plate away. "I thought it tasted weird."

Cummings ignored him. "Lorraine and I worked hard on this cake, Tozzi. The least you could do is try it."

Tozzi glanced up at the front door. He thought he saw Stacy coming in, but it was someone else with hair sort of like hers.

"My God," Cummings said, licking frosting off her fingers, "is this what happens when you turn forty? Snap out of it, Tozzi. You're in a fog. If this is what I have to look forward to in three years, I'll shoot myself first."

"Want help?" Gibbons grinned behind his bottle.

Cummings flashed a saccharine smile.

"I'll get around to the cake," Tozzi said. "I'm just not hungry right now." He sipped his beer and checked the clock again.

"Maybe we can send a piece to Sal Immordino," Lorraine suggested. "He might appreciate it right now."

Gibbons coughed up a sarcastic laugh. "Stick a file in it, why don'cha? He'll give you a great big kiss when he gets out. *If* he gets out." Gibbons sucked on his beer. "Hey, why don't we all go over and see him? Bust his balls a little more. He's right down the street at the Metropolitan Correctional Center. Whattaya think, Toz?"

Tozzi pictured the dark streets outside this place. He remembered the side street a block south of here where he was attacked and shot in the leg. He remembered being down on the ground after he'd been shot, seeing Stacy's misty silhouette under the streetlight, hearing her scream.

Cummings brought another forkful of cake to her mouth. "I don't think Sal Immordino deserves any of our cake. If the judge wouldn't grant him bail, why should we give him cake?"

Gibbons snorted. "I suppose you'd rather drive down to Trenton and bring a piece to that lunatic, Emerick."

Cummings's eyes shot open. "Certainly not. That poor man has enough problems. He doesn't need sugar shock to add to his woes." She looked at Lorraine. "Emerick had to have been a hyperactive child. Sweets must've made him wild. They didn't understand the effect sugar has on hyperactive kids back in those days."

Gibbons narrowed his eyes. "I thought you said you didn't use any sugar in this cake."

Lorraine and Cummings both looked guilty. "Only in the frosting," Lorraine admitted.

Tozzi tuned them out. He stared down at all the candles scattered on the table, the wicks burnt and black, the butt ends smeared with frosting. Forty candles. It had been like a goddamn forest fire when they brought it out. They didn't have to have the exact number of candles. A couple would've been fine. He glanced up at the bar. Another long-haired blonde just came in, but it wasn't Stacy. He picked up one of the half-melted candles and twirled it between his fingers.

"On second thought, maybe we should bring a piece to Immordino," Gibbons said. "Could be his last piece of birthday cake ever. Word on the street is that Juicy Vacarini put out another contract on him, which is no big surprise. Sal's not long for this world. They may not get him where he is now, but once he's convicted and sent to a federal pen, somebody'll get to him."

Lorraine looked skeptical. "You mean another prisoner would do the hit? Does that happen?"

Gibbons sipped his beer and nodded. "All the time."

Tozzi broke off a dried line of wax that had dripped from the candle. "Yeah, but Sal may not get convicted. Someone must've pocketed that tape recorder when it flew into the crowd. Sal's doing his rope-a-dope routine again, and his public defender's getting red in the face, yelling that his client's not competent to stand trial. We still don't have any hard evidence to prove that Sal's not nuts, so basically we're back where we started with him."

Gibbons banged his bottle on the table. "What the hell're you talking about? We've got your testimony. You heard him talking like a normal person. So did Stacy and Cummings. *You're* the one who's gonna put him away, Toz."

"Without the tape, I'm not so sure our testimony alone will do it. Remember, Sal's been declared incompetent by the court three times before this, so there's a precedent. His lawyer will argue that taking Stacy hostage and waving a gun in church was all part of his craziness."

"Yes, but what about Sister Cil?" Cummings said. "Given the way she feels about her brother, she may very well testify against him, especially if the prosecutor is willing to drop the charges against her in exchange for her cooperation."

Gibbons shook his head. "What's she up for? Aiding and abetting? You tell me what grand jury is gonna indict a nun. And if she's not indicted, she has no reason to make any deals. Besides, Sister Cil believes in mercy and forgiveness. She's not gonna put her own brother away, no matter what he did to her."

Cummings pushed her glasses up her nose and speared another morsel of cake. "I'll go talk to her. She wanted me to counsel her girls at the Mary Magdalene Home. I think she may trust me. I may be able to persuade her."

Gibbons looked at her. "Yeah, right. And Ted Bundy was just a mixed-up kid."

"Gibbons!" Lorraine was frowning.

Cummings shrugged and kept eating. "It's all right, Lorraine. I've gotten used to his pointless sarcasm. It doesn't bother me anymore."

Gibbons snorted up a laugh. "Congratulations. You want a merit badge?"

Cummings set down her fork. "You're going to miss me when I go back to Quantico, Gibbons."

"And when exactly will that be, Doctor?"

"Next week. Didn't I tell you? I was called back to fill in for someone."

Gibbons leaned over the table. "How's about I put you on a train tonight, then I can start missing you right away?"

She flashed her saccharine smile again.

He bared his teeth.

"*Hey, Tozzi!*"

They all looked toward the bar. Roy, the muscle-bound bartender, was waving Tozzi over.

Tozzi scanned the room for Stacy before he got out of the booth, but he didn't see her. "Excuse me for a minute."

He walked over to the bar. Roy was the one who'd set up the prank with Stacy that first night. He knew her. Maybe she'd called. "What's up, Roy?"

Roy leaned over the bar and lowered his voice. "Someone wants to see you. Alone."

"What?" Tozzi looked back at Gibbons in the booth. He was suspicious. What did these two come up with this time? A belly dancer in the back room? Maybe a stripper? He wasn't in the mood. He wanted to see Stacy. "No more birthday surprises, okay, Roy?" He started to head back to the booth.

"No, wait. It's not what you think, Toz. It's Stacy. She wants to talk to you alone. No joke." Roy rolled his eyes toward the door next to the juke box. "She's out back in the storeroom. She called and asked me to let her in through the alley."

Tozzi stared at the door across the room. There were people drinking and eating at all the tables between the bar and that door, but he didn't see any of them. All he saw was the door. His stomach clenched. Why didn't she come in the front? Why was she acting like a spy?

"Go 'head," Roy said. "It's not locked."

Tozzi nodded and faced the door, wondering what she was thinking. He knew she was mad at him, but he was pretty sure he could fix that. He could explain why he'd acted so bizarre with her. The morning of the funeral he had no choice, he *had* to leave. And before that, well . . . he could tell her about his little problem now. He'd make her understand.

He wandered across the room, then stopped in front of the door. The neon pink-and-blue lights on the juke-box tinted his hand on the doorknob. The jukebox was playing some Madonna song he didn't know the name of. It was the one where she's got short bleached-out hair in the video, the one where she's wearing the dog collar and the torpedo bra, dancing in a peepshow, all these horny guys in glass booths drooling on their shoes and pulling their puds for her. He thought about his own pud. Thank God, he didn't have that problem anymore.

He opened the door. She was standing next to a stack of Budweiser cases. It was dim in there, just one low-watt bulb hanging from the ceiling. Her hair didn't sparkle in this light the way it usually did. Her eyes were moist, but they weren't sparkling either. She was wearing a blue jeans jacket over black jeans and a white cowboy shirt.

"Hi. How ya doin'?"

"Shut the door," she said.

"I called your machine—"

"I know." She stared into his eyes.

He couldn't read her. Her expression was intense, but he wasn't sure if she was angry or hurt or what. "Stacy, I—"

"No. Don't talk." She shook her head. "Let me talk. I know what I want to say."

He swallowed hard. He didn't like the sound of that.

"You saved my life, Tozzi, and I guess I should be grateful. . . . Well, I am grateful. For saving my life, that is. But what I'm feeling is something else."

She looked down at the floor, and Tozzi stayed still. She was just getting warmed up.

"I feel like a real fool, Tozzi. I feel stupid. I came on pretty strong to you at the apartment that morning when you were trying to get dressed. I wanted you so bad. I thought you were trying to put me off when you told me you had to get to a funeral. I thought you were just making it up to get rid of me." She stopped for a moment. "I didn't realize you were on duty—or whatever you call it. That's why I followed you out there. I thought you were making it all up. I guess I was pretty selfish."

"No, Stacy, I wasn't trying to get rid of you. I wanted you, too, but—"

"Don't talk. Let me finish what I want to say."

Tozzi nodded. "Okay."

"In church, when you told Sal Immordino that you loved me and that you wanted to marry me so that he'd let me go, I really believed it. I mean, I knew you were just saying it to fool him, but I *wanted* to believe it. I felt really stupid afterward, and it's been bothering me. Why was I so anxious to believe something I *knew* was a lie?"

"Well—"

"Please. Let me finish." She wiped under her eye with one finger and sniffed. "For the past two days I've been thinking about what it would be like to be with you, to be married to you. It's a weird thought." She shook her head and tried to laugh. "Now I'm sort of glad we didn't sleep together. It would never have worked out between us."

"Whattaya mean? Why do you say that?"

"Because you're too macho for me, Tozzi. I don't know why, but whenever I'm with you, I end up feeling like I'm the little girl and you're the big daddy there to protect me."

Great. Tozzi stared up at the light bulb.

"You're very male, Tozzi. Maybe a little too male for me. I have a feeling you're very dominating when you make love."

If you only knew.

She let out a long sigh. "I guess, deep down, I always knew it wouldn't work. I mean, you're a pretty straight guy, being an FBI agent and all. And then there's the age difference, which does kinda bother me. It's just that after I saw you get shot and I got to know you, I began to fantasize about you. You're really a very romantic character on a certain level. You know, guns and chasing bad guys and doing undercover work and all that. You just don't get to meet people like you every day." She forced a smile and shrugged. "But that's not real. Not for me. Your life is like a roller coaster, Tozzi, and I don't want to just go along for the ride. I want to pick my own rides."

Tozzi looked at the floor and nodded. "Yeah . . . I hear what you're saying." He sighed and resigned himself to the fact that he was gonna be a lonesome scrotum —again.

They stood there under the dim light bulb, neither one knowing what to say next. She'd pretty much said it all.

He jerked his thumb at the door. "We've all been waiting for you, Stacy. There's still plenty of cake left. You wanna—"

"No. I don't think I could handle that right now. Apologize for me."

Tozzi nodded. "Okay."

She moved forward tentatively, then put her arms around him and hugged him, resting the side of her face against his shoulder. The long bronze corkscrew curls covered his arm like a blanket. "I'll be in touch, Tozzi. Not right away. But I will call you sometime." She pulled away, looked him in the eye, and pressed her lips into a smile. "We're still gonna be friends, right?"

"Yeah . . . of course." He stared at the light bulb, blinking back a tear.

She pulled away from him and walked backward toward the other door. When she opened it, the clash and clatter, bright lights, and steamy smells of the kitchen invaded the dim peace of the storeroom.

"See you around, Tozzi."

"Yeah . . . See you around."

She went into the kitchen and shut the door behind her. It was dim and quiet again. Tozzi was all alone in a roomful of cardboard boxes with her smell on his shoulder.

Shit.

When he went back out, Gibbons was sitting by himself at the bar, staring up at the ball game on TV. Tozzi went over and took the stool next to him. "I just talked to—"

"I know," Gibbons said. "Roy told me. Whatsa matter? Can't afford a motel?"

Tozzi didn't answer. He wasn't in the mood for snappy repartee.

Gibbons nodded back toward the booth. "Lorraine and her buddy are yakking about college again. I couldn't take any more."

"Oh, yeah?"

"Listen, I wanna buy you a drink for your birthday. Something special. From me to you." He waved to the bartender. "Hey, Roy, you got any of those nice single-malt Scotches? You know the ones I mean? The names all start with 'Glen.'"

"I've got Glenfiddich and Glenlivet."

"Whichever one is better. For both of us. Straight up."

"You got it." Roy flipped two rock glasses onto the bar, grabbed a bottle from the rows lined up against the mirror, and poured. Normally Tozzi would've preferred his on the rocks, but the way he was feeling right now, straight up sounded properly medicinal.

Gibbons picked up his glass and looked at his partner. "I don't believe in bullshit toasts, Tozzi. You know, long life and happiness and all that fortune-cookie crap. It's all wishful thinking and false hopes as far as I'm concerned. But this one's just for us, Toz, for no particular reason at all. For us and all the Joe Blows in the world who get up every morning, put on their pants, and do what has to be done. To hell with worrying about what the future brings and to hell with getting older. Don't even bother thinking about it. The secret to life is simple: You just gotta keep moving, Toz. Keep your hands on the wheel, your eye on the road, and just keep going." He clinked Tozzi's glass.

Tozzi nodded and sipped his drink. It went down smooth with a warm afterburn. He held up his glass to the light and stared into the amber liquid.

"Tell me something, Gib. You think Stacy and I could've made something together? Something more permanent, I mean."

"I'm not following you."

Tozzi nodded toward the back room. "She just gave me my walking papers."

"Oh . . . Sorry to hear that."

"What I'm wondering is, could a guy really have a serious relationship with a woman half his age? I mean, it's not like I would've been the first guy in the world to try it."

Gibbons savored his second sip as he considered the question. "Nope. Not the first guy, and not the last."

"So you really think it could've worked out?"

"Hey, I was rooting for you. It was those two"—he nodded back toward the booth—"who thought it was so awful. And not because of her age. They just think you're a pig, that's all."

Tozzi nodded and glanced up at the TV. Some guy was taking a shower, smiling like he'd just won the lottery. A soap commercial. "Well, no use crying over spilled milk. I mean, she still wants to be friends, so something could happen later on down the line. But I sorta doubt it." He took another sip of his Scotch as he stared up at the TV. "Stacy Viera. She's a good person. If the circumstances had been different, I bet we coulda made a go of it. But anyway . . ." He looked down into his drink. "I have a feeling her face is gonna be in the back of my mind for a long, long time."

"Her face? That's the part you're gonna remember?"

Tozzi scowled at his partner. "Shut up, you dirty old man, you."

The commercial changed then, and the familiar bass line started thumping out of the TV. They both looked up at the same time. On the screen, the camera panned that gleaming gym until it found Stacy in her metallic purple tights, curling that barbell up and down, up and down, smiling seductively into the camera as her boobs jiggled like Jell-O.

Tozzi shook his head. He didn't need this now.

Roy rushed over and reached up to change the channel. Tozzi stopped him. "It's okay. Leave it, Roy." The bartender lowered his arm and shrugged, then went back to what he was doing.

Tozzi watched the rest of the commercial, staring at Stacy's face, wondering . . . just wondering.

"At Knickerbocker Spas, we want you to come on in and PUMP IT UP!"

Stacy kept curling the barbell, smiling into the camera as the music faded and the commercial ended. The next image was a live shot of the groundskeepers at Shea Stadium picking up the trash that the fans had thrown into the outfield.

Gibbons was humming to himself. It took Tozzi a minute to recognize that the tune was "My Way."

Tozzi stared at him. In all the years they'd been partners, he didn't think he'd ever heard Gibbons hum, sing, or whistle. But what was more surprising was the song he'd picked. "I thought you hated Sinatra."

"I do. This is the Elvis version." He continued humming.

Tozzi recalled the lyrics then, the stuff about the guy looking back over his life and all the regrets he doesn't have. "You're not funny, Gib. Not funny at all."

Gibbons stopped humming. He crinkled his eyes, shook his head, and clapped Tozzi on the shoulder. "Welcome to middle age, goombah." He knocked back the rest of his Scotch and banged the empty glass on the bar. "Now you can buy *me* a drink."

Tozzi just shook his head, went into his pocket, and laid a twenty on the bar. Gibbons had his thumb and index finger over his eyes, his shoulders bouncing as he laughed like a set of squeaky, worn-out brakes.

Tozzi was just about to take his twenty back and tell Gibbons he could buy his own goddamn drink when something caught his eye in the mirror behind the bar. She was blond, straight hair, older than Stacy, a more mature look—

"Thinking with your dick again, Toz?"

Tozzi shot him a dirty look in the mirror. "Mind your own business."

Gibbons shook his head, showing his teeth. "Face it, Tozzi. You're never gonna grow up."

Tozzi killed his drink, then waved to Roy, pointing at

their empty glasses. "I hope you're right, Gib. Who wants to end up like you?"

"Go scratch, will ya?"

Tozzi looked at his partner sideways, then glanced up at the ball game on TV. He was smiling like a crocodile.